...n author **Abby Green** ended a very glamorous career in film and TV—which really consisted of a lot of standing in the rain outside actors' trailers—to pursue her love of romance. After she'd bombarded Mills & Boon with manuscripts they kindly accepted one, and an author was born. She lives in Dublin, Ireland, and loves any excuse for distraction. Visit abby-green.com or email abbygreenauthor@gmail.com.

Melanie Milburne read her first Mills & Boon novel at the age of seventeen, in between studying for her final exams. After completing a master's degree in education she decided to write a novel, and thus her career as a romance author was born. Melanie is an ambassador for the Australian Childhood Foundation and a keen dog-lover and trainer. She enjoys long walks in the Tasmanian bush. In 2015 Melanie won the HOLT Medallion, a prestigious award honouring outstanding literary talent.

KT-464-259

000003077230

BRIDE BEHIND THE DESERT VEIL

ABBY GREEN

ONE HOT NEW YORK NIGHT

MELANIE MILBURNE

MILLS & BOON

DUDLEY LIBRARIES		all not, ed out e publisher it is published
000003077230		adition
Askews & Holts	29-Mar-2021	emark owner tered with the armonisation s.
AF ROM	£6.99	
2SE		blishers

MIX
Paper from
responsible sources
FSC **FSC® C007454**

www.fsc.org

BRIDE BEHIND THE DESERT VEIL

ABBY GREEN

This is for Ellen Walsh.

We've been best friends since we were
skinny little nippers running around the back fields and
cliff ways of Ballybunion.

I treasure our friendship and the roots
from which it came.

Love you lots, always.

PROLOGUE

'YOUR WIFE MAY now reveal her face.'

Sheikh Sharif Bin Noor Al Nazar waited with bated breath as his new wife's attendants came forward to unhook the elaborate face mask that had covered her face for the duration of the wedding ceremony.

Not even her eyes had been visible.

Sharif couldn't care less what she looked like—he had no intention of consummating this marriage; it was to be in name only for as short amount of time as possible—but if she was at least passably attractive that would certainly make things easier for him.

The delicate chains and gold medallions of the face covering clinked as it was removed and her face was revealed.

The first thing Sharif noted somewhat dispassionately was that he didn't have to worry about her being passably attractive—because she was stunningly beautiful.

The second thing was more of a visceral reaction. Shock, followed quickly by anger. Because his new wife, far from being the stranger he'd expected, was not in fact a stranger.

Not at all. In fact he knew her intimately.

One word resounded in Sharif's head. He wasn't even sure if he uttered it out loud. *'You!'*

CHAPTER ONE

Two weeks ago

'YOU'RE SAYING YOU don't even know what your bride-to-be looks like?'

The horrified expression on Nikos Marchetti's face was almost comical. Sharif Marchetti's younger half-brother was on a video call from his home in Ireland, where Sharif could see his wife, Maggie, pregnant again, pottering in the background with their eight-month-old baby son, Daniel, on one arm. For some strange reason Sharif found the domestic scene presented before him…distracting.

Because it was catching at something inside him. A place it shouldn't be catching. Because he found such domesticity utterly alien and unwelcome.

He focused on his brother. 'No, I don't know what she looks like. I know nothing about her and I'm not interested. I'm marrying her because of a diplomatic agreement between Al-Murja and Taraq that has to be honoured. And,' he tacked on with studied nonchalance, 'because settling down appears to be good for business.'

That was an understatement. Since both his younger half-brothers had recently taken wives—Maks, their youngest brother, had married his wife in a private civil ceremony in London just before Christmas—the Marchetti Group's stock value had gone through the roof.

But Sharif knew it could go even higher, reaching a stability and value that would finally bring him close to achieving all he'd set out to achieve when his father had died. When the old man had finally relinquished his control over the company that had been built off the backs of the

fortunes of others. Namely, each one of his three wives—
Sharif's mother, and the mothers of Nikos and Maks.

Maggie's face, and Daniel's cherubic one, appeared over
Nikos's shoulder. 'Al-Murja and Taraq? An arranged marriage? It all sounds so exotic!'

Sharif wrangled his focus back to the present moment.
Nikos was reaching for his son, tucking him competently
against his chest while commenting drily to his wife, who
had come to perch on his knee, 'Sharif doesn't operate at
the level of mere mortals. On this side of the world he's a
Marchetti, and merely one of the world's most successsful
billionaires, but in his mother's desert home of Al-Murja
he's a royal sheikh and even goes by a different name.'

Maggie's big blue eyes opened wide. 'Ooh, Sharif, I
never knew that. What's your other name?'

There was a knock on the door of Sharif's office in
Manhattan. He welcomed it, not liking how this familiar-
ity was impacting upon him. Over the last few months he
and his brothers might have developed more of an affinity than they'd ever had before, but they were still far from
being truly functional as a family.

'My car is here. I'll be in touch, Nikos, as soon as I'm
back.'

His brother shook his head. 'Why are you doing this
again?'

Sharif forced a smile he wasn't feeling. 'Because I'm
envious of what you and Maks have, brother. I want to be
as happy as you.'

But as Sharif terminated the connection on Nikos's sharp
burst of disbelieving laughter, his deep-seated cynicism
rubbed against something raw. Something he knew would
only be made less raw when he stood over the dismantled
pieces of the Marchetti Group and ground his father's legacy to dust.

His conscience pricked as he sat in the back of his chauffeur-driven limousine a few minutes later, thinking of his half-brothers and how they might react if they knew his plans. But he quashed the feeling. They had no more allegiance to their father than he had. And, as much as they might have developed an affinity, he didn't trust anyone with his plans. Not even them.

When the time came he would tell them and they would walk away with wealth beyond their means.

What more could they want?

One week ago, Taraq

'Why should I let you take your sister's place for this marriage?' asked the King.

Aaliyah Binte Rashad Mansour did her best to stay calm, but she was gritty-eyed from lack of sleep after the frantic journey she'd just taken from England back to her desert home in the middle of the Arabian Peninsula, after an hysterical phone call from her beloved younger half-sister Samara.

'Because I'm your eldest daughter. Samara is only nineteen.'

And she was in love with the son of the King's chief aide.

Liyah's father said nothing more for a moment, and she pressed on while she had a chance. 'Samara hasn't even met this man you want her to marry. Clearly they're strangers. What does it matter if it's me and not her?'

Her sister had told her, *'He just wants a wife. He doesn't care who that is, as long as it's someone from this family.'*

Her father made an indistinct sound. He wasn't a very tall man. Liyah was almost taller, at five foot ten. She'd always felt that he disapproved of her less than delicate proportions. Among the myriad other things that she'd never understood.

Her mother had been his first wife, and she had died when Liyah was a toddler. Liyah had only the vaguest memories of being rocked, and a lullaby being sung, but she'd long since convinced herself that was just a weak fantasy to make up for the fact that when her father had married again and had his other children, Liyah had been effectively sidelined and forgotten about. Neglected.

The only family member Liyah had ever allowed close was Samara who, since she was tiny, had followed Liyah around like a faithful shadow, crashing through all of Liyah's barriers.

As soon as she'd known Samara was in distress, and why, Liyah hadn't thought twice about coming home and offering herself in her sister's place. But now that she was here in front of her father a sense of panic gripped her.

'Who is he, anyway? And why is he happy to marry a woman he doesn't even know? I thought we'd moved on from arranged marriages.'

'Don't be naive, Aaliyah. The best marriages are still primarily the ones that are arranged for the benefit of two parties—in this instance two neighbouring kingdoms that have a long history of enmity.'

'But it's been years since anything—'

Her father interrupted. 'He's the cousin of the King of Al-Murja and he's honouring a decades-old diplomatic agreement by marrying into this family and providing a dowry. His mother was meant to marry your uncle, but she took off to Europe and married an Italian playboy instead, giving him her dowry. That marriage fell apart and she came home in disgrace with a baby son. She died when he was still young and his father brought him up.'

That story rang a few vague bells in Liyah's head. But her father had stopped pacing and now looked at her. There was a gleam in his dark eyes—very unlike Liyah's green ones.

'His mother ran off to Europe just as you did. Clearly you share her rebellious spirit, Aaliyah.'

Indignation made Liyah's spine tense. 'It's hardly rebellious to want to—'

Her father held up a hand, cutting her off again. 'No, I think this will work very well, actually. Sheikh Sharif Bin Noor Al Nazar controls a vast luxury conglomerate in Europe. He will not stand for a rebellious wife. He is just what you need to learn some control, Aaliyah. To learn respect.'

A million things bubbled in Liyah's blood, chief of which were a very familiar hurt and the need to defend herself, but she forced herself to swallow it all down and ask, 'So does this mean that you'll let me take Samara's place?'

Her father looked at her for a long moment. There wasn't a hint of warmth or approval in his eyes. Just the cool disdain that had become so familiar. Then he said, 'Yes, you will be the one to marry Sheikh Sharif Bin Noor Al Nazar. And you will use this as an opportunity to redeem yourself in the eyes of this family.'

Liyah's relief was tempered with panic at what she'd just done, but she couldn't back out now. Not when Samara's happiness was at stake. She would do anything for her sister.

Her father was turning away from her, clearly done with the conversation, and shock that he could dismiss her so easily after all but handing her over to a complete stranger for the rest of her life made Liyah blurt out, 'Why do you care for me so little, Father?'

He stopped. He faced her again, and for the first time in her life Liyah saw something flicker to life in his eyes. Incredibly. It was only after he spoke that she realised what it was: acute pain.

He said, 'Because your mother was the only woman I loved and you look exactly like her. So every day that you're alive and she isn't is a reminder of what I have lost.'

Yesterday

Sharif saw the falcon first. A peregrine falcon. Mature. He guessed at least ten years old. Magnificent. Feathers reflecting golden tints in the dying rays of the sun. Its grace and seemingly lazy circles in the air didn't fool Sharif. It was looking for prey and would swoop and kill within a split second.

He was about to find his binoculars to have a closer look when he heard the sound of a horse's hooves. One horse.

He shrank back into the shadows of the trees around the natural pool at the oasis where he'd set up camp for the night, en route to the palace at Taraq. His team had gone on ahead. He needed some time alone in the desert. It never failed to ground and recharge him, and he knew the coming weeks would require all of his focus…

A horse and rider thundered into the small but lush oasis, shattering the peace. In an instant Sharif assessed the young man to be an expert horseman, his body moving as one with the horse. The enormous stallion came to an abrupt halt under a twitch of the reins, nostrils flaring, body sheened with a light film of sweat. He'd been ridden hard.

The young man slid off athletically, patting the horse's neck and leading it over to the pool where it drank thirstily. He looped the reins around a nearby tree, tethering the horse.

Sharif wasn't sure why he stayed hidden in the shadows, but some instinct was compelling him to remain hidden for now. He sensed the stranger's desire to be alone. Like him. Also, he presumed the rider would move on once the horse had drunk and rested for a moment.

He couldn't make out the man's—the *boy's* face. He had to be a boy. He was tall, but too slight to be a man. His head and face were covered in a loose turban.

The falcon swooped low at that moment and Sharif saw

the rider lift up his right arm. The bird came to rest on a leather arm-guard. So it was a pet falcon. Impressive.

The stranger fed the bird what looked like a piece of meat out of a pouch at his hip and then, with a flick of his arm, let the bird fly off again.

The young man stood at the edge of the pool. A sigh seemed to go through his slender frame. And then he lifted his hands to undo his turban.

Sharif moved to announce himself, but stopped in his tracks when the turban fell away and a riotous mass of dark unruly curls was unleashed, tumbling down a narrow back. *Narrow back. Long hair. Curls.*

It hit Sharif. This wasn't a young man—it was a young woman, and as he watched, struck mute and unable to move, she started to take off all her clothes.

The gallop to the oasis had only taken the smallest edge off Liyah's turmoil—a potent mixture of anger and helplessness. It was the eve of her wedding and she was hopelessly trapped. And she'd put herself in this position for the sake of her sister, which only made her feel even more impotent. It wasn't as if she was being forced into this. She could have ignored her sister's call. Stayed in Europe.

Yet, she couldn't have. She adored her sister—the only family member who had ever shown Liyah love and acceptance. Liyah would do anything to secure Samara's happiness. Even this.

And, after extracting a promise from her father that he wouldn't stand in the way of Samara marrying her sweetheart, Javid, at least Liyah's sacrifice wouldn't be in vain.

But it wasn't even that sacrifice that was uppermost in her mind. She was still reeling from what her father had revealed a week ago. That he'd loved her mother. And that Liyah reminded him of her.

Knowing the reason why she'd always been shunned by

her father wasn't exactly a comfort. It only compounded her sense of dislocation. Isolation. Love had done this to her father—made him bitter.

In a way, discovering this had only confirmed her belief that love was not to be trusted. It made you weak and vulnerable.

If anything, she more than most should agree with a marriage based on the sound principles of practicality and necessity. She just hadn't ever figured that she would have to put it into practice. She'd relished the prospect of an independent life. Free to make choices of her own.

Living in Europe for the past couple of years had given her a false sense of freedom. That freedom had been an illusion. Even if she hadn't come back here to take her sister's place, her family's neglect and disapproval would have always cast a long shadow, reminding her of how unlovable she was.

Since her father had mentioned that her husband-to-be was the CEO of a luxury conglomerate, Liyah imagined him to be the sort of individual who gorged himself on rich food, beautiful women and vacuous pleasures.

She didn't want to blight her last days of freedom— *ha!*—by thinking of a future she couldn't change, so she hadn't even bothered to look him up. Which she knew wasn't exactly rational—but then she hadn't been feeling very rational for the last week as the full enormity of what she'd agreed to sank in.

The water of the deep pool looked inviting and cool and she felt hot and constricted. Panicky.

She let the turban that had been wound around her head and face to protect her from the sand drop to the ground. She started to take off her clothes, knowing she was safely alone because no one ever came here. It was too close to the palace to be a stopping point for travellers. And the Sheikh—her future husband—had arrived just before she'd left, with an entourage. Not that she'd hung around to see him.

She undid the buttons on her shirt and it fell down her arms with a soft whoosh. The cooling evening air made her skin prickle. She undid her bra, let that fall too. She opened the button on her soft leather trousers—trousers that her father would never approve of as they were not feminine. Which was precisely why Liyah loved them. Apart from the ease of movement they gave her.

She shimmied them over her hips and then down her legs, stepping out of them. She pulled down her underwear.

Now she was naked.

Her horse whinnied softly. The sky was a dark bruised lavender, filling with stars. A crescent moon was rising. A swell of emotion made her chest tight. Would she ever be back here again? She loved this place. It was where she felt most at peace. Cantering over the sand with her bird high in the sky above her. Wild. Free.

Liyah stepped into the water, still warm after the day's intense heat. It glided over her skin like silk as she walked in up to her waist and then dived deep, where the depths were cooler and darker.

Only when her lungs were about to burst did she kick her way back up and break the surface, sucking in deep gulps of air. It took a second for her ears to clear before she heard a man's voice.

'What the hell were you doing? I was about to rescue you.'

At the sound of the voice Liyah whirled around in the water to face the shore. Shock at the sight of the very tall, broad and dark stranger almost made her sink under the surface again.

His hands were on his hips and he stood in the shallows, the end of his long white robe drifting in the water. He had short, thick dark hair. His jaw was stubbled. But even through her shock Liyah could see that he was breathtakingly handsome. And powerful.

His eyes looked dark too. High cheekbones. A firm mouth. Currently in a disapproving line.

That line of disapproval snapped Liyah out of her shock. She'd had enough disapproval to last a lifetime. Her peace had been invaded. Her last night of solitude.

'I don't need rescuing.' A thought occurred to her and an acute sense of exposure made her ask, 'How long have you been there?'

'Long enough.' He sounded grim. 'You need to come out.'

Indignation filled her at his autocratic tone, reminding her of how little autonomy she had over her own life. 'I don't *need* to do anything, actually.'

'You're going to stay there all night? You'll freeze.'

It was true. The scorching desert temperatures fell precipitously at night. Liyah could already feel the chill of the water creeping into her bones.

'I can't come out. I don't have any clothes on.' Strangely, she didn't feel unsafe, even though this man was a complete stranger.

'I know.'

Liyah stopped treading water. 'You did spy on me.'

Yet, strangely again, the thought of him watching her strip and dive into the water wasn't making her feel indignant. It was making her feel…aware.

In the dusky half-light Liyah couldn't be entirely sure she wasn't dreaming. She could have sworn there had been no one else here when she'd arrived, but then, she hadn't exactly checked her surroundings thoroughly.

When she looked over the man's shoulder now, she could make out the shape of a tent amongst the trees on the far side of the oasis. And a horse. It whinnied softly and her horse answered.

'You're camping here?'

'For the night, yes.'

His voice was deep. Deep enough to reverberate in the pit of her belly. He had an accent she couldn't place. Mid-Atlantic, but with a hint of something else—something foreign. But also familiar to here. An intriguing mix. Yet she knew she'd never seen him before. He was a total stranger.

She should ask who he was, but for some reason the words wouldn't form on her tongue.

And he was right: she couldn't stay treading water all night.

'I need something to wear.' Her own clothes were scattered along the shoreline, but instead of going to pick them up the man reached behind his head and pulled off his robe.

Liyah's breath caught in her solar plexus when his bare chest was revealed. Massive and tightly muscled, with dark hair curling over his pectorals and a dark line dissecting his abdominals to disappear under the loosely fitting trousers that hung low on his lean hips.

'Here, take this.'

He held his robe outstretched to her from the shore. She swam towards the shallows until she could feel the ground beneath her feet. The water lapped around her shoulders.

She could see that the bottoms of his trousers were in the water. 'Your trousers are getting wet.'

'They'll dry.'

Again, Liyah wondered if she was in a dream. But no dream she'd ever had came close to this. She started to walk forward, feeling the resistance of the water against her body.

The waterline dropped lower, now just covering her breasts. Liyah stopped. She expected the man to turn around, to show some respect. But he didn't. *He'd already watched her.* Albeit from behind.

Again, it didn't make her feel violated in any way—it excited her.

If she was being rational for a second, *excited* was the last thing she should be feeling. Scared. Wary. Insulted. Indignant. Those were the things she should be feeling. Yet she wasn't.

She should also be asking him to turn around. But, again, the words wouldn't form in her mouth. She was filled with a fire that made her feel rebellious and reckless. Surely just a reaction to everything that was happening to her—everything that was expected of her? But she had a sense that she was somehow regaining some control over a life that had veered wildly out of control.

She also had an overwhelming compulsion to go towards this complete stranger as she was. Naked.

She took another step forward. The water broke just over her breasts. Another step. Now her breasts were bared to the man's dark gaze. She could see him more clearly now. His eyes dark. His jaw defined. Tight. His gaze dropped. Her nipples were already tight and hard from the water. They tingled.

She kept moving forward and the water lapped at her belly, then her hips, the tops of her legs and thighs. Between her legs, where the centre of her body pulsed with heat.

In some corner of her brain she was aghast at herself for behaving with such wanton confidence. She wasn't this person who would allow a stranger to see her naked body. But here, in this place—this place that had been a sacred refuge to her for her whole life—she felt removed from reality. Removed from the confines of normal behaviour.

And this man was more than just a random stranger. She'd sensed it the minute she'd laid eyes on him. He held himself with the arrogance and confidence of a born leader. Entitled. Proud.

She stepped into the shallows and reached for the robe

he held out. She pulled it on over her head, aware of that dark gaze watching as the fine material settled over her body, the bottom wet from the water.

The heat from his body lingered on the robe and made her skin prickle even more. Her breasts felt heavy. Tight.

'Thank you.' She sounded breathless.

'You're welcome.'

Strangely, even though she was covered again from neck to toe, she didn't feel any more protected from that penetrating gaze. Up close, she realised he was even more magnificent. A virile man in his prime. Tall. Broad. With dark olive skin that gleamed under the rising moon, stretched taut over hard muscles.

He held out a hand and Liyah looked at it for a long moment. The air was heavy around her. Heavy with a tension that had nothing to do with conflict or conversation. It was a tension that came from the crackling energy between them. A tension that came from this whole improbable situation.

In all her years of coming here she'd never met anyone else. Ever. But tonight, on the eve of her wedding to a man sight unseen, here was this compelling stranger. She wasn't usually prone to superstition, but it felt somehow…fated.

Tomorrow her life would change for ever, but tomorrow wasn't here yet… There was a whole night between now and then. A whole night of tantalising freedom left. The last piece of freedom she would have for some time.

Before she could think about it she put her hand into his. It was big. Slightly callused. Something about that evidence of hard work thrilled her. His fingers closed around hers and he tugged her out of the shallows and onto the sand.

Sharif had wondered if he was hallucinating. If he'd conjured up the goddess who had disappeared into the black depths of the oasis pool. But then she'd emerged, like Aphrodite, dark olive skin glistening like satin as the water sluiced over her body.

She was no marble statue, cold and rigid and pale. She was all woman. Flesh and bone. Limbs long and sleek.

And the hand in his now felt real enough.

Instinctively his thumb felt for her pulse and it throbbed at her wrist, echoing the throb in his blood.

'You are real...' he said, almost to himself.

Even though she was covered again, her naked image was imprinted on his brain. For ever, he suspected. He had watched her disrobe, too transfixed to say a word. Her body was carved from an erotic fantasy he hadn't even realised he'd had—strong and supple, athletic, but with curves that pronounced her a fertile woman in her prime.

Wide hips, small waist, long legs, lush bottom. And her breasts... Bigger than he would have guessed. Firm. Perfectly formed, with dark nipples that made his mouth water.

Dark tight curls at the juncture of her legs—he wanted to spread her there, see if she glistened...

'I am real.'

Her voice, husky, cut through the fever in Sharif's head. His hand tightened around hers and he tugged her towards him. He caught her scent—roses and earth and sand and heat.

The other thing that slammed into his awareness now, up close, was the fact that she was stunningly beautiful—and tall. The top of her head would graze his jaw. Dark eyebrows framed huge almond-shaped eyes. He couldn't make out their colour in the light, but they weren't as dark as his. Straight nose. High cheekbones. That dark olive complexion.

His fingers itched to reach out and touch her, explore to see if her skin felt as satiny as it looked.

But her mouth...

His avid gaze stopped there. Her mouth was beyond provocative. A lush invitation to taste and explore. To crush under his as he enticed her to give up all her secrets.

Sharif felt dizzy. He had met and slept with some of the world's most beautiful women and not one had ever affected him like this. On a visceral, primal level. He knew that if he didn't have this woman—

He couldn't even finish that thought. *He would have her.* He had to.

Her thick, wild hair was wet, but he could see that it was already showing a tendency to curl again.

'Where did you come from?'

A man not remotely prone to superstitions or fantasies, Sharif felt for the first time in his life as if the world around him wasn't entirely...concrete.

'I could ask the same of you.'

The fact that she sounded equally at a loss to explain this set of events was little comfort.

'Does it matter?'

Sharif knew as soon as he asked it that it was a rhetorical question. They were here now. That was all that mattered.

She shook her head. 'No, it doesn't. Who we are doesn't matter either.'

Sharif barely heard the thread of desperation in her voice. It was only afterwards that he would recall it. Long afterwards.

But right now he felt a weight lift off his chest and shoulders. For the first time since he could remember he was with someone who had no idea who he was. There was no preconception, no misconception, no judgement, no expectation.

'Would you like something to eat?'

She blinked. 'Yes...okay. I'd like that.'

Keeping hold of her hand, Sharif led the woman over to his tent.

* * *

The tent that was set up in the shelter of the trees was larger than Liyah had expected, but the man still had to duck his head a little to go in. He had to be six foot five at least. Tall enough to make her feel small. And she was used to towering over most people.

Men in particular seemed to find her height a provocation. But not this one. The way he'd looked at her so intently just now... Her heart hadn't slowed down since she'd laid eyes on him.

Her eyes adjusted from the falling light outside to the golden glow of lots of candles. There was a table set up with food, and a place-setting for one. There was a bed in the corner, large and luxurious, with jewel-covered throws.

Liyah looked away quickly, suddenly ambushed by the memory of how it had felt to walk out of the water naked, with his dark gaze on her. She didn't want him to see her looking at the bed. He'd already crossed about a dozen boundaries that, if her rational brain was working, she would never have allowed anyone to cross. Not to mention a complete stranger.

He let her hand go and went over to the chair and pulled it out. 'Please...sit down.'

Liyah looked around. 'There's only one chair.'

'I'll find something. Please.'

It was so surreal that Liyah did as he bade, moving around the table to sit down. She felt him behind her, his hands close to her shoulders. Her hair was still damp. Heavy. It was too long, too unruly, but every time she got frustrated and determined to cut it she would think of the pictures she had of her mother, with the same long hair, and she'd lose the will to let it go.

Any memory or connection with her mother was so tenuous. And precious.

The man had disappeared behind a screen that presumably hid the washing area. And now he reappeared, taking Liyah's breath away with his sheer physicality.

He had put on a plain white T-shirt and it made his dark olive skin look even darker. It highlighted the musculature of his chest, somehow making it more provocative than if he'd still been bare.

He put down a wooden stool on the opposite side of the table. For the first time she could look at him up close in the light and she was mesmerised.

He was breathtaking. His face was lean and sculpted, the low flickering candlelight casting shadows and making his skin gleam like burnished bronze. Hard jaw defined by stubble. Nose like a blade. Deep-set dark eyes. Fathomless.

His mouth was as strong as the rest of him, but wide. His lips were full, more than hinting at a sensual nature—as if Liyah hadn't noticed that as soon as she'd seen him. He oozed a sexual magnetism that had stunned her as effectively as if he'd shot her with a dart from a gun.

'Are you sure you don't want to take the chair? That doesn't look very comfortable.'

He shook his head and put an empty plate in front of her. 'Help yourself.'

At that moment Liyah realised she was famished. In the stress of the last week she'd barely eaten, and she didn't do well on low food supplies. The food looked... amazing. There was hummus and flatbread. Dolma vine leaves stuffed with meat. Succulent pieces of lamb with balls of spiced rice.

She picked a selection and put them on her plate. She heard a cork and saw him pour white wine into a glass.

He handed it to her. 'Drink?'

Liyah took it, and watched as he poured himself a glass. He raised it. The candles imbued the whole scene with a golden glow that didn't go anywhere near helping her to keep a grasp of reality.

'Here's to…unexpected encounters.'

Liyah lifted her glass. She could feel any desire to try to restore sanity, to remember who she was, where she was, fatally slipping away, to be replaced by a wholly different and far earthier desire.

She touched her glass to his and it made a low melodic chime. She echoed his words. 'To unexpected encounters.'

He lifted his glass to his mouth, and just before he took a sip he said, 'And what we make of them.'

CHAPTER TWO

'AND WHAT WE make of them.'

Liyah took a sip of her wine as she absorbed that comment. This man was altogether too bold and confident, but he'd woken something inside her. Something equally bold. If not as confident.

'Your eyes are green.'

Liyah looked at him. 'My mother's eyes were green.'

'Try the lamb. It's delicious.'

Liyah picked up a piece of lamb, along with some of the rice, and popped it into her mouth. The meat practically melted on her tongue and the spices in the rice made her taste buds come alive.

'You know this place well.'

It wasn't a question. Liyah swallowed her food and nodded. 'I've always come here. It's usually empty. It doesn't serve as a stopping point as it's so close to the city.' *To the palace.* She pushed her mind away from that reminder.

'Your bird is very tame. How old is he?'

Liyah bit back a smile. *'She.'*

The man smiled and she nearly fell off her chair. It changed him from being merely stupendously gorgeous to something not of this earth.

'I shouldn't have presumed.'

Liyah recovered her wits. 'She's been mine since I was a child. I trained her out here in the desert.'

'Does she have a name?'

Liyah felt self-conscious. No one had ever cared about her bird except for the falconer at the palace. 'Sheba.'

'Like the Queen? She is a beautiful bird.'

'Yes, she is.'

'Almost as beautiful as her owner.'

Liyah's mouth dried. Her heart thumped. He thought she was beautiful. But she knew that she wasn't really. She was too tall. Her hair was too wild. She couldn't fade gracefully into the background like other women. She always stuck out. Which made her think of her time in Europe. Her dark skin and height had marked her out from the start. Making her a target for people who wanted to exploit her for fun.

Others had told her she was beautiful back then too. And she'd lapped it up, starved of attention and in a new world where she'd felt out of place. But it had been a cruel lie.

This was a timely reminder. She had no idea who this man was and yet she was lapping up his attention like an eager puppy, having learnt nothing.

Liyah put down her napkin and went to stand, but the man caught her hand in his. He was frowning.

'Hey, where are you going?'

'I should leave. I don't know what I was thinking.'

Liyah pulled her hand free. The man stood up.

Just before she got to the opening to the tent, he said, 'Wait. Stop. Please.'

She didn't know him, but she sensed that he didn't say the word *please* much. It sounded rusty. Unused. She stopped and felt him come close behind her.

He said, 'Usually when I compliment a woman she doesn't run away.'

Liyah whirled around, incensed. 'I'm not running away. I've just realised that this is…' She stopped. She didn't even have words for what this was.

He supplied one. 'Crazy?'

'I didn't come here this evening expecting to find…you.'

'And yet here I am. I wasn't expecting company either. Far from it.'

Liyah looked up at him. He was too tall. So broad. He eclipsed everything around him.

'If I wanted to leave now, would you let me?'

He took a step back, looking almost affronted. 'Of course. You're free to go.' But then his expression changed and he said, '*If* you want to. But I don't think you do want to…'

He sounded so sure of himself. Part of Liyah wanted to prove him wrong. She wanted to turn, go outside, pick up her clothes and leave. But a much bigger part of her—the part that had felt little or no compunction about revealing her naked body to him—wanted to stay.

As if sensing her vacillation, he said, 'This thing between us…this connection…is not usual. You do know that?'

Of course she didn't. She'd believed that she'd wanted a man before—*correction, a boy*—but what she'd felt then had been nothing remotely like this swooping exhilarating rollercoaster of sensations. Even the food had tasted more delicious than anything she'd ever tasted before.

Fearing for her very sanity, she almost whispered, 'Are you actually real?'

He took a step towards her again and she could smell him, spicy and musky. He took her hand and lifted it up, placed it on his chest, over his heart.

She felt the strong rhythmic *thump-thump* under her palm. It sent a veritable tsunami of emotions through her. It was so illicitly intimate, yet reassuring at the same time.

Her father ran a conservative household. He didn't approve of displays of affection in public, or in private either. Any physical touch Liyah had experienced growing up had come at the brusque hands of nannies, or the women in the palace hammam.

She'd been in the hammam the day before, and to her eternal shame—because she didn't usually indulge in self-pity—a sense of loneliness and vulnerability had gripped her. She'd found tears running down her face. The only saving grace had been that she'd known they wouldn't be noticed during the ancient full-body-washing ritual.

Tears were a weakness that Liyah rarely indulged in. She had no reason to feel sorry for herself. She'd been born into a privileged world, albeit one that came with responsibilies and duties. She'd had a moment of believing she might escape them—when she'd been in Europe—but deep down she'd always known that her fate was not her own. She just hadn't known how that would manifest, or that it would manifest so dramatically.

And yet here she was, with her palm on this man's chest, his heart echoing the drumming of her blood. A sense of fatality gripped her. She had no idea what her husband-to-be was like, or who he was beyond a name—her own stubborn fault for not wanting to know…as if that might stop it happening—but tomorrow she would no longer be *this* anonymous woman.

No longer free to feel the heartbeat of a stranger under her palm. No longer free to swim naked or to take off on her horse when the whim took her. No longer—

'Kiss me, please,' she blurted out, the words rising up from an unstoppable place inside her.

Sharif's blood leapt. He wanted nothing more than to kiss this woman. And a lot more. But he forced himself to stop for a second.

He put his hand over hers on his chest. It felt incredibly feminine and delicate. 'Are you sure?'

He had seen the turmoil on her face just now, as if she was agonising. But now it was clear, determined.

She nodded. And said, 'Yes. I'm sure.'

Sharif took his hand from hers and put his hands on her upper arms, tugging her gently towards him until he could feel the heat of her body through the thin robe.

Her hair was already starting to curl wildly again. Her

green eyes were huge. Unusual, and adding to her striking beauty. Not many had light-coloured eyes in this region. He wondered again for a second who she might be, but then pushed it aside. It didn't matter. All that mattered was this.

He pulled her closer until he could feel the lush curves of her body come into contact with his. *Dio.* He felt like a schoolboy with his first woman all over again. What the hell was *that* about?

She was looking up at him, both hands splayed on his chest now. Lips parting, trembling slightly, her breath coming in little pants that made her breasts move against him.

He bent his head and covered her mouth with his, and even as a part of him was telling himself that this was no different from any other kiss he knew it was a lie.

Her lips were soft, but firm. Like her. All over. And he'd barely touched her but he was drowning. His hands tightened on her arms as if that would help anchor him as he deepened the kiss and tasted her sweetness.

She was hesitant at first, and that only heightened the eroticism of this relatively chaste kiss, but then she became bolder, matching his exploration with her own, nipping his tongue with her teeth. She wrapped her arms around his neck and came even closer…so close that he could feel the tantalising thrust of her hard nipples through the fabric of their clothes.

He pulled back, dizzy. He needed to see her, feel her. Now.

He must have spoken out loud because she took down her hands and arms and stepped back, dislodging his hold.

And as he watched she pulled his robe up and over her head, and dropped it to the floor of the tent.

He was looking at her as if he'd never seen a woman before. Which was ridiculous, because he had already seen her and she would be an idiot to think for a second that a man like this, who oozed sexuality and confidence, hadn't looked on lots of naked women.

Liyah's mouth felt swollen after that kiss. She could still taste him, dark and explicit, on her tongue.

But that black gaze devoured her now, lingering on her breasts, her belly, her waist. And down to the juncture between her legs. Her thighs.

'Turn around,' he ordered gruffly.

Liyah did so, welcoming momentary escape from that avid intensity. She heard movement behind her and then felt his heat before she felt him. *He was naked.*

He pulled her hair aside and over one shoulder. His hands came to her arms again and she felt his breath against her before his lips touched her bare skin.

'Okay?' he asked.

His consideration was not something she'd anticipated when she'd behaved so impetuously.

She nodded, and whispered, 'Yes. Please.'

Please keep going. Transport me from this world, from myself, for tonight, so I don't have to—

Liyah sucked in a gasp when the man's arms came under hers and he cupped her breasts in his big hands. His hair-roughened chest was at her back. And she could feel the potency of his hard body. Hard for her.

Heat grew at her core, making her wet. She groaned softly and fell back into him, her legs turning to jelly as one hand left her breast and travelled down, exploring her curves, over her belly to that place between her legs.

He drew her up against him, his erection cupped by her buttocks. With one hand, he explored her breast, fingers finding and trapping her nipple, his other hand gently encouraged her to part her legs, so that he could explore her there. Find the seam of flesh that was the last barrier to the evidence of how much she wanted him. Wanted this.

And then he was there, his fingers opening her up, sinking deep. She clutched at his arm, his hand. Pushing and pulling at the same time. Wanting him to keep doing what he was doing between her legs, but not wanting him to see how much she wanted it.

He whispered against her skin. 'It's okay... I know...'

She gave up fighting her response and opened up even more, allowing him to move his hand between her legs, his fingers seeking and finding and thrusting deep into her clasping flesh.

Liyah might have screamed—she wasn't even sure. All she knew was that he was turning her head so his mouth could fuse with hers as her whole body quivered and shook in his arms, the precursor to the storm he unleashed with a flick of his fingers.

Liyah was floating...and it was only when he laid her down on the bed that she realised she hadn't been floating at all. He'd just carried her over to the bed.

Her whole body was suffused with lingering ecstasy, the waves of orgasm making her inner muscles clench in reaction. She hadn't had an orgasm before...and now she understood.

A wave of gratitude swept through her, and before she could stop herself she said, 'Thank you.'

He came down on the bed beside her, long lean muscles rippling under all that dark skin. 'What for?'

Liyah clamped her mouth shut. She didn't want to admit she hadn't had an orgasm before, despite having had sex once. She didn't want to admit that she'd felt there must be something wrong with her because she hadn't enjoyed the experience, at all. It had been humiliating on so many levels and then afterwards—

She shut her mind to that.

She shook her head on the pillow. 'Nothing... Just, thank you.'

The man smiled.

Liyah bit her lip, wanting his mouth on hers again, drugging her, transporting her.

To mask her desire, she looked at him. She hadn't seen his naked body before...he'd been behind her. But now, as he lay alongside her, she let her gaze move down over the hard planes of his chest and his taut belly. To the dark hair between his legs and the rigid length of his erection. Veins ran up along the shaft, pulsing with blood. His thighs were thick and muscled.

Liyah felt dizzy, even though she was lying down. She glanced at him, feeling shy. He was watching her. She came up on one arm. 'Can I...? Touch you...?'

He lay on his back, his smile turning lazy. Knowing. 'Be my guest.'

Liyah came up on her knees. She tentatively put out a hand and placed it on his chest, feeling his heart beat again. It was thumping hard. Fast. She trailed it down over his belly. His muscles clenched. She looked at him quickly. He wasn't smiling any more.

He said, 'Go on.'

She was too intimidated by the silk and steel length of him to explore there just yet, so she traced her fingers over his thigh, marvelling at the sheer strength. His hips were narrow, where hers flared out. She'd never been so aware of a man and a woman's innate differences.

His body jerked at her touch, as if tempting her to touch him more intimately.

Her heart-rate leapt and after a moment of hesitation, she gave in to temptation, touching him experimentally.

He made a sound and she stopped.

He looked pained.

She asked, 'What is it?'

'Nothing, just...don't stop.'

Liyah curled her hand around him—as much as she could. There was a drop of moisture at the head and she had the inexplicable urge to lick it, taste his essence. She blushed at the thought.

'Let me see you.'

His voice sounded thick. Not sure what he meant, Liyah looked at him. He sat up slightly, muscles contracting. He took her arms and gently encouraged her to straddle him, placing her so she was spread across his thighs and facing him. Nowhere to hide. Exposed. Her skin prickled with excitement.

His hands moved down to her hips. He sat back against the plumped-up cushions. 'You have beautiful breasts.'

Liyah blushed again. She'd never thought much of her breasts. She'd always been a bit self-conscious of their size, wishing she had a more petite frame like her younger half-sisters. They felt heavy now.

He sat up and cupped them, looking at her briefly before bringing his hot mouth to first one and then the other, teasing her with open kisses and gentle nips on her skin, before placing his mouth where she was screaming internally to be touched.

He sucked one nipple and then the other, tugging at her flesh and making her head fall back at the sensation. He fed her flesh into his mouth as if savouring the most succulent food.

And then, with one hand, he touched her between her legs, where she was so exposed, and without warning she fell over the edge again, gasping in surprise and not a little terrified at this control he could wield so easily over her. It was as if he knew her body better than she did. A stranger.

When her world had stopped spinning she realised that he was lying back and her hands were digging into his chest. He pulled her down so that her breasts were crushed into his chest and then he moved her hair back, finding her mouth and kissing her.

Excitement built again when she felt his erection straining between them. Her body was moving instinctively against his, seeking friction. Seeking *more*.

He expertly manoeuvred her body so that she was sitting up again, poised over him. He held himself in his hand, the head nudging the entrance to her very core. She couldn't breathe. It was as if her body wept with the need to feel him inside her.

She let herself sink onto him slowly as he took his hand away and gripped her hip. He was big. She sucked in a breath but he lay still, letting her dictate the pace as she allowed her body to absorb all that heat and strength.

She held her breath as momentary discomfort made itself felt.

His hands tightened on her hips. 'Are you...?'

She focused on him, her vision blurred by all the sensations coursing through her body. What was he asking? If she was a—?

She shook her head. 'No, I'm not.'

But she'd only had sex once before, and she wasn't even sure if the experience counted, because it had felt nothing like this.

The discomfort had become something else—something much sharper and more pleasurable. Liyah started to move up and down slowly, letting her body get used to his.

They were both breathing heavily now, and Liyah felt sweat sheening her skin. Her movements became faster, and he held her hips lightly, but she could feel the need in him to hold her so that he could take control.

She felt infinitely powerful in that moment. But then her own frustration grew because she couldn't find the perfect rhythm that her body craved.

In a split second he'd manoeuvred them so that she was on her back and he looked down at her, his body still deeply embedded in hers.

He pulled out and her every muscle tensed, waiting

for the delicious slide of his body into hers again, but he stopped.

Hoping she didn't sound as desperate as she felt, Liyah said, 'Is something wrong?'

He pulled out fully and her body protested.

'Protection. I have no protection here.'

Liyah didn't understand for a second, and then she did. Relief flowed through her. 'It's okay. I'm on the pill.'

Sharif looked at the woman under him. Her wild hair was spread around her head. Her skin was flushed dark red, her eyes like bright green jewels. Lips plump.

The effort it had taken him to pull free from the clasp of her body made him shake. No woman—*ever*—had had this effect on him. Sex for him was usually a transitory physical satisfaction. Like scratching an itch. He'd always derived more pleasure out of the chase and the conquest than the actual *act*. He'd always been able to hold himself slightly aloof…

But here—now—that ability to remain aloof was incinerated. He'd almost forgotten his own rule. *Never sleep with a woman without protection*—because he had no intention of revisiting the sins of his father on an innocent child.

In another instant, with another woman, Sharif would have taken this as a wake-up call. His natural cynicism and distrust of people would have flatlined his desire.

But his entire being ached with the need to sheath himself inside her again and throw caution to the wind, following the dictates of his body, mind and soul to seek an oblivion he knew instinctively would eclipse anything he'd felt before.

He didn't even know her name.

He would never see her after this night.

Even more disturbing was this instinct that he had to

trust her. Or was that just needy desperation because he wanted her so badly?

'You're on the pill?'

She nodded. 'For over a year now. I wouldn't lie about something like this. The consequences for someone like me would be…unthinkable.'

Any sliver of sanity that might have pulled Sharif back from the edge melted into a heat haze. In this moment he believed her—and not just because he wanted to.

He said, 'I'm clean. I got checked recently.'

Even though he never made love without protection.

Her hands went to his chest, palms flat. 'I trust you.'

I trust you.

No women—*no person*—had ever said that to him before. He had never been in the business of fostering enough intimacy to invite statements like that. *Until now.*

But he didn't want to dwell on that. Not when every muscle in his body was screaming with the need to join his body with this woman's.

He forced himself to say, 'Are you sure?'

She nodded. 'Please—I want this. I want you.'

He found the slick folds that parted, oh, so easily when he pushed against her, and couldn't help the low groan of intense satisfaction when he sheathed himself inside her silky tight embrace again. The fact that this didn't just feel like *sex* was also something he didn't want to dwell on.

He forced himself to control his thrusts, letting her get used to his body. He knew he was big, and he could tell she was inexperienced—even if she wasn't a virgin.

Gradually he felt her body adjust to his, saw the way her cheeks flushed a darker pink. The way she bit her lip. The way she moved under him, lifting her hips. Her hands explored him, and if she wasn't careful she was going to push him off the edge way before he was ready.

He caught her hands and raised them above her head, linking their fingers. He said, 'Spread your legs wider for me.'

She did, and he sank even deeper. She let out a low moan. Sharif let her go and slid his hand under her back, arching her up so that he could find and suck one hard nipple into his mouth, rolling the taut peak before nipping gently.

Her movements became more frenzied, and he felt the telltale flutters along his length as he drove deep and hard. Sweat sheened their skin as they raced to the pinnacle, and it took more control than Sharif had ever had to call on in his life to ensure that she reached it before he did.

She arched up, her whole body taut like a bow, as her orgasm held her high before ripping through her body all the way to her inner muscles, which clenched so hard around Sharif that he was no longer capable of holding back the flood of ecstasy that wiped his brain clean of every single coherent thought.

Today

Liyah woke with a start. She was lying in an unfamiliar bed in unfamiliar surroundings and her body felt...

A rush of heat flashed through her mind when she recalled where she was.

And with whom.

The nameless man.

He was lying on his front beside her, but not touching her. One arm was carelessly hanging over the edge of the bed, the other was bent up over his head. His face was turned to the side, towards her.

Even in sleep he looked fierce. Strong. The stubble lining his jaw was darker...

Her wide awake gaze—tracked down over the sleek

muscles, no less impressive at rest. Those narrow hips.
His buttocks—firm. A pulse throbbed between her legs
when she thought of the sheer power of his body thrusting
into hers, so deep she'd seen stars.

A wave of emotion took her by surprise. After her first
dismal sexual experience in Europe she'd suspected that
there might be something wrong with her. But after last
night...

This man had restored a very wounded part of her soul.
And her confidence. He'd looked at her as if he'd never
seen a woman before. He'd touched her as reverently as
if she was infinitely precious, and then he'd made love
to her as if he had been starving for something only she
could give him.

She'd fallen into a pleasure-induced coma after that first
time and had woken in his arms to find him carrying her
over to a steaming hot bath that had been hidden behind
the screen.

She hadn't even been aware of how tender her muscles
were until she'd felt the hot water soothe them. Still stunned
after what had happened, she'd been incapable of speech.
He'd climbed into the bath behind her, spreading his legs
down alongside hers, and had tucked her hair up in a knot
before soaping her all over, his big hands making her feel
delicate and precious for the first time...*ever.*

She'd turned her head, afraid of the clutch of emotion in
her chest—afraid of what it meant and that he'd see it —
and had found his mouth. Firm and hot. She'd turned in the
bath until she was straddling him, the silky water making
it easy to glide over him and sink down onto his erection.
The movement of their bodies, as if they'd been made for
each other, had quickened as the fever of lust had taken
them over, the water splashing all around the tub going
unnoticed in their race to find nirvana again.

She had only the vaguest memory of him lifting her out

of the bath, rubbing her down briskly with a towel and laying her back down on the bed, of his steely warmth surrounding her, his hand on her breast…

Yet here she was now. Her bones felt liquid.

She noticed, almost lazily, that there were pink trails in the sky outside, just visible above the opening in the tent.

Pink trails heralding dawn.

The dawn of her wedding day.

Suddenly Liyah wasn't feeling lazy any more. Panic gripped her belly. She was due to have henna painted on her hands and feet this morning, in preparation for the afternoon's ceremony.

She had to go. *Now.*

She managed to leave the sumptuous bed without waking him, and stole to the opening of the tent. But there she stopped, giving in to temptation and taking one last look, knowing she'd never see him again. Knowing that she might always wonder if she'd dreamt this night up.

Her eyes devoured his majestic form. Even though he was sprawled in louche splendour across the bed, he was no less impressive or intimidating. His body and his face would be imprinted on her memory. For ever.

That clutch of emotion caught at Liyah again. What had happened here had been so…unexpected. Unprecedented. And magical. It would be her secret to carry with her, deep inside, where no one would ever find it.

Least of all her new husband.

When Sharif woke his head felt fuzzy, as if he'd had too much to drink. And his body felt pleasantly achy. Heavy. But also light.

But he hadn't had too much to drink.

He'd just had the most intensely erotic experience of his life.

Sharif jacknifed up to sit in the bed as vivid memories assailed him.

But beside him was an empty space. No sign of the wild-haired temptress with the green eyes who had rendered him insensible with desire.

Desire? He grimaced at that. Desire was too ineffectual a word for what he'd felt for her from the moment he'd seen her revealed by the pool.

A wave of lust gripped him as the previous night came back in glorious Technicolor. The way she'd sat astride him, taking him deep into her body, the look of awe on her face, her cheeks darkened with pleasure. And how it had felt when her secret inner muscles had milked him—

Dio. Sharif never dwelled on sex with lovers. He had it—he moved on.

He got out of the bed, feeling dizzy for a moment. Dizzy after a night of unbridled pleasure. He sensed the tent was empty and walked to the entrance, pulling back the material over the opening.

Dawn was bathing the oasis in deep pinks and golds. Sharif stepped out. Naked. The cool air made his skin prickle, but so did the fact that there was no sign of the woman.

Her horse was gone.

She was gone.

He walked over to the pool. Its serene surface left no hint of the unearthly goddess who had disappeared into its depths only to emerge and prove that she'd been all too earthly.

Sharif's skin prickled even more, and it had nothing to do with the cool air and everything to do with a sense of exposure. Had she in fact existed at all? Or had it been a particularly lurid dream? Was he so jaded that he'd conjured up an erotic fantasy to entertain himself on the eve of his wedding to a woman sight unseen?

In fact the more he thought about it, the more he found it almost easier to believe it hadn't happened. He was no saint, but neither was he inclined to 'instalust' or casual sex with a stranger. Usually his women were carefully vetted.

Not that it stopped them from crying to the tabloids when he ended their liaisons, a snide inner voice reminded him.

He ignored the voice. And then went cold as he thought of something else. They hadn't used protection. He'd taken her at her word when she'd mentioned being on the pill.

He shook his head. It couldn't have happened. He *never* indulged in unprotected sex. A man like him was a magnet for women who wanted to secure their lives by having his baby. And he was not in the market for babies. Not now. Not ever.

In a bid to wake himself out of this reverie and come back to sanity, Sharif stepped into the water and dived deep into its inky depths. The shock of the water made his brain freeze, and only when his lungs were ready to burst did he come back up to the surface.

As he sucked in deep breaths his mind cleared. It *had* been a dream. Lurid and very real, yes, but a dream. That was the only way he could explain it. And he always had crazy dreams when he was in the desert. Admittedly, never like that...

Sharif walked out of the water, a sense of almost relief coursing through him. Relief that it hadn't been real, but also a tinge of regret. But of course she hadn't been real—a woman like that couldn't possibly be...

Just then something caught his peripheral vision. Something white. He went over to it. It was near the shoreline, on the ground.

Sharif stooped down and picked it up. A scrap of material. White. Cotton. Plain. Underwear.

A flash of memory came back to him—the woman stepping out of her clothes. Diving into the water.

She *had* been real.

The relief that coursed through him made a mockery of his assurance that it had all been a dream, but Sharif's mouth firmed. It might have been real, and he might have acted completely out of character, but she was gone now, like a ghost, and she would have to remain that way. Within a few hours he was to marry a woman he'd never met. He didn't need the distraction of an erotic temptress.

It was time to avenge his mother's betrayal and her death, and nothing would get in his way.

CHAPTER THREE

'YOUR WIFE MAY now reveal her face.'

Liyah's heart was thumping so hard she was surprised no one else could hear it. It had taken off like a racehorse, obliterating the escalating dread, the minute she'd seen her husband-to-be and recognised him as her nameless lover from the previous night.

No longer nameless.

He was Sheikh Sharif Bin Noor Al Nazar. Or, as he was better known in America and Europe, Sharif Marchetti, CEO of a vast luxury conglomerate.

This information had been supplied to her by the gossiping women at the henna painting ceremony earlier that day, while there had also been mention of how handsome he was.

Liyah's head had been too full of the previous night to take much notice.

He was resplendent in Al-Murja royal dress, which made him look even taller and broader. The cream silk of his royal robes, with gold thread piping, enhanced his dark skin tone. He wore no headdress. But Liyah noticed that his hair had been trimmed since last night. And his jaw was clean-shaven.

She remembered the graze of his stubble against her inner thighs...

She slammed a door on that incendiary memory.

The shock that had hit her like a body-blow as soon as she'd recognised him still gripped her, keeping her in a sort of paralysis. The only thing that had given her the time to absorb that shock was the fact that he hadn't yet recognised *her*. But he was about to...

The women came forward—her sister Samara was one

of her attendants today—and they deftly and far too quickly removed the elaborate face shield that was a traditional part of weddings in Taraq, and had been for hundreds of years.

Liyah blinked as her eyes adjusted to the brightness of the throne room in the royal palace. A grand description for what was really a modest fortress.

She looked up at her husband with dread lining her belly and saw the expressions chase across his face as if in slow motion. Recognition. Confusion. And then shock, disbelief. Anger.

And then his mouth opened and he uttered one word. *'You!'*

Somehow—miraculously—no one seemed to have caught Sharif's exclamation of recognition, and the ceremony finished as Liyah's hand was placed over his—the moment when she was deemed to be his wife.

Her hand was covered in the dark, intricate stains of henna. The red swirls swam a little in front of her eyes and she had to suck in a breath, terrified she might faint. The heavy robes and headdress she wore weren't helping.

Her gaze had slid away from his as soon as he'd spoken, but she could feel those dark eyes on her, boring into her, silently commanding her to look at him.

She felt numb, and she welcomed it, because if the numbness wore off then she knew she would be subjected to an onslaught of sensations and memories.

When she'd returned to the palace earlier, and undergone the pre-wedding bathing ritual, she'd lamented her mystery lover's touch and smell being washed from her body, even though she knew how inappropriate it would have been to go to another man while his imprint was still on her.

But he was no longer a mystery. He was her husband. And that fact filled her with so many conflicting feelings that she felt dizzy all over again.

They were led in a procession with the guests and both

families into another formal room. The ballroom. Where a lavish feast had been laid out.

Normally weddings in Taraq would be three and four-day affairs—but, as her father had told her, this was to be a much briefer celebration.

Liyah and Sharif were seated at the top table, side by side. She took her hand from his and sat down, studiously avoiding looking to her right, where he sat. The ring that had been placed on her finger during the ceremony felt heavy. She'd barely looked at it—a thick, ornate gold ring, with a bluish stone in a circular setting surrounded by diamonds.

The King of Al-Murja, a man as tall and dark and handsome as Sharif, sat nearby, looking austere. As austere as her husband.

Husband. She felt dizzy again, even though she was sitting down.

Liyah cursed herself now for not having looked him up. If she had, she would have known who he was at the oasis.

And would that have changed her behaviour?

Liyah couldn't say how she would have reacted last night even if she'd known who he was. It was all too much to process.

And then, from her right, came a low and steely tone. 'Look at me, *wife.*'

Liyah gulped and slowly turned her head to meet those far too memorable dark eyes. She noticed now that there were gold rings around his irises. So not totally dark. Golden. Molten.

'So what was that last night? Were you trying out the wares before you committed to marriage with a stranger? Should I be flattered you deemed me suitable?'

His voice was cold enough to make her shiver—a big difference from how he'd sounded last night. The mid-

Atlantic twang mocked her now. As did her instinct last night that he was not just *anyone*.

'No,' she croaked. 'It wasn't like that. I had no idea who you were.'

He made a rude sound. 'I find that hard to believe.'

His accusing tone broke Liyah out of her shocked paralysis. 'Wait... Did you know who I was?'

'No.'

A dart of hurt lanced her. He'd been equally disinclined to know about her. But she shouldn't be surprised—after all her sister had told her. *He just wants a wife. He doesn't care who that is.*

'Then I could accuse you of the same—maybe you did know who I was and you wanted to make sure *I* was suitable.'

'You weren't a virgin. That would make you very unsuitable to some.'

Liyah flushed at that. In this part of the world he would be within his rights to reject her on those grounds... Except the time to do it would have been the moment he'd recognised her.

'Are you going to say something?' Liyah immediately thought of the potential repercussions for her younger sister, who might be denied the husband she wanted to punish Liyah.

But Sharif shook his head slowly. 'No. I'm not a hypocrite. I'm far from a virgin. I don't expect my wife to be. Anyway, that's not what this marriage will be about.'

Liyah looked at him. She frowned. 'What's that supposed—?'

But she was cut off when the music started, drowning out what she'd been about to say. She had to face forward to watch the traditional dancers.

Her brain was racing, wanting to know what Sharif had meant. She cursed herself again for not having looked him up. She would have been better prepared. But it was too late to dwell on regrets. Or on reckless decisions made in the heat of the moment.

She'd never expected to see him again but now he was her husband. And she would have to deal with the consequences.

Sharif's blood was boiling as he sat beside his brand-new wife. Aaliyah. She now had a name. The woman who had driven him senseless with lust only a few hours ago. The same woman he'd suspected of being a figment of his imagination.

He didn't believe for a second that she hadn't known who he was last night. It was too conveniently serendipitous that she'd just happened to visit the oasis when he'd been there.

Someone must have told her that he hadn't arrived at the palace with his entourage. And she'd come to investigate her future husband. The thought that she'd been laughing at him the whole way through the marriage ceremony, behind her veil, set his nerves on edge.

Little happened in Sharif's life that he wasn't in control of. And this was not how he'd envisaged his marriage starting—with his blood boiling over with shock, anger and, even worse, *lust*.

Even though her body was now covered in the voluminous red and white traditional wedding robes of Taraq, Sharif could picture every dip and hollow. How she'd looked when she'd stepped out of the water in front of him, water sluicing down over endless curves and gleaming skin. The long sleek limbs. Her breasts, perfectly shaped and heavy... the juncture between her legs where dark hair curled enticingly, inviting him to explore—

Dio. He'd planned on making the most of his wife in the coming weeks, having her by his side at as many events as possible to ensure that the Marchetti Group brand was at its most stable and valuable for when he put his plans into motion.

By his side. Not in his bed. And most definitely *not* under his skin.

The last woman in the world he'd ever expected to see again, who he wanted nowhere near him, was in fact now his wife. And as his wife, she would be in close proximity at all times. Whether he liked it or not.

'Liyah…you look so sophisticated. I've never seen you like this.'

Liyah grimaced at her reflection in the mirror. The shift dress and matching jacket were in pastel pink. She hated pink. She hated anything too girly and always had, preferring a far more relaxed and casual tomboy aesthetic.

She'd barely even taken notice of the women who had measured her up the day after her father had allowed her to take Samara's place as Sharif's bride. She'd been too impatient to see her horse, whom she hadn't seen in months, while she'd been in Europe.

But now she knew why she'd been measured up.

Because her…her *husband* had provided this going-away outfit. And another bag containing a change of clothes, sleepwear, underwear and toiletries.

She thought she looked ridiculous. Her hair was too wild and unruly for an outfit like this, but it was too late to try and tame it. And, even worse, suddenly she felt nervous. She'd managed to avoid Sharif while the reception had been underway and they'd been surrounded by a hundred people, but now she would be stepping onto a plane with him and there would be nowhere to hide.

'My hair…my hair is too much.'

Samara stepped up behind her and pulled her hair back

into a low ponytail. 'Your hair is beautiful, Liyah, like the rest of you.'

Samara rested her chin on Liyah's shoulder and she met her sister's dark gaze in the mirror. Liyah didn't even share the same eye colour as her siblings. She really was the cuckoo in the nest.

Samara's pretty face was serious. 'Thank you, Liyah, for what you've done. You have no idea how much—'

A rising swell of emotion made Liyah turn around. She clasped her sister close before the emotion became too much to push down. 'I know,' she whispered. 'I know. Just be happy, Sammy, okay? Marry Javid and be happy.'

At that moment Liyah truly wished for her sister that she wouldn't be disappointed by love. Or destroyed by it, like their father.

Her sister nodded against her. She pulled back, dark eyes bright with tears. But she forced a smile. 'I'll miss you.'

'And I'll miss you. But call me any time, okay?'

Samara nodded again.

Maids entered to take Liyah's bags down to where her husband waited in the royal courtyard and Liyah followed them. Samara was the only one who had come to say good-bye. Liyah hated it that it still hurt. That some small vulnerable part of her had still hoped that she'd be important to her family. To her father.

She stopped in the shadows just under the massive stone archway that led outside. Sharif was pacing back and forth. He saw the maids coming out with the bags and flicked his wrist to look at his watch, clearly impatient. But Liyah couldn't move.

Gone were the elaborate gold and cream robes of the regal Sheikh—and gone was the wild nameless man who had seduced her into a place of heated insanity last night. In their place was another incarnation...this one even more intimidating.

His tall, lean body was sheathed in an immaculate three-piece dark suit. A white shirt, open at the neck, highlighted his dark skin. He *should* have looked more civilised. More urbane. But if anything he looked even more elemental. Wild. Dangerous.

Even though she'd slept with him, she felt in that moment that she'd never truly know him, and a little shiver skated over her skin. A kind of premonition that as soon as she stepped out of this shadow and into the sunlight, under his gaze and his protection, her life would never be the same. And she knew it wouldn't—for obvious reasons, and also for much deeper and more secret reasons that she really did not want to investigate right now.

The self-protective walls she'd cultivated her whole life suddenly felt very flimsy.

The sun was setting, bathing everything with a golden glow. It had been around this time yesterday that Liyah had left the palace to ride out to the oasis.

Suddenly, in spite of everything, she had a sense that she didn't regret what had happened at the oasis. It had been too earth-shattering to regret. It had changed something inside her.

A man who looked like an aide hurried over to Sharif's side, and Liyah heard Sharif speak in a low, harsh tone.

'Find her.'

Steeling herself, Liyah stepped forward out of the shadows. 'I'm here. Ready to go.'

Sharif turned around, his whole body reacting with a jolt of awareness just to hearing her husky voice.

Damn.

She had changed out of the traditional wedding robes that dated back to when her family had been Bedouin nomads. Sharif had asked an assistant to ensure she received appropriate clothes for her transition into his world as his wife, but clearly he hadn't researched much about her, or what she looked like.

Nor did you, reminded an inner voice.

He quashed the sting of his conscience when he thought of how little it had registered when he'd been asked if he would mind marrying the eldest Princess of Taraq and not her sister.

He'd agreed, and in the same instant moved on to the next item on his agenda—because it really didn't matter to whom he was married. All he needed was a wife.

But now he was aware of the significance of having chosen another woman, however carelessly.

Would the other sister have been sent to the oasis to seduce him, too?

The pastel pink did nothing for her skin tone, and the plain design of the dress effectively hid the spectacular curves that he couldn't stop seeing in his mind's eye. All he could think about was the fact that this woman needed to be dressed in bold and vibrant colours. With jewels at her throat and ears. Her wrists. Arms. And with silk and satin clinging to every luscious inch of her body.

Nothing could really detract from her sheer luminous beauty, though. Not even her unstyled pulled-back hair, or the fact that her face was scrubbed clean. Sharif couldn't recall the last time a woman had made so little effort for him.

Irritation at his reaction to her and this whole situation, which had morphed beyond what he'd expected, made his voice sharp. 'We should leave. My plane is waiting at the airfield.'

He noticed how she lifted her chin at his tone and something flashed in those stunning green eyes. A flash of defiance. His blood sizzled and he gritted his jaw.

He ignored his driver standing to attention and opened the back door of the Jeep himself. 'Please.'

He'd said *please* more than he'd ever said it in his life within the past twenty-four hours.

Aaliyah moved forward, the nude high heels making her legs look even longer and more lissom, reminding him of how strong her thighs were. Firm and lean from riding her thoroughbred stallion to deserted oases so she could swim naked and tempt men. Tempt *him*.

Suddenly the thought that he might not have been the only one to see her like that made his blood spike to dangerous levels.

He gritted his jaw even harder as her clean, unmanufactured scent tickled his nostrils as she got into the car and her dress slid up, revealing a taut and silky-smooth thigh. He'd noticed that the heels put her tantalisingly closer to his mouth too.

He closed the door and walked around the vehicle to get into the front beside the driver. The sooner they were back in his world, on his turf, where he could regain some sense of control, the better.

Liyah woke with a start, not sure were she was. There was a voice.

'Mrs Marchetti?'

Who was Mrs Marchetti?

It came again, insistent, along with a peremptory knock on wood.

She was on her husband's private jet.

It all came rushing back.

'Mrs Marchetti? We're landing in half an hour.'

Liyah sat up in the bed. The voice was on the other side of the bedroom door. 'Thank you. I'm awake,' she croaked out.

'Would you like some breakfast?'

Liyah saw the pink trails across the sky outside. They'd chased the dawn from the Middle East to the west.

'Just some coffee would be lovely, thank you.'

She was about to land in a whole new world and life. She'd expected this to be happening with a stranger. Well, he still was a stranger. But one she knew intimately.

Liyah saw the en suite bathroom and went in, groaning when she saw the frizz ball her hair had become. Her face was creased too, from where she'd lain down. She felt sticky.

She noticed that someone had left her bags in the bedroom and took the opportunity to freshen up, pulling out a pair of dark trousers and a long-sleeved cashmere top. Simple, elegant. Better than the powder-pink dress.

She took a quick shower, tying her hair up out of the way. It was too much of a job to get into washing and drying it now.

When she'd dried off and changed, she found a mercifully flat pair of shoes and took a breath and went into the cabin.

She could see Sharif's dark head over his seat-back. When she came closer he was engrossed in his laptop. He glanced at her as she came alongside him and slid into the seat on the other side of the aisle. She only realised then that she'd left her hair in a knot on the top of her head, too wild to let loose.

The steward came over with a steaming coffee and Liyah smiled her thanks, accepting it gratefully, hoping she didn't look too dishevelled.

She took a sip, relishing the hot tart taste, and then risked another look at Sharif. He closed his laptop and she noticed stubble on his jaw. He'd taken off his jacket but still wore the waistcoat of the suit. Shirtsleeves rolled up. He was utterly civilised and *un*civilised all at the same time. A potent mix.

'Did you work all night?'

He accepted a coffee from the steward too. He looked at her, arching a brow. 'Concerned about me, Aaliyah?'

His voice made her insides tighten with awareness. This man was so dangerous. And he already knew so much about her. Too much.

Up until the cataclysmic moment when she'd realised who her husband was, she'd felt safe in the knowledge that her uncharacteristic behaviour would never be scrutinised in the cold light of day. But the universe was laughing at her now. Not only would her behaviour be scrutinised, but she'd married a man whose only impression of her was based on the illicit night they'd shared together. And she had no defence. She'd been bolder and more brazen than at any other time in her life.

'Don't call me Aaliyah. It's Liyah. Please.'

'Liyah, then.' His gaze dropped, taking in her change of clothes. 'Dark matte colours and pinks do nothing for you,' he observed. 'We'll remedy that. I have lots of events lined up that you'll be required to attend by my side.'

Liyah flushed at the way he assessed her so coolly, as if she was some kind of mannequin. Feeling defensive she said, 'I didn't choose the clothes. They were picked for me.'

'Well, you didn't offer any information on what you preferred,' Sharif pointed out.

Liyah said nothing, because she had scant interest in fashion or trends, and she wasn't sure she would have been adept at knowing what *did* suit her. The fact that she suspected this man did made her feel defensive all over again. She really knew next to nothing about him.

'My father said you control a…a luxury conglomerate?'

His dark gaze narrowed on her face. She felt very bare. Not that she was used to wearing make-up, but she'd like some kind of armour right now.

'Yes, I run it with my two half-brothers.'

So, he had family. Liyah absorbed that.

Sharif frowned. 'You really didn't know who I was at the oasis?'

She shook her head. 'I figured there would be plenty of time to learn about who you were. After all, we're married now, for better or worse. For a long time.'

'You weren't much interested in the prenuptial agreement. My staff told me you only glanced through it before signing.'

Liyah shrugged. 'I thought that would please you?'

'It intrigues me. I don't know a woman who wouldn't have gone through the document with a team of lawyers and dissected it to within an inch of its life before engaging in negotiatons for the maximum they could get their hands on.'

'The women you know don't sound very nice.'

A muscle in his jaw ticked. 'That could very well be the case, but as one of the wealthiest people on the planet I do tend to attract a certain type. So what makes you different? I know you don't have your father's fortune to fall back on, because your family is all but bankrupt—like your country. Hence the eagerness to marry you, or anyone, off.'

Liyah blinked. 'So it's true...the rumour about the fiscal debt in Taraq?'

Sharif nodded. 'Your father and his ministers have over-extended themselves hugely in redeveloping the country.'

Liyah had heard the rumours—especially when she'd been abroad—but hadn't known if they were true or not. Naturally her father would never share such information with her. Not even when she was helping dig her own country out of debt with this marriage.

'I don't depend on my father for an income or an inheritance,' Liyah said. 'He wrote me out of the family will long ago.'

'Why?'

'Because my mother left an inheritance to me, her only child. My father couldn't touch it, and I inherited when I was eighteen. It's probably nothing compared to the wealth you command, but it's enough to keep me secure.'

'That's the only thing you checked in the prenup—to make sure that our marriage didn't give me any rights over the money you have independently.'

Liyah nodded. 'So I don't need anything from you.'

An expression crossed his face, too fast to decipher, but Liyah thought it was scepticism.

He said, 'That's refreshing to know. But let me know how you feel when I initiate our divorce and you've become used to a life of comfort and luxury beyond your wildest dreams.'

'Divorce?' They'd only just got married.

'You really should have read that prenuptial agreement properly. It's all in there. When you signed the contract, the day before the wedding—hours before we met at the oasis—you agreed to a divorce at the earliest in six months and at the latest in a year's time. This is a marriage in name only—purely for appearances.'

Liyah let this sink in. She should be feeling relief right now, at the thought that not only was this a marriage in name only but that it was also to be shortlived. But what she was feeling was more ambiguous. Curiosity...

'Why such a specific timeframe?'

'Because I only need a wife until such time as I don't need one any more. Once certain...objectives have been met.'

The air steward approached them again, to inform them that they'd be landing any minute and to ask them to make sure they were buckled in.

Liyah's head was buzzing with this information. If what Sharif was saying was true, then within a year at the most she'd have her freedom again. And by that time Samara would be married into her new family, so Liyah wouldn't have any reason to return to a place that had never really welcomed her. She really would be free.

So why didn't that induce joy?

The wedding ring on Liyah's finger felt very heavy all of a sudden, and she twisted it absently on her finger.

Sharif asked sharply, 'Does it not fit?'

Liyah looked at him. She shook her head. 'It fits fine… it's just…*big*.'

The plane touched down smoothly at that moment. As the roar of the throttle eased, and the plane made its way to the hangar where they would disembark, Liyah asked, 'This really was always intended to be a marriage in name only?'

Sharif nodded. 'As per the prenuptial agreement—it's all there in black and white.'

'But what…?' Liyah stopped, suddenly hesitant.'

Sharif lifted a brow. 'What…?'

Liyah could feel herself getting hot again. 'What about the fact that we…?' She stopped again, unable to articulate the words.

'Slept together?'

She nodded.

Sharif's expression hardened. 'That was a mistake. It won't happen again. This marriage isn't about that.'

Liyah couldn't look away from Sharif's hard expression. *'It won't happen again.'* A word trembled on her tongue. *Why?* But she stopped herself from letting it slip out, cursing herself for not realising sooner.

She'd been inexperienced. He hadn't. Clearly what had been a transformative experience for her had not been nearly as earth-shattering for him, and she felt mortified now for assuming otherwise.

She should be welcoming this development. The fact that he didn't really want a wife. He'd seduced her so easily.

She'd lain down and bared her entire body and soul to him. She'd behaved totally out of character. Did she really want to risk revealing herself to him again? *No.*

The plane had come to a stop now, and staff were opening doors. Liyah gathered her things and avoided Sharif's eye, terrified that he might read something she couldn't hide.

Disappointment.

CHAPTER FOUR

ABOUT AN HOUR after they'd landed at the airfield Sharif watched Liyah walk around the vast space of his penthouse. A helicopter had brought them from the airfield to the building Sharif owned, where he had an apartment at the very top.

Liyah had looked mesmerised as they'd flown over the iconic city.

'Have you been to New York before?' he'd asked her.

She'd just shaken her head, eyes wide and glued to the canopy of tall sparkling buildings below. It had made Sharif look down too, for the first time in a long time. Normally he was in such a hurry to get to the next place, next meeting…

Now she walked through the vast open living space, and Sharif noted it dispassionately through her eyes. Impeccably decorated, with a neutral background of varying shades of grey. The furniture was sleek and elegant—antique. Works of art, on the walls and dotted around the room on tables, provided pops of colour and texture.

It struck him now that he'd never really felt fully connected with this space. He had no more attachment to this apartment than he did to any hotel suite.

Massive curtains were pulled back from floor-to-ceiling windows and a huge set of French doors that led out to a terrace overlooking Central Park. Liyah stood at the window and looked out.

Her hair was still up in a messy knot. The trousers and top she'd changed into did little to hide her body. She could be a model, with her height and proportions. But, her generous curves would put her in the plus size bracket —which was ridiculous, Sharif knew, because she was a perfectly healthy weight.

It was an aspect of the fashion industry that was slowly changing to reflect a far more accurate depiction of women's bodies, and not before time.

He didn't welcome the hum of electricity that seemed to have become a permanent fixture in his blood since she'd been revealed at the wedding. *Since last night.* He defended himself. She was truly stunning, even as pared back as she was right now. And he was only human. He'd always appreciated a beautiful woman.

But something prickled over Sharif's skin as he contemplated what a knockout she would be when she was dressed to impress. He had a feeling that she would easily transcend the most beautiful women he'd ever seen. And he inhabited a world where beauty wasn't just a given. It was expected. Demanded.

He resolved to speak to his team about making sure there were no skeletons in her closet that might derail his plans. But he was sure there weren't. The Mansour royal family weren't renowned for creating headlines—which was one of the reasons he'd decided to make the most of the diplomatic marriage.

Liyah was still trying to get her bearings after the helicopter ride that had whisked them over to the island of Manhattan, to this tall, gleaming spire of steel where they'd landed on the roof. She looked over the expanse of Central Park nearby—less lush than usual at this time of year, in late winter, but still beautiful.

A tiny bubble of hysteria rose inside her as she realised that it was no wonder she couldn't get her bearings. Her feet had literally hardly touched the ground since they'd landed. And was this how her new husband lived? In the clouds? Far above the mere mortals below? He probably got whatever was the opposite of a head rush if he had to go down to ground level.

She could feel him behind her, albeit a few feet away. Looking at her. Was he trying to figure her out? Or was she so inconsequential to him that she wasn't even worth that?

She turned around and felt an immediate rush of awareness when she found that he *was* looking at her. Hands in pockets. Supremely at home against this luxurious backdrop. She might be from a royal family but she knew that whatever riches and privileges she'd grown up with could never have prepared her for *this* world. They were at another level now. Literally. He could probably buy and sell her entire country a few times over and still have change.

Liyah folded her arms, feeling self-conscious. 'If you don't mind me saying, you look as if you were doing just fine without a wife.'

Sharif moved then, with a fluid athletic grace that made Liyah's mouth go dry. He took off his jacket and draped it gracefully over a chair and then sat down on a couch, his large body all at once relaxed and yet alert. Primed. He had a stillness about him that was seriously unnerving, but also mesmerising. Like a predator that looked benign until it struck with deadly precision.

He put out a hand, 'Please, sit—make yourself at home.'

Liyah's mouth compressed as she took in the vast array of sumptuous couches and chairs covered in smooth soft velvet. Tactile and yet intimidating. Because they looked as if they'd never been touched. She chose an armchair at a right angle to his couch and sat gingerly.

Sharif said, 'I can assure you that I do indeed need a wife at this particular juncture. But tell me something…why did you offer yourself up in your sister's place?'

The thought that he could be here right now with Samara and not *her* sent a dark shard of something very disturbing deep into Liyah's gut. *Jealousy?*

Liyah felt prickly after that disturbing revelation. 'Samara is only nineteen.'

'Which, as you know, in Taraq and Al-Murja is a perfectly respectable age to get married.'

Liyah responded stiffly. 'I just think it's too young to throw away your independence.'

Sharif raised a brow. His mouth quirked. 'I've married a feminist?'

'Is that a problem?'

Sharif laid an arm across the back of the couch and it pulled the material of his shirt and waistcoat across his broad chest. Distracting Liyah. She cursed him, because he probably knew exactly what he was doing.

He answered, 'Not at all. I don't see how any woman can say she's *not* a feminist.'

Liyah's prickliness and scattered thoughts disappeared. She looked at him.

He said, 'Don't look so surprised. My mother was a strong woman, and if it hadn't been for her I would have had to spend even more time with my father.'

'How old were you when she died?'

Sharif didn't move a muscle, but Liyah sensed his reticence.

'Nine. It was a long time ago.'

Clearly they'd been close. Liyah felt a pang to think of how different her own life might have been if her mother hadn't died so young.

'So,' he repeated, 'why did you take your sister's place?'

Liyah hesitated at the prospect of telling Sharif the truth, but then reminded herself that he hadn't even cared which sister he married. 'Because she's in love with someone else and wants to marry him.'

'But you just said you think she's too young to give up her independence...isn't it a contradiction to approve of her marrying someone else?'

Liyah's conscience pricked. She *had* just contradicted

herself—spectacularly. She felt like squirming. No one had ever questioned her this closely about anything. 'I just want her to be happy... But I'm afraid she'll be disappointed. Because love doesn't exist—or, if it does, it's a destructive force.'

'That's a very cynical view to have.'

'Something tells me that a man who is prepared to seduce a stranger the night before his arranged marriage doesn't exactly hold love in high esteem,' Liyah observed drily.

Sharif acknowledged that with a dip of his head. 'Touché.'

For a moment Liyah felt a heady rush of exhilaration. Here was a kindred spirit. Was that why she'd been so drawn to him on sight? Because she'd sensed an unconscious affinity? It would certainly help explain her uncharacteristic behaviour.

And yet, even though she recognised and welcomed the sense of affinity, the exhilaration faded to leave a hollow echo inside her to know he was as cynical as her.

'So, who hurt you?'

Liyah's breath stopped for a second at his question. She wondered if she'd heard correctly. 'Excuse me?'

'You're not innocent, but you're not experienced. So, whoever your lover was, he either hurt you badly enough to spark your cynicism or he merely confirmed it. And he didn't ensure that you were satisfied.'

Liyah wanted to slide under the chair and into the floor. Had it been so obvious? No wonder he didn't want to repeat the experience.

'You think you see a lot.'

He practically smirked. 'I know I do. It is a skill honed over many years.'

The need to know how and why he'd developed such a skill hovered on Liyah's tongue, but before she could say a word there was a sound and they both blinked, as if taken by surprise at the way their conversation had engrossed them.

Liyah looked to the door, where a middle-aged gentleman stood. She hadn't even known anyone else was in the place, but it was so vast she wasn't surprised.

Sharif stood up. 'Liyah, I'd like you to meet Thomas Burke, the house manager here.'

Liyah stood up and met the man halfway. Shaking his hand, she smiled, feeling suddenly shy.

'Mrs Marchetti, it's a pleasure to welcome you to New York.'

Sharif glanced at his watch and said, 'I have to go downtown for some meetings and to catch up on my calls. Thomas will show you around and take note of any dietary requirements. You should settle in, Liyah, I'll be back for dinner.'

'Take note of any dietary requirements.' As if she was literally an employee.

Which she pretty much was.

Sharif walked out, taking his jacket with him, and Liyah breathed out fully for the first time since they'd arrived at the apartment.

She dutifully followed Thomas around the different rooms and tried not to let her jaw drop too obviously. There were two dining rooms—informal and formal. A massive kitchen with its own elegant dining area. There was a gym, with a lap pool, and a media centre, complete with a cinema that could seat about fifty people.

There were numerous bedrooms.

She noticed that Thomas didn't show her into Sharif's, but she was given a room just across the hall and it was show-stopping. Decorated in dark blues and greys, with a shag pile carpet, it was decadent and glamorous.

It had its own terrace and a dressing room, and en suite bathroom that was about as big as the hammam back in Taraq.

Thomas stood in the doorway, not a hint of curiosity about the fact that the new Mrs Marchetti and her husband were obviously not traditional man and wife showing on his face.

'As Mr Marchetti said, let me know if you have any specific dietary preferences and I'll pass them on to the chef.'

The chef!

Liyah balked. 'How many staff are here?'

Thomas calculated for a second. 'Daily, about three—the housemaid, the chef and myself. Then weekly there's a few more—the florist...people like that.'

Liyah had seen the gorgeous colourful blooms in the hall... Thomas was looking at her. She hadn't answered. 'Oh, sorry—nothing. No preferences. I eat anything.'

Thomas looked almost comically taken aback for a moment, and then he bowed ever so slightly and smiled. 'Very good. Dinner will be served at seven, and Mr Marchetti will be in the lounge for an aperitif at six-thirty. Just press the bell by your bed if you need anything in the meantime.'

Thomas left and Liyah investigated her space. Her luggage had been magically unpacked and put away, and she tried not to wince at how shabby her things looked in the pristine space.

She had sisters who wouldn't be caught dead in anything without a designer label, but that had just been one of the many differences between them and Liyah.

She explored the terrace, taking in the truly stupendous view. The sidewalk looked many miles below her, where people scurried like ants. The sky was bright blue and the air was sharp and cold. But there was no snow.

Liyah had never seen snow. It hadn't ever been that cold when she'd been in Europe.

Despite her sleep on the plane, Liyah felt weary. It had been a tumultuous couple of days. And this was supposedly her wedding night with her new husband. Except it was morning—daytime—and they were on the other side of the world. And he obviously had no intention of sleeping with her again.

Thoroughly discombobulated, and not wanting to dwell on the revelations of her new situation, Liyah took off her clothes and crawled into the enormous bed between sheets that felt like silk to the touch. She was asleep in seconds.

That evening Sharif looked out over the view of a lowering grey sky. He'd never really got used to the cold winters in New York, but as this was where he'd moved the headquarters of the Marchetti Group's operations after his father's death he'd come to tolerate them.

Moving here from the main hub in Rome had been his first step in breaking all ties with his father's legacy. His first step in stamping out his father's influence. The next steps would be the final death knells and would wipe Domenico Marchetti's name out of existence, reducing his legacy to dust.

But even now, as he reminded himself of all that was at stake and all that was to come, Sharif couldn't focus. He was distracted. He'd been distracted all day. Thinking of *her*. His new wife. The woman who was also his mysterious temptress from the oasis—who had lured him like a siren and then kissed him like a novice.

But now he knew better. She'd been no novice.

She'd known exactly what she was doing at that oasis and she'd taken him for a complete fool—

A sound from behind him brought his thoughts to a stop. He turned around slowly. His wife stood in the doorway. She looked hesitant. She was wearing a long cream traditional Taraqi tunic. V-necked, it dipped just low enough to show the top of the curve of her breasts. She also wore slim-fitting matching trousers and flat sandals. He noticed there was still henna on her feet. If this was a traditional marriage he would be taking her to his bed tonight.

A skewer of need twisted in Sharif's gut and he crushed it. This was *not* a traditional marriage and he would *not* be taking her to his bed. Ever again.

Her hair was down, curling wildly around her shoulders, parted in the middle to reveal the effortless beauty of her face. Those huge almond eyes. Wide, generous mouth, lush lips. High cheekbones.

Sharif could imagine her as a teenager, all coltish limbs and awkward grace. But now she was a grown woman, and he had seriously underestimated her.

'Would you like a drink?' He forced civility into his voice when he felt far from civil.

She nodded and walked in.

Sharif couldn't help but notice the soft sway of her breasts under the material of her tunic. *Dio.* She wasn't wearing a bra. Considering what he knew now, he suspected that was on purpose. Her talk of not needing money from him had been a cute deflection from her true nature.

'A soda and lime would be nice, thank you.'

So demure. So deceptive.

Sharif poured her drink, handed it to her, and then poured himself a Scotch.

She hovered, as if unsure what to do or where to go.

Her apparent reticence irritated him now. It was all an act. He cursed himself for not investigating her sooner. But he *had* investigated her sister, and nothing untoward had come back, so he'd just assumed she would be the same. A serious lapse in Sharif's usual attention to detail.

'Please, sit, Liyah. You don't need permission.'

Liyah sat on one of the couches, sending him a slightly inquisitive look, which he ignored.

Sharif chose a chair. Instead of demanding that she explain herself straight away, he decided to play dumb. 'Did you rest this afternoon?'

She nodded and took a sip of her drink. 'Yes, thank you.'

But Sharif knew he couldn't string this out—he was too angry. 'You don't have to thank me for everything. This is your home now too, and you're free to come and go. But...' He paused for a moment, watching her carefully. 'I will not tolerate the kind of behaviour you have displayed on your hedonistic jaunt around Europe over the last couple of years.'

Hedonistic jaunt.

Liyah had just taken a sip of her drink and she nearly choked, but she managed to swallow before she did.

She looked at her husband.

He'd seen the papers and the paparazzi photos.

The hurt that she'd felt the first time she'd realised she'd been so betrayed felt fresh again. The fact that she wasn't similarly armed with information on Sharif made her feel very defenceless now. But then she told herself she was being paranoid.

'What exactly are you talking about?'

His mouth thinned. 'The nice little portfolio my assistant put together for me, featuring your various and myriad exploits last summer in Europe, mainly on the Côte d'Azur.'

She wasn't being paranoid. Liyah's insides cramped. 'Those pictures weren't—'

He cut in. 'Weren't what they looked like? Spare me the excuses, Liyah. It was pretty clear what they were—pictures of an entitled royal socialite living to excess. But I couldn't care less what you got up to, or that you seem to like to affect this act of faux innocence and naivety. What I do care about is that you do not repeat that behaviour while you are married to me. Luckily the pictures didn't get picked up by the wider gossip sites. And we're going to keep it that way.

You won't be hooking up with any of your Eurotrash party friends while you're with me.'

Liyah felt sick. She could see the pictures in her mind's eye. Lolling on the deck of a massive yacht in the sparkling Mediterranean Sea drinking champagne. Falling out of famous nightclubs being held up by so-called friends. Shopping in the most famous shops and streets of Spain, Italy, Paris... You name it, she'd been there.

Except she hadn't.

Because the girl in those pictures hadn't been her.

The words to try and explain this to Sharif trembled on her tongue, but he was like a stone. Disgusted. Disapproving. And a need to protect herself rose up. She would only be with this man for a year at the most. He didn't deserve to know the real her—the woman far removed from those pictures.

And how could she defend herself when his first impression of her had been the wanton woman he'd met at the oasis, who had shown no hesitation in jumping into bed with a complete stranger? No wonder he believed the worst.

She forced the emotion out of her voice. 'You can rest assured that I won't be a liability while we're married.'

Thomas appeared in the doorway at that moment, with perfect timing, to announce dinner.

Liyah preceded Sharif out of the room and tried not to feel like a chastened child. But it was hard when she wanted to stamp her feet and tell him that he had it all wrong. The injustice made her breathless, but she felt a stronger need not to let him see the soft, vulnerable part of her that very few had ever seen.

To Liyah's relief, Sharif hadn't brought up those lurid paparazzi shots again over their deliciously cooked dinner of tender chicken and rice infused with herbs and spices. But it appeared that he wasn't prepared to let everything go.

He leant back now, a nearly empty wine glass in his hand, and looked at her. 'I believed that someone must have hurt you, but if anything it's more likely to have been the other way around. Who was he?'

Liyah kept her face expressionless, even as she sucked in a breath at the barb. He thought she'd been acting the whole time. Feigning her reticence and lack of experience.

An image came into her head. A young man—her age. Tall, handsome. Cheeky smile. Charming. Intelligent. How easily he'd swept her off her feet and made her believe that he was truly interested in her. How easily she'd let him breach barriers she'd never allowed anyone else to, so self-protective and distrustful.

But when she'd first arrived in Europe a couple of years ago she'd been hungry to experience this new world and be a modern, independent woman. So one night she'd allowed him the ultimate intimacy.

She hadn't told him she was a virgin, too embarrassed and shy, and eager to relieve herself of the burden of innocence. But when she'd tensed at the unexpected pain on penetration he'd stopped, a horrified look on his face, clearly not expecting a fellow university student of twenty-two to still be a virgin.

For a moment she'd thought he'd force himself on her, but he'd jumped up and hurled a string of profane insults instead. And then she'd discovered that she was the butt of a random drunken bet between him and his friends to see how quickly he could get her into bed. Apparently he'd won his bet.

After that Liyah could remember covering up with tomboyish clothes. Tying her hair back. Wearing her glasses all the time. Diminishing herself as much as possible to avoid sticking out on the university campus. Drawing attention.

And yet Sharif had just had to look at her and she'd forgotten the painful lessons she'd learnt in a heartbeat. Sheer instinct had overridden every rational bone in her body, proving that there was still a shameful hunger inside her, ready to expose her weakness for connection and intimacy at all costs. She'd learnt nothing. And this man wasn't about to believe what she had to say in her defence. So she would protect herself by playing to his low regard of her.

She pushed the hurt down and lifted her chin. 'He was nobody. I don't even remember his name.'

'I almost feel sorry for him.'

'He really doesn't need your sympathy,' Liyah forced out. Seeking desperately to get the focus off her, and ruffle Sharif's irritatingly judgemental and cool demeanour, she said, 'Considering our experience of each other, and the fact that this is a marriage in name only, will you be discreet?'

Sharif's gaze narrowed on her. Liyah's face grew hot.

He said, 'Taking lovers and causing headlines is the absolute antithesis of what I'm aiming to achieve by marrying you. I've got more important things to worry about.'

'Like what, exactly? Why is it so important to you to have a wife right now, when clearly it's not something you relish?'

Sharif looked at Liyah. Her cheeks had darkened with colour. Her eyes were flashing and he could see her chest moving up and down. She was agitated. Because he'd caught her out? Because he was setting parameters? Whatever the reason, it was having an incendiary effect on his blood and he had to shift discreetly in his seat.

He had to focus on what she'd asked. His first instinct was to give her some platitude, but something stopped him. He'd never been in this situation before, with a woman who was ostensibly going to be by his side for the foreseeable future. The longest liasion he'd ever had had lasted about two weeks.

'I'm at a crucial juncture in the development of the Marchetti Group and having a wife by my side will take me—*us*—to the next level. That is the most important thing, and it drives every decision I make.'

Was it his imagination or had she flinched slightly when he'd said that? Her eyes were huge and very green. Then she looked away and it irritated him, because usually he was the one to avoid eye contact. And why did he feel the need to justify why the Marchetti Group was so important when he'd never felt the need to before?

He wanted her eyes back on him. 'I've got a team lined up to come here tomorrow and set you up.'

She looked at him again, and Sharif felt a moment of satisfaction even as a spike of need made his body tighten.

She said, 'Set me up?'

He nodded, imagining her in a sleek satin and lace concoction before he could stop himself. 'A stylist and a hair and beauty team. A few others. To make sure you're prepared for our first event on Wednesday evening.'

The colour drained out of her face slightly. 'That's the day after tomorrow!'

Sharif nodded. 'A press release will be issued tomorrow, announcing our marriage. We've flown under the radar so far, which is how I wanted it. But you need to be ready to face the world I inhabit. This is going to be far removed from the tacky haunts you frequented in Europe and that dusty palace in Taraq.'

Her cheeks flushed again and her jaw tightened. 'It wasn't me in those—' She stopped suddenly.

'It wasn't you in what?'

She shook her head, letting her hair fall forward. 'Nothing.' Then she looked at him again and pulled at a wayward strand. 'There's not much I can do about this unless you want me to cut it off.'

To Sharif's surprise he felt a visceral rejection of that

notion even as he wanted to tame it somehow, because it reminded him too much of the wildness she aroused inside him.

He shook his head. 'No need. I have the best in the business lined up—they'll make sure you're presentable.'

'Thanks.'

Sharif almost smiled at her sarcastic tone. 'Believe me, you're going to need all the armour you can get. As the wife of the Marchetti Group's CEO, your every move and item of clothing will be scrutinised with a magnifying glass. But it shouldn't be too daunting. After all, you are a princess, so you were always going to be on display to a lesser or greater extent.'

A short while later, after Sharif had excused himself to go to his study and make some calls—did the man never stop working?—Liyah was curled up in a chair in front of one of the big windows, her hands around a mug of herbal tea delivered to her by Thomas.

Manhattan looked like a magical carpet of diamonds outside. She could see the blinking lights of all the helicopters flying in the sky. Delivering more billionaires to their luxurious apartments?

Sharif's words resounded in her head. *'You were always going to be on display.'* Was she? She knew he was right, but somehow, she'd believed that by escaping to Europe to go to university she'd somehow slip under the radar. And then Samara had needed her.

The thought of being moulded to fit into Sharif's world filled her with dread. She'd always preferred being in the background, even though she'd inevitably stood out. When she'd been a teenager she'd been gangly and uncoordinated, and then, seemingly overnight, she'd developed curves that she'd had no idea what to do with.

The women of the palace had always used to pass comment that she was too tall. Too ungainly. Not delicate and feminine like the rest of her sisters.

That had been one of the things that had attracted her to the guy who had shown her attention at university. The guy she'd trusted with her innocence when she shouldn't have. He'd been tall, although not as tall as Sharif. He'd seemed glad that she was tall, even making a joke about how nice it was not to have to bend down to kiss someone.

It had all been smooth lies to fulfil a bet.

Liyah cringed now to think of how desperate she'd been to forge a life for herself, to fit in, and how starved of attention. *Weak, for affection.*

But Sharif hadn't had to say anything. He'd just looked at her as if he wanted to devour her. She shivered now, even though the apartment was at the perfect temperature for comfort.

On an impulse, she went and retrieved her laptop from her luggage and brought it back to the living room. Sitting cross-legged on the chair, she did what she should have done days ago. She looked up her husband.

She was immediately bombarded with a slew of paparazzi shots of Sharif with women. Lots of women. And each one absolutely stunning. Redheads. Blondes. Brunettes. All pale and sleek and elegant.

None like Liyah, with her wild untameable hair and dark skin. Something twisted painfully inside her. She clearly wasn't his type. What had happened between them at the oasis had been an anomaly. No wonder he didn't want anything more to happen.

She delved further and noted that he was rarely seen with the same woman more than a handful of times. And then she came across the recent spate of 'kiss and tells'. Women clearly unhappy with the way he'd unceremoniously ended their liaisons.

Liyah shivered again. She could imagine only too well

how it must feel—like being under the scorching rays of the sun only to be suddenly thrust into the icy winds of the Arctic.

She shook her head at her fanciful imagination. It was a *good* thing to know what kind of a man he was and realise that she'd escaped relatively unscathed.

Unscathed? mocked a voice in her head. *Unscathed doesn't quite account for the fact that he's ignited a wicked hunger inside you.*

Liyah ignored the voice and purposely clicked on a link relating to the Marchetti business, moving away from incendiary images and thoughts. She read about Sharif's deceased father, who sounded like a larger than life character, bullish in his ambition to build a global brand from a handful of boutiques in Rome. He'd been a dark, masculine man. Undeniably handsome. But there was something about him that Liyah thought looked cruel.

Then she read about the speculation that he would have been nothing without the vast fortunes of each of the women he'd married. Sharif's mother was mentioned and pictured—Princess Noor, a stunningly beautiful woman. Liyah recognised her beauty in Sharif's features. The deepset eyes. High cheekbones. Proud, regal nose.

She read about how Sharif had rebuilt the company after his father had died, having left it tainted with scandals and rumours of corruption. She read about Sharif's ruthlessness in going after legacy brands, only to strip them of everything but their name before hiring whole new teams to revitalise them.

She read about his half-brothers. Nikos and Maks. From different mothers. Both were gorgeous. Nikos was being called 'a reformed playboy', after marrying and settling down with a young family. There was a picture of him with his pregnant wife and a dark-haired baby that looked to be nearly a year old. Apparently, he hadn't known about his son until after he was born.

Maks seemed to be much more elusive. But Liyah found a picture of his recent wedding to a petite and very pretty woman with honey-blonde hair. They were coming out of a civil office in London and smiling at each other. They looked as if they were in love, and Liyah felt a flash of envy that she quickly told herself wasn't envy. It was pity—because their apparent happiness would undoubtedly be an illusion. Even staged for the cameras.

She thought of what Sharif had said about needing to marry to take the Marchetti Group to the next level. Perhaps that was why his brothers had married too. A joint effort to stabilise the brand. That made a lot more sense to Liyah than the fanciful notion that perhaps Sharif's brothers were different from him and had married for love.

How could they possibly believe in love when they'd all come from broken marriages?

Clearly Nikos had married his ex-lover and the mother of his child only to protect the reputation of the company. What about Maks, though? And how had Sharif become the sophisticated and ruthless CEO of a vast conglomerate if he'd grown up on the other side of the world in a desert kingdom?

Liyah shut the laptop abruptly, not liking the swirl of questions in her head precipitated by the online search. She didn't need to know about Sharif or his family. She just needed to get through the next year and then she would finally be free to pursue her own goals and her own life.

She waited for a spurt of excitement and joy at that prospect, but she felt nothing except a kind of…flatness.

She scowled at herself and put it down to weariness. In spite of her nap earlier, and the nap on the plane, she was tired, and a lot had happened. It was no wonder she couldn't drum up much enthusiasm.

However, when she crept past Sharif's office door a few minutes later, and heard the deep rumble of his voice on the other side, the instant rush of adrenalin and excitement made a complete mockery of any notion that her sense of anti-climax was fatigue-related...

CHAPTER FIVE

TWO DAYS LATER, Sharif waited for Liyah to appear in the apartment's main reception room. He'd hardly seen her since that first evening—he'd been busy catching up on what he'd missed during his few days' absence.

The irony wasn't lost on him that if he was a regular person he would still be on his honeymoon. But before his brain could be flooded with tantalising images of what a honeymoon with Liyah might look like—*feel like*—he reminded himself that he wasn't a regular person, and hadn't been since the moment his father had seduced his mother with one eye on creating an heir and another on stealing her vast dowry.

Sharif put two fingers behind his bow tie and his top button in an effort to loosen them slightly. He felt constricted when he normally never did. There was a hum in his blood too—a hum of anticipation. Something he usually only associated with the prospect of bettering a rival in business or making a spectacular acquisition.

He heard a sound and instinctively tightened his fingers around the small tumbler of whisky he'd poured himself. He turned around slowly to see Liyah standing just inside the door, looking unbelievably hesitant.

And stunning.

Sharif didn't even realise his breath had stopped until his body forced him to breathe in.

His gaze followed the outline of the satin dress from the thin straps over her shoulders to the line of the bodice that cut across her chest, where the swells of her breasts were just tantalisingly visible. It went in at her slim waist and then curved out again over her hips, falling in a straight, elegant line to the floor.

It was an earthy olive-green, and it enhanced the colour of her skin exactly as he'd imagined. The design couldn't have been more simple. Deceptively simple, as he knew. He recognised haute couture as soon as he saw it. It could have been made for her, but he knew it hadn't been as there hadn't been enough time. But the material moulded to her body in a way that looked indecent enough to be bespoke.

He felt dizzy. Her hair had been straightened into a sleek fall of black silk and tucked behind her ears, where drop diamonds sparkled. But the absence of her usual unruly waves failed to diminish the incendiary memories of that night when she'd been a wild, untamed goddess, emerging from the depths of a black pool. He found this version of her more than provocative when it should be less.

He noticed that the only other jewellery she wore was a simple diamond bracelet. She held a matching green clutch bag in her hands.

She cleared her throat. 'Is it...? Am I...okay?'

Sharif was used to women fishing for compliments, and was accustomed to handing them out without even thinking, or really meaning them. Empty platitudes. Exactly what he was expected to say. But this was uncharted territory for him.

'You are...perfect, Liyah.'

She looked away. He saw that the hands on her bag weren't quite steady.

A spike of concern made him say, 'What is it? Is something wrong?'

She moved one slim shoulder up and down. 'I guess I'm not really used to this level of attention.'

Sharif thought of those photos of her cavorting on yachts and falling out of clubs in slinky short numbers that were most definitely *not* haute couture. The spike of concern faded. Yes, she came from a royal family, but he appreciated that his world was a step up in levels of sophistication. Still, he had no doubt that she'd become accustomed to his world very soon.

Sharif put down his glass. 'We should go. My driver is waiting.'

He crossed the space between them and was about to take Liyah's elbow to guide her out when he stopped. Her scent filled Sharif's nostrils. A new scent. Tones of heady musky flowers conjuring up images of the hot dry desert, where exotic flowers bloomed in the most unlikely places. *Like deserted oases.*

'My ring. My wedding ring. I forgot to put it on.'

Liyah was looking up at him and Sharif realised she must be wearing heels, because her plump, lush mouth was close enough for him to see that it was slicked only with a nude sheen. Nothing as garish as red or pink lipstick.

Close up, he could see that the green of the dress made her eyes pop, and that kohl and dark shadow had turned them a light smoky green. All in all, her make-up was subtle, merely enhancing her natural beauty.

He blinked. *The ring.* 'You don't like wearing it?'

She made a face as she pulled away. 'Sorry, it's lovely— I'm just afraid I'll lose it or something.'

She turned to go back to her room—presumably to get it—and presented Sharif with a view of her smooth back. He swallowed a sound of frustration that she was getting to him like this, and forced out, 'Wait. I have something here.'

She'd distracted him enough that he'd forgotten. He'd ordered a replacement ring, because he'd seen that the other one didn't seem to fit.

She turned around and came back.

Sharif took a small box out of his inside pocket. He opened it and she looked down. He saw her inhale. It made her breasts swell against the dress. Blood surged to his groin and he clenched his jaw.

'Try it on.'

He took it out of the box and held out his hand, not even sure why he was insisting on doing it himself. Her hand was cool in his. Small. He slid the ring onto her finger. She drew her hand back and the ring sparkled, making him feel like a fraud. He cursed himself. Since when had he grown a conscience?

She looked at the ring. 'You didn't have to change it.'

Sharif put the empty box down on a nearby table. 'It's fine, I should have consulted with you in the first instance. Let's go.'

Liyah sat in the warm cocoon of the sleek car, with a couple of feet between her and Sharif. A couple of feet that she was grateful for, because she still hadn't quite recovered from seeing him waiting for her dressed in a classic black tuxedo.

The suit was clearly bespoke, showcasing the powerful lines of his body. It made him look even taller and broader than he usually did. But, while he wore the suit with the utmost elegance and propriety, Liyah wasn't fooled by the sophisticated veneer for a second.

He'd placed a voluminous fur coat over her shoulders before they'd left the apartment. She'd looked at it suspiciously, and he'd said drily, 'Don't worry—it's fake. We only work with designers who reject the harming of animals for their designs.'

She'd been grateful for the luxurious warmth when the cold Mahattan air had hit her like a slap in the face upon emerging onto the street. But after the initial shock, she'd breathed in the sharp air gratefully. It was her first time out of the apartment since she'd arrived. Till now, her only encounter with the outside world had been from her terrace, many floors above the streets, heightening the sense of unreality, which had only been compounded by the activities of the last two days.

She glanced at the new ring on her finger again. He'd

surprised her, noticing that she hadn't felt comfortable with the other one. Except this one made her uncomfortable too—but for very different reasons.

It was…beautiful. And relatively discreet.

It was a diamond in a circular setting, surrounded by small baguette emeralds that extended outwards on either side. It was unusual, and something she might have actually picked for herself. But she chastised herself for thinking even for a second that he'd put any thought into it. Not when a veritable army of people had attended to every aspect of her 'look' for the last forty-eight hours.

She'd been pulled, squeezed, trimmed, measured, massaged and used as a mannequin upon which hundreds of different dresses, trouser suits, jumpsuits, casual clothes, swimwear, coats and shoes had been tried.

She'd even been consulted on what scents she preferred by a perfumier, and a signature scent had been mixed and sent to her within twenty-four hours in a beautiful crystal bottle with her name on it, embossed with gold leaf.

And underwear… Underwear so delicate and fine that it made her blush just to look at it.

The previous night Liyah had dreamt of Sharif's big hands, flicking aside wispy bits of lace from her body so he could get to her skin. She'd woken trembling and hot. Aching inside.

Liyah slid Sharif a quick furtive look. He was looking out of his window, his jaw hard. Remote. His thick hair was brushed back, curling on the collar of his coat slightly. He looked like a remote stranger. She could scarcely believe he was the same man who had led her into that tent at the oasis and fed her, before laying her down and showing her that she wasn't a freak. That she had capacity to feel such pleasure that—

'The press release has generated some interest. You

should expect intense attention from the press when we arrive. Just stick close to me.'

Liyah's thoughts scattered. Sharif was looking at her and his face was cast in shadow, making the lines leaner and harsher. His eyes glittered. She gulped. No doubt he thought she was used to the paparazzi, because he believed she'd been courting their attention over the last two summers in Europe.

'Okay.'

Flashing lights in her peripheral vision made Liyah turn her head. She could see they were approaching an impressive building, with red-carpeted steps leading up to an ornate entrance. Men in tuxedoes and women in shimmering gowns were making their way into the building.

'Where is this?'

'It's the Metropolitan Museum.'

Liyah sucked in a breath. She'd heard of the famous building. Suddenly she felt very unprepared. 'What exactly is this event?'

'It's an annual gala to raise funds for a range of charities.'

The car was pulling to a stop at the bottom of the steps now. Liyah wanted to slide down to the floor of the car and avoid the masses of paparazzi lined up along each side, and the glamorous crowd. This was far removed from anything she'd ever experienced before. In terms of royalty, the Mansours were definitely country bumpkins.

But Sharif was already out of the car, leaving a blast of icy air in his wake. And then her door was opening and he was holding out a hand.

Liyah had a flashback to when he'd held his hand out to her at the oasis. This couldn't be more different...

She forced it out of her mind, took a deep breath, and let him help her from the car to join him at the bottom of the steps.

Immediately it seemed as if everyone—the guests arriving and walking up the steps, the paparazzi, the myriad men and women in black suits with headsets, ushering the guests towards the entrance—turned as one to look at Sharif and Liyah.

Liyah was barely aware of Sharif's hand wrapping tightly around hers. Or his frowning look as he took in her face. Or his words. 'Just stay by my side.'

They started to move forward, and the crowd parted like the Red Sea to let them pass. There was a strange hush, and then all hell seemed to break loose.

'Sharif! Sharif! Let us meet your new wife!'

'Princess Aaliyah—over here!'

'Please, Princess, look over here. Who are you wearing?'

'Marchetti! Now that all of you are settling down, does this mean you're taking your eye off the ball? Losing your edge?'

Sharif stopped so abruptly that Liyah stumbled at his side. He turned to the bank of photographers to see where that last question had come from. She could feel the tension in his form.

He addressed the faceless people behind the flashing lights. 'The Marchetti Group is only getting stronger. I can assure you of that.'

And then he was tugging Liyah to his side and all but carrying her as they made their way up the rest of the steps.

As they reached the main doors, a golden glow emanated from inside a large marble foyer. More stairs led up to another level. Flaming lanterns lit their way and exotic fresh flowers scented the air. Uniformed staff expertly divested Liyah of her overcoat, so that by the time they reached the top she looked like every other woman in her glittering gown and jewels. It was opulent, and decadent, and so glamorous that she was afraid to breathe in case she made it disappear, or ruined it in some way.

Sharif held out his arm. She looked at it stupidly for a moment, before realising he wasn't holding her hand any more. She stepped forward and put her arm through his. She could feel the steely strength of his muscles against her, under his clothes. His heat. She tried to numb herself against the effect, but it was hard not to give in to the urge to cleave to his side.

And even more so when they walked into a room that was bathed in the golden light of hundreds of chandeliers. Ornate flower arrangements made up the centrepieces of round tables. People milled about chatting, networking. Soft, easy jazz came from a band near the top of the room.

They hadn't moved but a few feet forward before Sharif was stopped by someone. He introduced her to every person who approached them, and Liyah's face started to ache from forcing a smile. She gave up trying to remember names. They weren't really interested in her though—they only wanted Sharif.

He despatched all the sycophants with ruthless efficiency, indulging in no kind of small talk. Charming he was not…and yet that didn't stop people flocking to him. No, what he was, was something far more compelling…

It was somewhat comforting for Liyah to realise that she didn't feel as out of place or conspicuous as she usually did. Not with Sharif by her side. He eclipsed everything around him. Nevertheless, she wasn't unaware of the sly looks she received—mainly from other women—and the whispers as they passed by. But she held her head up and pretended not to notice.

Eventually they reached their table, which was at the top of the room, and Liyah sat down gratefully.

'Okay?'

She looked at Sharif as he spoke, taking his seat beside her. She realised she must have made a face. 'High heels aren't really my thing.'

He frowned at her, and she immediately realised that what she'd said would be at odds with the woman he thought she was. But before she could say anything else the music came to a stop and the people hushed.

Speeches were made as they were served plates of food that looked more like art installations. Liyah sipped at sparkling wine and it only added to the general feeling of unreality.

And then Sharif's name was mentioned by the MC.

Liyah's ears pricked up.

'Year on year, the biggest philanthropic contribution comes from the Marchetti Group…please welcome Sharif Marchetti.'

Thunderous applause rang in Liyah's ears as she watched him get up, adjust his jacket and climb the steps to the stage. He moved with such fluid animal grace that she couldn't take her eyes off him.

Sharif's speech was brief, succinct, and surprisingly passionate. Liyah might have expected to hear cynicism in his voice, but she could tell that he actually cared about what he was saying.

After another round of rapturous applause, Sharif returned to the table. The MC wrapped up the speeches and people started to stand up and move around.

Sharif looked at Liyah, 'Ready?'

'For what?'

'To go.'

Liyah had been prepared to settle in for a long evening of boredom as Sharif batted away more sycophants, but apparently that wasn't how he rolled.

She stood up. 'Sure.' What else was she going to say?

Sharif took her hand and started to lead her through the crowd. Liyah faltered when she saw an anteroom where people were starting to dance to a popular tune. She loved dancing. She'd developed a surprising interest in, and love for clubbing when she'd been in Europe. Liking the sense of being anonymous in a crowd. Liking the music.

Sharif stopped and looked from her to the room. 'I don't dance, Liyah.'

She opened her mouth to say something—she wasn't sure what—but Sharif had already turned and begun leading her away.

They were stopped just as they reached the main door by a smirking older gentleman.

He said, 'Callaghan.'

The man inclined his head. 'Marchetti. I'd offer you congratulations, but I have to admit that the cynic in me thinks that it's a very opportune moment for you to appear with a convenient wife in tow. Your brothers and now you…allaying the jitters of the board so you're in peak position to launch—what, exactly? I haven't found out what you're up to yet, Marchetti, but I will…don't worry.'

Sharif said, 'With an imagination like that, Callaghan, you're clearly a frustrated novelist. And have you met my wife, whom you accuse of being a pawn?'

His easy, drawling tone belied the tension Liyah felt in the hand that was wrapped around hers.

The man had the grace to look sheepish as he acknowledged Liyah.

She held out her hand. 'Pleased to meet you. I'm Liyah.'

The man shook her hand perfunctorily, muttering something unintelligible, and walked off.

Sharif said something unsavoury under his breath and they walked out of the room.

'Who was that?' Liyah asked, when it became obvious that Sharif wasn't about to elaborate on the exchange.

'Him? Oh, just a freelance business reporter.'

'What did he mean about an "opportune moment"?'

'He's just looking for a story.'

Liyah wasn't convinced, but they were at the main doors

leading outside now, and an attendant appeared with Liyah's coat. Sharif took it and helped her into it. Liyah couldn't help shivering when Sharif's fingers brushed the back of her bare neck when she lifted her hair out of the way.

He stilled for a moment, and then said, 'We'll be back at the apartment soon.'

He'd obviously mistaken her shiver as an indication of feeling cold. Not awareness. Thankfully. She shivered all over again under the coat at the thought of him realising just how much he affected her.

In the back of the car, Sharif heard Liyah ask, 'Do you always leave these events early? Or was it just tonight?'

He forced his jaw to unlock. It had gritted tight on the sight of that reporter. Actually, it had been gritted all evening, as he'd tried to remain unaware of Liyah beside him, sinuous and sultry in that dress—which was now, thankfully, covered up.

This was unprecedented territory for Sharif. He wasn't used to women having such a visceral pull on him. He was used to desiring women, of course, but also to relegating it very much to a place he had total control over.

He'd almost fumbled his speech because he'd been so aware of Liyah, sitting just feet away, her skin gleaming against the green of the dress. And, even more distractingly, he'd been acutely aware of the attention she'd drawn from other men. Which usually didn't bother him in the slightest, because the women he dated impacted on him only in a very peripheral way.

But Liyah is your wife, so it's natural that her effect is different.

Sharif relaxed his jaw some more. That was it.

He reached for his bow tie, loosening it. He looked at her and almost forgot what she'd asked. The soft lights in the back of the car made her seem unreadable, infinitely mysterious. All he wanted to do was clamp his hands in her hair and tug her towards him, so that he could crush that provocative mouth under his and punish her for proving to be such a distraction.

He forced his blood to cool. 'Did you want to stay and dance? Pretend you were back in the clubs of Europe?'

'I do like dancing, actually. That's not a crime, is it?'

'Only if you end up being carried out by the bouncers.'

He watched that full mouth compress and felt his body jerk in response. He shifted in his seat.

She said, 'You didn't answer my question. Do you normally leave events early?'

Sharif instinctively chafed at the question. He didn't indulge women who wanted to know more about him. He hadn't shared his inner thoughts and motivations with anyone since his mother had died and the one person he'd trusted had gone. He kept things strictly superficial. Sexual. And then it was over. Which women did not appreciate... Hence the recent media attention, after his last lover had decided to lash out in the papers, branding him a heartless monster.

But Liyah was different. They were married. And for some reason he had a compulsion to tell her. 'I don't particularly enjoy them. And I don't see the point in hanging around when what I've needed to do is done.'

Liyah moved back into her corner of the car, as if she wanted to get a better look at him. It made Sharif's skin prickle with awareness and something else. Exposure.

'You're a bit of a lone wolf, aren't you?'

'You don't need anybody else, Sharif!'

Those words had been hurled at him too many times to count over the years. His mother had said them too, but with the emphasis on it being a good thing. She'd said, *'You don't need anybody else Sharif. Don't trust anyone. Trust yourself. You are your own best friend. You'll know what to do.'* She'd learnt a harsh lesson at the hands of his father, when he'd betrayed her trust, stolen her inheritance and broken her heart.

So, yes, Sharif was a lone wolf. He'd become one to survive. So why was it that Liyah's observation snagged on him like a splinter piercing his skin?

'I trust myself and I ask for no one's opinion or help unless I want another perspective.'

'What about your brothers?'

A heavy weight settled in his gut. 'We didn't spend time together when we were growing up, so we're not close. But they trust me.'

As he said those words the weight got heavier. He'd never really acknowledged that before. But they did trust him. They had from the moment their father had died and he'd called them to the board and convinced them that it was in their interest to work together.

He knew that they might not admit they trusted him, and they certainly had their own reasons for wanting to work for the company their father had built up—but deep down there'd always be an affinity. Because they'd all suffered at the hands of their father.

'But you don't trust them?'

Sharif frowned sharply. Liyah was skating far too close to the truth, making guilt spike. 'I trust them as much as you trust *your* family.'

She flushed at that. He could see her skin get darker. Blood rushing to the surface. His body tightened. What was he doing...provoking her when he had no intention of slaking this lust?

'You don't know enough about me to know who I might trust.'

'Your sister? You sacrificed yourself for her.'

Sharif suddenly had an image of Liyah's pretty, but far less compelling sister. He couldn't imagine being in this situation with her and feeling this throbbing, desperate need. Which was not what he'd intended for this marriage.

'Yes, my sister. I do trust her.' She sounded defensive.

The car was pulling up to the kerb outside his apartment building now, and Sharif almost lamented the interruption. He found that he was enjoying parrying with Liyah because he didn't know what she might say next. She was unpredictable.

His door was opened by the driver and he got out and went around to open Liyah's door. She put her hand in his, the wedding ring glittering in the dark.

His insides clenched as he closed his fingers around hers. He'd never imagined putting a ring on any woman's finger. But it looked good on her. Better than the other one, which he'd only used because it was an heirloom from his mother's side of the family. He found that seeing his ring on her hand didn't make him feel as claustrophobic as he might have expected.

She stepped out, close to Sharif. For a moment he didn't move, drinking in her scent. Soft, musky. She smelled of heat and flowers.

And then suddenly she wrinkled her nose and looked up, and Sharif saw snowflakes landing on her face. Settling on her cheek.

A slow, awed smile bloomed across her face. 'It's snowing!'

Sharif found a smile tugging at his own mouth. 'That's usually what happens in New York this time of year.'

She didn't seem to hear him. She was looking up, totally transfixed. Closing her eyes and laughing softly as more flakes fell, leaving little wet trails down her cheeks.

Surprised, Sharif said, 'You've never seen snow before?'

She shook her head, making her hair ripple over her shoulders like black silk. She opened her eyes. They were a darker green in the dim light. 'Never! It feels like being kissed.'

Sharif's gaze dropped to Liyah's mouth. Soft, infinitely tempting. He was about to reach for her, put a hand under the coat to find her waist, tug her towards him so he could—

Stop. The voice sounded in his head. What was he doing, being tempted by such rudimentary tactics? She was trying to entice him.

Of course she must have seen snow before—she'd been in Europe.

But they were out on the street, with people passing. No doubt paparazzi lurking. And it was for that reason and that reason only that Sharif decided he would give in to her ruse and tug her closer, cover her mouth with his.

He heard her surprised little gasp. For a second he revelled in the feel of her yielding, melting against him, head tipping back, mouth softening. He ran his tongue along the seam of her mouth and had to stop a growl of satisfaction when she opened to him and he delved deep into her sweetness, fast forgetting why he had decided to kiss her in the first place when he knew it was a bad idea.

He sensed the change in her just before she tensed, her hands coming up between them. Sharif lifted his head. It was snowing harder now, with thick, fluffy flakes landing all around them and on Liyah's hair, face.

She blinked. 'Why did you kiss me?'

Because you couldn't not, whispered a sly voice.

In his peripheral vision Sharif saw a flash of light. 'Paparazzi. Shame to waste an opportunity to give them something to print tomorrow.'

Liar.

Sharif let Liyah push him back. She took a step to the side but then made a sudden jerking movement when her foot slipped on the icy ground.

Without even thinking, Sharif scooped her up into his arms and carried her into the apartment building, where the door was being held open by his security staff.

Liyah was still too much in shock to say or do anything as Sharif carried her into the building as if she weighed no more than a bag of sugar—when she knew she was no delicate flower.

Paparazzi.

She hadn't noticed anything. But then with Sharif standing so close and that decadent, sexy scent winding around her like invisible silken thread it was no wonder.

Delayed mortification rose inside her. She hadn't even put up a modicum of resistance. It was as if she'd been waiting for him to kiss her all evening.

They were at the elevator now, and she said stiffly, 'You can put me down now.'

At least there was the voluminous coat between them. The thought of Sharif carrying her while she was wearing just the flimsy dress was far too reminiscent of when he'd lifted her out of the bath at the oasis and carried her over to the bed.

He put her down and the doors opened. Liyah stepped in, dismayed at how shaky her legs were. Sharif got in beside her, instantly dominating the space and sucking up all the oxygen, turning it hot and making it hard to breathe. Liyah was suddenly sweltering in the coat but didn't want to take it off.

When the doors opened into the penthouse suite Liyah stepped out and finally shucked off the coat with relief. Thomas appeared as if from nowhere, and Liyah smiled her thanks as he took it and faded into the background again.

She turned to Sharif, avoiding looking at him directly. 'Please don't do that again without warning me first. I know

I'm little more than an employee, but you can't just…man-handle me when it suits you.'

Liyah winced inwardly at her choice of words. It hadn't felt like manhandling. At all. It had felt delicious to be standing in the freezing cold, with snowflakes falling like feathers on her skin and Sharif's mouth on hers, incinerating her from the inside out. She could still almost feel the imprint of his hand on her waist.

He was silent for so long that Liyah risked a glance. He was smiling. *Smiling!*

He said, 'Manhandle?'

Liyah's mortification turned to anger. She crossed her arms. 'Yes—manhandle. As in put your hands on me, and your mouth, without asking permission.'

She thought then of all the women who'd given her sly looks earlier. No doubt they wouldn't complain if Sharif *manhandled* them. In fact she was fairly certain that it was something he'd never been accused of before.

It wasn't really fair to level it at him now…but if he thought he could just kiss her like that in public with no forewarning…

Liyah went hot and cold at the same time at the thought of constantly being exposed in her desire for him.

Sharif's mouth straightened. 'Please accept my apologies. In future I will ask your permission first.'

Liyah was sorry she'd said a word now. Sharif Marchetti, also known as Sheikh Sharif Bin Noor al Nazar, was not a man who asked permission for anything. He demanded and people acquiesced. As she'd acquiesced all too easily.

Struggling to maintain a modicum of dignity, Liyah tipped up her chin. 'I'm quite tired now. I'm going to bed.'

'Goodnight, Liyah.'

She turned, and walked away as gracefully as she could, aware of Sharif's eyes boring into her back.

He was probably still laughing at her.

* * *

Sharif watched Liyah walk away, his gaze drawn helplessly to the sway of her hips. The smooth expanse of her
skin above the neckline of the dress. Her bare shoulders.

She'd certainly proved to be a complementary foil this
evening. If she kept it up like that she would be the perfectly convenient wife he'd wanted.

*If it wasn't for the irritating fact that you want her so
badly you had to kiss her on the street like a crass boy.*

Sharif ignored the inner voice and focused on the niggle
of disquiet that told him a society party girl didn't change
her spots so easily.

Your brother Nikos did.

He ignored that reminder too. His brother had been one
of the world's most notorious playboys until he'd met his
wife Maggie and then a year later had discovered he had a
son. But, as Sharif liked to goad him all the time, he was
sure it was only a temporary state of affairs before Nikos
realised what he was missing and went back to his old ways.

After all, they were both their father's sons, and their father hadn't had a committed bone in his body. Unless you
counted his commitment to fleecing his wives and using
their money to build up the company...

But in the end their father hadn't even had the commitment to further his own ambitions—had become drunk
and corrupt on success, wealth and status. He'd died in the
arms of his latest lover, any reputation he'd built up shot to
pieces. And that was when Sharif had realised the extent
of his father's betrayal.

He hadn't stolen from his mother and effectively killed
her for the good of anything. He had done it only to satiate his intense greed and to prove that disinheriting him
had been a mistake.

Domenico Marchetti had never got over the fact that he'd
been passed over in his father's will for his younger brother.

Sharif's father had arrogantly assumed he'd inherit, even though he'd put no time or effort into the modest family business, but it had been left to his brother instead.

Part of Domenico's bid for power had included getting revenge on his brother by ruining the business. *His own family's inheritance.* Sharif even had a memory of his uncle—a broken man—coming to Domenico, begging for help, for mercy. Sharif's father had slapped him across the face and thrown him out on the street.

Sharif shoved aside the unwelcome rush of memories. Liyah might have been a compliant foil this evening, but she was probably just lulling him into a false sense of security before she displayed her true colours again and reverted to type.

And that would not happen. Not while she was his wife.

CHAPTER SIX

'SHE'S *WHERE*?'

Sharif stood up from the boardroom table and a dozen faces turned towards him expectantly. He waved a hand to indicate they should go on without him and walked over to one of the floor-to-ceiling windows, shoving his free hand in the pocket of his trousers.

The disembodied voice came again. 'She's in Central Park, sir…playing in the snow.'

Sharif couldn't see Central Park from where he was. It was north and he looked south, towards lower Manhattan. He cursed.

'Playing with who?'

'Er…some kids, sir.'

Sharif absorbed this.

Liyah had sent a text from the phone he'd furnished her with earlier, wanting to know if there were plans for that evening. He'd informed her that, yes, there were. They were due to attend a dinner. And then she'd asked if she could have a few hours to go out. He'd said of course she could. He wasn't her gaoler.

He'd fully expected that she would use the car to drive her from designer boutique to designer boutique. Not that she would ditch the car and insist on walking. To Central Park. To play in the snow.

'Send me a picture,' said Sharif, then terminated the conversation with his security officer and went back to the table, sitting down again. He vaguely tuned in to the discussion, but when his phone vibrated in his pocket he took it out again.

He couldn't quite believe what he was seeing. An image of a wrapped-up Liyah, her hair reverted to its wild and unruly state since the other night, flowing from under a woollen hat around her shoulders. She was grinning at what looked like an army of small children as they launched themselves at her. In the next picture she was on the ground, covered by the same children, with snow spraying all around them.

Sharif found this utterly incomprehensible. And it was hard to compute how it made him feel. Envious? He rejected that thought. Why on earth would he be envious of—

'Sir... *Sir?*'

Sharif looked up from his phone. His chief financial advisor was looking at him with a frown.

'If we want to put these plans in motion by the end of the month, we need to sign off on this today.'

A jolt went through Sharif. What was he doing? He never let anything distract him from his endgame. And certainly not a woman.

He put his phone away—but not before sending a terse text to Liyah.

Make sure you're ready at six p.m. It's a formal dinner, cocktail dress. The styling team will meet you back at the apartment.

Sharif threw his phone down. Why did he suddenly feel like a buzz-kill?

That evening Liyah was the one waiting for Sharif to finish getting ready for dinner. Apparently he was hosting an exclusive event to welcome the new head designer of an iconic fashion house.

Liyah stood at the window, her image reflected back to her, but she wasn't seeing that.

When Sharif had arrived back, a short while ago, he'd immediately said, 'Why didn't you go shopping today?'

Liyah had been genuinely perplexed. 'Was I supposed to? I have more clothes than I could possibly wear.'

'Why did you go to the park?'

'Why not? I wanted to see the snow.'

'And those kids?'

It had been more like an interrogation than a catch-up on the day's events. But then she'd reminded herself that this was hardly a regular marriage situation. And Sharif had probably assumed she'd spend the day in a beauty salon or perhaps an opium den.

Liyah had folded her arms, glaring at Sharif, hating how even in a plain dark suit and a white shirt open at the neck he still managed to pack the same punch as if he was wearing a tuxedo.

Or nothing at all.

'They saw me in the snow. They laughed at me when I told them it was my first time seeing it. And then they started a snowball fight.'

Eventually he'd said, 'Okay.'

'Okay?' Liyah had repeated testily. 'I am allowed to go outside and play in the snow?'

His gaze had narrowed, become dark and unreadable. Liyah had noticed his unshaven jaw and deep inside a pulse had picked up pace.

'Don't provoke me, Liyah. And don't forget that you're most likely being followed by paparazzi at all times. We leave in half an hour.'

Liyah's hair and make-up had already been done, so she'd just had to put on the dress. It was snowing again outside, making Manhattan pristine.

The sight of the snow mocked her. There'd been something poignant about experiencing it for the first time on her own in the park, despite the kids. And that had freaked her out—because throughout her time away from home over the past couple of years she hadn't ever felt lonely before. And yet today she'd found her mind wandering to Sharif. Wondering what he was doing. Thinking of the way he'd moved through that room full of people last night. So alone. Tense.

He intrigued her. He seemed so different here from the man she'd met in the desert.

She moved slightly, and the reflection of the dress glittered back at her. It was a simple elegant design—A-line, tea-length, strapless. Dark bronze silk over cream tulle. She wore matching shoes and her hair had been straightened again, slicked back into a low bun at the back of her head. Kohl made her eyes seem bigger, and gold hoops in her ears swung and caught the light.

She didn't feel like herself. But she could appreciate that Sharif wouldn't want her to look as wild as she had at the oasis, or even on her wedding day—and, even though she mightn't want to admit it, this new version of herself wasn't entirely…unwelcome. In spite of her avowed tomboy tendencies, Liyah couldn't help but feel…pretty. Maybe even a little beautiful.

The sparkling green of the small emeralds in her wedding ring caught her eye. She hadn't taken it off since Sharif had put it on her finger and a prickle skated over her skin. At that moment she caught sight of him behind her, reflected in the window.

How long had he been there?

He was wearing a three-piece suit. And suddenly there didn't seem to be enough air in the room. She was glad she wasn't facing him directly, because her heart was practically jumping through her chest. It was so mortifying that he had this effect on her, when all she'd been to him was a random hook-up in a desert oasis before he had to commit to a convenient marriage.

'Ready to go?' he said from behind her.

Liyah steeled herself and turned around. 'Yes.'

She had a sudden vision of how this marriage would play

out—days spent on her own interspersed with sterile social events. Playing dress-up in haute couture. She clenched her hands into fists. Why did that suddenly bother her? When the thought of her imminent freedom and independence should be enough to see her through this short period?

She moved forward, very aware of Sharif's eyes on her, coolly appraising. He held out a long camel coat and helped her into it. A classic design, it belted around her waist. She picked up her clutch bag.

In the back of the car a few minutes later, cocooned from the bitterly cold air outside, Liyah said, 'I looked you up today.'

He turned, arched a brow.

Her face grew hot. 'I mean I looked up your company. So, you basically own all the biggest luxury designer brands and labels in the world?'

Sharif inclined his head. 'Along with the oldest and most exclusive champagne and Irish whiskey brands.'

'You have a distillery in Ireland?'

He nodded.

'Is that something you always wanted to do? Follow in your father's footsteps?'

Sharif tensed visibly, his eyes widening, and then he made a sound that was half-laugh, half-growl. 'Follow? I had no choice but to take over—or everything he'd built up would have been destroyed and all for nothing.'

Feeling her way, she said, 'You weren't close?'

She thought he wasn't going to answer, but then he said, 'Do you know when I saw snow for the first time?'

She shook her head.

'In Scotland, at a boarding school so remote you needed a boat to get to the mainland. That's where my beloved father put me after he'd had me kidnapped from my mother's home in Al-Murja.'

'Kidnapped?' Liyah was shocked. She hadn't seen anything about that in the stories she'd found online. 'Why would he kidnap you?'

'Because my mother wasn't going to just hand me over. She knew what he was like. He'd seduced her and married her just to get her dowry and set himself up. He'd humiliated her and broken her heart. She knew he only wanted me as a pawn to use in the future. Someone he could mould into doing his bidding.'

His voice was hard. Cold. Liyah couldn't push away the image of a young boy with dark hair, shivering against the forbidding backdrop of an icy country. The culture shock would have been traumatic. Especially coming from the desert. The very thought of it made her own heart ache.

'How did your mother die?'

'He killed her.' Before Liyah could respond to that, Sharif added, 'Or as good as. She got sick. She needed urgent expensive medical treatment in Europe. Her family didn't have the necessary cash—it took years for them to recover financially from the loss of her dowry, and from the humiliation of her not fulfilling the agreement to marry your uncle—and my father refused to help. When he eventually did agree to fly her to Paris for an operation it was too late. She'd died.'

'How old were you?'

'I'd just turned nine. I hadn't seen her in a year.'

A lump formed in Liyah's throat. She forced it down, sensing that Sharif was not looking for sympathy or comfort. She just said, 'That's rough.'

Sharif shrugged. 'It was what it was. It's in the past now.'

But she sensed it was not forgotten. Not by a long shot.

They were coming to a smooth stop outside a restaurant now, and Liyah could see officious-looking people springing forward with clipboards, and umbrellas to ward off the snow.

Sharif got out and opened Liyah's door. She steeled herself against the inevitable reaction when she put her hand into his, but it was no use. By the time she got into the warm space of the restaurant her skin was hot, and she pulled away from Sharif in case he saw how weak she was.

Someone discreetly took her coat and she followed Sharif into the restaurant, gasping a little when she saw the elaborate setting. There was a long table laid with gold cutlery. An arrangement of winter flowers ran down the centre of the table in green, gold and decadent red. There were hundreds of flickering candles.

Everything became a bit of a blur as she and Sharif were swept into a round of meeting people and air-kissing before they were seated for dinner. Liyah had to stop her jaw dropping to the floor more than once when she recognised several movie stars. One of whom had won multiple awards the previous year.

To her relief, she wasn't seated beside Sharif, who was at the top of the table. The new designer and his assistant were next to him. It gave her a chance to regain her breath after the revelations he'd shared on their journey here. A chance to observe him for once. She saw how he interacted with the designer, giving him the totality of his attention, but every now and then his gaze would slide to Liyah and she'd immediately feel flustered and look away.

In a bid to avoid Sharif's eye, she got into a conversation with the woman beside her who turned out to be very pleasant. She was a stylist who regularly worked with the designer, and Liyah was able to ask her lots of questions about the fashion industry that Sharif would never have had the time to indulge.

After Sharif had given a speech, and the dinner party had started to break up, people moved into another room, from where Liyah could hear the infectious beat of disco music. Clearly the party was continuing. But when she looked around, Sharif was approaching with her coat.

'You really don't like to hang around, do you?' Liyah observed drily as he helped her into it.

'This is work for me.'

When they were back in the car, Liyah couldn't help probing. 'So, if you take a woman on a date, what do you usually do?'

Sharif didn't like the way he suddenly felt defensive. For the whole of the dinner he'd found himself distracted. Distracted by the play of golden light on Liyah's skin. The slope of her bare shoulders. Her arms, slender but strong. The graceful curve of her neck and jaw. The regal line of her profile and those ridiculously lush lips. The way she'd made everyone else look pale and listless in comparison. The way she'd listened attentively to the person beside her when everyone else in the room had been darting looks all around to see who was looking at them, or if someone more important was on the horizon.

He didn't like it that he'd noticed so much. It made him prickly on top of feeling defensive. 'Do you feel hard done by because I haven't taken you on a date, Liyah?'

Her eyes flashed. 'I know this isn't a conventional relationship. I don't expect...that.'

'That?' He mimicked her. 'You mean romance? I don't offer women romance, Liyah—as you might have noticed from the recent salacious headlines you must have seen in your research. I offer them a very straightforward transaction.'

'Sex.'

He shrugged unapologetically. 'In a word. I'm not interested in a relationship. Hence this...' He gestured between them to indicate their arrangement.

She was silent for a moment, and then she asked, 'Why are you so consumed by building the business if you hated your father so much?'

Revenge. Retribution. Redemption.

How did this woman get so close to his edges every time? He barely knew her, but she seemed to be able to see into a place inside him where no one else ever dared venture. Not even his brothers—and if anyone could guess at the darkness inside him it would be them.

And, worse, why did he feel the need to tell her anything? The story about him being kidnapped was in the public domain and yet he never spoke of it. Never spoke of that terrifying moment when a Jeep had come hurtling towards him over the sand in the desert. He'd been going to set up camp for the night on his own. At the age of eight. Because he'd wanted to prove to his mother that he could be trusted.

He'd thought at first that it was his cousins, or his uncle, but it had been white-faced strangers with scarves covering their mouths. Private mercenaries with rough hands. Too strong for him to fight.

They'd hauled him off his horse.

To this day he cursed himself for not cantering away when he'd had the chance. They'd bundled him into the Jeep and taken him to a helicopter. And then a plane. First to Rome, where his father had laid out what was expected of him, and then to that gothic monstrosity of a school in Scotland.

He refused to visit Scotland even now.

And here was this woman, shining a light onto things he never discussed with anyone and making him aware of…what? That perhaps there was some lack in his life? Something missing?

Sexual frustration bit at his veins like the craving for a drug too long denied. He could kiss Liyah right now, give in to the carnal urge to slake his lust, and in so doing stop her looking at him as if she could see into all his hidden corners. And, more importantly, stop the irritating questions falling from those far too tempting lips.

But he knew that to give in would be to display a fatal weakness. So he said, in a tone that invited no further questions, 'I might have hated my father, but I don't allow emotions to cloud my judgement when it comes to business.'

Or when it comes to relationships, Liyah mused to herself silently as the car made its smooth progress through the streets of Manhattan.

She avoided Sharif's eye for the rest of the journey, not wanting him to see how his words had affected her, because she wasn't even sure why she felt this hollow sensation in her chest, when the fact that the man had closed his heart off long ago should have no impact on her whatsoever.

When Sharif returned to the apartment late the following night, he was uncomfortably aware that for the first time in his life he'd felt a sense of resentment at being kept at the office by work, when usually the thought of coming back to an empty apartment was unappealing. But he'd been watching the clock since late afternoon. Texting his security team to see what Liyah was doing.

She'd gone to the New York Public Library and spent hours inside.

And now, as he walked into the living area and was confronted with the sight of Liyah sitting cross-legged on a chair, in sweat pants and a soft, clingy cashmere top, with her hair piled on her head, reading a book, he knew that something wasn't adding up.

But he didn't feel inclined to worry about it right then.

He leant against the doorframe. 'I didn't know you wore glasses.'

She looked up, startled. And as he watched, her cheeks flushed darker. It had an immediate effect on his blood, bringing it to the boil after simmering all day. It was getting harder to keep his sexual frustration under control.

The glasses suited her. They made her look serious. Seriously sexy. But, as if hearing his thoughts, she took them off.

She closed the book. 'I wasn't sure what time you'd be back…if you'd have had dinner. I'm not sure how this works.'

Sharif straightened up and walked into the room. Its soft lighting gave everything a golden glow, including her. She watched him approach and desire coiled tight in his body. He undid his tie, and the buttons on his waistcoat, aware of her eyes following his movements as if she couldn't help herself.

He sat down on a chair near hers and picked up her book from where she'd put it down. A weighty tome on the history of New York.

She said, a little defensively, 'I wanted to read up about the city.'

Sharif put the book down. 'Perfectly commendable.' Although annoyingly inconsistent with the kind of person he thought she was. Right now she looked about as far removed from a partying socialite as it was possible to get.

Sharif made a mental note to get his team to make a more thorough investigation into what she'd been doing in Europe, suddenly suspicious as to why she was behaving so differently.

'Have you eaten?' he asked.

She nodded. 'Paul, the chef, made me a delicious beef stew. There's loads left over if you're hungry.'

A pang caught Sharif unexpectedly in the chest. No one had ever worried about saving him food before.

He shook his head. 'I had take-out in the office.'

Liyah made a face. 'That's not very healthy.'

Sharif smiled mockingly. 'Concerned for my welfare, Liyah? I told you—I don't need a wife, except on paper.'

Those mesmerising green eyes sparked and narrowed.

'Don't worry. I won't concern myself with your wellbeing again.'

Sharif cursed himself for goading her. Before he did something he'd regret, he stood up and put his hands in his pockets. 'You should go to bed, Liyah, it's late. And we're going to be taking a flight to Paris tomorrow night.'

Liyah was still trying to control her heart, which had been racing since she'd seen Sharif in the doorway, looking sexily dishevelled. Jaw stubbled. He loomed over her now, and she scrambled up from the chair and moved to the window, putting some distance between them.

Whenever he was around it felt hard to breathe.

She felt prickly—because she'd been unprepared to see him again, even after a day apart. *Not* prickly because she'd felt a little abandoned. She didn't like the sensation that she was in control of so little. Not helped by Sharif's effect on her.

'I have no objection to going to Paris, but a bit of forewarning would be nice.'

A muscle in Sharif's jaw pulsed. But he said equably, 'I'll arrange for my assistant to forward you my schedule, so you know what's coming up.'

'Thank you.' Now she felt as if she was overreacting.

Sharif shrugged minutely. 'No problem. I should have thought of it before now.'

'What's happening in Paris?'

'Some meetings with my brother and our team there, and there's an event to attend.'

'What kind of event?'

'A charity ball.' Sharif glanced at his watch. 'I have some more work to do this evening. The stylist will come tomorrow to make sure you have all you need for the trip.'

Liyah felt a spurt of relief that she wouldn't have to figure it out herself, but at the same time she felt indignation that he didn't trust her to pack the right things.

He turned and left the room, and Liyah's eyes were drawn helplessly to his fluid grace. All that taut energy. She turned around, disgusted with herself, and then groaned when she saw her reflection in the darkened window.

She imagined how Sharif had seen her just now. Hair piled up. Leisurewear. No make-up. Wearing glasses, reading a book. It was no wonder he didn't desire her any more. And that was fine with her.

Just fine.

Paris

'You like to be high up, don't you?'

Liyah couldn't keep the amused tone from her voice as she looked around Sharif's Paris apartment. It was on the top floor of a stunning nineteenth-century building, with views from almost every window of the Eiffel Tower in the near distance. It had a terrace and an elegantly modern interior design.

'I appreciate a good view.'

Liyah turned around to face him. 'Yes, but how often do you actually look at it?'

'Has anyone ever told you that you ask a lot of questions?'

Liyah blanched as a nanny's voice came back into her head. *'Always with the questions, Aaliyah. No one wants a princess who asks too many questions for a wife.'*

She'd been about six, and even at that young age she'd decided that if she couldn't ask questions then she didn't want to be a princess, or anyone's wife.

'What is it?' Sharif's voice was sharp.

Liyah shook her head. 'Nothing—just a moment of déja-vu.'

He looked at his watch. 'I'm afraid I have to go straight

to the office, but I'll take you to lunch in a few hours. You should get some rest.'

Liyah had slept on the plane—an overnight flight, bringing them into Paris early in the morning. She'd noticed that Sharif hadn't slept. He'd been on his laptop or his phone the whole time. He evidently didn't need sleep, like mere mortals.

'I'm okay. Actually, I might take a walk around...stretch my legs.'

Sharif shrugged. 'Whatever you want. One of the security team will go with you.'

Liyah opened her mouth to object, but shut it again when she saw the look on Sharif's face. It wasn't worth arguing. Even though she came from a royal family, they'd never been important or rich enough to merit serious protection. But she was at another level now.

He left the apartment, and after Liyah had freshened up she explored a little more, finding a media room and a gym with a lap pool. It looked very inviting, but she wanted to get out into the fresh air and see Paris again. It was one of her favourite cities.

She bundled up against the cool late winter breeze and set out to the Eiffel Tower, which was further away than she'd thought. An optical illusion.

When she reached it, she stood in the plaza among lots of other tourists milling around, and looked up at the majestic structure. Paris had been the first foreign city she'd visited after London, and she'd adored wandering around, getting lost in the *arrondissements*, sitting in cafés and lingering over coffee, watching the world go by.

You were lonely, though.

Liyah pushed the voice aside. *Not* lonely. Independent. Happy.

She saw her security man a few feet away, on his phone, his face towards her, his eyes hidden behind black shades.

Liyah went over. 'Is that Sharif?'

The man hesitated before nodding.

Liyah held out her hand, and he gave her the phone with clear reluctance. She said into it, 'Hello, Sharif.'

There was silence at the other end, and then a sigh. 'Yes, Liyah?'

'If you're so concerned about where I am and what I'm up to you should leave your stuffy meeting and come and see some sights for yourself.'

He had said he would meet her for lunch, but she didn't believe that. Anyway, she was used to occupying herself.

But then Sharif said, 'I'll meet you there. Wait for me.'

He terminated the call and Liyah handed back the phone, a little stunned. And excited. She turned away from the security guard, who pocketed his phone again and resumed his stony-faced position. Liyah tried but failed to block out the fluttery feeling in her belly.

Sharif saw her before she saw him. She was sitting on a low wall facing the Eiffel Tower. She was wearing jeans, Chelsea boots, and a dark green turtleneck under a leather bomber jacket with a sheepskin lining. Her hair was pulled up into a bun, with curling wayward strands framing her face. She also wore sunglasses. No different to many of the monied tourists around her, but a world apart at the same time.

She was drawing attention just sitting still. Her natural beauty too obvious to ignore. But she appeared not to notice. Before, Sharif would have immediately been cynical about that, believing that she was well aware of the attention she attracted. But now...he couldn't be sure.

He'd been right to investigate her more thoroughly. The fact that she'd flipped the tables on him *again* was becoming irritating in the extreme.

CHAPTER SEVEN

'How did you get a table here at such short notice?' Liyah asked, taking in the astounding views all around them from the ultra-exclusive restaurant in the Eiffel Tower. Then she rolled her eyes and answered herself. 'Stupid question, don't bother answering.'

She looked at Sharif, who was still in the three-piece suit that he'd changed into on the plane before landing. He looked as fresh as if he'd just woken from a ten-hour sleep.

The waiter came and took their orders. Even though they weren't near the top, they were still high enough that people looked like ants down below, milling around at the bottom of the tower.

Liyah said, 'I was only joking when I said that you should come. I didn't mean to break up your day.'

'I said I'd meet you for lunch.'

The waiter returned with white wine and poured two glasses. Sharif lifted his and said, *'Santé.'*

Liyah clinked her glass with his. *'Santé.'*

She took a sip, but was very aware of Sharif's gaze, which had turned calculating. She suddenly felt nervous and had no idea why.

He said nothing at first. Over a delicious starter of asparagus, and a main course of chicken breast, he lulled Liyah into a false sense of security by conducting a light conversation regarding her likes and dislikes—everything from movies to books and art.

Apparently he too enjoyed twisty dark thrillers, and he revealed a surprisingly nerdy interest in comic books.

He said, 'There were tons of them in my Scottish boarding school. I used to take piles of them and hide in one of the gardener's sheds, and get lost in them for hours.

It was worth the punishment when the staff thought I'd run away.'

Liyah gasped. 'They punished you?'

Sharif's mouth flattened. 'It wasn't a good place.'

He put down his glass of wine and leant forward.

Liyah was still thinking of that dark-haired young boy, being subjected to some awful humiliation, far from home, griefstruck, so when Sharif asked, almost idly, 'When were you going to tell me that it isn't you in those paparazzi shots?' Liyah almost missed it.

Her skin went clammy. Maybe she'd heard wrong. She'd been distracted. 'What did you say?'

'You heard me. It wasn't you in those paparazzi pictures.'

'How do you know?'

'Because I looked at them properly after I realised you weren't behaving like a spoiled socialite. Far from it.'

Liyah felt as if a layer of her skin had been stripped back. Incredibly vulnerable.

Sharif sat back. 'What I want to know is why you wouldn't tell me the truth when I confronted you about it? Why pretend to be something you're not?'

Liyah admitted defeat. 'The day you brought it up...it seemed easier just to let you believe what you wanted. I barely knew you. Everything had happened so fast.' She avoided his eye and plucked at her napkin. 'I guess it felt like a kind of armour. I wasn't ready to let you know who I was, and you didn't seem inclined to want to know.' She looked at him. 'You were too busy telling me that I was pretty much a bought companion, purely for public appearances.'

Sharif had the grace to look slightly discomfited. 'Yes, well... I was still coming to terms with the fact that *you*, the mystery woman from the oasis, and my new wife were one and the same. And you have to admit that your behaviour that night—*our* behaviour,' he amended, 'didn't exactly dissuade me from believing the worst.'

'That was part of it too,' Liyah admitted. 'I didn't think you'd believe me.'

'So, if you weren't tripping on and off yachts and spending up a storm and falling out of nightclubs, what *were* you doing?'

Sharif's gaze was direct and unwavering. Liyah tipped up her chin. 'I do like to dance, and I did go to nightclubs.'

'But, like most people, you probably managed not to fall out of them. Who's the girl in the pictures?'

'She's a Middle Eastern model. One of my sisters spotted that she looked like me. Same hair. Height…'

'She's totally different. She's about half your weight and she has no breasts.'

He glanced at her chest, making Liyah all too conscious of her larger than fashionable breasts under the soft fabric of her sweater. And her nipples were reacting to his look right now, growing hard, tingling…

She said in a strangled voice, 'I think we look totally different too, but she worked for what my father wanted and so he paid her to behave like a spoiled socialite and then tipped the press off that it was me.'

Sharif—thankfully—lifted his gaze back up to Liyah's face. 'Why would he do that?'

Liyah tried to ignore the familiar pang of hurt. 'Because telling people I was misbehaving all around Europe was preferable to admitting that I had left Taraq to try and live an independent life, which is all I've ever wanted.'

'What were you doing?'

Liyah's heart was beating fast. She hated it that it mattered to her what Sharif thought. 'I got a place at Oxford. I did a Master's in Economic and Social History over two years.'

'A Master's? Had you done an undergraduate course?'

Liyah shook her head. 'No, I'd studied for the Bacca-laureate with a tutor in Taraq, and I did an interview, and they accepted me.' Liyah's mouth twisted. 'I'm sure being an international student with ready funds helped.'

Sharif shook his head. 'They're more discerning than that at Oxford. How many languages do you speak?'

'Arabic—obviously. English, French, and passable Italian and Spanish.'

'And if you were here for the summer holidays, and not falling out of clubs and onto yachts, what were you doing?'

'One summer I worked in a vineyard in France, picking grapes, and I also worked in the library at Oxford.'

'And your family were *angry* that you were doing that?'

'My father is conservative. He doesn't approve of my desire for independence. To be honest, I didn't expect them even to notice that I was gone.'

Liyah looked directly at Sharif, daring him to pity her. This wasn't about self-pity—even if her family's disregard for her had brought pain.

'My father turned his back on me a long time ago—after my mother died. He moved on with his other wives and children.'

Sharif said tautly, 'That's why I have no intention of having children. I've only known a father to be a destructive force, and I wouldn't wish that on anyone else.'

Before, Liyah would have agreed with Sharif, but something rogue made her say now, 'We're not our fathers.'

'Do you want children?'

In all honesty, Liyah wasn't sure any more. 'I want a life of freedom and independence. I don't see how children fit into that. And I'm aware that's selfish.'

Sharif shook his head. 'It's not selfish to want what most people take for granted. You'll have all the freedom you want within a year at the latest, Liyah. You'll be wealthy enough to do whatever you want, wherever you want.'

Once again, instead of relief, Sharif's words precipitated an ominous ache inside her. It was the same hollow sensation she'd felt when he'd laid out so succinctly that he didn't want a relationship...

There was a low beeping sound and Sharif picked up his phone, which had been face-down on the table. Liyah blinked and looked around. She'd been so caught in the bubble of Sharif's focus that she hadn't noticed that the restaurant had emptied around them.

He was speaking into his phone now. 'Okay, we'll see you there.' He put his phone away and said, 'That was my brother Nikos. He and his wife Maggie will also be at the charity ball tonight, so you'll get to meet them.'

'They live in Paris?'

Sharif nodded as he gestured to one of the staff for the bill. 'They also have a house in Ireland, and they spend a lot of time there. Maggie's Scottish, but was brought up in Ireland. They have a son, Daniel, who is about eight months old, and Maggie is pregnant with their second child.'

Liyah squinted at Sharif. 'So, you have a nephew and another one, or a niece, on the way?'

Sharif made a face. 'It's a girl, apparently. And my other brother Maks has just announced that his wife is pregnant too.' He stood up. 'I'm afraid I have to go back to the office, but my driver can take you to the apartment. We'll leave for the ball at seven p.m.'

Liyah stood up too, still absorbing the fact that Sharif's brothers seemed to be well on their way to creating families. Surely if they had only got married for appearances' sake, like her and Sharif, they wouldn't be actively having babies?

As they walked back outside Sharif put on his overcoat and sunglasses. Liyah saw the women nearby—and the men—doing double takes. And then third takes. She rolled her eyes.

Sharif said again, 'Take my car.'

Liyah said, 'It's okay. I'll walk back to the apartment.'

'Suit yourself. A stylist will bring some dresses by for you to choose from. It's a black tie event.'

Liyah was turning away when Sharif called her name. She stopped. He came and stood in front of her. She couldn't see his eyes behind the dark shades.

He said, 'Don't let them touch your hair. Leave it loose.'

Liyah's heart hitched. 'Why? It's so messy—'

'Just…don't touch it.'

He turned and walked away, long strides putting distance between them within seconds. Liyah looked after him, afraid of the very tender sensation she could feel near her heart because he wanted her to look like…*her*. Especially after what she had just revealed—the truth about her European trip. The truth of who she was.

A bit of an academic nerd. Someone who wanted to travel. And read. And be independent. Someone most of her family didn't really care about.

The fact that Sharif had realised himself that she wasn't the girl in the photos had hit Liyah in a very deep and secret place, where she hid her hurts and vulnerabilities. It was all too seductive to read a deeper meaning into Sharif's comment about leaving her hair in its natural unstyled state.

But then Liyah castigated herself and turned abruptly and walked away in the opposite direction. She was being ridiculous. There was no deep or hidden meaning in Sharif wanting her to leave her hair alone. Absolutely none. No matter how much she might want there to be.

And *that* was something that she definitely was not going to acknowledge.

That evening, Liyah took a deep breath as she stood in front of the mirror. It was crazy—she knew she was a princess—but increasingly she actually *felt* like a princess.

The dress was strapless, with a sweetheart neckline and low back. How it stayed up was a feat of engineering and bodice work that Liyah didn't understand, but it felt secure. It was in the most delicate shade of blush pink, almost nude with a golden embroidered overlay. It had a cinched-in waist and a full, long tulle skirt and a small train that made it dramatic without being too loud.

The dress shimmered and glistened when she moved, and with it she wore gold hued high heels.

A very nice girl had appeared with the stylist, to do her hair and make-up, and the stylist had brought her pink diamond earrings and a matching bracelet.

The women had left not long ago, and now Liyah looked at herself again. Her hair was down, as requested, and the girl had brushed it until it flowed like ripples of silk over her shoulders, the unruliness tamed somewhat.

There was a knock on the door. Liyah's heart slammed against her breastbone. She opened it, and her eyes widened as she took in Sharif in a white tuxedo jacket, with a white shirt and black bow tie. He looked dark and sexy.

There was silence. And then Sharif said, 'You look… stunning, Liyah.'

She felt shy. 'Thank you. So do you.'

They went down to the foyer of the building, where the concierge held open the door and their driver was waiting, helping Liyah into one side of the car while Sharif got into the other.

The dress had a thigh-high slit and Liyah held the edges together over her thigh for the duration of the journey. Not that Sharif would even notice if she stripped naked, she was sure.

When they arrived at a seriously opulent-looking hotel, Sharif got out and came around, opening her door. He helped her out and kept hold of her hand, leading her onto the red carpet.

They stopped for the ubiquitous pictures. Liyah tried not to flinch every time a flash went off, wondering if she'd ever get used to it.

Beside her, Sharif said, *sotto voce*, 'That was one of the first things to make me suspect that perhaps there was more to you than you'd told me.'

'What was that?'

'Your lack of ease in front of the photographers. I noticed it at the Met.'

She looked up and met his gaze. A moment passed between them—a sense of affinity, delicate and ephemeral. His eyes moved to her mouth and he lifted a brow in question. Liyah knew what he was asking and she gave one tiny nod, her skin prickling all over in anticipation.

His head descended and his mouth brushed hers, light enough to tease, but strong enough to make her move closer, making a small sound. Her free hand went to his chest and he caught it there.

Then he pulled back. The world was a deafening clatter of sound and flashing lights.

'Mr Marchetti, another kiss, please!'

'Princess Aaliyah—over here. Who are you wearing?'

Liyah felt dizzy, but she watched as Sharif calmly faced the photographers and said, 'Mrs Marchetti is wearing Elie Saab couture.'

He moved forward and Liyah followed unsteadily, trying to get her hammering heart back into a normal rhythm. He'd barely kissed her, and it had been purely for the cameras, but she was reduced to jelly. What would happen if he kissed her in private?

Not going to happen, she reminded herself.

By the time they reached the main reception she was marginally under control again.

Sharif stopped suddenly and said something in Italian that she didn't catch. Then he turned to her, pulling his phone out. 'There was something I wanted to show you before we left the apartment, but I got distracted.'

Liyah's heart sped up again. Had she distracted him? She hoped so, because he distracted *her* all the time.

He handed her his phone. It was a press release, headed with the Marchetti Group's logo.

We accept the apology from Celebrity! Magazine, which published photos of a woman last year, claiming them to be of Princess Aaliyah Binte Rashad Mansour.

It was, in fact, a model called Ameera Sayam.

Celebrity! Magazine have agreed to donate an undisclosed amount of money to a charity chosen by the Marchetti Group, and extend their apologies for having caused Mrs Aaliyah Marchetti any distress.

The words swam ominously in front of Liyah's eyes and she quickly blinked. Until that moment she hadn't realised how hurtful it was that her own father had betrayed her in such a way. And now Sharif had gone out of his way to clear her name.

She handed back his phone. 'Thank you…you didn't have to do that.' Her voice was husky.

'I did, actually. Your reputation now affects me and the Marchetti Group.'

Liyah's emotions shrivelled. He'd done it for pragmatic reasons. Not for *her*. 'Of course.'

A waiter approached and Sharif took two glasses of champagne, handing Liyah one. She avoided his eye and took a quick sip, hoping he wouldn't notice anything. What was it about this man? She'd been more aware of her emotions in the past couple of weeks than she had her whole life.

And of your desires, pointed out a wicked inner voice.

Sharif took her hand again and led her into the crowd.

She'd never seen so many beautiful people in her life. Women in shimmering dresses like hers. Blinging with jewels... The smell of perfume was almost overwhelming...

And then from behind them Liyah heard a voice.

'There they are! Sharif!'

Sharif turned around and Liyah followed him to see a man approaching. He was as tall as Sharif and very dark, with thick curly hair. He was also astonishingly good-looking, with a classical beauty that reminded Liyah of a Greek statue. She recognised Nikos from the pictures she'd seen on the internet.

And the woman beside him. Tall—as tall as Liyah, if not taller—and very pale, with golden russet hair piled high, huge blue eyes.

She looked at Liyah and exclaimed, 'You must be Aaliyah!' She stuck out a hand. 'I'm Maggie. It's so nice to meet you.'

Liyah instinctively relaxed. Maggie was so friendly and open that it was impossible not to smile.

She shook her hand. 'It's Liyah, please—only my father calls me Aaliyah, and that's not a good thing.'

Maggie shook her hand and widened her eyes even more. She leant forward and whispered, 'Say no more. I understand all about Daddy issues. And as for these two...' Maggie gestured with her head towards Sharif and Nikos, who were watching them.

Liyah stifled a giggle. Nikos was rolling his eyes, but a smile played around his mouth as he wrapped an arm around Maggie's waist and pulled her to his side, whispering something in her ear that made her blush. It was then that Liyah noticed the bump under the form-fitting silk of her beautiful black evening dress.

'Congratulations,' she said.

Maggie put a hand on her neat bump and made a face. 'Thanks. It won't be easy, having two under two, but I like the idea of Daniel having a sibling close to his own age. I was an only child, and I always wanted brothers and sisters.'

Liyah was tempted to mention the fact that having a lot of siblings didn't exactly spell happy families...

'Liyah, this is Nikos.'

Sharif was introducing her to his brother. Liyah shook his hand, shyer than she'd been with Maggie. Nikos was smiling, and she could see how charming he was, but she could also detect that Marchetti steeliness.

These two were so clearly in love that Liyah felt bad for having entertained cynical doubts. She was very aware of the chasm between her and Sharif. Which was crazy, because love had no place for them.

Maggie was easy to talk to, and refreshingly normal in a world that Liyah barely recognised any more. She noticed that Sharif was tense around Nikos, but also how he couldn't help smiling at whatever Nikos said. She sensed that Sharif wanted to let his guard down, but wouldn't. Or couldn't.

They gradually moved closer to a central ballroom, where waltz music was playing. Maggie nudged her husband. 'You should ask Liyah to dance, Nikos—after all, we never got to celebrate the wedding.' She sent a look to Sharif, who just arched a brow.

Liyah was embarrassed, but before she knew how to respond Nikos was bowing before her and saying, 'If you would do me the honour, I'd love to have this dance.'

Relieved by the distraction, and wondering how much these two knew about the reality of her marriage with Sharif, Liyah put her hand in her brother-in-law's and let him lead her onto the dance floor. It was something of a respite to spend time with a man who didn't affect her so acutely. Who didn't look at her and make her skin feel tight and hot.

Nikos was a good dancer, fluid and strong. And she breathed out and let him take control.

He said above her head, 'That bad, eh…?'

She looked up. 'Excuse me?'

He winked. 'I heard that sigh of relief. And I know how tough it is spending time with Sharif, so I don't envy you.'

Immediately Liyah felt defensive. 'He's really not that bad.'

At all.

Nikos looked at her and she blushed. 'You…you do know? That the marriage isn't…'

'All I know,' he said diplomatically, 'is that I think you'll be good for him. He works too hard and he's too serious. I'd imagine that any adjustment in his life to accomodate someone else is a good thing.'

'He's told me you didn't grow up together?'

Nikos made a face. 'No, our beloved father didn't approve of us half-brothers actually getting to know one another. He had plans for us all in the business, and was counting on us competing against one another to keep the Marchetti Group on its toes. The fact that he wouldn't approve of us working together is something that makes things even sweeter now. Sharif was the one who pointed out to Maks and I that it was *our* legacy to protect.' Nikos shook his head 'But after what happened to him and his mother, I don't know how he didn't destroy it all at the first opportunity.'

'You wouldn't have minded?'

Nikos grimaced. 'I didn't care about much until I met Maggie again and knew I had a son. Now everything is changed.' He looked at Liyah and smiled. 'I blame my wife for the fact that I can't seem to keep anything to myself these days.'

Liyah smiled too. 'She's very sweet.'

Nikos looked over her head, presumably at his wife,

and said, 'Yes she is.' And then, in an ominous voice, 'Incoming—behind you. I warn you now: the man is a terrible dancer.'

Nikos disappeared into the crowd just as Sharif appeared in her eyeline. He was glowering after his brother. They stood in the middle of the dance floor, with couples moving around them.

Sharif took Liyah's hand and moved to walk off, but she dug her heels in and hissed, 'It's the middle of the song.'

Sharif faced her. 'I told you I don't do this sort of thing.'

Liyah stepped close to him. Lifted her hands. For a moment Sharif looked so like a petulant little boy that she had to bite back a laugh. But then he muttered something and took her into his arms.

Instantly flames raced along Liyah's veins. Her core grew heavy and hot with desire. Sharif didn't have his brother's fluidity, it was true, but he moved with competent grace for such a big man.

Liyah looked up. 'Why do you hate dancing so much? You're not as bad as—' She cut herself off at Sharif's sharp look.

'Nikos oversharing again? Marriage and fatherhood have turned his brain soft.'

When he didn't say anything else, Liyah prompted, 'Well...?'

Sharif sighed. 'My father made me go to the Bal des Débutantes, here in Paris.'

'I know of it... I didn't go, but my sisters did.'

Liyah felt the familiar prickle of shame and tried to ignore it. The Bal des Débutantes was an invitation-only exclusive event, designed to introduce prominent young men and women of the world to society. Obviously she hadn't been deemed prominent enough by her family.

Sharif said, 'You were lucky. My father and I were both invited. Except my father didn't turn up. I missed the waltz class before the event and I was the only *cavalier* at the ball who didn't know how to dance. Throw in the fact that my father was reaching nuclear levels of press coverage at the time, and my mixed race heritage among the blue-eyed Princes of Europe made me stand out like a sore thumb... It didn't end well.'

Liyah's eyes widened. 'You got into a scrap?'

Sharif lifted the hand holding hers and pointed at a scar by his jaw.

Liyah reached out and ran her finger along the small indentation.

The moment Liyah's finger touched Sharif's skin an electric jolt went right down to his solar plexus. He stopped moving. She looked up at him, eyes huge. Her hair flowed over her shoulders, marking her out amongst all the other women with their complicated up-dos and overdone faces.

He didn't know what had compelled him to tell her to leave her hair down.

Yes, you do. You wanted to see her again as you saw her that night. Naked. Wild.

He shoved the provocative thought aside.

Once again she made everyone else pale in comparison. She was vibrant. Full of an earthy sensuality that called to him on such an urgent and deep level that Sharif knew he was fighting a losing battle.

She barely had to touch him and he burned. He felt volatile, and it hadn't been helped by seeing Nikos and Maggie.

Being around his brothers, and now their wives, always put him on edge, left him filled with mixed emotions. Protectiveness, regret, affection... But also a strong instinct not to trust—and guilt. Because he hadn't told them everything he was planning.

Just seeing Liyah dancing with Nikos, smiling at whatever he was saying, had made the darkness inside him lash and roar, even when he knew for a fact that Nikos had eyes only for Maggie. He'd learnt not to test Nikos's loyalty in that regard, and now, with Maggie pregnant again, they inhabited a place that Sharif could not understand.

Seeing them so happy brought back painful echoes of his relationship with his mother. Her unconditional love and his feeling of security. Something that he'd told himself he would never need again, because the pain of losing it had been so great.

Sharif gritted his jaw. He really wasn't in the mood for these introspective thoughts. And yet here was Liyah, her huge green eyes looking up at him and making him feel as if she was seeing all the way down to where he kept his darkness hidden.

He'd noticed the emotion in her eyes when he'd shown her the press release about those paparazzi photos claiming to be of her. He knew damn well that he could have left it alone…that his comment about her reputation hadn't been entirely true—those photos had barely made a dent in the mainstream gossip columns. But he'd seen how much it had affected her when she'd told him about it, and he'd wanted to avenge her. So he'd instructed his legal team to extract an apology and a retraction from the magazine or force them to face a lawsuit.

They'd issued the press release within hours.

Sharif was aware of the song coming to an end and the sense of exposure mixed with those other volatile emotions in his gut boiled over. He needed to shut out the voices and the swirling thoughts and refocus. And he knew only one way to do that.

Stop denying himself. Stop denying them both.

He led Liyah off the dance floor, his blood pounding. They were almost at the main entrance when he felt her pulling on his hand. He stopped, looked at her.

She said, 'I know you don't like to hang around, but we literally just got here.'

Sharif felt drunk with lust. The light made her skin gleam dark golden. The swells of her breasts above her bodice were a provocation he had no intention of resisting any longer. He'd forgotten why he'd ever thought it would be a good idea *not* to sleep with his wife.

He felt it in her too. She trembled whenever he touched her. Even now a blush was rising into her cheeks, staining them darker.

She said, 'Why are you looking at me like that?'

'I don't think this is working.'

She frowned. 'You don't think what isn't working?'

But Sharif was striding through the lobby of the hotel now, cutting a swathe through the throng of guests, Liyah's hand clamped firmly in his.

Liyah said from behind him, 'What about Nikos and Maggie? Don't we need to say goodbye? Don't you have people to meet?'

'Nikos can look after it. I'll send him a text.'

They walked outside and a valet scrambled to call Sharif's car and driver around. He felt Liyah shiver beside him and took off his jacket then put it on her.

He texted Nikos.

We've left. Will you cover for me?

He got a text back almost straight away.

Of course. Welcome to my world, brother.

There was a winking emoji, and then a laughing crying emoji.

Sharif scowled and shoved his phone back in his pocket. This, with Liyah, was nothing like what Nikos had gone through with Maggie. For a start, she'd had Nikos's son—when he'd met her again, he'd been a father.

Sharif felt desperate. Almost feral. Things he never usually allowed himself to feel. He was always so careful to show the world that he was not his wayward father. Or his playboy brother. But he didn't have a playboy brother any more. Right now he was channelling the Marchetti rebelliousness all by himself and he couldn't care less.

He wanted his wife.

CHAPTER EIGHT

LIYAH ABSORBED THE heat and scent from Sharif's jacket as the car pulled to a smooth stop beside them. He opened the door and she got in. She didn't know what was going on with him, but she desperately resisted the temptation to believe that the heated look in his eyes meant something.

They joined the crazy Paris traffic and Liyah said nothing at first. Waiting to see if Sharif would elaborate. But he was silent. Brooding.

Eventually Liyah had to break the growing tension. 'Um…what you said about something not working…what did you mean?'

Sharif turned to look at her, snapping out of his brooding mood. He lounged back against the side of the car. Liyah had never seen him like this. It intimidated her as much as it excited her. There was something careless about him. No… Something reckless. Dangerous.

'I meant that I don't think our current arrangement is working.'

The driver put up the privacy shield between the front and the back seats.

Liyah's stomach plummeted. She'd asked too many questions. She didn't fit into his world. She didn't look like those other effortlessly soignée women. He didn't want to dance. Not with her, anyway.

And why was her first reaction dismay?

Terrified he'd see how much he'd got to her, Liyah said stiffly, 'I think you're right. Obviously neither of us are really suited to this…arrangement—'

'I don't mean that—' Sharif interrupted her, but then broke off abruptly. He cursed.

Liyah realised the car had stopped moving, they were back at his apartment.

Before she could try to figure out what he *had* meant he was out of the car, opening her door and reaching for her, taking her hand and leading her into the building. When they were in the elevator he didn't let go of her hand. Still he didn't say anything.

Electricity crackled in the air between them. She was afraid to look at him, or put a name to it, or think about what it meant. But she could feel it in her gut. Desire. The flames were getting loose and licking at her insides. But what if she was wrong? What if—?

The elevator doors opened and Sharif led her into the apartment's foyer. The door closed behind her and Sharif let her hand go. She wobbled a little in her heels. Why was she out of breath all of a sudden?

Feeling incredibly nervous, she started to babble. 'I liked Nikos and Maggie. They're genuinely in love, aren't they?'

Sharif's expression was stark. He looked at her as if he'd never seen her before and then he said, 'I don't know much about love—but I know about *this*.'

Liyah frowned. 'About—?'

But her words were cut off when Sharif clamped his hands on her waist and pulled her into his body. All the air left her chest.

'This marriage in name only is not working.'

The look in his eye was explicit. His body was hard. His heart hammered under her hands, which were splayed across his chest. Liyah opened her mouth and then shut it again. The flames of desire licked higher. But even as they did, and as she became aware of the full meaning behind Sharif's declaration, she felt the need to resist.

'Are you sure that's a good idea?'

'I want my wife.' He growled the words.

It took a second for her to absorb that fact. To acknowledge how badly she'd wanted him to want her. How much it had flayed her inside to think that one night had been enough for him.

Then it sank in. Stark. Unvarnished.

'I want my wife.'

This was how he did it. No romance. He hadn't even said *I want you.* She was a commodity to him. He just wanted to scratch an itch—she was no different from his other lovers. Maybe seeing his brother with his wife had made him realise that he was missing convenient sex in his convenient marriage.

That suspicion made something close down inside Liyah.

She took a step back, dislodging Sharif's hands. 'Well, I don't think I'm prepared to renegotiate the parameters of this arrangement just because you want someone to warm your bed. I'm sure you have plenty of contacts you can call to alleviate your…urges.'

Deep inside, Liyah wondered what on earth she was saying. She was willingly pushing him into another woman's bed! But he'd never been hers in the first place. Not really. No matter how serendipitous or magical that night at the oasis had felt.

'I told you—I don't need any adverse press at this time.' He took a step towards her.

Panic at his proximity and her own weakness made Liyah put out a hand as if to ward him off. *Or grab him and bring him closer?* teased a sly inner voice.

She dropped her hand. 'So now I'm convenient not just for a marriage but also to scratch a physical itch?'

He took another step closer. His scent wrapped around her like a siren call. Woody and oriental. Infinitely seductive. She wanted to close her eyes, breathe him in until she was dizzy.

He made a sound like a strangled laugh. 'Believe me, there's nothing "convenient" about how you make me feel.'

Panic spiked. 'I don't mind if you want to take someone else to bed. I won't say anything.'

He came closer, as if she hadn't spoken. Liyah felt as if she was under water. His hands were opening his jacket that was still on her and pushing it apart, over her shoulders and down her arms. It fell to the floor at her feet with a muted swish of fabric.

He said, almost to himself, 'The problem is that I don't want anyone else. I only want you.'

You. Not *my wife.* Her. Liyah.

Treacherously, she felt her defences weaken.

Up close, he still towered over her, even in heels. His jaw was dark with stubble. He was so broad that he blocked everything else out.

And then he said, 'You really wouldn't mind?'

Liyah couldn't think straight. 'Wouldn't mind what?'

'If I slept with another woman?'

A raging hungry beast reared up inside her, and his scent and proximity made her defences crumble to dust. She had an image of him at the oasis, watching her emerge from the water, holding his hand out to her. Something very elemental moved through her.

This man was hers.

And right then she couldn't remember why it was so important to fight that.

'I would mind.'

Had she growled as she'd said that? She couldn't be sure, but she didn't care, because Sharif had his hands on her waist again and was tugging her towards him. It was only when their bodies touched that she realised she was shaking from the need overflowing inside her.

He went still. 'This doesn't change anything, Liyah. We're just letting our mutual chemistry burn out or else it'll drive us crazy. But that's all it is. It doesn't change what this marriage is.'

Not a marriage. A business arrangement.

'I know,' Liyah said, hoping she didn't sound too desperate. 'That's fine with me.'

She didn't want anything more either. She wanted her freedom. Independence. She certainly didn't want to risk her heart after a lifetime of learning that those who were meant to love you most either left you or rejected you. Or asked you to sacrifice your freedom for theirs.

This had nothing to do with emotions. It was desire. Physical. She could handle that.

To make sure he understood, she said, 'I want you, Sharif.'

As if a switch had been flicked, he muttered something guttural and dug his hands into her hair, clasping her head, tipping her face up to his. Liyah gripped his arms and his muscles bunched under her palms. Her legs nearly gave way and she had to lock them to stay standing.

When his mouth covered hers electricity shot into her veins and straight to every erogenous point. She was suddenly ravenous, reaching up and straining to get closer. There were too many clothes in the way. She scrabbled for Sharif's waistcoat, pushing it off, dislodging his hands. Then his bow-tie and shirt.

When his chest was bare she pulled back and put her hands on him. He was warm and vital. The hair tickled her palms. His heart was thudding heavily. She felt drunk. Even though she'd barely touched her champagne earlier.

'You… I want to see you, Liyah.'

She turned around and pulled her hair over her shoulder, presenting him with her back. He pulled down her zip, his fingers stopping just above her buttocks. The dress loosened around her chest. Sharif came close behind her. She shivered when his bare chest met her back and his arms went around her, his hands cupping and measuring the weight of her breasts. She moaned with need, her head falling back against his shoulder.

He caught her jaw, tipped her face up so that his mouth could meet hers as he found and caught a nipple between his fingers, lightly pinching and rolling it until Liyah couldn't breathe with her need. She twisted in his arms, facing him again, her hands scrabbling for his belt, undoing it, opening a button, pushing his trousers and briefs down over his hips.

They were still standing in the foyer of the apartment. They'd barely moved two feet. But she didn't even notice. She took his rigid flesh in her hand, feeling the size and weight of him, hearing his sharp sucked-in breath, revelling in a momentary feeling of power.

He took her hand away. She looked up and quivered inwardly at the expression on his face.

'No time to play. I need you now.'

He backed her up until her shoulders hit the door with a soft thud. The wood was cool against her heated flesh. He crowded her and she revelled in it, wrapping her arms around his neck, rubbing her breasts against his chest.

She felt curiously emotional in the midst of this onslaught of sensation. She'd thought she'd never see him again after that night at the oasis. And then there'd been the shock of discovering he was her husband, and the belief that he didn't want her again.

But that was all incinerated to dust now, under his mouth. She squeezed her eyes shut to avoid him seeing anything of her feelings.

After a deep, drugging kiss, he broke away to press his mouth against her skin, her shoulder, her neck, and then down. He lifted her breast and cupped it so that he could zero in on her throbbing nipple, sucking and pulling the taut peak into his mouth, nipping with his teeth until Liyah was squirming, her every nerve-ending on fire.

Suddenly Sharif reared back and said throatily, 'Put your legs around me.'

Liyah kicked off her shoes, and when he lifted her up she locked her legs around his hips. The centre of her body came into contact with his, the flimsy lace of her underwear no barrier. She bit her lip, fighting not to beg because she knew that he was going to ease the burning ache in her core right here, right now.

He reached between them and she heard a faint rip. Her underwear. She didn't care. He guided the head of his erection to her centre, to where she was weeping with need. He looked at her as he teased her, lubricating his own body with the slick evidence of her desire.

And then, just when she thought she could take no more, he thrust deep, stealing her breath and her sanity. She was so primed that it took only a few deep, hard strokes to push her over the edge, and then her body clamped around Sharif's as he found his own release, his hips jerking in the aftermath of a storm so fast and intense they couldn't move for long moments.

Slowly Liyah began to put the shattered pieces of herself back together. She became aware of Sharif's arm around her waist. His other hand was by her head, against the door. His face was buried in her neck, his breath uneven. Warm. Their hearts were pounding. Skin slick with perspiration.

Sharif lifted his head slowly. Liyah couldn't look away. She was aware that she'd never been more exposed, but she couldn't seem to care.

To her surprise, Sharif caught a piece of wayward hair and tucked it behind her ear. He said, 'Okay?'

She felt emotional again. She nodded quickly in a bid to distract him. To distract herself. 'Fine.'

When Sharif put her down gently, Liyah winced at the loss of connection. Her dress was ruched up to her waist and the top had fallen down, baring her breasts. Her underwear was strewn on the ground, as were her bag, Sharif's jacket and shirt and tie. Her shoes...

She pulled her dress up and bent to pick up her underwear. When she reached for the shoes Sharif took her hand and pulled her up.

'Leave them.'

He'd pulled his trousers up, but the button was still open. He looked thoroughly disreputable and dangerous, and Liyah's over-stimulated body pulsed back into life.

He tugged her behind him. She followed on legs like jelly, holding her dress up. 'Where are we going?'

He looked back at her and smiled wickedly. 'To continue discussing this renegotiation.'

Sharif stood looking down at the sleeping form of his wife for a long moment. She was sprawled on her front, one arm raised. He could see the plump flesh of one breast. Her lush bottom. Those long legs that had wrapped around him like a vice, holding him, pulling him so deep inside her that he'd seen stars.

His blood ran thickly in his veins in an overload of pleasure. He'd never experienced this after sex.

Liar.

He made a face to acknowledge the fact that he had. Once before. With the same woman.

The confirmation that her effect on him was still as potent was disturbing. Sex for him was usually a momentary thing, a passing release of energy. This was something else. Something he didn't want to investigate.

Because surely it would burn out.

It was nothing more than extraordinary chemistry.

He assured himself that he was merely taking advantage of an unprecedented situation—the fact that he wanted his convenient wife. If anything, not having to feign intimacy would help his cause. And, more importantly, it would defuse her ability to distract him.

But then Sharif became aware that he was still standing there, captivated by his sleeping wife. So much for not being distracted. He'd been due at a meeting half an hour ago.

With a scowl marring his features, and his body resisting leaving her behind, Sharif left the bedroom.

When Liyah woke she felt as if she was floating in a soft silken ocean. Every limb was heavy and utterly relaxed. There was a hum in her blood. A hum of satisfaction. But also of…hunger.

Her eyes snapped open as a rush of X-rated memories assailed her from last night. Sharif bringing her to his room, stripping her bare before stripping off his remaining clothes. Laying her on the bed and spreading her legs so that he could put his mouth to her…

Liyah put a hand over her face and groaned softly. She'd been so wanton. Begging for more. He'd made love to her over and over again. Until they'd been limp with exhaustion and pink trails had coloured the Paris sky outside.

She opened her eyes again. And now it was bright daylight. She felt disorientated. She was not used to sleeping in.

Not used to being ravished.

She lifted her head and looked around. The room was empty. She spread out an arm. The bed beside her was cold. Sharif had probably left hours ago. She felt at a disadvantage. Her skin prickled and she pulled the cover over her naked body, suddenly feeling a little exposed—as if instinctively aware that he'd observed her while she slept.

Now she was being silly. Sharif Marchetti was not a man who lingered over his lovers. His absence was proof of that.

Hating feeling at such a disadvantage, and feeling like a sloth, Liyah got up and grabbed a robe from the back of Sharif's bathroom door. It dwarfed her and it smelled of him. She resisted the urge to hold it up to her face and breathe deep, and gathered up her dress and shoes before creeping back to her own room as if she'd been engaged in some illicit activity.

Sharif watched Liyah from the other side of the room. They were in one of Paris's famous atelier salons, where painstakingly intricate work went into creating the most stunning dresses in the world, primarily for haute couture. Clothes that could literally only be afforded by the very few and very privileged. Clothes that were often likened to pieces of art rather than fashion.

He'd found himself quite unintenionally calling Liyah to see if she wanted to come here with him.

She was wearing a long rust-coloured corduroy dress, with buttons down the front and a brown leather belt. Leather high-heeled boots. Her hair was tied back, showing off that amazing bone structure.

She looked the part of wife of the CEO of the Marchetti Group. Casual, but elegant and stylish. And she was listening intently to an older French woman—one of the typically expert seamstresses who worked behind the scenes to create the astonishing confections that would be worn down a runway at some point in the future.

Growing bored of the conversation he was meant to be listening to, about stats and figures and projections—this kind of very specialised work was at constant risk of being eroded by newer inventions and ways of creating clothes—Sharif gravitated towards Liyah, telling himself that it had nothing to do with the pull he still felt in his blood, that hadn't cooled since last night.

He couldn't remember a night of such unbridled passion. He had been insensible to everything but the woman under him. One orgasm had led to another until he'd been too exhausted to move.

Their night at the oasis had been a mere prelude to the most amazing chemistry he'd ever experienced. And the fact that it was happening with a woman who was his wife...was mind-blowing.

Liyah was wearing special gloves to handle a dress, and speaking to the woman in French, exclaiming over the work. The woman was obviously pleased with Liyah's praise, her cheeks pink with pride.

'C'est vraiment incroyable...'

Liyah looked up at Sharif as he came to stand beside her. An electric frisson sizzled up his spine. Her eyes widened as if she felt it too. The buttons at the front of her dress were fastened just low enough for him to see the curve of her breasts, the V in her cleavage.

It was an effort to drag his gaze up and see that Liyah was speaking.

'Martine was telling me that it's taken six months to make this dress.'

Sharif tore his gaze off Liyah and smiled at the woman. 'Your work, as always, is sublime, Martine.'

The woman went even pinker now.

He took Liyah's hand and the hungry beast inside him seemed to calm somewhat. A niggling observation he chose not to investigate.

Just as he was bringing her back to where he'd been talking with the design team at the house, the head designer appeared in their path.

He exclaimed dramatically, 'Who is this creature?' while looking at Liyah.

Sharif felt his hackles rise—which seemed to happen a lot lately, whenever someone looked at Liyah. 'This is my wife, Liyah.'

'You are exquisite.'

The man walked around her, looking her up and down. She looked slightly bemused. Then he introduced himself to Liyah and took her hand, pressing a kiss to the back of it and bowing theatrically.

Liyah smiled at the dramatics.

Sharif's hackles went even higher.

The designer looked at Sharif. 'I have been looking for the right person to try on one of my newest designs and now I've met her. Please can I borrow your wife for ten minutes?'

Sharif wanted to growl at the man. *No.* But he knew he was being totally irrational. The designer was paying Liyah a huge compliment, and he would look petty if he refused.

'Of course.' He turned to Liyah. 'If you don't mind?'

She looked a little uncertain, but she shrugged. 'Not at all—if it'll fit?'

The designer looked excited as he grabbed Liyah's hand and pulled her away from Sharif. He said, 'Oh, it'll fit—I know it will. And you will look fabulous. Then all we have to do is convince your husband to let you wear it in public.'

The first thing that erupted into Sharif's head when Liyah emerged from behind a curtain some twenty minutes or so later was that there was no way in hell she would ever appear in public wearing the most provocative outfit he'd ever seen.

It was moulded to every dip, hollow and curve of her body. Being round-necked and long-sleeved didn't make it any more demure.

The designer stood beside him and said in an awed voice, 'Have you ever seen anything more perfect?'

Sharif got out a strangled, 'What is it?'

'A sequinned zebra print catsuit.'

Liyah looked like a feline goddess. Even the fact that she didn't have the confidence of a model couldn't detract from the overall look.

Sharif's phone rang at that moment and he picked it out of his pocket, actually relieved that he had a moment's distraction from the vision in front of him. It was his chief strategic advisor, reminding him of an invitation to go to the opening of a new nightclub in Paris that evening.

Sharif had dismissed the invitation originally, because he loathed nightclubs. But his advisor was saying now, 'I know you don't usually go to events like this, but the club is owned by Felipe Sanchez—who we both know is worth keeping an eye on because he's starting to encroach on our territory…buying up designer labels and luxury brands that are outside our sphere of interest. But, as we know well, today's undesirable brand could become tomorrow's behemoth. We need to keep an eye on him. If you went to the opening, perhaps your presence…and your wife's…would eclipse some of Felipe's bid to grab publicity. I don't think I need to tell you that Princess Aaliyah is attracting a lot of press attention. They want more of her…'

As much as Sharif hated the notion of doing anything in response to someone else's provocation, he knew his advisor was right. The last thing he needed was a rival upsetting his plans before he was ready to unveil them to the world. And, as much as he didn't want anyone else to see Liyah as she was right now, he knew that if she appeared in public in this outfit, on his arm, an eclipse would be guaranteed.

If not a nucelar meltdown…

That evening, central Paris

Liyah was naked in public. Well, not literally naked. But she felt naked—because she was so far out of her comfort zone that it was both terrifying and exhilarating at the same time.

She was wearing the catsuit she'd tried on earlier in the atelier and the material was gossamer-light, heightening her feeling of being exposed. She and Sharif had just stepped out of his car. Before them lay a red carpet, populated by well-known faces from the music world, actors and actresses... And at the other end of the carpet were the glittering lights of the newly opened nightclub. The pounding drum and bass of the music could be felt even from here.

Up till now, attending an event with Sharif had been a sophisticated and elegant affair. Tonight was something very different. Edgier, younger. Sharif wore a plain black suit and a black shirt, unbuttoned. Liyah saw a girl walk past wearing what looked like two slivers of silver lamé held together by pins.

Suddenly she didn't feel so naked, and when Sharif took her hand and said, 'Okay?' she looked at him and nodded, aware that for the first time she wanted to please him.

When he'd asked if she'd mind wearing this outfit to an event this evening, her first instinct had been to say *No way*. It was the kind of thing she would never wear in a million years. It had been one thing to try it on for the designer—but another entirely to wear it publicly, as if this was the kind of outfit, or event she took in her stride. When underneath it all, in spite of her metamorphosis over the last few whirlwind weeks, she was still just a nerdy academic who loved the outdoors and travelling and learning about the world.

But that wasn't entirely true. Because with Sharif she was discovering that she had a whole other side to her that she'd never explored before. A side that had been shut down after the experience with her first lover in England. A side that revelled in wearing something so provocative even as it terrified her.

Because she knew it had an incendiary effect on Sharif ...

After their visit to the atelier he'd accompanied her back to the apartment, and the evidence of just how provocative he'd found the catsuit had had him growling instructions into his phone to clear his schedule before taking Liyah to his room and making love to her with a hunger that had inflamed her. The after-effects lingered in her blood even now.

But now the world exploded in their faces as the wall of paparazzi caught sight of them and en masse trained their lenses on Liyah, in the glittering sequinned catsuit.

A couple of hours later, Liyah was sleepily curled into Sharif's side in the back of the car. to her surprise Sharif had deigned to stay for longer than a nanosecond at the club. He'd even—shock, horror—gone onto the dance floor with her. She smiled to herself at the memory.

Her ears were still ringing slightly after the loud music, so she was only half aware that Sharif was talking to someone on the phone. But then her ears pricked up.

'It worked very well,' he was saying. 'Felipe's reaction alone made it worthwhile attending.' And then, 'There are? Already? Send them to me.'

Sharif terminated the conversation.

Liyah sat up. He was looking at his phone and she saw an image of herself. She looked closer, not feeling sleepy any more. 'Is that me? From tonight?'

Sharif angled the phone towards her. There were a few images of them on the red carpet. And also some grainy ones from inside the club. A rush of hot exposure came back to her as she saw herself straining closer to Sharif on the dance floor, her arms twined around his neck, every point of their bodies touching. She was looking up at him and she looked utterly besotted.

'The pictures from tonight are already going viral. I think it's safe to say that the news of the opening of Felipe Sanchez's new club will fade into insignificance next to the pictures of you in that catsuit.'

'Who is Felipe Sanchez?'

'Someone who needs to be monitored. He's not a threat now, but if unchecked he could become one.'

Liyah felt sick as the evening took on another connotation. 'So he's a rival?'

Sharif said, 'You could describe him as that.'

'And this evening was about deflecting attention from him,' Liyah surmised flatly.

She handed back Sharif's phone and moved away, towards the car door. The rush of betrayal was all too familiar. Along with the sense of exposure. And self-recrimination for having thought for a second that tonight had been some kind of date.

She said, 'I'm under no illusions that this is a real relationship, but I would appreciate it if you would inform me the next time you're intending to use me as a pawn in your quest for world domination.'

Sharif felt the bite of his conscience. He heard the hurt in Liyah's voice. Impossible not to. And the fact that he was so attuned to another human being, probably for the first time since his mother had died, was an uncomfortable sensation.

She said accusingly, 'That's *my* image that's going to be plastered all over the internet tomorrow.'

'Your image has already caused quite a stir on the internet,' Sharif pointed out.

'Yes, but not while wearing a sequinned zebra print catsuit.'

Sharif felt the distance between them like a physical thing. He didn't like it. He wanted to reach for her, but knew not to.

'You look amazing. That's why you're currently breaking the internet.'

'Maybe I don't want to break the internet.'

Sharif shook his head. 'You have no idea how stunning you are, do you? Who taught you that you weren't beautiful?'

He could see Liyah flinch minutely, and he wanted to curl his hand into a fist and punch someone.

'Tell me again about that guy you were with.'

'He wasn't anyone important.'

'He made you feel insignificant?'

He saw her swallow. When she spoke her voice was husky.

'He was just a guy at my university. As you can imagine, coming from Taraq, I was less...worldly than most other girls my age. He singled me out—made me feel special. I thought he was attractive, but now I can see that I was confused by the attention he was showing me. I was used to standing out because of my height and my colouring. But he seemed to see beyond that.'

'What happened?' Sharif had to curb the violent urge he felt at the thought of such a man uncovering her sensual beauty and not appreciating it.

Liyah shrugged, looked down at her lap. 'He had a bet with his friends that he could get me into bed after one date. I... I was eager to live a modern life. I wanted to lose my virginity, to feel mature, independent...' She looked up. 'He won the bet.'

Sharif emitted a crude Italian swear word in response. He reached for Liyah, unable to resist any longer. She was tense, but she moved closer. She was sinuous under the delicate fabric and he had to curb the urge to rip it from her body there and then. He'd already given in to the storm of lust this bodysuit had unleashed earlier.

'He was an idiot. And he didn't deserve the gift you gave him.'

Liyah's heart hitched. She didn't doubt Sharif's sincerity.

She couldn't believe she'd told him of her humiliation, but the hurt she'd been feeling upon discovering how he'd manipulated and orchestrated this evening was

fading into insignificance next to the way he was looking at her right now.

His hands found where her hair was slicked back into
the bun and he undid it, letting it unravel down her back
and over her shoulders. He cupped her face in his hands.

'Never let anyone make you feel small, Liyah,' he said.
'You are stunning, and you have a power that I don't think
you even recognise fully yet. You're formidable.'

Liyah's heart did more than hitch this time. She quickly
tried to negate it. Remind herself who she was with—a man
who undoubtedly was a master at complimenting needy lovers. The thought of *lovers* made her want to hiss and spit...

'You don't have to say that.'

'I know,' he said simply. 'But it's true. And if the thought
of those pictures really upsets you then I'll have my team
take care of removing them.'

Liyah blinked. 'You would do that?'

He nodded. 'I could certainly limit them.'

Liyah asked, 'Will they be good for your business?'

Sharif hesitated for a moment, and then he said, 'In a
word? Yes. More than you know.'

'Then it's okay—leave them out there.'

'Are you sure? We have a window to limit this right now,
but if we wait till morning it'll be gone.'

Liyah shook her head. She put her hands on Sharif's
chest. 'No, it's okay. I know you're not used to answering
to anyone. But next time... Just let me know. Okay?'

Sharif's mouth tipped up on one side. 'Deal. Now, will
you let me make it up to you?'

'How?'

'Like this...'

He pressed the button to make the privacy screen go up
between them and the driver, and then he reached for the
zip at the back of the suit, pulling it down so that he could

peel the suit over her shoulders, down her arms and away from her chest, exposing her breasts to his hungry gaze.

'Sharif…' Liyah said weakly as he bent forward and cupped one breast.

He looked at her and arched a brow. 'Yes?'

'We shouldn't…not here.'

He blew on her nipple, before flicking out his tongue to taste the hard tip. It hardened even more. Liyah bit her lip.

'Do you want me to stop?'

Never. Liyah was on fire.

She moved back, drawing Sharif with her so he loomed over her supine body. 'No. Don't stop.'

He smiled and it was wicked. 'Your wish, Mrs Marchetti, is my command.'

And even in the midst of Sharif's lovemaking Liyah knew that something had happened here in the back of the car. Something that she didn't want to look at too closely. Because she sensed that, far from renegotiating this marriage as a purely physical thing, they'd moved way beyond that now.

Or, fatally, *she* had.

CHAPTER NINE

Two days later, London

LIYAH LOOKED OUT at a spectacular bird's eye view of London—naturally. Sharif's apartment was the penthouse of one of London's most exclusive hotels. On one side was the Presidential Suite and on the other Sharif's apartment.

Liyah could see the iconic Tower Bridge nearby, and all the way up the Thames to the London Eye.

As per Sharif's schedule, which was emailed to her now, they were here for the engagement party of Sasha and her fiancé. Sasha was Maks's younger sister, but no relation to Sharif or Nikos as she'd had a different father.

Liyah was curious to meet Maks and his wife—and Sasha. And to glean more nuggets of information about Sharif.

She still felt a little tender after Paris. Tender from the revelation that she could no longer ignore.

She'd fallen in love with Sharif. And it had happened in spite of everything she'd experienced that had made her want to protect herself from such vulnerability. She knew how those who were meant to love you most either left you or just…didn't love you.

It had happened with the speed and impact of an unstoppable train. And she knew why. Because, contrary to that first time, when Liyah had felt 'seen' by her lover, she now knew she had not been. That had been wishful thinking on her part—a need to justify allowing someone the ultimate intimacy. But with Sharif…she really did feel seen.

Literally, in her first interaction with him, she'd been naked.

But it was more than that. She felt an affinity with him

that she'd never felt with anyone else. Not even her sister. She saw a kindred spirit in his self-isolation. His lone wolfness. It resonated in her because she'd always been alone too.

Now, for the first time in her life she didn't feel alone.

And it was so dangerous—because for Sharif this was still very much physical. And she sensed that, while her own defences had ultimately been too weak to withstand him, his defences were far stronger.

His life was built around avenging his mother's betrayal and death. He hadn't spelt it out like that, but she'd guessed it. He had a singular ambition and Liyah was a momentary diversion, helping him to that end.

But what of that end? What would happen if and when he did avenge his mother? Would he have peace then? Or move on to the next challenge?

'Ready?'

Liyah turned around, startled out of her reverie. Sharif stood in the doorway to the palatial lounge in a black tuxedo. She sucked in a breath, still not used to the punch to her gut every time she saw him.

'Yes, I'm ready.'

This evening she was wearing a black silk dress. It had a high neck and long sleeves, and fell just below her knee. A gold belt cinched in her waist and the flowing fabric. It was paired with black high heels. She felt covered up and relatively demure, which was welcome after the other night in Paris and the catsuit.

The morning after that night at the club she'd woken to find it torn and in tatters. Much to her mortification. It hadn't survived intact after Sharif's lovemaking in the car, and then when they'd arrived back at the apartment, the zip had got stuck and Sharif had ripped the fabric asunder. Not that Liyah had objected at the time.

But, considering how viral those pictures of her in the

suit had gone after that night, Liyah figured the designer had got his value from it. She just prayed he wouldn't ask for its return.

'You've left your hair down,' Sharif commented.

Liyah walked over to him, growing warm from the heated look in his gaze. 'Did you want me to put it up?'

He shook his head and curved a hand around the back of her neck, tugging her towards him. He pressed a swift kiss to her mouth, and even that had Liyah moaning softly. Since the other night, it was as if any restraint was a thing of the past.

They'd even made love on the plane on the way from Paris to London. A flight that had taken less than two hours.

When he touched her like this, or made love to her, it was easy to pretend to herself that it was just physical, but she knew it wasn't. For her.

The engagement party was being held in one of London's most iconic hotels near Hyde Park. When they arrived in the main lobby, Sharif was approached by a man Liyah had never seen before. He introduced the man to her as the Marchetti Group's head of European PR. Liyah smiled, but lost interest as the two men engaged in a conversation about strategy.

She saw an eye-catching modern painting on the wall nearby and wandered over to take a closer look. When she felt a presence close by she looked up with a smile on her face, expecting to see Sharif, but it wasn't Sharif, and it took her a second to place who it was.

The man put out his hand. 'We met in New York, shortly after your wedding. I believe it was your first public event with your husband?'

Liyah instinctively recoiled, remembering the reporter who had confronted Sharif at that first event at the Metropolitan Museum. 'Mr Callaghan, isn't it?'

He smiled unctuously and she recoiled even further.

'Well remembered, Mrs Marchetti.' He took a card out of his pocket and held it towards her. 'I just wanted to give you my contact details, in case you ever feel you want to share what life is like on the inside of the world's most successful—'

The card was plucked out of Callaghan's hand before Liyah could touch it. She breathed a sigh of relief as Sharif pulled her close. His voice was icy.

'Aren't you a little far from home, Callaghan? And this is a private family event.'

The man stepped back and held his hands up in a mock show of humility. 'What can I say? I just happened to be in London at the same time.'

Sharif made a rude sound. 'Clear off, Callaghan. You're not welcome.'

Sharif led Liyah away, and threw the card into a bin as they passed through the lobby. She felt a prickling at the back of her neck, as if the man was still staring after them, but when she looked around he was gone.

In the elevator, Sharif said tightly, 'What did he want?'

'He wanted to give me his contact details. He seems to be looking for a story.'

She looked up at Sharif. His jaw was tight.

'There is no story.'

The elevator doors were opening now, and in a bid to try and move on from that unsettling encounter Liyah asked, 'What does Sasha's fiancé do?'

'His name is Dante Danieli. He's an award-winning photographer and film-maker.'

They stepped into a luxuriously decorated function room at the top of the hotel. Staff came and took their overcoats. Sharif took her hand and led her into the room, which oozed elegant sophistication, dressed in a theme of silver and grey and pink, with huge exotic blooms as centrepieces on the tables.

A waiter approached with a tray of champagne. Sharif took two glasses and handed her one.

Almost immediately Liyah recognised Maggie and Nikos, who had spotted them and were coming over. She was surprised at how pleased she was to see them again, greeting them warrmly.

Maggie said, 'I saw those pictures of you in that one-piece suit and I'm so jealous.' She pointed to her growing belly. 'I don't think I'll ever fit into anything like that ever again. Not that I would even be able to pull it off! You looked amazing.'

Liyah blushed. She felt Sharif's arm come around her waist.

'Didn't she?'

The warm feeling grew as they chatted companionably with Nikos and Maggie, and Liyah noticed that Sharif seemed less tense than he had before.

And then another tall man approached, with a petite woman by his side. He had dark blond colouring. Short hair. Gorgeous. Maks Marchetti.

'Sharif. I see that you're finally having some fun.' He looked at Liyah, smiling, 'And this must be the reason why you've taken that stick out of your—'

'Maks!' his wife exclaimed. She put a hand out to Liyah. 'Hi, I'm Zoe. It's so nice to meet you.'

Liyah shook her hand and Maks winked at her. 'Don't mind me. I just like to wind Sharif up at every opportunity, and it's nice to see him discover he's mortal too.'

Sharif made a rude sound beside her. Liyah shook Maks's hand, momentarily mesmerised by his grey eyes. Very different from Nikos and Sharif. She sneaked a glance between the men as they chatted. Each one as tall and imposing as the other. They packed quite a punch.

Liyah was drawn into a conversation with Maggie and Zoe. It felt quite natural, and she was unable to stay shy for long. They were both so down to earth. Zoe was pregnant too—almost out of her first trimester. She was very attractive, with honey-blonde shoulder-length hair. She had scars on her face that intrigued Liyah, but they didn't detract from her prettiness.

It was more than a little overwhelming to feel as if she was part of this group of people. And then she felt an acute pang as she acknowledged the fact that she wouldn't be part of it for long. She and Sharif would divorce and she wouldn't see them again.

Maks and Zoe excused themselves to go and check on Sasha, who Liyah guessed was the tall woman near the dais. She looked like Maks—a feminine version. Tall. Blonde hair. She was stunning. Wearing a blush-coloured strapless dress. Diamonds sparkled at her throat and wrists, and even from here Liyah could see the huge diamond on her finger.

A man joined Sasha. He was in a tuxedo. Tall and broad. Messy dark hair. He was very masculine, and savagely handsome. He pulled her to his side and whispered something in her ear that made her giggle and blush. She looked happy. Another couple truly in love…?

A dart of envy pierced Liyah before she could stop it. And, suddenly feeling a little too vulnerable to be around Sharif, in case he spotted it, Liyah made her excuses and walked over to where some French doors were partially open. She went outside to the terrace. It was cold, but the first hints of spring on the way could be felt. New life…

London sparkled under the moon. Vibrant and glamorous. It had always been her favourite city. But the desert… That was where her heart lay.

She was so wrapped up in her thoughts she didn't hear Sharif join her, but she felt him when her pulse inexplicably picked up.

'Penny for them?'

She looked at him, so tall and vital and handsome in his

tuxedo. She shrugged and looked back out over the view. 'I was just thinking of cities…and the desert. I miss it. I think it's where I feel most at home, even though it can be such an inhospitable place.'

Sharif placed his hands on the terrace wall. 'You miss your horse and your bird?'

She nodded. 'I feel free in the desert. Totally at peace.'

He turned and leant against the terrace wall, facing her. 'When my father sent those mercenaries to kidnap me I blamed the desert for a long time. As if it had somehow betrayed me by not protecting me.' He grimaced. 'Obviously I know better, but that's how the desert is for me—like a living organism.' His mouth quirked. 'I've since forgiven it.'

Liyah said, 'It's so vibrant and full of life, but it can turn on you in an instant. I got caught in a sandstorm once—scariest experience of my life.'

They stood in silence for a moment.

Then Liyah said, 'I know you said you took on your father's business because it was your due, and your brothers', and because you wanted to make something of it, but I can't imagine it was easy to take over from a man you hated so much.'

'It wasn't,' Sharif admitted. 'I despised it at first. Because I despised him and anything he touched. I thought his business was a vacuous world, full of vain people. I thought it had no value. Until I had access to the accounts and saw the spreadsheets. At first it was very much a means to an end for me—rebuilding it. But over time, as I got to know more, I came to appreciate the industry. I think there's a place for enduring brands in the world. And for fashion and art. We provide something aspirational. Inspirational. And I think we can do a lot of good in changing things for the better. In terms of the environment. Inclusivity. Diversity. Art and design and creativity is what civilises us.

If that disappears, or becomes eroded, we lose something very valuable.'

Liyah stayed silent, willing Sharif to continue.

'We had an intern in one of our offices from South Africa. He grew up in poverty in the townships. His mother cleaned in the big rich houses and she used to bring home copies of *Vogue*. For a young gay boy, who literally had nothing else, those magazines were a portal to another world, where he could fantasise about being someone else.'

Sharif looked at Liyah, and pride was visible on his face.

'He won Men's Designer of the Year at the fashion awards a few months ago.'

Liyah smiled. 'I love that story.'

People started clapping and cheering inside.

'We're missing the announcement,' she said. 'We should go back in.'

But Sharif caught her hand and stopped her, pulling her towards him until they were touching. 'I prefer it out here.'

'Do you, now?'

'Yes... I do.

He took off his jacket and placed it over her shoulders, before tugging on it so that she came even closer. Surrounded by his smell and his body heat, Liyah cast aside all her concerns and gave herself up to the moment.

Because she knew that when the time came all she would have to remember would be moments like this.

Later that night—much later—when they returned to the apartment, to Sharif's bedroom, Liyah wasn't prepared for the urgency that gripped her as soon as Sharif put his hands on her face and tipped it up so he could kiss her.

She realised she'd been waiting for this moment all evening.

She was ravenous.

She scrabbled to undo his clothes as his hands moved

over her body, undoing her dress, taking it off her. His kisses stole her sanity. She pulled back, dizzy, to see Sharif shed his clothes. A button popped. Liyah felt like giggling, but it was drowned out by the rush of blood to her head when she saw Sharif's magnificent body bared.

He was like a warrior. And she wanted to honour him.

She dropped to her knees in front of him and heard his surprised huff of air. 'Liyah, what are you—?'

But she couldn't resist that straining column of flesh. She wanted to taste him. The very essence of him. She wrapped her hand around him and heard him suck in a breath, whistling through his teeth.

He put his hands on her head, his fingers clamping tight as she inexpertly explored the thick, rigid flesh, running her tongue around the head before putting her mouth around him fully.

Sharif's legs were shaking…his hands trembling. He didn't recognise himself right now, having gone from civilised to carnal beast in about zero to ten seconds. It had taken all his restraint not to leave the party early, drag Liyah back to the apartment like some hormonal schoolboy.

He'd actually fantasised about her doing this, and now he was straining with the effort it took to keep his hips still.

Eventually it became too much. As much as he wanted to find oblivion in Liyah's far too tempting mouth, he wanted to be buried deep inside her more. And that was a revelation he refused to look at now—usually this form of release suited him just fine, feeling like a lesser form of intimacy.

He pulled back and Liyah looked up at him, her eyes unfocused. Her hair was wild and tumbling over her shoulders, almost obscuring her breasts.

Sharif couldn't even speak. He just pulled her up and lifted her, carrying her over to the bed before laying her down. He felt off-centre and, despite the clawing need to plunge deep and find satisfaction right now, he forced himself to go slow, to prove that he hadn't lost it completely.

Liyah was still dizzy from the headiness of what she'd just done, from how it had felt and tasted to have him in her mouth. At her mercy. She'd felt the tension in his hips, the way his hands had trembled in her hair. But now he seemed intent on proving that any notion she might have that she had the upper hand was sadly misplaced.

He came between her legs and pushed them apart, moving his big hands up to her thighs, spreading them even wider as he bent down, pressing kisses along the tender inner skin, his breath feathering closer and closer to the centre of her body, where her flesh pulsed.

And then he put his mouth on her flesh. She arched her back and grabbed the sheet with both hands, straining to contain the pleasure building at her core. But it was impossible. One flick of his wicked tongue and she was tumbling over the edge, and her body was still contracting when he reared over her and plunged deep, sending her into another spiral of ecstasy, showing her all too comprehensively who was the expert.

Liyah lay there for a long moment afterwards, her skin cooling and her breathing returning to normal. She was shell-shocked all over again at how this was between them. But surely it would begin to fade? This intense need and desire?

She heard Sharif's breathing return to normal beside her. She wondered if he was thinking the same thing.

And then he surprised her by saying abruptly, 'Actually, Callaghan isn't entirely wrong. I do have plans for the Marchetti Group. My plan is to destroy it.'

Callaghan. The reporter who had followed them to London. Liyah turned on her side to face him, shocked. 'What?'

Sharif didn't look at her. 'I'm going to reduce the Mar-

chetti Group to nothing. That's what I've been working towards. Building it up until it's powerful beyond anything
my father could ever have imagined and then selling it off,
piece by piece, until his legacy no longer exists. All the success he garnered off the backs of the women he seduced
and stole from will be forgotten.'

Liyah went very still. 'But…but all that stuff you told
me earlier about appreciating the industry…'

'This won't affect the industry at large. It'll cause a few
waves, yes, but the brands will continue to exist. Just not
under the Marchetti name.'

'But what if they don't survive without your support?'
Liyah thought of the women who worked in the atelier in
Paris.

'That's part of my reasoning in making sure we're in a
strong position. All the brands and labels will be desirable
lucrative concerns.'

Liyah came up on one elbow. 'What about your brothers? They don't know about your plans, do they?'

Sharif threw back the covers and got up from the bed in
a fluid movement. He walked over to a set of drawers and
pulled out a pair of sweat pants, put them on. They hung low
on his hips as he walked over to the window, arms folded.

Liyah sat up, pulling her knees up to her chest. Feeling
cold all of a sudden.

Eventually he said, 'No, they don't know.'

'Because you don't trust them?'

He turned around. 'In a word, no. Even if we do have
an accord now, I can't say for certain that they wouldn't
go against me—and I can't let that happen. Not when I'm
so close. They hated our father as much as I did. Nikos's
mother committed suicide because of him. Domenico made
Maks's and his sister's life hell when their mother had affairs and ultimately divorced him. I still can't trust that they

feel the same way I do, but they won't go without recompense. They'll be billionaires, no matter what.'

'You could talk to them,' Liyah suggested. 'Perhaps not telling them everything but sounding them out? They deserve that, don't they?'

She could see the lines of Sharif's body tense.

'They'd suspect in a second. They're not stupid.'

Liyah pulled up the sheet, feeling exposed. 'I think that you're underestimating them. I think you can trust them. Didn't they come into the group when you suggested it after your father died? They've helped you build it up.'

'They've helped you build it up.'

Sharif was so tightly wound that he felt as if he might crack open. Everything Liyah was saying was hitting him in a place that stung. And he had no idea what had compelled him to tell her any of this. It had started coming out of him before he could stop it.

The truth was that on some level he knew she was right. But he'd been alone for so long, living with his plan to grind his father's name and legacy to dust, that the prospect of it not happening was unconscionable. Too much of a risk.

As if reading his mind, Liyah said softly, 'Would you risk putting a rift between you and your brothers for this?'

'Yes,' he answered, swiftly and emphatically. Except this time it felt hollow.

He'd always figured a rift between him and his brothers would be the unfortunate outcome, but in the past couple of years he and Nikos and Maks had gravitated more and more towards one another. It was easier between them now. He felt...affection.

But he slammed down on all that now. Sentimental nonsense. This whole plan would only succeed with the element of surprise. No one could know.

Liyah got out of the bed, naked. She grabbed Sharif's

shirt from where it lay on the floor, slipping into it. It fell to her thighs. Her hair was tousled and she looked thoroughly bedded.

She held the edges of the shirt together. 'I'm going to take a shower and go to bed. Goodnight, Sharif.'

Sharif watched as Liyah left the room, an acrid feeling in his gut. For so long in his life he'd been certain that what he was doing was the right thing. The thing that would finally bring him a sense of vengeance meted out. And then peace.

And yet now all he could see were Liyah's huge eyes, looking at him reproachfully. He could hear her soft voice... *I think you can trust them.*

He turned around to face the window again and cursed. She was making him lose his focus. Damn her. Damn her for not being the wife he'd envisaged—unobtrusive and on the sidelines. Far from that, she was in his bed, under his skin, and every time he looked at her she made his mind go blank with lust.

Damn her for making him want to spill his guts.

And damn her for suddenly making him doubt everything.

Not even a hot shower could warm Liyah up. She wrapped herself in a towelling robe and curled up on the sofa in her bedroom. The extent of Sharif's ambition to avenge his mother and destroy his father even at the risk of alienating his brothers should have shocked her, but it didn't. After all, he'd been prepared to marry a total stranger purely to gain any advantage he could in the run-up to realising his ambition.

She felt cold at the thought of Sharif bearing this heavy, toxic burden for so long. And then she thought if she felt cold, how must *he* feel? He'd been alone for a lot longer than her. Trusting no one.

Obeying an instinct she couldn't ignore, Liyah went back

to Sharif's room. He wasn't in bed. And then she heard running water. He was in the shower.

She undid the robe and let it fall to the ground and opened the door. Sharif was standing with his hands on the wall, his head down between his shoulders. There was something so…isolated about his stance that Liyah's heart cracked for him.

She went into the shower and inserted herself between him and the wall. He tensed at first, and those dark eyes with gold around the edges stared at her as if he couldn't believe she was there.

She put her hands on his chest and rose up on her tiptoes, pressing a kiss to his mouth, which was in a hard, flat line. At first he didn't respond. She thought he was going to reject her. But then, as if a dam had burst, Sharif put his arms around her and lifted her up.

She put her legs around him and he leant her back against the wall, running his hand over her breasts, cupping one heavy weight before bending his head to suckle on her eager flesh.

He thrust up into her body, stealing her breath and her soul. It was slow, deliberate torture, as if he was making her pay for extracting a confession he hadn't wanted to make.

Liyah absorbed it all, and afterwards she wrapped her legs around him even tighter, felt him shudder his release into her body.

Manhattan

Sharif sat in the back of his car and pulled out his mobile phone. He texted Liyah.

I'm on my way home.

Then he stopped, deleted 'home' with a scowl and replaced it.

...to the apartment.

The woman was turning his brain to mush. Since that night in London, almost three weeks ago, they hadn't discussed the subject of his plans again. When Liyah had appeared that night in his shower he'd been consumed with so many tangled emotions that he'd almost told her to leave him alone, but then she'd put her hands on him and he'd lost the will to tell her to go.

It was as if she'd sensed what he needed and taken all of him, absorbing his need to exorcise what was inside him.

The following morning, when he'd woken, he'd felt as close to a sense of peace as he'd ever experienced before in his life.

His phone pinged with a response.

Good for you.

He smiled.

It will be good for me. And for you.

After a couple of seconds:

Promises, promises...

And an eye-roll emoji.

Sharif's blood leapt. He'd make her pay for that. He put his phone away, the smile still on his face.

The past three weeks had been...interesting. He'd had a few events to attend, accompanied by Liyah, and he'd found that as she'd grown more comfortable in his milieu she'd become quite happy to talk to people and not depend on him. If anything, he was the one looking for her now, and he didn't like how used he'd got to having her by his side.

He'd found her in a corner the other evening, talking to a septugenarian professor in Arabic about Taraq.

And one day, at the end of the working day—for normal people—she'd appeared in his office with tickets that she'd bought for a sold-out Broadway show. At first he'd been inclined to refuse, aware that he had enough work to keep him there for hours. But Liyah had looked so crestfallen that he hadn't had the heart to say no.

Sharif couldn't recall the last time he'd gone to a show that hadn't been a premiere, or part of a gala night. It had been revelatory...how such a regular thing could be so enjoyable. Although in truth he'd got more enjoyment out of watching Liyah enjoy the show. Wearing those glasses that made her look like a sexy academic.

And now he was going home—early, for him—because all day he hadn't been able to get the image of how she'd looked that morning out of his head. Sleepy and sexy. Hair in a wild tangle around her head.

She'd not slept in her own room since they'd returned from London. She shared his room. Which he'd never done with any woman. But he found that he liked seeing her things strewn around the space. Her creams and lotions in the bathroom. Her scent in the air...

He scowled again. He was definitely losing it. The sooner her allure started to fade—as he was sure it would—the better. It was coming closer and closer to the time when he would make the announcement about selling off the Marchetti Group, and he was aware that he was using Liyah as a distraction to avoid thinking about his brothers.

The car pulled up outside the apartment building and Sharif felt his anticipation build as he got nearer to the apartment door. This was also a novelty. Having someone waiting for him. Welcoming him. He'd always been so careful to keep women out of his private space before.

But not Liyah.

As soon as he walked through the door smells assailed him. Smells of Al-Murja. The desert.

He shucked off his jacket and loosened his tie. Explored the apartment, following the smells to the kitchen. He was prepared to see his chef but it wasn't his chef. It was Liyah. She was wearing jeans and a loose shirt. Bare feet. Hair up in a loose knot.

She was listening to jazz, humming to herself. And the smell of the food made Sharif's mouth water. He smelled spices and lemon. Chicken… Lamb?

He knew he should resist this vision of domesticity. It wasn't what he'd signed up for with this marriage. But it was more seductive than he liked to admit…

Liyah sensed Sharif and whirled around to see him standing in the doorway, leaning against the doorframe. Tie undone, shirt open at the top. Stubbled jaw. Her belly dipped and swooped. Her heart hitched. She felt shy. Which was ridiculous after what they'd done the previous night.

'Hi.'

'You're cooking.'

Liyah smiled. 'I can see why you're CEO—your powers of observation are truly impressive.'

Sharif made a face. He came in, nose twitching. 'What are you cooking?'

'I have a couscous, cherry tomato and herb salad. Lamb and pistachio patties. Harissa chicken. Hummus. Flatbread. Here.'

She handed him some flatbread and hummus. He tasted it.

'That's good. Really good. Where did you learn to cook?'

'I taught myself when I was at university. I felt homesick for Taraq and I found that cooking meals that reminded me of home helped.'

Sharif said, 'I'll have a quick shower and join you.'

Liyah looked at him. 'You're so sure you're invited?'

Sharif came around the ktichen island and pulled her close, covering her mouth with his. She felt the inevitable spark leap to life between them.

Still there. Not gone yet.

With every kiss now, every night of making love, Liyah was more aware that sooner or later there would come a time when Sharif wouldn't look at her in quite the same way. Wouldn't want her with the same desperation she felt.

He let her go and walked out of the room, leaving Liyah dazed and hungry. And, annoyingly, not for the delicious food she'd made.

Later that evening the movie's credits rolled and Sharif looked down to see Liyah curled up on the couch beside him, snoring softly, glasses askew on her face.

He turned off the TV—another first. Although he had a state-of-the-art media centre installed he rarely, if ever, watched anything except maybe the news.

He felt a sense of something he'd never experienced before, and had to take a few seconds to figure out what it was. *Contentment.* A sense of peace. This whole evening had been...easy. Pleasurable.

Normally, when he didn't have a function to attend, he would spend the evening in his study, with a sense of restlessness buzzing under his skin. A restlessness that was now gone.

He made a face. He was losing it. A little home cooking and his brain was scrambled.

He picked Liyah's glasses off her face and put them to one side. He gathered her into his arms and stood up. She made a sound...her eyes opened. Unfocused. Sleepy. *Sexy.*

She burrowed closer into his chest and Sharif's body reacted to her soft curves. As if he hadn't been in a state

of semi-arousal all evening, since he'd returned and found
her creating a veritable feast for the tastebuds and senses...

He felt his phone vibrate in his pocket, but by the time
he got to the bedroom with Liyah she was awake and wrapping her arms around his neck, pressing open-mouthed
kisses to his jaw. He forgot all about checking his phone
to see who was looking for him. He had more important
things to attend to.

CHAPTER TEN

WHEN LIYAH WOKE UP the following morning she stretched luxuriously, keeping her eyes closed, revelling in the after-effects of Sharif's lovemaking. Blinking blearily, she came up on one elbow and groaned softly when she saw the time on her phone. Nearly midday.

This man had turned her into such a sloth. But it was usually dawn before they were falling asleep, exhausted. Last night had been no different.

A voice from behind her said, 'You're awake.'

Startled, because she'd thought she was alone, Liyah looked over her shoulder to see Sharif at the window. The sun made her squint, but she could see he was fully dressed in a three-piece suit.

She sensed something was wrong and sat up, pulling the sheet to cover her chest, not even sure why she felt in-stinctively vulnerable all of a sudden.

'Morning... Why aren't you at work?' He was always gone when she woke.

Sharif stepped towards the bed, out of the sunlight. Liyah could see him now and his expression was stony.

'Sharif...what is it?'

He folded his arms. 'Tell me—when do you go into my study to send your messages to Callaghan? When I've left the apartment? Did seeing him in London give you the idea to go to him with the scoop?'

Liyah wanted to shake her head. Sharif was making no sense.

She sat up properly, clutching the sheet. 'What are you talking about?'

'Come and see for yourself.' He stalked out of the room.

Liyah scrambled to find something to wear, pulling on

Sharif's robe, which was hanging on the back of the bathroom door. She didn't even know where he had gone, but she heard the sound of the TV and went into the lounge. Where they had been last night... Until she had fallen asleep and woken in Sharif's arms...

Not now.

The TV was on. A news channel. Sharif stood before it, remote in one hand, his other hand in his pocket. She went and stood beside him. And her innards froze when she realised what she was watching.

As if she couldn't make sense of what the reporter was saying, she read the text that ran at the bottom of the screen.

Sharif Marchetti decides to sell the Marchetti Group... Brothers and fellow board members Nikos and Maks Marchetti...unaware of this development... An emergency meeting of the board is due to take place...

The reporter was talking again. 'Only days ago, Marchetti Group shares were at an all-time high. The company had the Midas touch. It could do no wrong. The question on everyone's lips is why on earth would Sharif Marchetti destroy his own company like this?'

Sharif switched off the TV. He faced Liyah, who was in shock.

'Well?'

She looked at him. She found it hard to speak. To articulate anything. 'How...how did they find out?'

'Really? You're really going to pretend it wasn't you? When Callaghan was the one who got the scoop? You met him—right under my nose in London.'

Liyah's brain felt sluggish as she recalled the man approaching her, trying to give her his card. 'Don't be ridiculous, Sharif. Of course I didn't say anything to him. I didn't even take his card. Why would I say anything?'

'Because you disapprove? Because you feel I'm not being fair to my brothers? Maybe you contacted Nikos and he called Callaghan, hoping to cause a bit of chaos so that I wouldn't go through with it. But I think it was because I gave you privileged information and that was an irresistible currency for you. A way to negotiate the end of our marriage well before time so you could get your precious independence early.'

Liyah's legs felt like jelly. She sat down on the chair behind her. 'That's such a twisted theory... I didn't do this, Sharif. I swear. Whatever I felt about your decision, your motives...that's between you and your brothers.'

'Not any more. It's now between me, my brothers and the entire world. Our stock has plummeted.'

'But...wouldn't this have happened anyway, when you made your announcement?'

'No, it would have been controlled. And I was always going to tell Nikos and Maks before I did anything. I just wasn't going to involve them until the last moment.' Sharif looked at his watch. 'I have to go. I have to give a press conference this afternoon and then I'm flying to Paris. I don't know when I'll be back.'

He went to walk out of the room and Liyah stood up. Before he disappeared, she said, 'You really believe it was me?'

Sharif stopped. He turned around. 'You're the only one who knew the full extent of my plans. I hadn't even revealed them to my own staff. They were kept in a safe in my office, and the only person who has the code is me.'

Liyah felt sick. Sharif walked out. She stared at the empty space for a long moment. Until she heard Sharif speak with Thomas and then the *ping* of the elevator doors.

He was gone.

Liyah was too numb to process what had just happened. She showered, dressed… Sat on the couch in the lounge and watched Sharif give his press conference a couple of hours later, trying to limit the damage.

Thomas enquired if she wanted to eat, but she had no appetite. At some point she went out and walked the streets for blocks and blocks. Always aware of the security man tailing her. She was almost surprised he was still there…

The speed with which Sharif had turned on her, choosing to believe that she could have possibly— Her stomach roiled.

When she finally returned to the apartment it was empty. She slept in her own bed for the first time since that first week she'd arrived in Manhattan.

When she woke at dawn she was gritty-eyed. She checked her phone. No calls, no messages.

Days passed in a hazy blur. Liyah saw news reports about how the board of the Marchetti Group were holding crisis meetings. She saw pictures of Nikos and Maks leaving the Paris office, as grim-looking as Sharif, and her heart ached.

They would hate him for not trusting them. The damage would be irreparable.

And then, just like a few months ago, when her sister had called her and begged her for help, Samara needed Liyah again.

And Liyah saw no reason not to go to her—because there was nothing for her here any more.

When Sharif arrived back at his Manhattan apartment all was quiet. He knew Liyah wasn't there. He knew she was in Taraq with her family. Her sister was getting married within the next fortnight, sooner than expected. He'd been invited, but he'd declined.

He shrugged off his jacket and undid his tie. He went

straight to his drinks cabinet and poured himself a stiff whisky. Not that whisky had done much to help in the last two weeks since he'd left. But it had blurred the edges and helped him forget the dreams that haunted him most nights. Dreams of *her*. And of treachery.

The liquid burnt its way down his throat. He poured another. The world was in flames around him. Everything he'd worked so hard to achieve was ruined. His father was laughing at him from his grave. His mother... His heart constricted. He'd failed her.

And all because he'd lost his focus. He'd let his brain migrate to his pants. He'd forgotten a lifetime of lessons in trusting no one but himself. He'd allowed a siren with huge green eyes to lull him into a false sense of security. To make a fool out of him.

His phone rang in his pocket and he took it out. Saw the name. He smiled mirthlessly and restrained himself from throwing the phone at the window.

He answered it, saying, 'Haven't you done enough damage, Callaghan? Tell me—did you know that first night that my wife would betray my trust? Did she come to you or did you approach her? Actually, I don't even want to know.'

He emitted an expletive and terminated the call, throwing the phone down.

It pinged almost immediately, but Sharif ignored it. He was bone weary.

He walked through his empty apartment, noting that it was exactly how he remembered, before Liyah had arrived.

He walked into her room. There was the slightest hint of her fragrance. But of course—she'd been sharing his room. Because he was the biggest fool on earth.

He went into the dressing room. All the clothes that he'd purchased for her were hanging up. Shoes lined up. Jewellery laid out. He was about to leave when he noticed something and turned back. Her wedding ring. The second one.

It was there. She'd never taken it off after he'd put it on her finger. But she'd left it behind.

He should be welcoming the sight of it there. Clearly she'd got the message that the end of this marriage was nigh. But it didn't feel good to see it. He felt as if it was mocking him. For being such a fool.

He turned and walked out, leaving the ring behind.

'You look so beautiful, Sammy—really. Everything will be okay...trust me.'

Liyah's sister was fighting back tears. 'Father threatened to kill him.'

Liyah said in soothing tones, 'Our father is many things, but he is not a murderer.'

Samara had fallen pregnant with her fiancé's baby. Hence the fast-tracked wedding, to mitigate the scandal of sex before marriage.

Liyah said now, 'You're marrying Javid, and that's all that matters. Once you're married our father can't say anything.'

Samara nodded and sniffled. Their other sisters fussed around.

Liyah took a step back for a moment, and saw her own reflection in the mirror. She was dressed in clothing very similar to her wedding day outfit. Traditional Bedouin robes. She quickly blocked out the thought, not welcoming anything that led to thinking about Sharif.

It had been almost a month now, and the pain and sense of betrayal were still acute.

Her sisters were covering Samara's face with the elaborate face veil. Samara put out a hand. 'Liyah?'

Liyah stepped forward, taking her sister's hand. 'I'm right here.'

They started to make the journey from the women's quarters to the throne room, where the wedding would take place. Against her best intentions, Liyah couldn't stop her mind deviating with sickening predictability to Sharif.

When her father had been told he wasn't coming to the wedding, he'd said, 'A husband should be with his wife. What did you do, Liyah? You don't please him?'

She'd actually received an email from Sharif today. But she hadn't opened it yet. She'd thrown away the phone he'd given her, so she had no idea if he'd been trying to contact her via that.

She didn't know what she would do, but she figured she would have to contact him again at some point to discuss the divorce. It was obvious that their marriage couldn't continue now—not when the very reason for her existence as his wife was no longer valid.

His grand plans for revenge had been ruined. And it wasn't as if their relationship was ever going to morph into a real marriage, no matter how hot the sex, or the fact that it had seemed as if Sharif was enjoying spending time with her.

She'd deliberately avoided looking at the international news, not wanting to see the Marchetti Group's demise. Or to see pictures of his brothers again, looking so grim. Had he told them that he blamed Liyah for the leak?

They were in the throne room now, and Liyah focused on her sister. This was what was important. Not her broken heart.

Much later that night, after the first day's festivities had ended, Liyah opened up her laptop. She was tempted to delete the email without opening it, but she was too weak.

There was nothing in the subject line.

She sucked in a breath and opened it.

Liyah, I've been trying to contact you. Please call me. We need to talk. Sharif.

No frills. No elaboration. No doubt he wanted to talk about the divorce.

Liyah typed back.

You can instruct your legal team to send me divorce papers. I am happy to proceed.

And then she sent her reply and shut the laptop.

Over the following days Sharif left messages with her father's aides, but Liyah refused to take any calls or return them. He sent her more emails, but she refused to look at them. And then one day one of her father's aides came to tell her that Sharif was at the palace to see her.

Liyah panicked. She wasn't ready to deal with Sharif and his accusations again. Especially not here, where her father's disapproval permeated the atmosphere.

She told the aide she would meet Sharif, and as soon as he left pulled a shawl from her wardrobe and wrapped it around her shoulders and head before leaving her room.

A group of female palace workers were heading towards the palace entrance and Liyah followed them, slipping between them. When they reached the main courtyard Liyah's step faltered.

Sharif was standing beside a four-by-four vehicle in a polo shirt and jeans. Sunglasses. She wasn't the only one who faltered. Sharif's gaze tracked to the women and Liyah averted her face suddenly, hurrying to keep up with them. She wrapped the shawl over her face to try and disguise herself.

She had no moment of warning, and the breath left her chest when her arm was taken and she was whirled around. Dark brown eyes ringed with gold met panicked green.

'I knew it was you,' Sharif breathed,

He pulled back the shawl, revealing Liyah's face and hair. Her heart slammed to a stop, before starting again at

an accelerated rhythm. She cursed her too-distinctive hair.
Of course she hadn't been able to blend in. She never had.

His gaze raked her up and down. 'What are you doing?
Trying to avoid me?'

Liyah pulled her arm free, conscious of her less than
glamorous outfit. She was wearing a traditional tunic over
slim-fitting trousers. Flat sandals. A far cry from the wife
he'd moulded to fit into his world.

'I find that I'm not all that keen on being accused of
espionage again. I told you to get your legal team to contact me.'

Sharif muttered something under his breath.

Her pulse was hammering and her insides were swooping and fizzing. Even though she hated his guts.

Liar.

She stepped back. 'Just leave me be, Sharif.'

She turned to go, and then he said from behind her, 'I
know you didn't do it, Liyah. I'm sorry. I just… Look, can
we talk? I need to talk to you.'

Liyah stopped in her tracks. She was breathing as if she'd
run a marathon. The other women were gone. She absorbed
what Sharif said. *I know you didn't do it.*

Her hurt and sense of betrayal were still acute. And she
didn't want him to see that. So she didn't turn around; she
kept moving.

Another muttered curse came from behind her and then,
before she could react, Sharif was in front of her and bending down. She only knew what he was doing when the
world was upended and she realised he'd flung her over
his shoulder.

His hand was on her bottom. She was so astounded and
indignant that she could hardly breathe, let alone speak.

He opened the back door of his vehicle and put her on
the seat. Liyah sprawled inelegantly, looking at him. 'What
the hell do you think you're doing?'

His jaw clenched. 'We need to talk.'

He closed the door before she could respond and strode around to the front. Liyah leapt for the door handle but it was locked. Both sides. And then the car was moving.

For a long moment she fumed in the back seat. Sharif was silent. Navigating his way out of the city and into the surrounding desert. Past the oasis. On into the desert. And on. And on. Further and further away. Towards Al-Murja.

Eventually she couldn't stay silent. She leant forward, doing her best to avoid looking at Sharif directly. 'Where are you taking me?'

'It's at least another half an hour. Make yourself comfortable. We'll talk when we get there.'

Liyah sat back and folded her arms over her chest. She caught Sharif's eye in the rearview mirror and pointedly looked away. But she couldn't help but wonder what he wanted if he really did now know she hadn't been the source of the leak.

Roughly half an hour later a structure appeared on the horizon. Despite herself, Liyah leaned forward to look. Gradually it was revealed as a modest fortress-type building, with turrets. Greenery dotted the ground outside. It must have been built on an oasis.

Liyah recognised the skyline of Al-Murja's capital city in the distance. She recognised where they were: the border between Taraq and Al-Murja.

Sharif drove straight up to the building, and to her surprise she saw the gates open to admit them. Her jaw dropped as they drove in. Inside the walls was a lush oasis. Flowers bloomed on almost every wall. Vines twined and tangled around columns. There were ponds and fountains. Palm trees.

The building itself was simple. Two-storey. She could see through it to corridors and columns, to inner courtyards around which she knew would be arranged rooms and quarters.

She wanted to ask *What is this place?* But she didn't want to give Sharif the satisfaction.

He came to a stop in the main courtyard, ringed with vibrant bushes and flowers. It was like an exotic outdoor hothouse. Liyah had never seen so many examples of desert plants in one place. It was magical.

He got out and came around and opened her door. She was tempted to stay put, but the thought of Sharif putting her over his shoulder again made her scramble out.

She looked behind her to see the main gates closing again. A man in a white *thobe* appeared and Sharif gave him the keys to the four-by-four. Then he kept on walking into the building.

With the utmost reluctance, Liyah followed.

Sharif knew she was behind him. He felt her presence in every cell of his body. Regret and self-recrimination burned in his gut. He didn't blame her for being angry. He had betrayed her in the worst way.

The moment he'd seen her trademark unruly hair, barely contained by the shawl, he'd known immediately it was her—as if he wouldn't have guessed from the way she moved. Or her green eyes when she'd looked at him.

He led her into a shaded courtyard, where a table was laid out with refreshments. He turned to face her. She was looking around her. Her body was tense.

'Please, help yourself.'

She looked at the table. And then at him. Folded her arms. 'I don't need anything. Can you just tell me whatever it is that can't be expressed through our legal teams?'

'Did you hear what I said back at the palace? I know you didn't do it.'

'I told you I didn't do it a month ago. You had a choice at the time to believe me or not. It's too late now, Sharif.'

She turned away, but Sharif caught her hand. That physical contact of skin on skin made his body tighten all over.

'Liyah, will you please let me explain…?'

CHAPTER ELEVEN

THE HURT THREATENED to overwhelm her, but Liyah pushed it down, not wanting him to see it.

As if she wasn't that bothered, she turned back, taking her hand from his. 'Fine—knock yourself out.'

She sat down on one of the chairs at the table, crossed her legs. She heard Sharif sigh and sneaked a glance. He was running a hand through his hair. She noticed belatedly that it was longer. And his jaw was stubbled enough to be halfway to a beard. She'd been too angry to notice before now. Too upset. She felt a dart of concern. Then quashed it.

'The truth is that as soon as I was informed of the leak I wanted to believe that you were responsible. I pushed aside any other possibility because I'd trusted you with information that I hadn't shared with anyone else. Not even my brothers, for fear my plans wouldn't proceed as I'd wanted.'

'How did you find out?'

Sharif sighed again. 'I think I always knew in my heart. But it was Callaghan who told me that it was one of my own aides. The man hacked into my safe and copied the documents. News of what I planned was too incendiary to make him resist leaking. He went to Callaghan, my brothers, the board, hoping that by doing so he'd stop the company from breaking up and save his own job in the process, or get promoted to a better position by one of my brothers, in return for the information.'

'How did your brothers react?'

Sharif emitted a caustic laugh. 'How do you think? They were livid. Exactly as you said. But, worse than that, they were hurt. I betrayed their trust badly. And yours. But now we've reached an agreement, and hopefully a solution. We're not dismantling the Marchetti Group. It's going to be rebranded The House of Noor—named after my mother. Dismantling everything my father had built up was always the focus of my revenge. I never really considered the legacy *we'd* built—me and my brothers—since he died. I was too blinkered. But you helped me start to see things differently. I had to acknowledge that my relationship with my brothers had changed. I didn't want to admit that, though, because I didn't want to admit that I cared about them as much as I did. I'm taking my mother's name too—officially. I'll be known by my Al-Murja title from now on. I've left it up to my brothers to decide if they want to hang on to the Marchetti name or not. Maks doesn't care too much. But I know Nikos will probably change his name too.'

A lump formed in Liyah's throat. She hated it that she cared about the fact that he'd managed to fix things with his family. And that he'd managed to honour his mother in such a profound way, by taking her name for himself and the company.

She finally looked at him. 'Why did you blame me if you had a shred of doubt?'

Sharif came and sat down on the other chair. He leant forward, hands linked loosely between his thighs. Liyah averted her gaze, but that was just as bad because she couldn't look away from his eyes.

'Because I realised how close you'd got. How much I'd instinctively trusted you. When I never trusted anyone in my whole life before. Yet within a month of meeting you I'm telling you my innermost secrets and sharing my life with you in a way that crept up on me.'

'I am your wife,' Liyah pointed out with an astringent tone. 'There's a certain amount of trust and cohabitation expected.'

Sharif stood up. Paced back and forth. When he spoke he sounded frustrated. 'I know that. But in my arrogance I believed I could marry someone—anyone—and not have them impact my life in any meaningful way except for the way *I* dictated.' He faced her. 'But then you came along and blew it all up. From that night at the oasis, nothing was the same again.'

And clearly, Liyah thought, not much had changed. He might have realised she was innocent of his accusations, but he still blamed her for upsetting his life.

Liyah stood up too. 'Look…thank you for your apology. You didn't have to go to all this trouble. I know that it's still over.'

Sharif looked at her. 'Over?'

'The marriage.'

Sharif shook his head. 'That's not why I brought you all the way here.'

Liyah's silly heart skipped a beat. 'Then…why?'

He took her hand. 'I want to show you something.'

He tugged her after him and, feeling bemused, she followed. He led her back out to the main courtyard and then around to the side, to the back of the complex. It was huge. With lush greenery blooming from every point. Liyah itched to explore, even amidst the turmoil in her gut.

'What do you think of this place?' Sharif asked.

'It's beautiful. Stunning.' It was like the dream she'd always had of a desert home. Not that she was going to admit that to Sharif…

She could see now that he was leading her to an area of stables and courtyards. More staff milled around. They addressed Sharif as *Sheikh*—Liyah had almost forgotten he was royalty too.

She heard a familiar whinny and stopped. It came again. Half to herself, she said, 'It can't be…'

She let go of Sharif's hand and followed the sound to see her beloved stallion's head poking out over a half-door. She went over, disbelieving until the moment she smelled him, and then she put her hand on his face and felt him nuzzle into her palm, looking for the apple she always brought.

She'd ridden him out from the Taraq palace only two days ago. She saw another stallion poke his head out from a neighbouring stable. Sharif's?

She looked at Sharif, who was standing a few feet away, watching her carefully. 'But…how is Aztec even here?'

'I had him transported yesterday.'

'You…? But why?'

Sharif didn't answer that. He said, 'Sheba is here too.' He pointed to the other side of the yard.

Reluctantly leaving Aztec, Liyah went over to a spacious shed where Sheba was in an enclosed structure far more luxurious and spacious than her home at the Taraq palace.

Liyah was too stunned for a moment to do much but stroke her soft feathers.

Sharif was in the doorway, blocking the light. Liyah turned to face him. 'But…why are they here?'

'Because this is yours, Liyah. I bought this fortress for you, so you'll always have your own home in the desert.'

She was stunned into speechlessness. The emotions his gesture evoked within her were too huge and confusing. Eventually she said, 'But I can't accept. It's too much.'

He was firm. 'It's yours. In your name. To do with what you will. A place where you can come and be free. Independent. Beholden to none.'

Liyah couldn't believe what Sharif was saying. He was literally offering her everything she'd ever thought she wanted and needed to be happy.

But that had been *before*. Before Sharif had come along and blown it all up. Exactly as he'd accused her. Except, for him, it was just a superficial wound.

She shook her head. 'I don't want it, Sharif. It's too much.'

'It's too late.'

Frustration, anger, love and pain all mixed together and threatened to overflow. She pushed past Sharif, moved back into the courtyard, needing air. Space.

'You don't get to do this,' Liyah said through her breaking heart. 'You don't get to buy me a dream castle in the middle of the desert just to salve your conscience so I can be here on my—'

She stopped and turned around, overcome. She felt Sharif close behind her.

'On your what?'

Something gave way inside her. A last defence. She was undone. Reduced to nothing. She had nothing left to lose.

She turned around again, let him see the emotion she was feeling, that was leaking out of her eyes. He went pale. 'On my own, Sharif. I've been on my own my whole life. Until I met you. You made me want more. You made me want things I'd never dared dream I could have. Like a relationship. Even after I'd vowed I would never let myself be so vulnerable. You made me fall in love with you and I'll never forgive you for that. I gave you the power to hurt me—and you did.'

The words hung in the air between them. Sharif didn't move. He didn't turn and get back into the car and disappear as fast as the wind could carry him. He stood there, looking at her with those dark unfathomable eyes.

Liyah couldn't take it any more. She moved to turn away, find somewhere in this vast place where she could lick her wounds, but Sharif said, 'Wait.'

She stopped, but didn't turn around.

He said from behind her, 'Would you forgive me if I said that all those things you mentioned… I want them too? With you. And,' he continued, 'if it's any consolation, I gave you the power to hurt me too. By accusing you of something you didn't do, I pushed you away before you could hurt me.

Except it didn't work. Because I hurt myself. And you. And I will never forgive myself for that.'

She turned around. His face was starker than she'd ever seen it.

He said, 'I love you, Liyah. I fell for you as soon as I laid eyes on you that night at the oasis, and I thank whatever serendipitous forces aligned to make you my mystery lover and my bride—because I know that if I had never met you again my life wouldn't have been worth living. I've had nightmares for the past month, and in each one it's our wedding day, and when your face is revealed it's not you. It's a stranger.'

Liyah looked at Sharif. She saw the truth written on his face and in his eyes. Saw the ravages of the past month. She saw them because she felt them too.

She took a step towards him, feeling the fragile, tentative beginnings of something like joy unfurling inside her. 'You really love me?'

He lifted a hand towards her. She saw that it was trembling. But he let it drop, as if he was still afraid to touch her.

'More than you could ever know,' he said. 'And now I know why I avoided it for so long. It's terrifying.'

Liyah took another step closer. Reached for his hand. Intertwined her fingers with his. For the first time in weeks she felt a sense of peace move through her, and also something much more profound. A sense of homecoming.

'I love you, Sharif. And I love this place. But I'll only agree to accept it on one condition.'

'Anything.'

'That you share it with me.'

He reached out, touched her hair reverently. 'I was afraid you wouldn't want that.'

'I do,' Liyah said fervently, moving closer until their bodies touched. 'But I have a question.'

'Anything,' Sharif said again, and smiled.

'If you're no longer Sharif Marchetti, then what does that make me?'

'If you consent to stay my wife then you will revert to your family name—Sheikha Aaliyah Binte Rashad Mansour.'

Liyah bit her lip, feeling emotional. 'Of course I consent. But I think I'd like to take my mother's name and yours—Aaliyah Binte Yasmeena al Nazar.'

Sharif's eyes looked suspiciously shiny. 'I think that is a very fine name.'

Liyah twined her arms around his neck. Desire rose, thick and urgent. 'I have one more very important question…'

Sharif framed her face with his hands. 'Anything,' he said, for a third time.

'Where are the bedrooms?'

'There are about twelve.'

'We only need one.'

He said, 'We should probably check them all, then, to make sure we pick the best one.'

Joy bubbled up and spilled out of Liyah's mouth in a spontaneous laugh as Sharif led her into the building. He turned to her and she could see the fragility of this moment written on his face.

He stopped and cupped her face. 'Is this real? Are you real? Or have I dreamt you up since that night at the oasis?'

If Liyah had had any lingering doubt it was eradicated in that instant. And, just as Sharif had put her hand over his heart that night, to prove he was real, she took his hand now and put it over her heart. 'I'm real. This is real. I love you, Sharif.'

He lowered his head and kissed her with a tenderness and a passion that left her trembling.

When he broke away, Liyah said breathlessly, 'I don't know if I can wait until the first bedroom.'

Sharif smiled and it was full of wickedness, his trademark arrogance returning. 'We're in no rush, are we?'

Liyah smiled. 'No rush at all.'

It was a month before they left the fortress...except for a couple of visits to a very special oasis.

EPILOGUE

Seven years later
Sharif and Liyah's desert fortress
on the borders of Taraq and Al-Murja

'Daniel, please don't do rabbit ears behind Luna's head this time. Can we just get one photo where we all look relatively normal, please?' Zoe made final adjustments to the camera, which was on a tripod. She pressed a button. 'Okay, everyone—ten seconds. Assume your positions and smile!'

She darted out from behind the camera and went over to where everyone was dutifully gathered in front of a wall of flowers. Maks tucked her into his chest. He stood beside Maggie and Nikos, who were beside Sharif and Liyah.

Nikos was holding a sleepy three-year-old Tessy in his arms—the latest addition to their family—and in front of them were Daniel and Luna, first cousins and as thick as thieves. Then there was Olympia, Daniel's sister, who was holding her four-year-old cousin Ben, Luna's brother, with one hand and four-year-old Stella, Sharif and Liyah's daughter, with the other hand.

Serenity reigned for about seven seconds—until the shutter clicked and children scattered with shrieks and yells, resuming whatever game they'd been playing before Zoe had gathered them all together.

Zoe went over and looked at the camera. She rolled her eyes to heaven even as she couldn't help but smile. 'That's it—I give up. You lot are impossible!'

When Sharif and Liyah looked at the photo later, they laughed. All the kids were making faces, and Daniel was, indeed, making rabbit ears again—this time behind his sister Olympia's head.

Maks was looking down at Zoe indulgently, and she was the only one smiling at the camera. Nikos was kissing Maggie. Sharif was looking at Liyah, who was smiling enigmatically. The fact that he had his hand placed over her abdomen was the first hint of the secret they'd just shared over dinner.

In seven months' time, the Marchetti/Al Nazar/Spiros clan was going to grow by two more little people.

After much congratulations, and tears and hugs and exclamations, Zoe had groaned theatrically. 'Twins? I'm definitely not signing up to take any more family photos. You can find someone else!'

But the next day Sharif and Liyah were due to welcome Sasha, Maks's sister, with her husband and their children. So inevitably another photo would be taken.

The sounds of the happy family gathering had faded into the night by now, and after putting Stella to bed Sharif found his wife standing at the wall of the terrace that wrapped around their bedroom suite—the one they'd spent a very enjoyable month choosing—which looked out over the desert beyond. The night sky was huge, lit up with a crescent moon and bright stars.

Sharif moved behind Liyah, wrapping his arms around her and resting his chin on her head. 'What are you thinking?'

Liyah wrapped her arms around his. Having a family hadn't happened straight away for them. It had taken a couple of years for Liyah to fall pregnant. They'd been about to make investigations when she'd become pregnant with Stella. So they didn't take this latest good news for granted for a second.

Liyah turned in his arms and looped hers around his neck. She wore a short silk nightdress and nothing else, and Sharif could feel every provocative curve. His blood simmered.

'You mean you can't read my mind?' she teased.

Sharif smiled. 'I would never presume to know what's going on in your head. From the moment I first saw you, you were a mystery, and you still are. You have the power to fell me—as you well know.'

Liyah made a disbelieving sound. And then she touched his jaw, traced the small scar. 'You fell me too—on a regular basis. But, since you want me to spell it out, I'm thinking that I love you, and I love Stella, and I love our extended family so much. I never knew what it was to be part of a loving family. I think I was too scared to admit I wanted one for a long time. We were so happy it felt like tempting fate.'

Sharif said huskily, 'I know.'

She put her hand on her belly. 'I love these babies already, but I'm also terrified because I don't want anything to ever harm them.'

Sharif lifted her hand and pressed a kiss to the centre of her palm. 'No harm will come to them—not from us anyway. And we will love them and protect them until they can fly away and be free to live their own lives. And then they'll come back…with their families.'

Tears sprang into Liyah's eyes. 'I love you so much.'

Sharif shook his head, his eyes shining too. 'Not half as much as I love you. You saved me, Liyah.'

Liyah pressed a kiss to his mouth, and whispered, 'We saved each other.'

'For ever.'

'Yes, my love.'

They turned and went into their bedroom, the vast night around them wrapping them in its protective cloak and echoing the sounds of their love.

* * * * *

ONE HOT
NEW YORK NIGHT

MELANIE MILBURNE

To Elida Yesenia DeHaan.

I hope you enjoy this book, specially dedicated to you!

Best wishes, Melanie xx

CHAPTER ONE

ZOEY SAW HIM the moment she stepped into the London auditorium where the advertising conference was being held. It wasn't hard to make out Finn O'Connell in a crowd—he was always the one surrounded by drooling, swooning women. At six foot six, he was head and shoulders over everyone else, with the sort of looks that could stop a bullet train. And a woman's heart. An unguarded woman's heart, that was.

But, just this once, Zoey allowed herself a secret little drool of her own. She might hate him with a passion but that didn't mean she couldn't admire some aspects of him—like his taut and toned body, his strong, powerful, muscle-packed legs, his impossibly broad shoulders, his lean chiselled jaw or his laughing brown eyes. Other aspects, not so much. If there were an Academy for Arrogance, Finn O'Connell would be top of the class.

As if he sensed her looking at him, Finn turned his head and glanced her way, his prominent black eyebrows rising ever so slightly above his eyes. Zoey was glad she wasn't easily provoked into a blush, as that mocking gaze moved over her in one slowly assessing sweep. His lips curved upwards in a smile that sent a frisson of awareness right through her body. It was the smile of a conqueror, a man who knew what he wanted and exactly how he was going to get it.

He moved away from his posse of adoring fans and strode purposefully in Zoey's direction. She knew she should whip round and dart out the nearest exit before he could get to her, but she couldn't seem to get her feet to move. It was as if he had locked her in place, frozen her to the spot with the commanding force of his dark brown gaze. She always tried to avoid being alone with him, not trusting herself to resist either slapping him or throwing herself at him. She didn't know why he of all people should have such an effect on her. He was too confident, too charming, too polished, too everything.

Finn came to stand within a foot of her, close enough for her to smell the expensive citrus notes of his after-shave and to see the devilish *ah, now I'll have some fun* glint in his eyes. 'Good morning, Ms Brackenfield.'

His bow and mock-formal tone stirred the hornet's nest of her hatred. The blood simmered in her veins until she thought they would explode. Zoey straightened her spine, steeled her gaze and set her mouth into a prim line. 'Looks like you've got your love life sorted for the next month.' She flicked her gaze in the direction of the group of women he'd just left, her tone rich with icy disdain.

His smile broadened and the glint in his eyes intensified to a sharp point of diamond-bright light that made something at the base of her spine fizz. 'You do me a disservice. I could get through that lot in a week.' His voice was a deep, sexy baritone, the sort of voice that made her think of tangled sheets, sweaty bodies, panting breaths, primal needs. Needs Zoey had ignored for months and would keep on ignoring...or try to, which was not so easy with Finn looking so damn sexy and standing within touching distance.

Being in Finn's company made her feel strangely out of kilter. Her usual *sang froid* was replaced with a hearty desire to slap his designer-stubbled face and screech a mouthful of obscenities at him. She raised her chin a fraction, determined to hold his gaze without flinching. 'One wonders if you have a revolving door on your bedroom.'

Finn's gaze drifted to her mouth, his indolent half-smile sending another frisson through her body. 'You're welcome to check it out some time and see for yourself.'

Zoey gripped the tote bag strap hanging off her shoulder for something to do with her hands, her heart skipping a beat, two beats, three, as if she had suddenly developed a bad case of arrhythmia. 'Does that line usually work for you?' Honestly, if her tone got any frostier, they would have to turn on the heating in the auditorium.

'Always.' His lazy smile sent a soft, feathery sensation down the back of her neck and spine, and her willpower requested sick leave.

Zoey could see why he had a reputation as a playboy—he was charm personified in every line of his gym-toned body. But she *would* resist him even if it killed her. She stretched her lips into a tight, no-teeth-showing smile. 'Well, I'd better let you get back to your avid fans over there.'

She began to turn away, but he stalled her by placing his hand lightly on her wrist and a high-voltage electrical charge shot through her body. He removed his hand within a second or two, but the sensation lingered on in her flesh, travelling from her wrist, up her arm and down her spine like a softly fizzing firework.

'I was expecting to see your dad here. Or maybe I've missed him in the crowd.' Finn turned and scanned the auditorium before meeting her gaze once more. 'He mentioned in a text the other day about catching up for a coffee.'

Zoey couldn't imagine what Finn would have in common with her father other than they both ran advertising agencies. And as to having a coffee with him, well, if only it was caffeine her father was addicted to. It was no secret her dad had a drinking problem—he had disgraced himself publicly a few too many times in spite of her efforts to keep him from harming the business.

Brackenfield Advertising was her birthright, her career, everything she had worked so hard for. She would do almost anything to keep the business on track, which meant sometimes feeling a little compromised when it came to managing her father. And right now, her father was at home nursing yet another hangover. And it wasn't from indulging in too much caffeine.

'My father is…catching up on work at home today.'

'Then maybe you and I could grab a coffee instead.'

'I'm busy.' Zoey lifted her chin and narrowed her gaze to flint. 'I didn't know you and my father were bosom buddies.'

His lips quirked in an enigmatic smile. 'Business rivals can still be friends, can't they?'

'Not in my book.' Zoey pointedly rubbed at her wrist, annoyed her skin was still tingling. One thing was for certain—she would *never* be Finn O'Connell's friend. He was a player, and she was done with players. Done for good. She pulled her sleeve back down over her wrist. She hadn't been touched by a man in months. Why should Finn's touch have such an impact on her?

She couldn't deny he was potently attractive. Tall, lean and toned, with an olive complexion that was currently deeply tanned, he looked every inch the sophisticated, suave self-made businessman. Enormously wealthy, today he was casually dressed—as were most delegates—his crew-neck lightweight cotton sweater showcasing the breadth of his broad shoulders and his navy-blue chinos the length and strength of his legs.

But, while Finn looked casual, nothing about his approach to business was laid back. He was focussed and ruthlessly driven, pulling in contracts so lucrative they made Zoey's eyes water in envy.

Zoey could sense his sensual power coming off him in waves. She was aware of him as she was aware of no other man. She had known him for a couple of years or so, running into him at various advertising functions. He had been her only rival for an account a few months ago and it still infuriated her that he'd won it instead of her, mostly because she knew for a fact he had a friend on the board of directors of the company— a female friend.

'I hear you're pitching for the Frascatelli account,' Finn said with another mercurial smile. 'Leonardo Frascatelli is only considering three ad companies' pitches for his campaign. A battle between friends, yes?'

Zoey blinked and her stomach dropped. Oh no, did that mean he was vying for it too? With only three candidates in the running, she'd been confident she was in with a chance. But what would happen to her chance if Finn was in the mix?

The Italian hotel chain was the biggest account she had ever gone after, and if she won it she wouldn't have to worry about her dad frittering away the business's assets any more. She would finally prove to her father she had what it took to run the company. She ran the tip of her tongue over her suddenly carpet-dry lips, her heart beating so fast it threatened to pop out of her ribcage. She could *not* lose the Frascatelli account.

She. Could. Not.

And most certainly not to Finn O'Connell.

Zoey was flying to New York that evening to present it the following afternoon. Her presentation was on her laptop in the cloak room along with her overnight bag. Did that mean he was flying over there too? 'I can't think of a single set of circumstances that would ever make me consider being friends with you.'

'Not very creative of you,' he drawled, his gaze sweeping over her in an indolent fashion. 'I can think of plenty.'

Zoey gave him a look that would have sent a swarm of angry wasps ducking for cover. 'I can only imagine what sort of ridiculous scenario a mind like yours would come up with—that is, of course, if you can get it out of the gutter long enough.'

Finn gave a rich, deep laugh that sent a tingle shimmering down her spine. Drat the man for being so incredibly attractive. Why couldn't he could have one just one physical imperfection? His mellifluous voice was one of the first things she had noticed about him. He could read out loud the most boring, soporific financial report and she would be hanging on his every word. His smiling dark brown eyes made her lips twitch in spite of her effort not to be taken in by his practised charm.

His mouth was nicely sculptured, his lips not too thick or too thin but somewhere perfectly in between. A mouth that promised erotic expertise in its every delicious contour. A mouth she had to keep well away from. No way was she joining the conga line to dive into his bed. No freaking way.

'I wouldn't dare to describe how my mind works.' He gave a slow smile and added, 'I might shock you to the core of your being.'

The core of her being was still recovering from his lazy smile, thank you very much. There was a fluttery sensation between her legs, and she hated herself for being so weak. So what if he was smouldering hot? So what if he made her feel more of a woman than she had ever felt just by looking at her with that sardonic gaze?

She *had* to resist him. She would be nothing more than a notch on his bedpost, a fleeting dalliance he would view as yet another conquest.

'Nothing about you would shock me, Finn. You're so boringly predictable, it's nauseating.' Not strictly true. He kept her on her toes more than any man she'd ever met. He constantly surprised her with his whip-smart repartee. She even—God forgive her—enjoyed their sparring. It gave her a rush, a secret thrill, to engage in a verbal scrap with him because his quick-witted mind more than matched her own.

Finn's eyes kindled, as if her carelessly flung words had thrown down a challenge he couldn't wait to act upon. 'Ah, well then, I'll have to lift my game to see if I can improve your opinion of me.' His lips curved in another smile that curled her toes inside her shoes.

'Finn!' A young blonde woman came tottering over in vertiginous heels with her hand outstretched, waving a business card held in her perfectly manicured fingers. 'I forgot to give you my number. Call me so we can catch up soon?'

Finn took the card and slipped it into his trouser pocket, his smile never faltering. 'Will do.'

The young woman looked as if she had just won the mega-draw lottery, her eyes so bright they could have lit up a football stadium. She gave Finn a fingertip wave and tottered back off to join her gaggle of friends.

Zoey rolled her eyes and, turning to one side, made vomiting noises. She straightened to lock gazes with Finn. 'Really?'

'She's an intern. I'm mentoring her.'

Zoey choked on a cynical laugh. She didn't know what annoyed her more—his straight face or his assumption she would be fooled by it. 'In the boardroom or the bedroom?'

His eyes never left hers, his mouth twitching at the corners with amusement. 'Your jealousy is immensely flattering. Who knew behind that ice maiden thing you've got going on is a woman so smoking-hot for me?'

Zoey curled her hands into fists, her anger flaring like a flame doused by an accelerant. It formed a red mist before her eyes and made each of her limbs stiffen like the branches of a dead tree. He enjoyed goading her—she could see it in his eyes. He liked getting a rise out of her and never wasted an opportunity to do so. He was playing her, and she was a fool to respond to him. But how was she supposed to ignore him? He wasn't the sort of man you could ignore. Oh, how she would love to slap his face. How she would love to kick him in the shins. How she would love to rake her nails—*her unmanicured nails*—down his face.

And, God help her, how she would love to sleep with him to see if he was as exciting a lover as gossip had it. Not that she would ever act on such a desire. Since being cheated on by her long-term boyfriend, Rupert, she was completely and utterly over men. She had given her all to her ex and had been completely blindsided by his betrayal. She didn't want the complications and compromises of a relationship any more.

But whenever she was anywhere near Finn O'Connell every female hormone in her body went into overdrive. She became aware of her body in his presence—of the tingles and flutters and arrows of lust almost impossible to ignore. But ignore them she must. Sleeping with the enemy was not in her game plan.

Zoey flashed him a livid glare, her chest heaving with the effort to contain her rage. 'I wouldn't sleep with you if you paid me a squillion pounds.'

His dark eyes danced and his confident smile irked her beyond endurance. 'Oh, babe, you surely don't think I'm the kind of man who has to pay for sex?' He stepped closer and placed two fingers beneath her chin, locking his gaze on hers. 'Can you feel that?' His voice lowered to a gravelly burr, his eyes holding hers in a mesmerising lock.

'F-feel what?' Zoey was annoyed her voice wobbled but her heart was leaping about like a mad thing in her chest, his fingers on her face sending a wave of scorching heat through her body.

Finn stroked his thumb over the circle of her chin, his warm minty breath wafting across her lips, mingling with her own breath like two invisible lovers getting it on. 'The energy we create together. I felt it the minute you walked into the room.'

No way was she admitting she felt it too. No way. Zoey disguised a swallow, her heart-rate accelerating, her inner core tingling as if he had touched her between the legs instead of on her chin. Why wasn't she stepping back? Why wasn't she slapping his arrogant face? She was under some sort of sensual spell, captivated by the feel of his thumb pad caressing her chin in slow strokes. Intoxicated by the clean, freshly laundered smell of his clothes, the citrus top notes and the sexy bergamot base note of his aftershave. She could feel the forcefield of his sensual energy calling out to her in invisible waves.

Her senses reeled from his closeness, his dangerously tempting closeness. She was acutely aware of his touch, even though it was only the pad of his thumb—it felt like a searing brand, the warmth seeping through her flesh travelling to her feminine core in a quicksilver streak.

Zoey had been celibate for months. She hadn't even thought about sex for weeks and weeks on end. Now, her mind was filling with images of being in bed with Finn in a tangle of limbs and crumpled bed linen, her body slick with sweat and glowing from earth-shattering pleasure. And she was in no doubt it would be earth-shattering pleasure. Being near him like this made her body pulse with longing—a raw, primal longing she wished she could block out, anaesthetise or bludgeon away. It was a persistent ache between her legs, a pounding ache in time with her heartbeat, an ache his touch triggered, inflamed, incited.

But somehow, with a mammoth effort, she got her willpower to scramble back out of sick bay. 'You're imagining it…' Zoey licked her lips and pulled out of his hold, rubbing at her chin and shooting him a frowning look through slitted eyes. 'If you ever put your hands on me again, I won't be answerable for the consequences,' she added through tight lips.

He gave a mock-shudder, his playful smile making his eyes gleam. 'Listen, babe, you'll be the one begging me to put my hands on you. I can guarantee it. *Ciao*.'

He walked away without another word and Zoey was left seething, grinding her teeth to powder, hating him all the more, because she had a horrible feeling he might be right.

CHAPTER TWO

FINN WAS STANDING in line waiting to go through the business class security checkpoint at London Heathrow airport when he saw Zoey Brackenfield two people ahead of him. He had sensed her presence even before he saw her—it was if something alerted him the minute he stepped into her orbit. It had been the same at the conference that morning— he had sensed her in the room like a disturbance in an electromagnetic field. A shiver had passed over his scalp and run down his spine, as if some sort of alchemy was going on between them—otherwise known as rip-roaring lust.

Finn always looked forward to seeing her at various advertising gigs. He enjoyed getting a rise out of her, which was amusingly easy to do. She was prickly and uptight, and flashed her violet gaze and lashed him with her sharp tongue any chance she got. But he knew deep in his DNA that underneath the prickly façade she was as hot for him as he was for her. Their combative repartee had been going on for months and he knew it was only a matter of time before she gave in to the desire that flared and flickered and flashed between them.

Zoey took out her laptop from its bag and put it on

a tray to go through the scanner, her striking features etched in a frown. He noticed the laptop was exactly the same brand and model as his—even the light grey bag was identical. *Great minds think alike,* he mused, and stepped up to take a tray from the stack.

She placed her tote bag on another tray and stood waiting—not all that patiently. She shifted her weight from foot to foot, pushed back her left sleeve and glanced at the watch on her slim wrist, then pushed her mid-length silky black hair behind one shoulder. She was dressed in black leather trousers that clung like a glove to her long, slim legs and taut and shapely little bottom. Her silky baby-blue V-necked blouse skimmed her breasts and, when she turned on an angle in his line of vision and bent over to take off her high-heeled shoes, he caught a glimpse of her delightful cleavage and a jab of lust hit him in his groin.

As if she sensed his gaze on her, she straightened and met his gaze, her frown intensifying, her eyes narrowing, her lips pursing.

Finn smiled and pushed his laptop further along the conveyer belt, then he reached to unbuckle his belt to put it on the tray with his watch and wallet and keys. Zoey's eyes followed the movement of his hands as he slowly released his belt, and two spots of colour formed on her cheeks. But then she bit her lip and whipped back round as if she was worried he was going to strip off completely. If only they'd been alone, he'd definitely have done that, and enjoyed watching her strip off too.

There was a slight hold-up, as one of the people in front of Zoey had forgotten to take the loose coins out of their pocket. By the time Zoey walked through to collect her things from the conveyer belt, Finn's things had come through as well. She barely gave him a glance, and snatched up her laptop and tote bag and scurried off, but she was soon stopped by one of the random check personnel. She blew out a breath and followed the uniformed man to be electronically swabbed.

Finn absently put his laptop back in the carrier bag, his gaze tracking to Zoey as if drawn by an industrial-strength magnet. She was so damn cute he could barely stand it. But the people coming through behind him in the queue meant he had to get his mind back on the task at hand. He hitched the laptop bag over his shoulder then put his belt back on and slipped his wallet and phone and keys in his trouser pockets.

His gaze flicked back to Zoey and the frustrated look on her face brought a smile to his lips. Those random checks were so random, he got called over every time he flew, but today was apparently his lucky day. No pat-down for him, but, hey, he wouldn't mind if it was Zoey doing the patting down.

Zoey was finally given the all-clear and gathered her things and stalked past, her head at a proud height, her gaze pointedly ignoring him.

'Got time for a drink?' Finn asked, catching up with her in a couple of easy strides.

'No, thank you. I don't want to miss my flight.' Even the sound of her heels click-clacking on the floor sounded annoyed.

'What flight are you on?'

She told him the carrier and the time, but it wasn't the same as his, and he was vaguely aware of a little stab of disappointment deep in his gut. Who knew what seven and a half hours in her company might have produced? He got hard just thinking about it.

'Good luck with your pitch,' he said with a smile. 'May the best person win.'

Zoey stopped walking to look up at him, her violet eyes like lethal daggers. 'If it were a level playing field, I would've won the last time we were pitching for the same account. Tell me, did you sleep with someone to swing the board's decision?'

'I don't have to resort to such tactics, babe, I just do a damn good job. Yours was a good pitch, though. And I really liked the dog food commercial you did a while back. Cute…real cute.'

She rapid-blinked in an exaggerated way, one of her hands coming up to her chest as if to calm her heart rate down. 'Oh. My. God. Did I just hear you give me a *compliment*?'

Finn chuckled at her mock-shocked expression. 'What? Doesn't anyone ever tell you how brilliant you are?'

'Not that I can remember.' She gave him a haughty look and added, 'But no doubt you've been hearing that said to you from the moment you were born.'

If only she knew how far from the truth that was. Finn had rarely seen either of his parents since he was six years old. They'd found the task of raising a child too restrictive for their hippy-dippy lifestyle—especially when he'd got to school age. They hadn't been able to handle the responsibility of waking up early enough after a night of drinking and smoking dope to get him ready for school or to pick him up afterwards, so they'd dumped him on distant relatives.

They had been given another couple of chances to get their act together during his childhood, but Finn had finally got tired of it by the time he was thirteen. He'd soon been shipped back to his relatives, who hadn't exactly welcomed him back with open arms. He couldn't recall too many compliments coming his way growing up, but he had got the message loud and clear that he'd been an encumbrance, a burden no one had wanted but kept out of a sense of duty.

'You'd be surprised,' Finn said with a hollow laugh.

Zoey looked at him for a beat or two longer, her forehead still creased in a slight frown. Then she shifted her gaze and glanced at her boarding pass. 'I'd better get to my gate...'

She walked off without another word and Finn felt again that strange little niggle of disappointment. He gave himself a mental shake and strode towards his own departure gate. He needed to get a grip. Anyone would think he was becoming a little obsessed with Zoey Brackenfield. He wasn't the type to get too attached to a woman—to anyone, when it came to that. His life in the fast lane left no time for long-term relationships. A long-term relationship in his mind was a day or two, tops. Any longer than that and he got a little antsy, eager to get out before it got too claustrophobic. Maybe he was like his freedom-loving parents after all. Scary thought.

It was almost three in the morning by the time Zoey got to her New York hotel. She had slept a little on the flight and watched a couple of movies rather than tweak her pitch on her laptop. She knew from experience that last-minute tweaks often did more harm than good. Her nerves would take over, her self-doubts run wild, and before she knew it the presentation would be completely different from her original vision.

Besides, she really loved travelling in Business Class. The way her father's business was currently going meant that travelling in style and comfort might not be something she would be doing too much longer, so she figured she might as well enjoy it while she could. No doubt Finn O'Connell had no worries on that score. She could just imagine him lying back on his airbed, sipping French champagne and chatting up the female cabin crew. *Grr.*

Zoey had a shower to freshen up and dressed in a bathrobe with her hair in a towel, turban-like, on her head, placing the laptop bag on the writing desk in the suite. She unzipped the bag and took out the laptop and laid it on the leather protector on the desk. She opened the screen and turned it on and waited for it to boot up. A strange sensation scuttled across her scalp as the screen became illuminated. She leaned forward, blinked her weary gaze and peered at the unfamiliar screensaver.

The unfamiliar screensaver...

Zoey's heart leapt to her throat, her legs went to water and her hands shook as though she had a movement disorder. This wasn't her laptop! She was in New York without her laptop. The laptop with her pitch on it.

Don't panic. Don't panic. Don't panic. She tried to calm herself down but she had never been a star pupil at mindfulness. Fear climbed her spine and spread its tentacles into her brain like a strangling vine. She was going to lose the contract. She was miles away from her laptop. What was she going to do? *Breathe. Breathe. Breathe.* Zoey took a deep lungful of air and stared at the laptop, praying this was a nightmare she would wake from at any moment.

But wait…all was not lost. Her presentation was in the cloud. But still, her laptop had a lot of personal information on it, and she didn't want to lose it. Besides, her pitch was first thing tomorrow morning and she couldn't be sure there would be another laptop she could use. And it would look unprofessional to turn up so ill-prepared.

Who owned this one?

Her mind spooled back to the security check at Heathrow and something cold slithered down the entire length of her spine. Could this be Finn O'Connell's laptop? Her stomach did a flip turn. Oh, no. Did that mean he had hers? She had a sticker on the back of her laptop with her name and number on it but there was nothing on the back of this computer.

The screensaver was asking for a password. She drummed her fingers on the desk. Did she need a password to check if it was his computer? Maybe there was something in the laptop bag that might be enough of a clue as to whose computer it was. She reached inside the bag and took out a couple of pens and a collection of business cards. One, from a woman called Kimba, had a red lipstick kiss pressed to the back with a handwritten message below it:

Thanks for last night, Finn. It was unbelievable.

Zoey wanted to tear it into confetti-sized pieces and only just stopped herself in time. Double *grr*. What a player. He probably had lovers all over the world.

But at least it solved the mystery of whose computer Zoey had in her possession…or did it? The bag was the same as hers. No doubt there were other laptop bags exactly the same as this one. How could she know for sure this was Finn's computer inside his bag? It had been crowded at the security checkpoint and so many laptops looked the same. Besides, he hadn't phoned or texted her to tell her he had hers. Maybe someone else had hers and this was a complete stranger's!

Zoey searched further in the laptop bag and pulled out a bright orange sticky note attached to a computer technician's card. The sticky note had the words 'temporary password' written on it and below it a series of numbers and letters and dashes and hashtags. She stared at it for a long moment, a host of rationalisations assembling in her head. She needed to know for sure if this was Finn's laptop. She had a password but whether it was Finn's or not was still not clear. This could easily be someone else's laptop accidentally put in his laptop bag.

She had to know for sure, didn't she? She had to check to see if it was actually Finn's laptop, right? She would call the airport once she knew one way or the other. She figured, if it turned out to be his, all she had to do was call him and ask him to meet her for a quick swap-over. There wouldn't be any delay that way, as he was probably in New York by now too.

Zoey stuck the note to the screen of the laptop and held her fingers over the keys. *You shouldn't be doing this.* She rolled her left shoulder backwards, as if she was physically dislodging her nagging conscience. Her fingers moved closer to the keyboard and her heart began to thud, a fine sweat breaking out across her brow. She could only imagine how nauseating it would be to read his emails. No doubt hundreds of gushing messages from his many lovers telling how wonderful he was. Could she stomach it? No. Definitely not.

Zoey got up from the desk, folding her arms across her body to remove them from temptation. It would be wrong to read his personal messages—anyone's, for that matter. Was it even a crime?

But then a thought crept into her brain… Could she just click on Finn's pitch? Just a teensy-weensy little peek? No. That would be taking things a little too far. She was a morally upright citizen. She believed in doing the right thing at all times and in all circumstances. And yet…this was her chance to get a heads-up on what his pitch looked like. He would never know she'd checked…

But *she* would know, and that was something that didn't sit well with her. The competition had to be fair and equal and, if she looked at his pitch and made last minute changes to hers once she got her laptop back and subsequently won the account, how victorious would she actually feel? It would be a hollow victory indeed. She wanted to win the pitch on her own merit. She had fought too hard and for too long to be taken seriously. If she were to cheat to get to the top, then she would be devaluing everything she had worked so hard for.

Zoey glanced back at the laptop, her teeth chewing at her lower lip. 'You can stop looking at me like that, okay?' She addressed the laptop sternly. 'I'm not doing it. I would hate it if he did it to me.'

Yikes! But what if he was doing it to her at this very moment?

Zoey let out a stiff curse. Those last few emails she sent to her ex were not something she wanted anyone else reading, and certainly not Finn O'Connell. She walked back to the computer and slammed it shut. 'There. Who said I can't resist temptation?'

As long as she could resist Finn O'Connell just as easily.

After dinner was served and then cleared away on the flight, Finn took out his laptop and set it up before him in his business class seat. But as soon as he opened it he knew something wasn't right. For one thing, there were food crumbs all over the keys, which was strange, because he never ate at the computer. Besides, it had only just come back from his tech service people, who had serviced one of his faulty programs, and they always returned it spotless.

He pressed the 'on' button and an unfamiliar screen-saver came up. Shoot. He had someone else's laptop.

Someone who had gone through the security check at the same time.

He turned the computer over and found a sticker on the back with Zoey's name and number on it. A smile broke over his face and he closed the laptop with a snap. What were the chances of them switching laptops?

As much as he was tempted to have a little snoop around Zoey Brackenfield's laptop, he was going to re-sist. Who said he couldn't be a chivalrous gentleman? She had a right to her privacy; besides, he could do without any more animosity from her. He genuinely liked her. She was feisty, determined and talented, and he admired her all-in work ethic. She was in a still largely male dominated field, but she didn't let it intimidate her. A couple of her projects he'd seen had been nothing short of brilliant.

Finn showered and shaved once he got to the penthouse suite of his hotel. He had yet to call Zoey about the laptop mix-up, but considering it was the middle of the night he figured it could wait until a decent hour. Clearly, she hadn't discovered the mix-up because he had no missed calls or text messages from her.

He had got a text message from Zoey's father, however, mentioning something about a business matter he wanted to discuss with him. Finn couldn't decide if it was one of Harry Brackenfield's increasingly regular drunken, middle-of-the-night texts or if there was a genuine reason behind his request for a meeting. Either way, it could wait. He had much more important business on his mind—getting his laptop back and seeing Zoey again.

But as Finn was coming out of the bathroom his phone buzzed from where he'd left it on the bedside table earlier. He walked over to scoop it up and saw Zoey's name come up.

'Good morning,' he said. 'I believe have something of yours in my possession.'

'Did you do it deliberately?' Her tone was so sharp, he was surprised it didn't pierce one of his arteries. 'Did you switch them at the airport?'

Finn walked over to the windows to look at the view of the city that never slept. The flashing billboards and colourful lights of Times Square were like an electronic firework show. 'Now, why would I do that? It's damned inconvenient for one thing and, secondly, dangerous to have my personal data in the hands of someone who doesn't have my best interests at heart.'

'I want it back. Now.' Her tone was so strident and forceful, he could almost picture her standing in her hotel room visibly shaking with anger.

He let out a mock-weary sigh. 'Can't it wait until morning?'

'It *is* morning,' she shot back. 'Where are you staying? I'll come to you right now.'

'Now is not convenient.'

There was a silence in which all he could hear was her agitated breathing.

'Have you got someone with you?' Zoey asked.

'You might not believe this but I'm all by myself.' Thing was, he was all by himself more often than not just lately. He was the first to admit his sex life needed a reboot. The hook-ups were not as exciting as they used to be. None of his lovers captivated him the way he wanted to be captivated. The way Zoey captivated him. His focus on her was stuffing up his ability to sleep with anyone else. But that was easily fixed—he would convince her to indulge in a hot little hook-up. Problem solved.

Zoey made a scoffing noise, as if in two minds whether to believe him about his solitary status. 'Then there's no reason I can't come by and get my computer and give you yours.'

'Why can't you wait until a decent hour? Or are you worried I'm going to hack into your computer, hmm?'

There was another tight little silence, punctuated by her breathing.

'Y-you wouldn't do that…would you?'

Finn let out an exaggerated sigh. 'Your low opinion of me never ceases to amaze me. Look—I'll compromise and bring your laptop to you rather than you come out in the wee hours. Where are you staying?'

She told him the name of the hotel, which was only a block away. 'How long will you be?' she added.

'Don't worry, babe. I know you're impatient to see me, but I won't keep you waiting much longer.'

'It's not you I want to see, it's my computer.' And then the phone clicked off.

Zoey tugged the damp towel off her head and threw it on the bed, her fury at Finn knowing no bounds. She wouldn't put it past him to have deliberately switched their computers. He never failed to grasp an opportunity to get under her skin. No doubt he'd been trawling through her emails and photos and pitch presentation without a single niggle of his conscience. She, at least, had felt conflicted enough not to do it, even if it had been a close call in terms of self-control. She shut down his computer and put it back in the laptop bag and firmly zipped it up.

But deep down she knew she had made the choice not to snoop because she respected him professionally, even if she had some issues with how he lived his private life.

Or maybe her issues with his private life were because she was envious of how easily he moved from one lover to the next. She had been unable to stomach the thought of sharing her body with anyone since her ex had cheated on her. Well, apart from Finn, which was both annoying and frustrating in equal measure, because he was the last person she wanted to get naked with under any circumstances. However, it was a pity her body wasn't in agreement with her rational mind.

The doorbell sounded before Zoey had time to change out of the hotel bathrobe into clothes. She clutched the front opening of the bathrobe together and padded over to the door. 'Is that you, Finn?'

'Sure is.'

Zoey opened the door and found him standing there with her laptop bag draped over one shoulder. He didn't look one bit jet-lagged—in fact, he looked ridiculously refreshed and heart-stoppingly gorgeous. He had recently showered and shaved, his brushed back thick, dark hair still damp. The tantalising notes of his aftershave drifted towards her, reminding her of a sun-baked citrus orchard with crushed exotic herbs underfoot. She held out her hand for her computer. 'Thank you for dropping it off. I won't keep you.'

He held firm to the laptop resting against his hip, one prominent dark eyebrow rising in an arc. 'Aren't you forgetting something?'

Zoey looked at him blankly for a moment. He flicked his gaze towards the writing desk behind her, his expression wry. 'I'll give you yours, if you give me mine. Deal?'

Zoey was so flustered at seeing him at this ungodly hour and looking so damn hot, she'd completely forgotten she had his computer. 'Oh…right, sorry…' She swung round and padded over to the desk to pick up the laptop. But then she heard the soft click of the suite door close behind her and a tingle shot down her spine. She turned to face him, her pulse rate picking up at the sardonic look in his eyes. 'I don't remember asking you into my room.'

'I know, and it was most impolite of you to not at least offer me a drink, since I walked all this way in the dark to bring you your laptop. I could have been mugged.' His eyes had a devilish gleam and her pulse rate went up another notch.

Zoey gave him a look that would have withered a plant. A plastic plant. 'Fine. What do you want? Erm, to drink, I mean.'

She was in no doubt about what he really wanted. She could see it in eyes, could feel it in the air—a throbbing pulse of sexual energy that pinged off him in waves, colliding with her own energy, stirring a host of longing and need that threatened to consume her. She felt it every time she was in his presence, the dark, sensual vibration of mutual lust. It horrified her that she was in lust with him. Horrified and shamed her. How could she possibly think of getting it on with him? He was a playboy. A man who had a freaking turnstile on his bedroom door. It was lowering to admit she was so attracted to him. What sort of self-destructive complex did she have to lust after a man she didn't even like?

'Coffee. I'll make it.' Finn sauntered over to the small coffee percolator near the mini-bar area. His take-charge attitude would have annoyed her normally, but she was tired and out of sorts, and the thought of someone else making her a coffee was rather tempting.

'Fine.' She sank to the small sofa in front of the television, wondering if she should have put up more of a fuss and insisted on him leaving. She realised, with a strange little jolt, she had never been totally alone with him before. There had always been other people in the background such as at conferences or at the airport the previous day.

One thing she did know—being alone with Finn O'Connell was dangerous. Not because he posed a physical threat to her safety but because she wasn't sure she knew how to handle such a potently attractive man at close, intimate quarters. At six-foot-six, he made the hotel room seem even smaller than it actually was. And, while she was no midget at five-foot-ten, she was currently barefoot and wearing nothing but a bathrobe.

Being so minimally attired made her feel at a distinct disadvantage. She needed the armour of her clothes to keep her from temptation. And temptation didn't get any more irresistible than Finn O'Connell in a playful mood.

Within a short time, the percolator made its gurgling noises, and the delicious aroma of brewed coffee began to tantalise Zoey's nostrils. Finn poured two cups and brought them over.

'Here you go. Strong and black.'

Zoey frowned and took the cup from him. 'How did you know how I take my coffee?'

His eyes twinkled. 'Lucky guess.'

Her lips twitched in spite of her effort to control her urge to smile back at him. The last thing she wanted to do was encourage him...or did she? The thought trickled into her head like the coffee had done in the machine just moments ago.

The dangerous thought of exploring the tension between them hummed like a current. It was a background hum, filtering through her body, awakening her female flesh to sensual possibilities. Possibilities she had forbidden herself to consider. Finn was a player, a fast-living playboy who had 'heartbreaker' written all over his too-handsome face. She had already had her heart broken by her ex. Why would she go in for another serve? It would be madness…

But it wouldn't be madness if she set the terms, would it? Why shouldn't she allow herself a treat now and again? She had given so much to her ex and got nothing back. Why not indulge herself this time with a man who didn't want anything from her other than hot no-strings sex?

Finn picked up the writing desk chair and placed it close to the sofa where she was sitting. He sat on the chair and balanced his right ankle over his other thigh in a casual pose she privately envied. Zoey had never felt more on edge in her life. Edgy, restless…excited. Yes, excited, because what woman wouldn't be excited in Finn's arrantly male presence?

Zoey sipped her coffee, covertly watching him do the same. Her eyes were drawn to the broad hand holding his cup, her mind conjuring up images of those long, tanned fingers moving down her body…touching her in places that hadn't seen any action for months on end. Places that began to tingle as they woke up from hibernation.

She sat up straighter on the sofa, almost spilling her coffee. 'Oops.' She caught a couple of droplets rolling down the side of her cup before they went on the cream linen sofa.

'Too hot for you?' Finn asked with an enigmatic smile, his eyes glinting.

You're too hot for me. Zoey put her cup on the lamp

table next to the sofa, her hand not as steady as she would have liked. 'No, it's fine. I'm just jet-lagged, I guess.'

He leaned back in his chair until it was balanced on the back legs only, his gaze measuring hers. 'Did you sleep on the plane?'

Zoey nodded. 'I'm glad I did now. If I'd realised you had my computer on the plane, I would have been in a flap of panic. It was bad enough finding out when I did, but at least it was only for a short time.'

There was a pulsing silence broken only by the sound of his chair creakily protesting at the way it was balanced. Finn rocked forward and the front legs of the chair landed on the carpet with a thud. 'So, how did you figure out it was my computer?'

'There was a business card in the laptop bag with a lipstick kiss on it from a woman called Kimba.' She picked up her coffee with a roll of her eyes. 'I'm surprised there was only one card. I was expecting hundreds.'

He gave a laugh and leaned forward to place his coffee cup on a nearby table. 'I do clean it out occasionally. But that wasn't all that was in the bag.'

Zoey brought her gaze back to his. 'You're crazy for leaving your password on a sticky note. What if someone else had got your laptop?'

His mouth curved upwards in a smile, making his eyes crinkle attractively at the corners. 'I had my laptop serviced yesterday and they reset the password. I haven't had time to reset it again.' He reached for his coffee cup, took a small sip and then balanced it base-ball-style in his hand. 'So, did you read my emails? Have a little snoop around?'

Zoey could feel heat storming into her cheeks and put her coffee back down on the table. 'Of course I didn't. Did you read mine?'

He placed his hand on his heart. 'Scout's honour, I didn't. I was tempted, sure, but I figured it was a pretty low thing to do.'

She bit down on her lower lip before she could stop herself. For reasons she couldn't explain, she believed him. He might be a charming player in his free time, but he was scrupulously honest in business. He had built from scratch an advertising empire that was one of the most successful in the business. She might not like him, but she couldn't help admiring him for what he had achieved.

Finn took another sip of his coffee. 'Did you look at my pitch?' His eyes held hers in a penetrating lock that made her scalp prickle.

Zoey sprang up from the sofa as if one of the cushions had bitten her on the bottom. 'I admit I was tempted, seriously tempted, but I didn't do it. Besides, I already know you're going to win.' She was doomed to fail with him as an opponent. It was galling to think he was going to win over her yet again. Would she ever get a chance to prove herself? She drew in another breath and released it on a defeated sigh. 'I think I haven't got a chance against you.'

'Come now, it's not over till it's over.' He got up off the chair and placed his coffee cup on the table with a loud thwack. 'You haven't even presented yours and you're giving up? What sort of attitude is that in this business? You have to believe in yourself, Zoey, no one else will if you don't.' His tone sounded almost frustrated, a frown deeply carved on his forehead.

His unexpected reaction surprised Zoey into a defensive mode. She curled her lip, her eyes flashing. 'Thanks for the pep talk, O'Connell. But I don't need you to tell me how to live my life.'

He raked a hand through his hair, leaving track marks amongst the thick strands. 'Look, I know things are a little messy with your father right now. But...'

Messy? She didn't need Finn to tell her how messy things were—she lived the cringeworthy reality every single day. Watching her father go from hero to zero, picking him up after every binge drinking session, covering for him when he missed a deadline, making excuses to clients when he failed to show up for a meeting... The list went on. Zoey tightened her arms around her middle until she could barely breathe. 'I'd like you to leave. Right now.'

Finn held her stormy gaze with unwavering ease. 'I admire your father. In his day, he was one of the best in the business but—'

'Get. Out.'

'I'd leave if I thought that's what you really wanted.'

Zoey thrust up her chin, her eyes blazing, her body trembling with forbidden longing. A longing she was desperately trying to control. 'Oh, so now you're an expert on what I want? Don't make me laugh.'

Finn stepped up to within a few centimetres of her, not touching her but standing so close she could see the detail in his eyes—the tiny flecks of darker brown like a mosaic, the pitch-black rim of his irises as if someone had traced each circumference with a felt-tip marker. He said nothing, did nothing, his expression almost impossible to read except for a diamond-hard glint in his eyes. Her eyes drifted to the sensual contour of his mouth and something deep in her core fluttered like the wings of moth—a soft, teasing reminder of needs she had ignored for so long. Needs Finn triggered in her every time she was near him, erotic needs that begged to be assuaged.

Zoey became aware of the heat of his body, aware of the energy crackling in the small distance between their bodies. *Touch him. Touch him. Touch him.* The mental chant sounded in her head, the need to do what her instincts demanded a relentless drive she suddenly couldn't control. Her hands went to the rock-hard wall of his chest, her fingers clutching at his T-shirt until it was bunched in both of her hands.

One part of her brain told her not to get any closer, the other part said the exact opposite. The push and pull was like a tug-of-war in her body. She was drawn to him like an iron filing to a powerful magnet, the sheer irresistible force of him overwhelming any blocking tactics on her part—if she could have come up with one, that was. Her rational mind was offline, and her body was now dictating the way forward. It had taken control and was running on primal instinct, not on rationality and reason.

One of her hands let go of his T-shirt and went to the back of his head. She stepped up on tiptoe and got her mouth as close to his as was possible without actually touching it. She didn't know why she was flirting so recklessly with danger. She didn't know why she was putting herself so close to temptation when her ability to resist him was currently so debatable.

But some wicked little imp inside her egged her on to see what would happen. She knew it was dangerous, infinitely dangerous, but oh, so wickedly thrilling to have him teetering with her on a high wire of self-control, not sure who was going to topple off first.

Her heart was beating like a tribal drum, the same erotic rhythm that was pulsing insistently between her legs. 'You think I can't wait for you to kiss me, don't you? But do you know what's going to happen if you so much as place your lips on mine?'

Finn still didn't touch her; his hands were by his sides but his hooded gaze communicated the effort it took not to do so. 'I'm going to kiss you back like you've never been kissed before, that's what.' His voice was deep and husky, his sensual promise sending a shiver cartwheeling down her spine.

Driven by that same little inner demon, Zoey moved a fraction closer, breathing in the vanilla and coffee scent of Finn's breath, her senses rioting. 'You think you're irresistible. That no woman with a pulse could ever say no to you. But I can resist you.'

Could she? Maybe, but why did she have to? They wanted the same thing—no-strings sex, an exploration of the lust that flared between them. What could be wrong with indulging her neglected senses in a simple hook-up with him?

Finn nudged his nose against hers—the tiniest nudge, but it sent a shockwave through her entire body. 'You're not saying no to me, you're saying no to yourself. You want me so badly, I can feel it every time I see you.'

Zoey fisted her hand in his hair in an almost cruel grip. 'I didn't think it was possible to hate someone as much as I hate you.'

His lips slanted in an indolent smile. 'Ah, but you don't hate me, babe. You hate how I make you feel. And I make you feel smoking-hot.'

'I feel *nothing* when I'm around you.' *Liar, liar, pants literally on fire.* On fire with lust.

He gave a low, deep chuckle and placed his hands on her hips, tugging her forward until she was flush against his rock-hard body. 'Then let's see if I can change that, shall we?' And his mouth came down firmly, explosively, on hers.

CHAPTER THREE

ANY THOUGHT OF pushing him away flew out of Zoey's head the moment his mouth crashed down on hers. Besides it being too late, deep down she knew she had intended this to happen from the get-go.

She wanted him to kiss her.

She wanted to push him over the edge.

She wanted him to be as desperate for intimate contact as was she.

His lips were firm, insistent, drawing from her an enthusiastic response she hadn't thought herself capable of giving to a man she didn't even like.

But what did like have to do with lust? Not much, it seemed.

The sensual heat of his mouth set fire to hers, his tongue entering her mouth with a bold, spine-tingling thrust that made her inner core contract with an ache of intense longing. His tongue duelled with hers in an erotic battle that sent her pulse rate soaring. She kissed him back with the same fierce drive, feeding off his mouth as if it was her only source of sustenance. Never had a kiss tasted so good, felt so good. It made every cell in her body throb with excitement.

One of Finn's hands went to the small of her back, drawing her even closer to his pelvis. The rigid press of his erection sent another wave of longing through her body. She made a sound at the back of her throat, a desperate whimpering sound of encouragement, and pushed further into his hardness, her arms winding around his neck, her fingers delving into the thickness of his hair.

Finn tilted his head to gain better access to her mouth, one of his hands cupping the side of her face. His tongue flicked against hers, calling it back into play, teasing her to a point where she was practically hanging off him, unable to stand on her own, for her legs were trembling so much. Never had she felt such ferocious desire. It pounded through her with each throbbing beat of her blood.

The taste of his mouth, the texture of his skin against her face, the feel of his hands on her hip and her cheek, sent her senses sky-rocketing. She needed to be closer. Ached to be closer. Would die if she didn't get closer.

Zoey unwound her arms from around his neck, tugging his T-shirt out of his jeans and placing her hands on his muscled chest, still with her mouth clamped to his. Her tongue danced with his in a sexy tango that made hot shivers go down her spine like a flow of molten lava.

Finn lifted his mouth off hers, looking at her with his dark, mercurial gaze. 'How am I doing so far? Have I changed your mind, or shall I stop right now?'

'Shut up and keep doing what you're doing,' Zoey said, dragging his head back down so her mouth could reconnect with his.

The kiss went on and on, more and more exciting,

more and more intense, leaving her more and more breathless, aching with want and wondering why the hell she had rebuffed him earlier. *This* was what she wanted. This passionate awakening of her senses, catapulting her into a maelstrom of delicious feeling. Feelings that she had forgotten she could feel but which she was feeling now even more intensely than ever before.

Finn lifted his mouth off hers only long enough to haul his T-shirt over his head, tossing it to one side before his lips came back down on hers with fiery purpose. His breathing was heavy, the primal, growling sounds he made in his throat ramping up her own arousal. One of his hands slipped between the front opening of her bath robe to claim her left breast. She gasped at the contact of his hands on her naked flesh, her body erupting into flames.

'Yes…oh, yes…' Zoey hadn't realised she had spoken out loud until she heard the sound of her desperate plea. 'Don't stop.'

Finn's eyes blazed with lust and he brought his mouth down to her breast, circling her nipple until it rose in a tight bud. He took it in his mouth, sucking on her with surprising gentleness, the sensation sending her senses spinning out of control. She grasped at his head, her spine arching in pleasure, her lower body tingling, tightening in anticipation of his intimate possession.

He lifted his mouth off her breast and held her gaze in an erotically charged lock that made the backs of her knees tingle and flames leap in her feminine core. 'I want you.' His bald statement was the most exciting, thrilling thing she had ever heard.

'Yeah, I kind of guessed that.' Zoey rubbed against

him, shamelessly urging him on. 'But I don't want to talk. I want to do this.' She placed her mouth on his chest, circling her tongue around his hard, flat nipple, delighting in the salty taste of his skin. She began to go lower, drawn to the swollen length of him, driven by some wicked force within her. She had to taste him. *All* of him.

Finn made a rough sound at the back of his throat and captured her by the upper arms. 'Wait. I have other plans for you right now.'

He ruthlessly tugged the bath robe fully open, sliding it down her arms and untying the belt so it dropped to the floor at her feet. His hungry gaze devoured every inch of her flesh but, instead of shrinking away from him, Zoey stood under his smouldering gaze, relishing every heart-stopping moment of seeing the raw, naked lust on his face. She was empowered by the way he was looking at her, as if she was some sort of sensual goddess that had materialised before him. She was giddily excited by the rampant desire she triggered in him—the same out-of-control desire he triggered in her.

'I want to see you naked. Fair's fair.' Zoey surprised herself with her boldness. Who was this wild and wanton woman blatantly stating her needs?

Finn held her gaze with his smouldering one. He unsnapped the stud button on his jeans and rolled down the zipper, the *zzzrrruuppt* sound sending a shiver skating down her spine. He stepped out of his jeans, and then out of his black form-fitting undershorts, and her heart rate went off the charts.

Zoey sucked in a breath, devouring every proud inch of him with her gaze. 'Mmm...not bad, I suppose.'

Finn gave a laugh and grasped her by the hips again, tugging her against his potent heat. 'I've wanted to do this for months.' He began to nibble on her earlobe, the teasing nip of his teeth making her shudder with pleasure.

'So, let's do it.' Zoey could hardly believe she was saying it, but it was all she wanted right now. *He* was all she wanted right now. To have his potent, powerful body ease the desperate, clawing ache of her female flesh.

Finn pulled back a little to look into her eyes with a searching expression. 'Are you sure this is what you want?'

Zoey rubbed up against him again, her gaze sultry, delighting in the way he snatched in a breath as if her body thrilled him like no other. 'I want you, Finn. I don't know how to make that any clearer.'

'While we're on the topic of clarity—you know I'm not in this for the long haul, right? I don't do long-term relationships. It's not my gig—never has been, never will be.'

Zoey stroked her hand down his lean jaw. 'Yes, well, that's lucky, because I don't either. Or at least, not any more.' She stroked the length of his nose and then outlined the contour of his mouth and added, 'This is exactly what I need right now. A one-night stand with a man who won't call me tomorrow and want a repeat.' She tapped his lower lip with her fingertip. 'Deal?'

Something shifted at the back of his gaze—a tiny flicker, like a sudden start of surprise, but quickly concealed. 'Deal.' His mouth came down to hers in a hard, scorching kiss, the heat inflamed all the more by the erotic press of their bodies.

Zoey opened to the commanding thrust of his tongue, her arms winding around his neck, which brought her tingling breasts tighter against his chest. The sprinkling of his chest hair tickled her soft flesh and his guttural groan as he deepened the kiss made her toes curl into the carpet at her feet. She had never felt such overwhelming desire for a man, such intense longing, it consumed her from head to foot.

Finn walked her backwards to the bed, his mouth still pressed firmly against hers. He laid her down and stood looking at her for a long, breathless moment, his body in full arousal making her inner core coil and tighten with lust.

Being taller than most of her friends, Zoey had her share of body issues, always feeling gargantuan compared to her petite friends. But with Finn's ravenous gaze moving over her she felt like a supermodel and, for the first time in for ever, proud of her feminine curves and long limbs. 'Had your fill?' she asked in a coquettish tone.

'Not yet.'

He leaned down over her, resting his hands either side of her head, his gaze capturing hers. 'You're beautiful—every delicious inch of you.'

'Yes, well, there are quite a few inches of me.'

He smiled and stroked a lazy finger down between her breasts, his eyes darkening to pitch. 'And I am going to kiss each and every one of them.'

Zoey shivered, her need for him escalating to the point of discomfort. She reached up to grasp his head with both of her hands. 'If you don't have sex with me soon, I'm going to scream.'

His brown eyes glinted. 'Then it looks like I'm going to make you scream either way.'

A frisson passed over her body at the erotic promise of his statement, the same erotic promise she could see in his eyes. She had never been all that vocal during sex with her ex. Their love life had become a little routine over the time they'd been together, but she had put that down to the increasing demands of their careers. If she were to be perfectly honest, it had even been a tad boring at times.

'I'm not a screamer, as it turns out.' Zoey wasn't sure why she was spilling such personal information to him.

Finn came down beside her on the bed and placed his hand on her mound. 'Then I guarantee you soon will be.'

He brought his mouth down to her folds and she arched her spine like a languorous cat, unable to speak for the sensations flowing through her. Electric sensations sent ripples of pleasure to every inch of her body. His tongue stroked against the swollen bud of her clitoris, delicately at first, gauging her response, before he increased his rhythm and pressure.

Zoey gasped as lightning bolts of delight coursed through her flesh, the tension building inexorably to a point of no return. A part of her mind drifted above to look down at her body being pleasured by Finn, and was a little shocked at how vulnerable she had made herself to him. The intimacy of what he was doing to her was way beyond what she had experienced before. Rupert had occasionally gone down on her, but he never stayed long enough for her to feel anything more than a few vague flutters.

But with Finn her body was on fire, and the flames were licking at her flesh with tongues of incendiary heat. Zoey arched her spine even further, her legs trembling as the wave of pleasure hit her with a booming crash. Her breathless whimpers became cries, and then an almost shrill scream, as the waves kept coming, one after the other, pummelling her, pounding through her, until she was thrown out the other side, limp, satiated, in a total state of physical bliss.

'Oh, dear God…' She was lost for words, her breathing still out of order, her senses still spinning.

Finn moved back up her body, his eyes shining like dark, wet paint. 'Ready for more?'

'You can't be serious? I'm a come-once-only girl.'

A wicked glint appeared in his gaze. 'Let's see what I can do about changing that.' He sprang off the bed and went to get a condom from his wallet in the back pocket of his jeans. Zoey relished watching him, his gloriously naked body stirring a new wave of longing in her. He tore the foil packet with his teeth, tossing away the wrapper, and then rolled the condom over his erection, glancing at her with that same dancing, devilish glint in his eyes. And Zoey almost climaxed again on the spot.

Finn came back over to her and she reached up and tugged him back down so he was lying over her, his weight balanced on his arms, one of his powerful thighs hitched over hers. He leaned down to kiss her and she tasted herself on his lips, the raw and earthy intimacy of it blowing her mind. His tongue entered her mouth, teasing hers into a duel that mimicked the throbbing energy of him poised between her thighs. He ran one hand down the flank of her thigh in a slow stroke, and then back again, his mouth moving against hers with deeper and deeper passion.

He lifted his mouth off hers to gaze down at her, his breathing heavy. 'I don't think I've ever wanted someone more than I do you at this moment.' His voice was rough-edged, his eyes holding hers in an intimate lock that heralded the sensual delights to come.

Zoey placed her hand at the back of his head, her fingers toying with his hair. 'I bet you say that to everyone you sleep with.' Her tone was teasing but a part of her realised with a twinge of unease—their one-night stand agreement notwithstanding—she didn't want him to look on her as he looked on his other lovers. She wanted to stand apart, to be someone who wouldn't just disappear into the crowd of past lovers, the nameless women he had pleasured and then walked away from without a backward glance. The sort of women who gave him business cards with lipstick kisses and 'thanks for the memories' messages.

But exactly what *did* she want?

Zoey didn't want a committed relationship with Finn, or with anyone else for that matter. That part of her life was over. Dead and buried. She could never trust another man, let him into her life, into her body and then find he had betrayed her. She wasn't that much of a fool to lay herself open again to such ego-shredding hurt.

But she did want to feel alive and, right now, she had never felt more so.

Finn brushed a wayward strand of her hair back off her face. 'I haven't said it to anyone and meant it the way I do right now. You drive me crazy.'

'You drive me crazy too.'

'Good, because I would hate it if things weren't equal between us.' He nudged at her entrance, his eyes darkening as he surged into her with a throaty groan.

Zoey gasped in bliss as he drove to the hilt, her body welcoming him, wrapping around him, gripping him as he started thrusting. She was quickly swept away with his fast-paced rhythm, her senses reeling as the friction increased. Sensations shot through her female flesh, darts, flickers and arrows of pleasure that increased with every deep thrust of his body. She gripped him by his taut buttocks, unable to think, only to feel. And, oh, what exquisite feeling. Tingles, fizzes and starbursts of pleasure rippled through her. The tension grew and grew in the most sensitive nub of her body, but she couldn't quite tip over the edge.

Finn brought his hand down between their bodies and began to stroke her swollen flesh with his fingers, the extra friction, right where she needed it, sending her into outer space. Her orgasm was like a meteor strike exploding in her flesh, sending ripples and waves and rushes of pleasure through her body so fast and so furiously, it was almost frightening. Her body had never felt so out of control. It was spinning and thrashing and whirling with sensations that went on and on, the sweet torture making her throw her head back and bite back a scream.

The muffled scream turned into a sob—a laughing sob of disbelief. How could she have experienced such a tumult of the senses with a man she viewed as the enemy?

Finn gave another deep groan and surged deeply, his movements fast, almost frantic, before he finally let go. Zoey gripped him by the buttocks, a vicarious frisson of pleasure passing over her body as she felt the intensity of his release. He collapsed over her, his breathing still hectic, the slightly rougher skin of his jaw tickling her cheek.

After a few moments, he propped himself up on one elbow to look down at her, his body still joined to hers. He brushed back a stray hair from her face, his expression difficult to make out. His eyes moved between hers, back and forth, back and forth, every now and again dipping to her mouth and back again. He brought his index finger to her mouth and tapped her gently on her lips. 'You rocked me to the core.'

'I'm not finished rocking you.' Zoey captured his finger with her teeth, biting down with just enough pressure to see his pupils flare. She opened her bite just enough so she could glide her tongue over the pad of his finger, holding his smouldering gaze.

'Whoa there, babe. I have some business to see to.' He sucked in a breath and pulled away to deal with the used condom.

Zoey lay on her side with her elbow bent, resting her head on her hand, and followed him with her gaze, drinking in the sight of his lean, tanned build and firm muscles. 'Do you have any more condoms with you?' She could barely believe she had asked such a question. Who was this insatiable woman? It was certainly nothing like her former self.

Finn winked at her and picked up his wallet. 'Enough.'

'How many is enough?'

He walked back over to her and sat beside her, one

of his hands running up and down her leg. 'What time's your pitch?'

Zoey glanced past him at the bedside clock and her stomach nose-dived. How could so much time have passed? She had completely forgotten about her pitch at nine a.m. 'Oh, shoot. I have to rush.' She brushed his hand away and scrambled off the bed, grabbing the bath robe off the floor and bundling herself into it. 'I have to shower and do my hair and make-up.' And get her scattered senses under some semblance of control.

Finn rose from the bed with an inscrutable look on his face. 'Then I won't keep you any longer.'

Zoey stood toying with the belt of her bath robe as he dressed, her teeth chewing at her lower lip, her body still tingling from his intimate possession. He picked up his laptop bag and slung it over his shoulder, his expression still masked.

'Erm…thanks for bringing me my laptop,' Zoey began but found herself floundering for what else to say. *Thanks for the memories? Thanks for giving me the best two orgasms of my life? Can I see you again?* No. She definitely was *not* saying that. No way. She had scratched the Finn O'Connell itch and it was time to move on. 'Hope you have a good flight back home,' she added. Urgh. Of course he would have a good flight home, no doubt with the Frascatelli account firmly in his possession.

Finn gave a brief smile that didn't reach his eyes. 'It was my pleasure.' And then he walked out of the suite and closed the door behind him with a definitive click that made Zoey flinch.

CHAPTER FOUR

FINN'S PITCH PRESENTATION didn't go as he'd envisaged. For one thing, his mind was replaying every moment of making love to Zoey Brackenfield instead of focussing on selling his vision for the ad campaign to the client's representative.

The second thing was a niggling sense of irritation that Zoey hadn't expressed a desire to see him again for a repeat session or two. He had expected her to say it before he left her hotel room. Expected it so much that when it hadn't been forthcoming it had stung him in a way he had not been stung before. It was ironic, as usually it was he who sent a lover on her way with no promise of a follow-up. But it was her call, and he had a feeling it wouldn't be long before their paths crossed once again. And he would make the most of it.

The sex had been nothing short of phenomenal, a totally mind-blowing experience, and he wanted more. Ached to have her in his arms again with a throbbing ache so deep and intense, it was distracting him from his work. So much so, he didn't realise the representative from the Frascatelli Hotel corporation was speaking to him.

'I'm sorry,' Finn said. 'I missed that last bit. What did you say?'

The representative closed their meeting with a stiff smile. 'Once Leonardo Frascatelli has a look at the three candidates' presentations for himself, and my order of preference, he will make a final decision and be in touch on who gets the contract. It will be a few days, I should think.'

'Thank you.' At least he might be in with a chance if Leo Frascatelli had the final say, Finn thought with an inward sigh of relief. It was a big account, and he knew there would be ongoing work once this initial campaign was over. He liked to win when he set his mind on a goal. It was why he loved the advertising business—it was an adrenalin rush, a fast-paced creative process with big dividends. He enjoyed the team work and he had some of the best in the business working for him.

But the biggest adrenalin rush he'd experienced lately was his one-nighter with Zoey. The hunger she had triggered in him hadn't gone away in spite of their hot night of sex. It hadn't defused anything. Instead, his hunger for her was even more ravenous than before. She stirred a fervent sexual energy in him, an energy unlike anything else he had experienced with anyone else.

He didn't know what it was about her, but he wanted more. Zoey had said she hated him, but it didn't change the fact that she desired him. And what a scorching-hot desire it was. He shuddered every time he thought of her silky warmth gripping him so tightly, her breathless gasps and cries of pleasure, the almost desperate clutch of her hands on his body. He had felt the same desperation to be as close as it was physically possible to be.

Finn walked out of the meeting room, sure he could pick up a faint trace of Zoey's perfume lingering in the air from when she had pitched earlier that morning. He closed the door on his exit and blew out a long breath.

Boy, oh, boy, did he have the lust bug bad.

Zoey flew back to London later the same day, determined to stick to the plan of no repeats of her completely out-of-character hook-up with Finn O'Connell. But the deed was done and now it was time to move on and not allow herself to think of him. Anyway, he was probably in bed with someone else by now.

As for her pitch, well, it was Finn's fault she had stumbled and garbled her way through it like a rookie intern on her first project. How was she supposed to perform at a peak professional level with her body still tingling from head to foot from Finn's off-the-scale lovemaking?

But then a thought dropped into her head... Maybe that had been his plan right from the start. Maybe he had wanted to sabotage her pitch by scrambling her brain, short-circuiting her senses, until all she could think about was the stroke and glide of his hands on her skin, his powerful body deep within hers, the starbursting orgasms that had left her body still tingling even hours later.

Maybe even the laptop switch had been deliberate. Seeing him in the queue at Heathrow had certainly flustered her. She had been so intent on getting through security without betraying how much he unsettled her, she had grabbed a computer off the conveyor belt without properly checking if it was hers.

But, as much as she was annoyed with herself over that little mix-up, how could she regret sleeping with him? It had been more hate sex on her part than anything else, but it had totally blown her mind and sent her senses into haywire from which they had yet to recover. How could she regret having the most incredible sex of her life?

Erm...because it's Finn O'Connell?

Zoey closed her eyes in a 'why was I such an idiot?' manner. But she consoled herself that it was only the once and it would not be repeated. There was no way she was going to hanker after him like his posse of fan girls. She had way too much pride.

In fact, she was not going to think about him at all.

Finn had only been back at his office a few minutes when his receptionist-cum-secretary, June, informed him Harry Brackenfield was waiting to speak to him in the conference room. 'He said it's highly confidential and he didn't want to be seen waiting for you in the waiting room,' she added. 'He wouldn't even make an appointment to come back at a more convenient time.'

'That's okay, I'll see him,' Finn said, wondering if he was in for a lecture about sleeping with Harry's daughter. But surely Zoey wouldn't share such private details of her love life with her father? Besides, Harry Brackenfield didn't seem the devoted and protective dad type.

Harry's attitude to Zoey troubled Finn at times. He had overheard Harry at a cocktail party a couple of months ago denigrating a project Zoey had worked on early in her career. Personally, Finn had thought her early work showed enormous talent. It had been a little rough around the edges but that was normal for a new-bie. Her later work was nothing short of brilliant, but he had a feeling she wasn't allowed to shine too brightly at Brackenfield, in case her work eclipsed her father's.

Finn walked into the conference room to find Harry seated on one side of the long table, his hands clasped together.

'Morning, Harry,' he said, taking the seat at the head of the table. 'I missed you at the conference the other day. I thought we were going to have coffee to discuss something.'

Harry's eyes shifted to one side. 'Yes, well, I thought it was too public there to discuss what I want to discuss with you.' His gaze moved back to Finn's. 'I want out.'

Finn frowned in confusion. 'Out?'

Harry separated his hands and laid them on the table. Finn noted both of them had a slight tremble. 'I'm of-fering you a takeover of Brackenfield Advertising. I know you've done takeovers in the past, and I thought you might be interested, since you've been asking me over the last couple of months about how things were going. I'm done. I'm tired of the long hours and my creativity has dried up. I want to take early retirement.'

A tick of excitement ran through Finn's blood. A friendly takeover was the ideal way to acquire a com-pany, but it concerned him that Zoey hadn't mentioned anything about it during their time in New York. And it begged the question as to why. 'Does Zoey know about this?'

A dull flush rose on the older man's cheekbones. 'No. And I insist the deal is off if she's told before the deal is signed off. It's my company and if I want to sell it, then I'll sell it. This is an exclusive offer to you but, if you don't want it, then I'll offer it to someone else.'

The trouble was, Finn did want it. Brackenfield Advertising would be a nice little coup to add to his empire, but it didn't sit well with him that Zoey was in the dark about the takeover. But business was business and, since Harry was the owner and director, what else was Finn supposed to do? Confidentiality was a cornerstone of good business deals and he wanted that company before one of his competitors got it.

Besides, his one-night stand with Zoey was exactly that—a one-night stand. Even if part of him wished it could be repeated. Would this takeover ruin the chances of seeing Zoey again? A niggle of unease passed through him, but he forced himself to ignore it. He wasn't interested in anything long-term even if Zoey was the most exciting lover he had been with in years…possibly ever.

Finn made a generous offer and readily Harry accepted it. It seemed to confirm the older man's keenness to do other things with his life other than work.

'Right, then, it looks like you've got yourself a deal,' Finn said, rising from his seat to offer Harry his hand. 'I'll get my legal people in contact with yours to get the paperwork written up.'

Harry shook Finn's hand. 'Thank you.'

Finn waited a beat before asking, 'Why the secrecy from Zoey? Surely as your only daughter she has the right to know what your plans are going forward?'

Harry's expression became belligerent. 'If she were my son, then maybe it would be different. But she's not.

She'll get married and have kids one day soon and then what will happen to the company?'

'Men get married and have kids too and still successfully manage companies,' Finn felt compelled to point out, even if he didn't place himself in that category. The marriage and kids package had never appealed to him, mostly because he had seen first-hand the damage when it didn't work out. 'Anyway, isn't Zoey more a career woman? That's the impression I've always had when speaking with her.'

It was weird because Zoey reminded him of himself—career-driven, single and wanting to stay that way, yet up for a bit of no-strings fun now and again to relieve the tension. The only trouble was, he didn't like the thought of her having fun with anyone else. If she wanted to have fun, then he wanted to be the one to have it with her. For now, at least. Not for ever.

'I'll tell her as soon as the deal is done and dusted,' Harry said. 'And not before.'

'Your call, but I think you're making a big mistake.'

Harry narrowed his eyes. 'Since when have you been such a champion for my daughter? She hates your guts, or haven't you noticed that small detail?'

Finn suppressed a smile. 'Let's say we've been working at our differences.' And having a hot lot of fun doing it too.

'Hey, how did your pitch in New York go?' Millie, one of Zoey's previous flatmates, asked at their bridesmaid dress fitting a few days later. 'I meant to ask you earlier, but I've been distracted by things...'

'Things' being Millie's recent engagement to hot-shot celebrity lawyer Hunter Addison. Madly in love, Millie had already moved out of their flat to live with him. Ivy Kennedy, Zoey's other previous flatmate, had also moved out a few weeks ago to live with her fiancé, Louis Charpentier. They were getting married next month, and Zoey and Millie were both going to be bridesmaids. And, when Millie and Hunter got married a couple of months after that, Ivy and Zoey would be maid of honour and bridesmaid, along with Hunter's young sister, Emma.

'I haven't heard back yet,' Zoey said, twirling from side to side in front of the full-length mirror in the bridal store's fitting room. 'I don't think this shade of blue suits me.'

'Are you nuts?' Millie laughed. 'You look stunning in it. And it really makes your violet eyes pop.'

What had made Zoey's eyes pop was seeing Finn O'Connell naked in her hotel room. Even though she had insisted their hook-up be a one-off, it still rankled a bit he hadn't called or texted her since. It was perverse of her to hope for a repeat when she had been the one to issue the once-only terms.

'I don't know…' She swished the long skirt of the dress from side to side, her mind wandering back to how it felt to have Finn's hands gliding over her naked body…

'Hey, earth to Zoey,' Millie said. 'You've got such a far-away look in your eyes. Did something happen while you were in New York?' She waggled her eyebrows meaningfully. 'Like with a man, for instance?'

Zoey flattened her mouth and frowned. 'What on earth makes you think that?'

Millie's face fell at her sharp tone. 'Sorry. Is it your father, then?'

Zoey let out a serrated sigh. 'I didn't mean to snap at you, it's just…'

'Tell me.' Millie touched her on the arm, her expression concerned. 'Has your dad been binge drinking again?'

'I haven't seen him since I got back from New York, so I don't know, but on balance I would say probably he has been.' She chewed at her lip and then added, 'I had a one-night stand.'

Millie's eyes went so wide, they could have moonlighted as Christmas baubles. 'Seriously? Who was it? How did you meet? What was it like? Will you see him again?'

Zoey twisted her mouth and fiddled with the shoestring strap of the bridesmaid dress. 'I'll probably see him again, but not like that.' She met her friend's eyes in the mirror. 'It was Finn O'Connell.'

Millie frowned. 'Your competitor for that other project? But I thought you hated him.'

Zoey gave her a wry look. 'Yes, well, it wasn't so long ago that you hated Hunter Addison and look where that led.'

Millie's expression was sheepish but glowing with happiness too. *'Touché.'* But then her frown came back. 'Are you saying you *feel* something for Finn O'Connell?'

'Of course not!' Zoey laughed. 'What a crazy question to ask.'

'You must have felt something otherwise you wouldn't have slept with him. You haven't had a date since you broke up with Rupert. Finn must have made you feel something to—'

'I felt lust.'

'And now?'

Zoey unzipped the dress. 'And now, nothing. It was a one-night stand and I don't want to repeat it.'

'Was it that bad?'

'Unfortunately, no.' Zoey sighed and stepped out of the dress and hung it back on the padded hanger. 'No wonder that man has a conga line of women waiting to fall into bed with him.'

'That good, huh?'

'Indescribable.' Zoey stepped into her jeans and pulled up the zip. 'But I'm not getting involved with a playboy.'

'They make wonderful fiancés once they fall in love,' Millie said. 'You only have to look at Louis and Hunter to see that. You couldn't ask for a more devoted partner. Did I tell you Hunter is helping my mother with her literacy problems? He's so patient with her, and I love him all the more for being so wonderfully supportive.'

'Hunter is a one-in-a-million guy and I'm happy for you.' Zoey reached for her top and pulled it over her head, then shook out her hair. 'But I'm not interested in a long-term relationship. Been there, done that, thrown away the trousseau.'

Millie gave her a long, measuring look. 'I know Rupert broke your heart cheating on you the way he did. But you can't stop yourself from falling in love with someone again out of fear. I wake up each day feeling so blessed I found love with Hunter. It would be so wonderful to see you happy again too.'

'Yes, well, maybe I wasn't all that happy with Rupert,' Zoey said, slipping her feet back into her shoes.

It was slowly dawning on her that her relationship with her ex had had some serious flaws which she had chosen not to notice at the time. It was sleeping with Finn O'Connell that made her realise how boring and routine things had become with Rupert. But, rather than address it at the time, she had blithely carried on until it had got to a humiliating showdown, finding him in bed—in *their* bed—with another woman.

'But you were with him for seven years.'

'Yeah, don't remind me,' Zoey said, rolling her eyes. 'I wished I'd left before he made such a fool of me.' She blew out a breath and added, 'I think I got too comfortable in my relationship with him. He told me he loved me daily and I believed it, more fool me. I should know by now you can never trust a word a man says.'

'Not all men are like Rupert.'

'Maybe not, but you only have to look at my father to see he's cut from the same cloth,' Zoey said. 'Says one thing, does another. He told me he was going to rehab the last time we had dinner. But did he do it? No. And lately he's been avoiding me. Ignoring my texts and not answering my calls. I should be relieved at the reduced contact with him, but I know him well enough to know he's up to something he knows I won't approve of. Fingers crossed it's not a new lover young enough to be his daughter. Urgh.'

'Oh, Zoey, I'm sorry you've been let down so much by your dad. But losing your mother when you were so young must have really devastated him.'

Zoey hated being reminded of the loss of her mother

when she'd been only four years old. One day her mum had been there, the next she wasn't. Carried away in an ambulance after falling from her horse while Zoey had been at kindergarten, dying three days later from severe head injuries, never having regained consciousness. Zoey hadn't had the chance to say goodbye. She hadn't even been allowed to go to the hospital or to the funeral. Her father had insisted she stay at home with the hastily engaged nanny—one of many, along with various stepmothers who had come and gone during her childhood.

'Yes, well, I lost her too, and do you see me drinking myself into a stupor and making a complete and utter fool of myself? Besides, his drinking has been a fairly recent thing. His last marriage break-up with his wife Linda seemed to be the trigger. She was the first woman he really cared about since mum. Another good reason not to fall in love. It's not worth it.'

Millie sighed. 'I'm sure your mum would be so proud of how you watch out for your dad and of all you've achieved professionally.'

Zoey picked up her tote bag from the chair. 'Yes, well, all I've achieved will be for nothing if I don't get this contract. Come on. I need a coffee.'

All this wedding preparation stuff was seriously messing with her head. Her two best friends had fallen in love with wonderful men—even a hardened cynic like her had to admit Hunter Addison and Louis Charpentier were worth giving up singledom for. But she had been so stung by Rupert's betrayal, and wondered if she would ever allow herself to trust a man again. She had given so much to her relationship with him, been there for him in every way possible, only to find it had all been for nothing. How could she open herself again to such excruciating pain and humiliation?

Finn was in his home office a couple of days later reading through the now mutually signed takeover contract Harry Brackenfield's lawyer had sent via courier. There was a cooling off period of a week, but he knew Harry wouldn't back away from the deal—not with the eye-watering amount of money Finn had paid. But Finn had made plenty of money over his career and the odd gamble now and again wouldn't harm the coffers. Brackenfield Advertising needed a thorough overhaul and a bit of dead wood would have to go. It was a business, after all, and a business was all about profit. That was the bottom line.

Finn's rescue cat, Tolstoy, was sitting on his desk with a scowl on his face. The battle-scarred Russian blue hadn't quite forgiven him for leaving him with the housekeeper when he flew to New York. Tolstoy had pointedly ignored him for the first three days and now, on day five, was only just softening towards him, in that he now tolerated being in the same room as him.

Finn slowly rolled a pen across his desk. 'Go on, you know you want to.' The pen rolled in the direction of the cat's paw, finally coming to a stop against a paperweight, but all Tolstoy did was give him an unblinking stare.

'Still mad at me, huh?' Finn opened the top drawer on his desk and took out a length of string and dangled it in front of the cat's face. 'What about this?'

Tolstoy continued to stare at him, his one green eye nothing short of scathing.

'You know something?' Finn said, dropping the string back in the drawer and closing it. 'You remind me of someone. She looks at me just like that.' He went back to the paperwork on his desk, reading through the fine print with studied concentration... Well, it would have been a lot easier to concentrate if his mind hadn't kept drifting to Zoey.

His phone buzzed beside him on the desk and he picked it up with a quick glance at the screen. It wasn't Zoey but Leo Frascatelli, which could only mean good news. 'Finn O'Connell.'

'Finn, I have a proposition for you,' Leo said. 'I've had a look at the three pitches and I've chosen you and Zoey Brackenfield as equal first. I couldn't choose between you, so I want you to work together on the campaign. Is that doable?'

It was doable but was it wise? Finn hadn't seen her since New York and with each day that had passed the ache to do so had got worse. It was so out of character for him to be hankering after a follow-up date with a lover. Working with Zoey would bring her back into his orbit but it would ramp up the temptation to sleep with her again. And again. And who knew how many more times? He wasn't normally one to mix business with pleasure. But he was prepared to risk it because the Frascatelli project was a lucrative one even if the profits would be split two ways.

'Sure. Have you talked to Zoey yet?'

'Not yet. I thought I'd run it by you first. Do you

think she'd be open to working with you? I've heard good things about her work.'

'She's extremely talented,' Finn said. 'How about I run it by her and let you know?'

'That would be great. Nice to talk to you, Finn.'

'You too.'

Finn clicked off his phone and looked at Tolstoy. 'Tell me I'm not an idiot for agreeing to work with Zoey on this account.'

The cat gave him a lugubrious stare.

Zoey decided to check in on her father on her way home from her dress fitting with Millie. Calling on him unannounced was always a little risky, not to mention stressful, but she was pleasantly surprised to find him in good spirits, and thankfully there was no obvious appearance that he'd been recently indulging in the alcoholic ones.

'Zoey, I was just about to call you. I have some good news.' He waved her inside, his face beaming.

She gave him the side-eye on the way in. 'Please don't tell me you're getting married again.'

'No, no, no.' He chuckled and closed the front door. 'It's way more exciting than that. I've sold the business. I got a takeover offer I couldn't refuse. I've just signed off on it.'

Zoey looked at him in shell-shocked silence, her thoughts flying off at tangents. *Sold?* How could the business be sold? She opened and closed her mouth, unable to find her voice for a moment. How could her father have done such a thing without even consulting her? Did she matter so little to him? Did he care nothing for her? She narrowed her eyes, her heart beating so heavily she could feel it pounding in her ears. 'What do you mean you've sold it? Are you sure you haven't been drinking?'

'Zoey.' His tone was that of an adult speaking to a cognitively dull child. 'I've only been drinking because of the stress of trying to run the business on my own. This will mean I can finally relax and—'

'But you wouldn't have had to run it on your own if you'd let me be a director!' She swung away with her hands clasped against her nose and mouth, trying to get her breathing under control.

How could this be happening? She had worked so damn hard. Covering for her father when he didn't meet a deadline. Filling in for him at meetings when he was nursing yet another hangover. She had compromised herself on so many occasions in an effort to keep the company's reputation intact. How could he go behind her back and sell the business without even talking it over with her first?

Zoey lowered her hands to stare at him with wild eyes. 'I can't believe you've done this. How could you... you betray me like this? You know how much the company means to me. Why didn't you discuss it with me? Why deliver it as a fait accompli?'

'Because I knew you would be against it, especially when you hear who's behind the takeover.'

Zoey stared at her father, her scalp prickling with unease. 'And are you going to tell me who this person is?'

'Finn O'Connell.'

'*Finn O'Connell?*' Zoey gasped. 'You can't be serious. Not him. Anyone but him.'

'I approached him and he jumped at the chance. He's had his eye on the company for a couple of months, asking me how things were going and so on. That's why I gave him first dibs.'

'A couple of months?' Zoey's voice came out as a shriek and her stomach churned fast enough to make butter. If what her father said was true, Finn had slept with her knowing he had his eye on her father's business. He had not said a word to her.

Not a single word.

Not even a hint.

Her father's betrayal suddenly didn't seem half as bad when she had Finn's duplicity to get her head around. Her hatred of him had gone on the back burner after their night of passion, in fact she had even wondered if it could be downgraded to mild dislike rather than pure unmitigated hatred.

But now her rage towards him was a tornado brewing in her body, making her physically shake with the effort to keep it under some semblance of control. Her head was pounding with tension, as if her temples were clamped in the cruel blunt jaws of a vice. She opened and closed her hands, her fingers feeling tingling and slightly numb, as if their blood supply had been cut off in the effort to keep her heart pumping. 'I—I can't believe that man would stoop so low.'

'Zoey, it's a business deal, there's nothing personal about it,' her father said in that same annoying 'adult to dull child' tone. 'Finn is keen to expand his business. He's done other highly successful takeovers. Anyway, I've lost the fire in my belly for the ad game. It's a perfect time for me to take early retirement, and you should be happy for me instead of harping on as if I've mortally wounded you.'

'You have mortally wounded me!' Zoey's voice rose in pitch, her eyes stinging with tears she refused to shed. She would *not* cry in front of her father. He would see it as a weakness and berate her for it, using her emotional response as yet another reason why he had sold the business out from under her. She took a couple of deep breaths and lowered her voice to a more reasonable level. 'What I'd like to know is, what happens to me? To my career?'

'You can work for Finn.'

Over my dead and rotting body. Zoey kept her expression under tight control but her anger towards Finn was boiling inside her belly like a toxic brew. She had never loathed someone more than she did Finn O'Connell at that moment. And she couldn't wait to tell him so to his too-handsome face. 'That's not going to happen,' she said. 'Not unless he gives me an offer I can't refuse.'

But she would refuse it anyway on principle. She would beg on the streets before she would have Finn lauding it over her as her boss. Oh, God, her boss. Could there be a worse form of torture?

'If Finn O'Connell wants something badly enough, he doesn't mind paying top dollar for it.'

Zoey gave an evil gleam of a vengeful smile. 'Oh, he'll pay for it. I'll make damn sure of it.'

CHAPTER FIVE

ZOEY DECIDED AGAINST calling Finn because she had a burning desire to see him in person. What she had to say to him was not suitable for a phone conversation. She wanted to see every nuance on his face, read every flicker of his expression, to gain some insight into whether he felt compromised by what he had done. She suspected not, but she had to know for certain. The fact he'd slept with her whilst knowing he was in the process of taking over her father's business churned her gut.

Why, oh why, had she fallen for his practised charm? Could there be a more humiliating experience?

But when she got to his office the smartly dressed middle-aged woman at the reception desk informed her Finn was working at home that day.

'What's his address, then?' Zoey asked. 'I'll see him there.'

The woman gave Zoey an up and down, assessing look, her lips pursing in a disapproving manner. 'I'm afraid I can't give you that information. But, if you'd like to make an appointment, Mr O'Connell will see you when he's next available. However, it might not be for a week or two.' She gave a tight smile that didn't reach her eyes and added, 'As you can imagine, he's a very busy man.'

Zoey ground her teeth so hard she thought she'd be on a liquid diet for the next month. She drew in a breath, releasing it in a measured stream, and leaned her hands on the desk, nailing the other woman's gaze. 'Listen, there's no point looking at me like that. I already have his phone number. What I have to say to him needs to be said face to face.'

'Then why don't you just video call him?'

'And have him hang up on me? No way. I want to see him in person. Today. Within the next half hour, if possible. I don't care how busy he is, either in his private or professional life, but I am not leaving this office until you give me his address.'

The receptionist arched her brows, her posture as stiff and as unyielding as a bouncer at a nightclub. 'Your name is?'

Zoey straightened from the desk, furious she was being treated like one of Finn's love-struck bimbos. 'Zoey Brackenfield.'

The woman's expression underwent a rapid change, her haughtiness fading to be replaced by a look of delighted surprise. 'Oh, so *you're* Zoey Brackenfield.' She shot up from her ergonomic chair and held out her hand across the reception counter, a smile threatening to split her face in two. 'How lovely to meet you. I just adored the dog food commercial you did a while back. I started feeding my dog that brand because of you. It was just fabulous.'

'Thank you,' Zoey said, briefly shaking the woman's

hand. But, compliments aside, she refused to back down and added in a pointed tone, 'His address?'

The woman shifted her lips from side to side, her eyes beginning to twinkle like fairy lights. 'I'd be happy to give it to you. No doubt you want to discuss the take-over.' She picked up a pen and wrote the address on a sticky note and handed it across the desk. 'It's about time Finn met his match.'

Zoey took the sticky note with a grim, no-teeth-showing smile. 'Oh, he's more than met his match.' And then she whipped round and left.

Finn lived in a leafy street in Chelsea in a gorgeous Georgian-style three-storey mansion. There was a small formal front garden with a neatly trimmed box hedge set behind a shiny, black wrought-iron fence. There were three colourful window boxes at the first-floor level, lush with vermillion pelargoniums and yellow-hearted purple pansies and trailing blue and white lo-belia. But Zoey wasn't here to admire the view, even if part of her was as green as that box hedge with envy. If the outside visage was any measure, it was a dream of a house. What a pity such an arrogant jerk owned it.

Zoey pushed open the front gate and marched up the path to the front door and placed her finger on the brass doorbell button and left it there. She heard it echoing through the house and after a few moments the sound of firm footsteps from inside.

Finn answered the door with a welcoming smile. 'Ah, just who I was about to call. Come in.'

Zoey pushed past him, her chest heaving. She waited

until he'd closed the door before she turned on him. 'You despicable, double-crossing jerk. How dare you buy—?'

'I take it you've heard about the takeover?' His expression was neutral, no sign of guilt, shame or conflict. Even his tone was irritatingly mild.

She clenched her hands into tight fists, her gaze blazing. 'I'm just dying to hear your explanation about why you didn't tell me you were taking over my father's company the night we...we...' She couldn't say the words without wanting to slap him.

'You've got it all wrong, babe. Your father approached me and offered to sell only a couple of days ago.'

Zoey stood rigidly before him, her blood boiling. How could she believe him? Why should she believe him? 'Did you do it deliberately? The whole laptop switch thing, the one-nighter, the secret takeover... was it all just a game to you? Was *I* just a silly little game to you?'

A muscle in Finn's jaw flickered just the once, as if he was holding back a retort. He let out a slow breath and made a placating gesture with one of his hands. 'Look, nothing was deliberate, other than I agreed to buy your father out when he came to me the other day. I couldn't tell you about the takeover because he didn't want me to. He insisted on absolute secrecy or the deal was off. If you want to be angry with anyone, it should be him.'

'I am angry with him!' Zoey said. 'But I'm even more furious with you. You should have given me the heads up. I had a right to know.'

'That's not the way I do business,' Finn said with

annoying calm. 'Your father wanted to keep it under wraps and, while I didn't necessarily agree with it, I respected his decision. Besides, you supposedly hate my guts, so why would I jeopardise the takeover by letting you in on it? You might have leaked it to someone to stop me from—'

'When did he approach you? Before or after we... we...had sex?'

'After.'

Zoey wasn't quite ready to believe him even though she found, somewhat to her surprise, that she desperately wanted to. 'But he said you'd had an eye on the company for a couple of months.'

'I'm interested in all of my competitors,' Finn said. 'I've run into your father a few times over the last couple of months and we talked shop, but I did not at any time make him an offer. He came to my office a couple of days after we got back from New York.'

'So...so why did you sleep with me?'

'I slept with you because it was what we both wanted.' His eyes contained a dark glitter that sent a shiver skating down her spine. 'And I would hazard a guess and say you want to do it again.'

Zoey coughed out a disdainful laugh. 'You're freaking unbelievable. Your ego is so big it deserves its own zip code. Its own government.' She jabbed her index finger into his rock-hard chest. 'You disgust me.' Jab. 'I hate you more than anyone I know.' Jab. Jab. 'You played me right from the start.' Jab. Jab. Jab. 'But I won't let you—'

'What?' He grabbed her hand before she could aim another jab at his chest. 'Tempt you into bed again?

You want me just as much as I want you. That night was something out of the ordinary for both of us. That's why you're here now instead of calling me on the phone to tear strips off me. What you want to tear off me is my clothes. You couldn't keep yourself away, could you, babe?'

Zoey tried to pull out of his hold but his grip tightened and a tingling sensation ran down the backs of her legs like a flock of scurrying insects. Not fear, not panic but lust. And how she hated herself for it. 'Let go of me before I slap your arrogant face.'

Finn tugged her closer, his gaze holding hers in a smouldering lock that sent another shiver scuttling down the backs of her legs. 'I'm not averse to a bit of edgy sex now and again but I draw the line at violence.' He placed his other hand in the small of her back, bringing her flush against him, allowing her to feel the potency of his arousal. And she almost melted into a liquid pool of longing right there and then. 'So, how about we make love not war, hmm?'

Zoey watched as his mouth came down, as if in slow motion, but she didn't do anything to resist. She couldn't. She was transfixed by the throbbing energy between their hard-pressed bodies. His body was calling out to hers in a language older than time. The language of lust—full-blooded, primal lust that craved only one outcome.

His lips met hers and something wild and feral was unleashed inside her. She opened her lips to the bold thrust of his tongue, welcoming him in, swept up in the scorching moment of madness, driven by desire so scorching it was threatening to blister her skin inside and out. Her lips clung to his, her free hand grasping the front of his shirt, her lower body on fire. Giant leaping flames of fire raged throughout her pelvis.

Never had she wanted a man like this one. He incited in her the most out of control urges, turning her into someone she didn't recognise. He turned her into a wanton woman who didn't care about anything but assuaging the raging desire overtaking her body. She fed off his mouth, her tongue playing with his in a catch-me-if-you-can caper, then sent another wave of heat through her female flesh. Her inner core flickered with sensations, hungry, pulsing sensations that built to a pulsating crescendo.

Finn released her other hand, winding both his arms around her, one of his hands going to the curve of her bottom, pushing her harder into his erection. 'No one drives me as wild with lust as you. No one.'

'I'm not sleeping with you again,' Zoey said breathlessly against his mouth. *But I want to so much!* Every cell in her body wanted him. Every pounding beat of her heart echoed with the need for more of his touch. Every inch of her flesh was vibrating with longing. Intoxicating, torturous longing.

'Who said anything about sleeping?' His mouth came back down firmly, desperately, drawing from her an even more fervent response.

Zoey placed her hands in his hair, tugging and releasing the thick black strands, relishing the sounds of his guttural groans as he deepened the kiss even further. One of Finn's hands moved up under her top, cupping her bra-clad breast, his thumb rolling over the already tightly budded nipple. Tingling sensations rippled through her flesh, the covering of lace no match for the incendiary heat and fire of his touch.

But somehow through the enveloping fog of desire a tiny beam of reality shone through. She was falling under his spell again, melting like tallow in his arms, and she had to put a stop to it while she still could. If she still could. Her pride depended on it.

Zoey pulled out of his hold and swiped a hand across her mouth as if to remove the taste of him from her lips. 'No. This can't happen. Not again.'

Finn shrugged as if it didn't matter either way and that made her hate him all the more. How dared he not be as affected by their kiss as her? Her whole body was quivering with need. A pounding need that threatened to overrule her self-control. 'Fine. Your call.'

Zoey stepped a couple of paces away, wrapping her arms around her still throbbing body. 'You must be out of your mind to think I would sleep with you again after what you've done.'

'All I've done is buy a company that was in danger of falling over,' Finn said. 'You know it's true, Zoey. Your father isn't capable of running the business any more. He's burnt out and ready to retire and he can do it more than comfortably with the price I paid to buy him out.'

'But *I'm* capable of running it,' she shot back. 'He had no right to sell it to you without even discussing it with me.'

'That's something you'll have to settle with him. But you and I have other business to discuss first.' He gestured to a sitting room off the large foyer. 'Come this way.'

Zoey wanted to refuse but something about his expression told her it would be wise to stay and hear him out. Besides, her job was on the line. She had to know what her options were, if there *were* options available to her. But her mind was reeling so badly with shock, anger and bitter disappointment she couldn't think clearly.

What would happen to her career now? She had pictured a long, productive career at Brackenfield Advertising, hopefully one day taking over as director. Proving to her father—and, yes, even proving to herself—she had the ability, drive and talent to do it.

But it had all been ripped out from under her.

All her plans, her hopes, her dreams and aspirations were hanging in the balance.

Zoey followed Finn down the long, wide hall into a beautifully decorated sitting room off the spacious hall. The polished timber floor was covered by a huge Persian rug that only left about a foot of the floorboards showing around the edges of the room. She stood for a moment, struck by the décor, the luxury carpet threatening to swallow her up to the ankles.

There was a fireplace with a marble mantelpiece above and two luxurious white sofas and a wing chair upholstered in a finely checked fabric for contrast. Various works of art hung on the walls—most of them looked like originals—and the central light above was a crystal chandelier with matching wall lights positioned at various points around the room to provide a more muted lighting effect.

The room overlooked a stunning, completely private back garden with espaliered pear trees along the stone boundary wall. Neatly trimmed, low border hedges ran either side of the flagstone pathway, which led to an outdoor eating area, the light-coloured wrought-iron setting in the French provincial style. No expense had been spared in making the property a showpiece. It was stylish, ultra-luxurious and commodious. The sitting room alone could have swallowed up half of her flat and left room to spare.

It occurred to Zoey that if she didn't keep her job in some form or the other she wouldn't have enough to pay her rent in the long term. Without Ivy and Millie chipping in now they had both moved out, it made for a very tight budget indeed. She would be able to manage for a few months, quite a few months, but what then? How long could she expect to survive? She certainly wasn't going to ask her father for any hand-outs, nor bunk down at his house. She would rather sleep under a sheet of cardboard on the streets.

Finn walked over to a cleverly concealed bar fridge in a cabinet below a wall of bookshelves. 'Would you like a drink?'

Zoey stood at some distance, not trusting herself to be any closer to him. 'A brandy—make it a double. I have a feeling I'm not going to like what you've got to say.'

'Now now, there's no need to be so dramatic,' he chided gently. 'You might be pleasantly surprised in what I have to tell you.' He poured two snifters of brandy into two ball-shaped glasses and then came over to her to hand her one. 'There you go.'

Zoey took the glass but wasn't able to avoid touching his fingers as she did so. The lightning bolt of sensual energy shot up her arm and went straight to a fizzing inferno in her core. Every moment of their scorching night of passion rushed back to her in a flash, as if her skin would never forget the intoxicating intensity of his touch. It was burned, branded into her flesh, and she would never forget it and never become impervious to it. How could the merest brush of his fingers cause such an eruption of longing? She took a large sip of brandy, but it burned her throat, and she began to cough and splutter.

Finn took the glass back from her and patted her on the back. 'Whoa, there. Better take it a little more slowly.'

Zoey shrugged off his hand and glowered at him, her cheeks on fire. 'I want to know what you plan to do with the staff, myself included.'

He idly swirled the contents of his glass, his gaze watching the whirlpool he created in a calm fashion before his gaze fixed back on hers. 'There will, of course, be some trimming—'

'And no doubt I'll be the first to go.'

He held her glare with the same implacable calm, his eyes giving nothing away. 'That will depend.'

Zoey narrowed her eyes to paper-thin slits. 'On what?' Whether she had a fling with him? Was he going to hold her to ransom, offering to keep her on the staff if she gave him access to her body? If so, he had another think coming. And, frankly, so did her body, which was already threatening to betray her and jump at the chance of another night in his arms.

One side of his mouth tilted in a sardonic smile, a knowing glint reflected in his eyes. 'Not on that.'

Zoey suppressed a shiver. 'I don't believe you.'

'I may be a little ruthless at times, but blackmail isn't my style.'

He probably didn't have to resort to blackmail since he only had to crook his little finger and women would flock to him. And Zoey had to be careful she didn't join them, which would have been a whole lot easier if he wasn't so impossibly, irresistibly attractive. She kept her gaze trained on his. 'At the risk of repeating myself, I don't believe you.'

Finn put his brandy glass down, as if he had lost interest in it. He met her gaze with his now inscrutable one. 'I had a call from Leo Frascatelli this afternoon.'

Zoey's heart sank like an anchor. Not just any old anchor—a battleship's anchor. She had lost the contract. Lost it to Finn O'Connell. Oh God, could her circumstances get any more humiliating? He had taken everything from her—her father's business, her career hopes and dreams and the Frascatelli contract. If it wasn't bad enough Finn had bought Brackenfield Advertising out from under her, now she would have to stomach his gloating over winning the account she had hoped would be hers.

She threw him a livid glare, her top lip curling. 'Congratulations. Who did you sleep with to nail that little prize?'

One side of his mouth curved upwards in a half-smile, his dark eyes shining with a mysterious light. 'No one. I was just about to call you about the call from Leo before you showed up on my doorstep in a towering rage.'

'Spare me the brag-fest or I might vomit on your nice cream carpet.'

'It would be no more than Tolstoy has done in the past.'

Zoey frowned. 'Tolstoy?'

As if he had heard his name mentioned, a Russian blue cat with only one eye came strolling into the room, the tinkling of his collar bell overly loud in the silence. The cat completely ignored Finn and came padding over to Zoey, winding around her ankles and bumping its head against her with a mewling sound.

'Zoey, allow me to introduce you to Tolstoy,' Finn said.

Zoey bent down to stroke the cat's head. 'Oh, you darling thing. But you look like you've been in the wars.' Tolstoy purred like a train and bumped his head against her petting hand. 'Aren't you a friendly boy, hey?'

'You have the magic touch, it seems,' Finn said. 'He normally hates strangers. He usually runs away and hides, or worse, attacks them.'

Yes, well, look who was talking about having the magic touch. Zoey was still tingling from head to foot from Finn's heart-stopping kiss. She straightened from petting the cat and met Finn's unreadable gaze. 'How long have you had him?'

'Five months. I found him injured on my way home one night and took him to a vet. They traced the owner via the microchip, but they no longer wanted him. So, I took him in. And paid the eye-watering vet bills.'

'Oh…that was…nice of you.'

Finn's mouth flickered with a wry smile. 'You sound surprised that I can be nice on occasion.'

Zoey elevated her chin. 'I'm sure you can lay on the

charm when you want things to go your way. But just for the record—it won't work with me.'

Finn waved to the sofa nearest her, his lips twitching and his eyes twinkling. 'Take a seat. I haven't finished telling you the good news about the Frascatelli account.'

Zoey sat on the sofa and some of the tension in her body dissipated as the deep feather cushioning dipped to take her weight. Tolstoy jumped up beside her, nudging her hand to get her to continue petting him. She absently stroked the cat, but she fought against the temptation to relax. She was in enemy territory and she had to avoid a repeat of what happened between her and Finn the other night.

Anyway, what good news could there be? She had lost the account to Finn. But why had he found out first and she had not even been told her pitch had been unsuccessful? 'Are you friends with Leonardo Frascatelli?' she asked, eyeing him suspiciously.

Finn sat on the opposite sofa, one arm resting on the arm rest. He hitched one leg over the other, resting his ankle on his bent knee in a relaxed pose. His gaze wandered to the cat she was stroking beside her and a flicker of a wry smile passed across his lips. 'We're casual acquaintances but he is too much of a professional to allow any nepotism to influence his decision. He couldn't decide between your pitch and mine, so he's asked both of us to do it. How do you feel about working with me on the account?'

Zoey stared at him in numb shock, a combination of dread and excitement stirring in her blood. 'You mean we *both* won it?' Her voice came out like a squeak and Tolstoy suddenly started and jumped off the sofa. And, twitching his tail, he stalked out of the room with an air of affronted dignity.

'Yep, and he asked me to run it by you first to see if you're willing to share the contract with me,' Finn said. 'It'll mean working together a fair bit but I'm game if you are.' The enigmatic light in his eyes played havoc with her already on-edge nerves. What would 'working with him' entail?

Zoey moistened her paper-dry lips, her heart kicking against her breastbone at the thought of being in Finn O'Connell's company for extended periods. Could she do it? Could she take on this project—this enormously lucrative project—and come out the other side with her pride intact?

'I—I'm having trouble understanding how this will work. I mean, you now apparently own Brackenfield Advertising. Am I going to be working under the Brackenfield banner or—?'

'The Brackenfield banner will no longer exist.' His tone was brutally blunt. 'I want you to work for me. The Frascatelli account can be your trial period. If all goes well, you can stay on with me. But if you'd like to explore other options, then that's fine too. It's up to you.'

Zoey sprang off the sofa and began to pace the floor in agitation. Brackenfield Advertising would no longer exist? Her job, her future, her career path was now under Finn O'Connell's control. Could there be anything more galling than to be totally under his command and authority? She spun round to face him, her chest pounding with rage. 'I didn't think it was possible to hate someone as much as I hate you. You've taken my future from me. You've stolen my father's company from me and—'

'I paid well above what I should have for your father's business,' Finn said, rising from the sofa with indolent ease. 'It's not been firing at peak performance for months and you damn well know it.'

'I've done my best, but my father wouldn't make me a director, so I was completely hamstrung,' Zoey fired back. 'Plus, I was always covering for him when he missed a deadline or failed to show up at a meeting. But I had it under control. I was bringing in a more or less steady stream of work and—'

'Look, all credit to you for caring about your father, but you're not helping him by covering for him all the time,' Finn said. 'He needs to face his demons and get some help before it's too late. And you're currently in the way of him getting that help.'

On one level, Zoey knew what he said had an element of truth to it. But she hated him too much to give him the satisfaction of telling him so. She thrust her hands on her hips and upped her chin, her eyes throwing sparks of ire at him.

'What would you know about my situation? You with your mouth full of silver spoons and oozing with privilege! You haven't any idea of the struggle it is to keep someone you love from making a complete ass of themselves.'

Something flickered over his face, a quiver of inner conflict at the back of his eyes. 'I know more about that than you probably realise.' His voice contained an odd note she had never heard him use before. A disquieting note, a chord of emotional pain buried so deep inside you could only hear its faint echo ringing in the silence.

Zoey opened her mouth but then closed it again when he turned to pick up his brandy glass from where he had left it. He studied the contents of the glass for a moment, then gave her a sideways glance. 'You speak of my privilege? There are no privileges, no silver spoons, when your parents drink and smoke every penny that comes in the door.'

He gave a grim smile and continued, holding the glass up. 'See this? One drink was never enough for either of my parents. If they had one, they had to have twenty.' He put the glass down with a dull thud. 'And don't get me started on the drugs.'

Zoey swallowed a tight stricture in her throat, ashamed of herself for making assumptions about his background. From what he had said so far, *she* was the one who had grown up with the silver spoons and privilege. 'I'm sorry. I didn't realise things were like that for you...'

Finn turned to put the glass of brandy down again, his expression becoming masked, as if talking about the past was something he found imminently distasteful. 'I'll give you five days to decide what you want to do regarding the Frascatelli project.'

His manner and tone had switched to brisk and businesslike efficiency with such speed, Zoey was a little slow to keep up. She was still musing over his disadvantaged childhood, marvelling at how he had built an advertising empire that was one of the most successful in the world. An empire she was being invited to join…if she could stomach working with him on the Frascatelli project first.

But how could she refuse? It was a project she had dreamed of working on ever since she'd first heard about it. She would have to keep strict boundaries around their working relationship. There could be no repeats of the other night. And her self-control would have to go to boot camp to get back in shape for the months ahead. Finn O'Connell was known to be a demanding boss, but a generous one.

Besides that, she needed a job.

'I'll give my answer now, if you don't mind.'

Finn held her gaze for a long beat, nothing in his expression suggesting he cared either way what her decision was. Zoey drew in a quick breath and released it in a single stream. 'I accept your offer. However, there are some rules I'd like to stipulate first.'

A marble-hard look came into his eyes and the base of her spine tingled. 'Come and see me in my office first thing tomorrow and we'll talk some more. But just to give you the heads up—I'm the one who makes the rules.'

'But I want to talk to you now.'

'Not now.' There was a note of intransigence in his tone and he pushed back his shirt cuff and gave his watch a pointed glance before adding, 'I have to be somewhere soon.'

Zoey gave him an arch look. 'A hot little hook-up waiting for you, is there?'

His unreadable eyes flicked to her mouth for a heart-stopping moment before reconnecting with her gaze. 'Tomorrow, nine a.m. sharp.' He gave a dismissive on-off smile and led the way to the door. 'I'll see you out in case you can't find your way.'

Zoey brushed past him. 'Don't bother. I can find my own way out.' And she marched out of the room, down the hall and out of the front door, giving it a satisfying slam on her exit.

Finn released a long breath and scraped a hand through his hair. He wasn't sure what had led him to reveal to Zoey the shabby little secrets of his parents' life choices. It wasn't something he bandied about to all and sundry. Everyone had a right to a little privacy, and he guarded that aspect of his life with religious zeal. He had spent too many years of his childhood wishing his parents were different. And, as Zoey did with her father, he too had enabled his parents at times in a bid to keep some semblance of normal family life together.

But it had backfired on him time and time again. His parents were addicts and they had only ever fleetingly taken responsibility for their cravings. A week or two here and there, a month, once even three months of being sober, but then they would drift back into their habits and he would be shipped off to relatives again. In the end, he had drawn a line in the sand and told them straight out—get clean or get out of his life. They'd chosen to get out of his life.

Tolstoy peered round the corner of the sitting room, his one-eyed stare wary. Finn bent down and scooped the cat up before it could turn its back on him. 'You're a traitor, do you hear me?' He stroked the soft fur of the cat's head and was rewarded with a rhythmic purr. 'But she is rather irresistible, isn't she?'

The cat nudged his hand and purred some more. Finn gave a crooked smile and continued stroking him. 'I'm glad you've forgiven me but I'm not sure if Zoey's going to.' He set the cat back down on the floor and Tolstoy sat and gave one of those gymnastically complicated leg-in-the-air licks of his nether regions.

Finn had all along considered Zoey's position when it had come to the takeover of her father's company, but he was a man of his word, and since Harry Brackenfield had insisted on secrecy that was what Finn had adhered to. There was a part of him that completely understood her angst and disappointment. Besides, didn't he know all about having your heart set on something only for it to be ripped away? But business was business and he didn't allow emotion to muddy the waters. He wanted to expand his own company and taking the best people from Brackenfield was a sure way to do it.

And Zoey was high on that list.

Finn had cut short his time with Zoey just now, not because he wanted to but because he needed to. There was only so much he was willing to reveal about his background and he was surprised he had revealed as much as he had. He wasn't used to letting people in to the darker aspects of his life. He didn't get close enough to people to share things he wished he could forget. There was no point revisiting the train wreck of his childhood. It never changed anything other than to make him feel even more bitter about his parents' lack of love and care for his well-being.

It was one of the reasons he had ruled out having a family of his own. Not because he didn't think he would do a good job as a father—after all, it wouldn't be too difficult to lift a little higher than the abysmal benchmark his father had set—but because he genuinely didn't want anyone needing him, relying on him, expecting him to be someone he knew he couldn't be. He didn't have the emotional repertoire for such a long-haul commitment. He was too ruthless, too driven, too independent and too self-sufficient.

He enjoyed being a free agent. He had never desired a long-term partner. The thought of developing lasting feelings for someone made him uneasy. Loving someone who didn't or couldn't love you back was too terrifying. He had been there as a child and never wanted to experience that sinking sense of loss again. He found that, within a week or two of being with someone, he began looking for a way out once the thrilling, blood-pumping chase was over. Time to move on to more exciting ventures.

But somehow, with Zoey, Finn sensed a different dynamic going on between them. She excited him in ways no one else had managed to do. Her stubborn prickliness both amused and frustrated him, and her feistiness was the biggest turn-on he had experienced. She was whip-smart and sharp-tongued and sensationally sexy, and he knew working with her was going to be one of the most exciting periods in his life. He didn't normally mix business with pleasure—the pitfalls were well-documented—but this time he was making an exception for an exceptional woman.

And he couldn't wait to start.

CHAPTER SIX

ZOEY ARRIVED AT Finn's office the following morning right on the stroke of nine a.m. She had spent a restless night ruminating over her situation, agonising over whether she was being a fool for agreeing to work with him. It would mean close contact, hours of close contact, and who knew what such proximity would produce? Another firestorm of lust? It must not happen. She must not give in to temptation. She must not be hoodwinked by Finn's charm and allure.

She. Must. Not.

Finn's middle-aged receptionist-cum-secretary smiled as Zoey came through the door. 'Good morning, Ms Brackenfield. Finn will be here shortly—something must have held him up. He's normally bang on time. Can I get you a coffee while you wait?'

Something had held him up, had it? Like a sleepover with one of his avid fans? Zoey painted a polite smile on her face while inside she was seething. No doubt some other foolish young woman had capitulated to his practised charm. No way was Zoey going to fall for it a second time—even if it had been the most spectacular sex of her entire life. 'No, thank you. Erm…please call me Zoey. Sorry, but I didn't catch your name the last time.'

'June,' the older woman said with a smile. 'Congratulations on the Frascatelli account. Finn told me you'll be sharing the contract with him. Are you excited?'

A part of Zoey was far more excited than she had any business being, but not just about the Frascatelli contract. The traitorous part of her that couldn't think of her night of passion with Finn without a frisson going through her body. The wild and reckless part of her that still smouldered and simmered with longing. 'I'm sure it will be an interesting experience,' she said, keeping her expression under tight control.

June's eyes danced. 'I'm sure you'll get on together famously.' She glanced behind Zoey's shoulder to the front entrance and added, 'Ah, here he is now.'

Zoey turned to see Finn striding through the door looking remarkably refreshed and heart-stoppingly handsome as usual. He obviously hadn't spent a sleepless night ruminating over what lay ahead. He had probably bedded some young nubile woman and had bed-wrecking sex while Zoey had spent the evening in a state of sexual frustration. One taste of him and she was addicted. How did it happen?

And how on God's sweet earth was she to control it?

He was wearing a charcoal-grey suit with an open-necked white shirt and looked every inch the suave man about town who didn't have a care in the world. Or did he? His revelation about his less than perfect childhood had totally stunned her. Never would she have envisaged him as the product of disadvantage. He had made such a success of his company, he had wealth beyond most people's wildest dreams and he had no shortage of female attention—hers included.

If only she could turn off this wretched attraction to him. If anything, it was getting worse, not better.

'Morning,' Finn said, encompassing both his receptionist and Zoey with a smile. 'Come this way, Zoey.' He glanced back at June and added, 'Hold my calls, June. And can you reschedule tonight's meeting with Peter Greenbaum? Zoey and I are having dinner instead.'

Dinner? Zoey ground her teeth behind her impassive expression. The arrogance of the man. He hadn't even asked her.

'Will do,' June said, reaching for the phone.

Zoey waited until she was alone with Finn in his office before she took him to task. She gave him an arch look. 'Dinner? Funny, but I don't recall you asking me to dinner.'

'I didn't ask.' He flicked her a glance on his way to his desk. 'But I'm telling you now. Take a seat.'

Zoey stayed exactly where she was. 'I'm not going to be ordered about by you. I have other plans for this evening.'

He shrugged off his jacket and hung it in a slimline cupboard against the wall. Then he came and stood behind his desk with his hands resting on the back of his ergonomic chair, a flinty look in his eyes. 'Cancel them. We have work to do.'

She folded her arms across her middle. 'Work? Are you sure that's what's on the agenda?'

His eyes drifted to her mouth and then back to her eyes, an indolent smile lifting up one side of his mouth. 'Work is on my agenda but who knows what's on yours?'

Zoey wasn't one to blush easily, but she could feel heat pouring into her cheeks. She lifted her chin and glued her gaze to his, determined not to be the first to look away. 'Before we begin working together, I think we need to set some ground rules.'

He rolled back his chair and sat down, leaned back and made a steeple with his fingers in front of his chest, his gaze unwavering on hers. 'I told you last night, I'm the one who makes the rules. You get to follow them.'

Zoey came over to stand in front of his desk and, leaning her hands on it, nailed him with a steely glare. 'Let me get something straight—I will *not* be ordered around by you.'

He slowly rocked his chair from side to side, his fingers still steepled in front of his chest. And, judging from his expression, he was seemingly unmoved by her curt statement. 'If you can't follow simple instructions then you won't have a future working for me once we finish this project.'

Zoey pushed herself away from his desk with an unladylike curse. 'Why do I get the feeling you only bought Brackenfield Advertising to have me under your control?'

He raised one dark eyebrow. 'My, oh my, what a vivid imagination you have.' He released his steepled fingers and leaned forward to rest his forearms on the desk. 'I told you why I bought it. It was about to go under. I was doing your dad a favour. And you too, when it comes to that.'

'I'm surprised you wanted to help him given he's nothing but a rotten drunk like your parents.'

The ensuing silence was so thick and palpable Zoey could feel it pressing on her from all four corners of the room. Nothing showed in Finn's expression that her words had upset him in any way, yet she got the sense that behind the screen of his eyes it was a different story. Shame coursed through her at her uncharitable outburst. She knew nothing of his parents' issues other than the small amount he had told her. And, given her own issues with her father, she understood all too well how heartbreaking it was to see a parent self-destruct, and feeling so useless to do anything to prevent it.

'I—I'm sorry,' Zoey said. 'That was completely uncalled for.'

Finn lifted his forearms off the desk and leaned back in his chair. 'What I told you last night was in confidence. Understood?'

She couldn't hold his gaze and lowered it to stare at the paperweight on his desk. 'Understood.' She bit down into her lower lip, wanting to inflict physical pain on herself for being so unnecessarily cruel.

Finn pushed back his chair and went over to the window overlooking a spectacular view of the Thames and Tower Bridge. He stood with his back to her for a moment or two, his hands thrust into his trouser pockets, the tension in his back and shoulders clearly visible through the fine cotton of his shirt.

He finally released a heavy-sounding breath and turned back to face her, his expression shadowed by the light coming in from the window now behind him.

'I probably don't need to tell you how hard it is to see your parents make a train wreck of their lives.'

'No…you don't.'

He took his hands out of his pockets and sent one through the thickness of his hair, the line of his mouth grim. 'My parents were hippies, flower children who suddenly found themselves the parents of a baby they hadn't planned on having, or at least not at that stage of their lives. They were barely out of their teens and had nothing behind them. So, when it all got too much, they drank or smoked dope to cope.'

He screwed up his mouth into a grimace. 'One of my first memories was trying to wake them both so I could have something to eat and drink. I think I was only three. It took me a long while—ten years, actually—until I realised they were completely unreliable. I gave them a couple of chances to lift their game but of course, they couldn't live without their addictions. So, I finally drew a line in the sand when I was thirteen and gave them a choice. It was no big surprise they chose the drink and drugs.'

Zoey's heart contracted at the neglect he had suffered, and another wave of shame coursed through her for being so mean. How awful for such a small child to witness his care-givers acting so irresponsibly. How frightening it must have been for him to not be sure if he was going to get fed each day. 'I'm so sorry… I can't imagine how tough that must have been for you. To not feel safe with your own parents. To not know if you're even going to be fed and taken care of properly. How on earth did you survive it?'

Finn made a gruff sound in the back of his throat. 'I

was farmed out to distant relatives from time to time. I would go back to my parents when they dried out for a bit and then the cycle would start all over again. By the time I got to my teens, I knew I would have to rely on myself and no one else to make something of my life. I studied hard, got a couple of part-time jobs, won a scholarship to a good school and the rest, as they say, is history.'

Zoey found herself standing in front of him without any clear memory of how she'd got there. But something in her compelled her to touch him, to reach out to him to show that she of all people understood some of what he had experienced. She placed her hand on his strong forearm, her fingers resting against hard male muscles, and a flicker of molten heat travelled in lightning-fast speed to her core.

'Finn...' Her voice got caught on something in her throat and she looked up into his dark brown eyes and tried again. 'I'm so ashamed of how I spoke to you. I admire you for overcoming such impossible odds to be where you are today. It's just amazing that you didn't let such an awful start in life ruin your own potential.'

His hand came down over hers and gave it a light squeeze, his eyes holding hers. 'For years, I did what you do for your father. I filled the gaps for them, compensated for them, made excuses for them. I just wanted a normal family and was prepared to go to extraordinary lengths to get it. But it was magical thinking. Some people aren't capable of changing, no matter how many chances you give them, so why wait around hoping one day they will?'

Zoey glanced at his hand covering hers and a faint

shiver passed through her body. His touch on her body was a flame to bone-dry tinder. She could feel the nerves of her skin responding to him, the tingles, the quivers, the spreading warmth. She brought her gaze back to his to find him looking at her with dark intensity, his eyes moving between hers then dipping to her mouth.

The air seemed suddenly charged with a new energy, a vibrating energy she could feel echoing in the lower region of her body. A pulse, a drumbeat, a blood-driven throb.

She hitched in a breath and went to pull out of his light hold but he placed his other hand on the top of her shoulder, anchoring her gently in place. Anchoring her to him as surely as if she had been nailed to the floor. 'Finn…' Her voice came out in a barely audible whisper, her heart picking up its pace.

Finn's hand moved from her shoulder to cradle one side of her face, his thumb moving like a slow metronome arm across her cheek. Back and forth. Back and forth. A rhythmic, mesmerising beat. 'I'm guessing this is not part of your list of rules?' His voice was low and deep and husky, his eyes dark and glinting.

Zoe moistened her lips, knowing full well it was a tell-tale signal of wanting to be kissed but doing it anyway. Her eyes drifted to his mouth and a wave of heat flooded her being. 'That depends on what you're going to do.'

He tilted her face up so her eyes were in line with his. 'What do you think I'm going to do?'

'Kiss me.'

'Is that a request or a statement?'

Zoey stepped up on tiptoe and planted her hands on his broad chest, her fingers clutching at his shirt. 'It's a command,' she said, just within a hair's breadth of his lips.

Finn brought his mouth down on hers with a smothered groan, his other arm going around her back like an iron band. Her body erupted in a shower of tingles as she came into contact with his rock-hard frame, every cell throbbing with anticipation. His lips moved with increasing urgency against hers, his tongue driving through the seam of her lips with ruthless determination.

Zoey welcomed him in with her own groan of delight, her tongue playing with his in a sexy tango that sent her blood thundering through the network of her veins. The scrape of his rough skin against the smoothness of hers sent a frisson through her body, the erotic flicker of his tongue sending a lightning bolt of lust straight to her core. Molten heat flooded her system. Desire—hot, thick, dark desire—raced through her female flesh and drove every thought out of her mind but the task of satisfying the burning ache of need.

How had she thought one night of passion was ever going to be enough? It wasn't. It couldn't be. She needed him like she needed air. Needed to feel the explosive energy they created together, to make sure she hadn't imagined it the first time. It didn't mean she was having a fling with him, it didn't mean she was like one of his gushing fans—it meant she was a woman with needs who wanted them satisfied by a man who desired her as much as she desired him.

And what fervent desire it was, firing back and forth between their bodies like high-voltage electricity.

Finn walked her backwards to his desk, bending her back over it, ruthlessly scattering pens and sticky-note pads out of the way. He stepped between her legs, his expression alive with intent, and she shuddered in anticipation. 'If this is on your rules list then you'd better say so now before it's too late.'

'It's not… Oh, God, it's not…' Zoey could barely get her voice to work, so caught up was she in the heart-stopping moment. She wrapped her thighs hard around his body, her inner core pulsating with wet, primal need.

He leaned over her, one of his hands anchored to the desk, the other tugging her blouse out of her skirt to access her breast through her balcony bra. There was just enough of the upper curve of her breast outside the cup of lace for his mouth to explore. But soon it wasn't enough for him and he tugged the bra out of the way so his lips and tongue could wreak further havoc on her senses.

Zoey writhed with building pleasure on his desk, a part of her mind drifting above her body to look down on the spine-tingling tableau below. It was like an X-rated fantasy to have Finn feasting on her body in such an unbridled way. But in a way he *was* a fantasy. He wasn't the type of man she could see a future with, even if she was interested in a future with a man. He was too much of a playboy, too much of a charmer, for her to want to be with him any length of time.

But she wanted this. Wanted him with a burning, aching need that was beyond anything she had felt before. It pounded through her body, hammered in her blood, throbbed between her legs.

'I haven't been able to stop thinking about this since

the last time we were together,' he said, kissing his way down her abdomen. 'Tell me to stop if you don't want me to go any further.'

Stop? No way was she letting him stop. Not while her body was quivering with longing, aching with the need to find release. 'Please don't stop…' Her voice was breathless, her spine arching off the desk as his hand drew up her skirt to bunch around her waist. 'Please don't stop or I'll kill you.'

A lazy smile backlit his gaze with a smouldering heat. 'Then, in the interests of occupational health and safety, I'd better do as you command.' He brought his mouth down to her mound, his fingers moving aside her knickers, his warm breath wafting against her sensitised flesh in a teasing breeze. 'So beautiful…' His voice was so low and deep, it sounded as if it came from beneath the floorboards.

His lips moved against her feminine folds, soft little touches that sent her pulse rate soaring. Shivers coursed down her legs and arms, flickers of molten heat deep in her core. He caressed her with his tongue, the slow strokes a form of exquisite torture, ramping up the pressure in her tender tissues until it was impossible to hold back the tumultuous wave. It crashed through her body as if a hurricane were powering it, booming, crashing waves that sent every thought out of her brain short of losing consciousness.

She bit back the urge to cry out, vaguely recalling Finn's receptionist was only a few metres away on the other side of the office door. Zoey was reduced to the pulsing pleasure of her primal body, transported to a place where only bliss could reside. The aftershocks kept coming, gradually subsiding to a gentle rocking through her flesh like the lap of idle waves on the shore.

Finn straightened her clothes into some sort of order, his expression one of glinting triumph. 'That was certainly a great way to start the day.' He held out his hand to help her up off the desk.

Zoey took his hand, her cheeks feeling as if they could cook a round of toast. She slipped down off his desk but grasped the front of his shirt. 'Not so fast, buddy. I haven't finished with you yet.'

Something dark and hot flared in the backs of his eyes. 'Now you've got my attention.'

Zoey pushed him back against the desk, stepping between his legs as he had done with her moments earlier. 'Lie down,' she commanded like a dominatrix, goaded on by the dark, sensual energy throbbing in her body— the same dark, sensual energy she could see reflected in his gaze.

Finn stood with his buttocks pressed against the desk, his hands going to her upper arms. 'You don't have to do this.'

Zoey planted a firm hand on the middle of his chest. 'I said, lie down.'

He gave an indolent smile, his eyes holding hers in a spine-tingling lock. 'Make me.'

Zoey kept her gaze trained on his and reached for his zipper, sliding it down, down, down, watching the flicker of anticipation in his eyes, feeling the shudder that rippled through him against the press of her hand. 'Here's one of my rules. You don't get to pleasure me unless I can return the favour. Got it?'

Finn gave another whole-body shudder, his eyes dark and as lustrous as wet paint. 'Got it.'

'Good.' Zoey pushed him down so his back and shoulders were on the desk, his strongly muscled thighs either side of hers. She freed him from his underwear and bent her head to take him in her mouth, teasing him at first with soft little flicks of her tongue against his engorged flesh. He groaned and muttered a curse, his body quaking as she subjected him to her wildest fantasy.

She stroked her tongue down his turgid length, then circled the head of his erection, round and round and round, until he muttered another curse. Then she took him fully in her mouth, sucking on him deeply, not letting up until he finally capitulated in a powerful release that rattled every object still sitting on his desk. It thrilled her to the core of her being to have him prostrated before her with the same blood-pounding pleasure he had given her.

Zoey stepped back from him with a sultry smile, feeling that at last she had him where she wanted him. Totally under her power. 'You're right. It was a great way to start the day.'

Finn dragged himself off the desk, but it looked as though his legs weren't quite up to the task of standing upright. He sent a hand through his hair, leaving deep grooves, his expression one of slight bewilderment. He gave a slow blink as if recalibrating himself, a mercurial smile lifting the edges of his mouth.

'I think I'm going to enjoy working with you way more than I anticipated.' He reached out his hand and picked up one of hers, bringing it up to his mouth, his eyes still locked on hers. He pressed a light kiss to each of her bent knuckles, the delicate caress sending a shower of shivers cascading down her spine.

The reality of what had just happened between them suddenly hit Zoey with the force of a slap. She pulled her hand out of his before she was tempted to do another round of off-the-charts office sex with him. How could she have let her wild side out to such a degree? The wild side she hadn't even known she possessed. It was like looking at a totally different person—a *femme fatale* who was driven by earthly drives and pleasures.

How long could this go on? She was supposed to be working on a project with him—an important project—not making out with him every chance she got. She didn't want to join the long list of Finn's temporary lovers. The flings who came and went in his life with such startling frequency. She hadn't had a fling in her life—she had only ever been in a couple of committed relationships before her ex. She wasn't even sure she liked the idea of casual sex. Where was the humanity in using someone's body to satiate her own desires? Where was the dignity of behaving like an animal without a theory of mind, only driven by raw, primal urges?

'Speaking of work...' Zoey straightened her clothes in a back-to-business manner before bringing her gaze back to his. 'I—I want to make something perfectly clear. I'm not having a fling with you. What happened here—' she waved her hand in the vague direction of his desk '—can't happen again. It's...it's totally unprofessional. It has to stop. Now.'

'Fine. Your call. But let me know as soon as you change your mind.'

Something about his smiling eyes told her he was

in no doubt of the struggle she was undergoing. The struggle to keep her hands off him, to be the disciplined professional she had trained herself for so long and hard to be. He had undone it with a single kiss, dismantled her armour like a hurricane through a house of cards.

'I won't be changing my mind,' Zoey said, pointedly ignoring his desk, for it seemed to mock her prim-sounding tone. So too did the secret, silent tremors of her body, the intimate muscles still flicking, kicking, tingling with tiny aftershocks. 'I don't want the distraction, for one thing, nor do I want everyone gossiping about me as your latest squeeze. It would be nothing short of humiliating. I'm here to work and that is what I intend to do.'

'We could always keep it a secret,' Finn said, his gaze unwavering on hers as if reading every betraying nuance on her face.

Zoey folded her arms across her body, desperate to restore some much-needed dignity. She had lost so much ground by falling yet again under his potent sensual spell. As tempting as it was to consider a secret liaison with him, what would happen once it was over? For it would all too soon be over—there was nothing more certain than that. Besides, neither of them wanted anything long-term. That part of her life was over. She had drawn a thick black line through it.

Now wasn't the time to erase it. Now was the time to concentrate on her career, to fulfil her ambitions without the distraction of a relationship. And a relationship of any duration with Finn would be one hell of a distraction. 'Secrets have a habit of becoming exposed,' she said.

'Not if we're careful.'

But that was the problem right there—she lost her ability to be careful when she was around Finn O'Connell. He triggered something reckless and dangerous in her and she *had* to control it. 'Thanks, but no.'

Finn gave an indifferent shrug and moved back to his desk. He straightened the objects he had pushed aside earlier with maddening casual ease, as if he made hot, passionate love to women on his desk every day. But then, he probably did, and Zoey had now joined their number. *Urgh.* Why had she allowed herself to be swept away on a tide of passion with a man she hated?

But you don't hate him.

The thought dropped into her head and stunned her for a moment. What did she feel for him apart from unbridled lust? Her hatred had cooled a little, more than a little, and in its place was a growing respect for all he had achieved given his difficult childhood. She even had to admit she actually liked some aspects of his personality. His drive and ambition were similar to her own. He worked hard, played hard and could be hard-nosed about business decisions, but didn't she secretly admire that single-mindedness?

And she couldn't forget about his battle-scarred cat. Finn had a caring side, a side he obviously didn't show to people too easily, but Zoey had seen it and liked what she saw.

But Finn had been late this morning and it niggled at the back of her mind that he could well have come straight from another woman's bed. Could she bear the thought of him delivering passionate, planet-dislodging sex so soon after being with another woman?

It reminded her too much of the humiliation of what her ex had done to her. Rupert had made love to her the very same morning before she'd come home and found him in bed with another woman later in the day. The discovery of them in her own bed had made her sick to her stomach. She couldn't rid her brain of the image of their naked bodies wrapped in each other's arms.

Finn pulled his chair out and indicated for her to sit on the chair opposite his desk, his expression now back in business mode. 'Let's nut out a few preliminary ideas for the Frascatelli project.'

Zoey sat on the chair and smoothed her skirt over her knees. 'Can I ask you something first?'

'Sure. Fire away.'

She ran the tip of her tongue across her lips, her gaze drifting to his mouth almost of its own volition. 'Erm...' She gave herself a mental shake and asked, 'Why were you late this morning?'

One corner of his mouth lifted in a half-smile. 'You can blame Tolstoy. I let him outside for a bit of sunshine in the garden, but he climbed up one of the trees and refused to come down.'

Relief swept through Zoey in a whooshing wave that made her slightly dizzy. He hadn't been with another woman. Yay. But then she thought about poor Tolstoy who didn't look strong enough to hold his own outdoors. 'Oh, did you get him back in?' She had a sudden vision of the poor cat getting run over or beaten up by another cat.

'Yeah, eventually.' His smile turned rueful. 'Next time, I'm getting a dog, they're way more obedient.'

'Why did you call him Tolstoy?'

'Because our relationship is one that oscillates between war and peace. We're currently in a war phase but there are peace negotiations in process.' He gave a grin and added, 'I'm hoping for a truce by this evening.'

Zoey laughed. 'Then I hope you're successful.' She was the first to admit he had a great sense of humour. 'I really liked him. He's quite adorable, notwithstanding his war wounds.'

'He was quite taken by you.' Finn's gaze held hers in a spine-tingling lock. 'His loving behaviour was completely out of character. I've had to stop entertaining at home because I'm worried he'll scratch someone. He only just tolerates my housekeeper because she feeds him fillet steak.'

'That must seriously cramp your style. I mean, not being able to have…erm…guests over.' She glanced at his mouth and wondered who would be the next woman to kiss those sculptured lips. Who would be the next woman to scream with pleasure in his arms?

His gaze dipped to her mouth and one side of his mouth came up in a half-smile. 'I manage.'

There was a moment or two of silence.

Zoey tore her gaze away from his mouth and shifted her weight in the chair. 'So, what's your vision for the project?' There—who said she couldn't be single-minded?

He leaned forward to pick up a gold pen from his desk and then leaned back in his chair, flicking the button on the top of the pen on and off. His gaze held hers in an unmistakably intimate tether that made her blood tick and roar in her veins. 'What are the four principles of advertising a product?'

Zoey disguised a swallow. 'Erm…attraction, interest, desire, action.' Exactly what Finn had done to her. Attracted her, piqued her interest, made her desire him and spurned her into action. Sensual, racy action she still couldn't quite believe she had taken. And—God forgive her for being so weak—action she wanted to take again.

A knowing smile ghosted his mouth, his dark eyes containing a smouldering glint that made her heart skip a beat and something topple over in her stomach. 'Foolproof, right?'

She licked her lips again before she could control the impulse. 'Yes.'

He tossed the pen he was clicking back down on the desk. 'We need to work on those principles but ramp up the heat. Most well-travelled people are familiar with the Frascatelli hotel chain in Europe, but we need to show the brand as never before. Leo, as you know, wants to build his brand here in the UK. We need to aim not just for the wow factor, but to convince people a Frascatelli hotel is the only place to stay. Agreed?'

Zoey nodded. 'Agreed.'

They discussed a few more ideas back and forth and Zoey was pleasantly surprised at how well he listened and took on board her opinions. He didn't interrupt or discount what she had to say but encouraged her to expand her ideas, to take them a little further out of her comfort zone. It was nothing like the brainstorming sessions she conducted with her father. Her father had dismissed her opinions, ridiculed her and belittled her when her ideas hadn't aligned with his. But with Finn it was an exhilarating process and she was disappointed when he brought the meeting to a close. The time had grown powerful wings and flown by.

Finn pushed back his chair to stand. 'Let's go away and each do our thing and we'll toss our ideas together some more over dinner tonight. Okay?'

'Okay.' Zoey rose from her chair and hunted around for her bag. She picked it up off the floor and hung the strap over her left shoulder, adding, 'Did you have somewhere in mind? I'll meet you there.'

'Let's do it at my place. It'll be more private. And Tolstoy will enjoy seeing you again.'

Do it? More private? The *double entendre* made Zoey arch her brows. 'We'll be working, not...not doing anything else.'

'But of course,' he said with an enigmatic smile. 'Your call, right?'

Zoey lifted her chin, determined to resist him no matter how irresistible he was. And on a scale of irresistible he was way up at the top.

And she had better not forget it.

CHAPTER SEVEN

FOR THE REST of the day, Finn found his thoughts drifting to the explosive little interlude with Zoey in his office. He couldn't look at his desk without picturing her there, nor could he get his mind away from the image of her going down on him. His whole body shuddered in remembrance, the pleasure so intense it had shaken him to the foundation of his being. Their mutual lust was heady and addictive, and yet Zoey seemed to want him with one hand but push him away with the other.

It was her decision. He wasn't the sort of man to force himself on a woman if she was feeling a little conflicted. But he suspected she was holding him off because she was frightened of the passion he stirred in her. When it came to that, he was a little frightened himself of the things she triggered in him.

Mixing business and pleasure was something he had always shied away from in the past but in Zoey's case he was prepared to make an exception. He wanted her and he knew damn well she wanted him. He was sure it was only a matter of time before she would be back in his arms. For how long, he couldn't say. His flings were short, brutally short, but he suspected a brief liaison with Zoey was not going to douse the flames of lust she evoked in him any time soon.

Their two explosive encounters had made him even more in lust with her. He wanted her with a ferocity that was all-consuming. She filled his thoughts like an obsession. Her wild sensuality sent a shockwave through his senses, making him thrum with the aftershocks for hours.

Somehow Zoey had done what no other woman had done before—she had taken control of their relationship, dictating when and even if, it would progress.

And the most disturbing thing of all was that he *wanted* it to progress. Wanted it badly. Not for ever, because he wasn't a for ever guy, but he wanted her for now. A fling was all he would offer, but so far, she was holding him at bay on that count. Was that why he was so captivated by her? The thrill of the chase had never been more exciting. The sex was beyond description. The drumming need to have her again was relentless, stirring his senses into a frenzy as soon as he saw her.

Yes, a short fling would be just the thing to get her out of his system. He couldn't allow a woman—even one as beautiful and delightfully entertaining as Zoey Brackenfield—to get under his skin for too long. Commitment of that sort was anathema to him, but then, apparently it was for her too.

Had someone broken her heart? Her father hadn't mentioned anything to him about a boyfriend, but then Harry didn't often talk much about Zoey other than to criticise her. Finn got the feeling Harry was one of those parents who had no idea how to love and value their offspring. And, unfortunately, Finn knew better than most how that felt.

Finn walked out of his office for the day, and June looked up from her desk with a twinkling smile. 'Zoey Brackenfield is rather stunning, isn't she? Those unusual violet eyes, that beautiful mouth, that gorgeous complexion. How on earth do you keep your hands off her?'

He kept his expression bland, but his lower body leapt at the mention of Zoey's physical attributes. Her beautiful mouth had been around him that morning and had just about blown the top of his head off with its wild magic. She had made him punch-drunk with pleasure. Shaken him, rattled him, scrambled him. And he couldn't wait for her to do it again.

'She's not the fling type.'

'And you're not the marrying type.' June gave a little shrug and added with a sigh, 'Pity.'

Finn affected a laugh. 'Well, nor is she, as it turns out.'

June's eyes danced as if they were auditioning for a reality TV dance show. 'Oh, even better.'

'Why's that?'

'Because she's nothing like all the other women who look up to you like you're some sort of rock god. She's seeing the real you, not the idealised you. She's seeing you as an equal, and that makes for a much better relationship in the long term.'

'Ahem.' Finn pointedly cleared his throat. 'Who said anything about a long-term relationship?'

June's smile was undented by his savage frown or curt tone. 'Just putting it out there.'

'I pay you to work for me, not to comment on my private life.'

'And just how satisfying has your private life been over the last few months?'

'Very satisfying.' But not before he had met Zoey. Finn suddenly realised he hadn't felt properly alive before he met her. His day to day, week to week, month to month routine had gradually become so humdrum. He hadn't noticed until Zoey had brought colour, energy and zing to his life. Their occasional meetings at various advertising gigs had been the bright spots in his otherwise routine existence. And just lately she had awakened a dormant part of him, stirring it into living, breathing vitality.

'Zoey Brackenfield is a breath of fresh air,' June said, as if reading his thoughts. 'I think she'll be an asset to the company.' Her smile became enigmatic. 'Who knows how she will shake this place up, hey?'

Who indeed? But, if what had happened between him and Zoey so far was any indication, all he could say was, *Bring it on.*

Zoey dressed with care for her dinner at Finn's house. She spent ages on her hair and make-up, making sure she looked her best. She wasn't game enough to question why she was going to so much trouble—after all, she was supposed to be keeping things strictly business between them.

But every time she thought of him—which was way too often for her liking—her mind filled with images of them in his office making mad, passionate love. Her body remembered every glide of his hands, every stroke

and flicker of his tongue against her most tender and
sensitive flesh. She shivered as she recalled the taste
of him, the feel of him, the velvet and steel power of
him and how he was completely undone by her ca-
resses. Which was only fair, seeing how undone she
had been by his.

She was starting to realise she had seriously mis-
judged Finn in every way possible. She had accused
him of betraying her over the takeover of her father's
company, but a subsequent conversation with her father
had confirmed what Finn had said—her father had approached Finn, not the other way round. There was so
much more to Finn than she had first thought. He had
a depth of character that intrigued her and pleased her.
He wasn't the shallow, self-serving man she had assumed him to be.

Zoey picked up her evening bag and gave herself one
more glance in the full-length mirror. The black dress
wasn't new, but it outlined her curves without revealing
too much cleavage. She had washed and blow-dried her
hair, leaving it loose and wavy around her shoulders.
Her make-up was understated apart from smoky eye-
liner and a vivid slash of red lipstick.

'You'll do,' she said to her reflection. 'But don't get
any funny ideas about tonight. It's a working dinner,
nothing else.'

Finn answered the door to her dressed in camel-co-
loured trousers and a casual white shirt that highlighted
the width of his shoulders. His hair was still damp from
a recent shower and his jaw freshly shaven. 'Wow. You
look good enough to eat,' he said with a glinting smile.

Zoey suppressed a shiver and stepped across the threshold, shooting him a narrow glance on the way past. 'Don't even think about it, O'Connell. I'm here to work, not play.'

'Spoilsport.' Finn grinned and then closed the door behind her. 'Come this way—I'm just putting the finishing touches to our meal.'

Zoey followed him to the well-appointed kitchen at the rear of the house, its bank of windows overlooking the garden. She looked at the various items he was preparing on the large island countertop—fillet steaks marinated in red wine and herbs, a melange of green vegetables, potatoes Dauphinoise, as well as a delectable cheese board with seasonal fruit. 'Impressive. I didn't know you were so domesticated. I thought you'd get your housekeeper to do that for you.'

'She only comes in to clean once a week and to look after Tolstoy when I travel.'

Zoey glanced around the room. 'Where is he?'

'Sulking upstairs.' Finn reached for a couple of wine glasses in a cupboard and then placed them on the countertop. 'I wouldn't let him go outside after this morning's *contretemps*.' He held up a bottle of red wine. 'I have white if you'd prefer.'

'Red is fine, thank you.' Zoey perched on one of the stools next to the island bench.

He poured two glasses of the red wine and handed her one, holding his up to hers in a toast. 'So, to working, not playing, together.' There was a hint of amusement lurking in the background of his dark brown gaze.

Zoey clinked her glass against his, something in her stomach pitching. But would *she* be able to stick to the rules? Her lower body quivered with the memory of his lovemaking, little pulses and flickers that reminded her of the exquisite magic of his touch. And how much she wanted to feel it again. 'Cheers,' she said, her gaze slipping away from the smouldering heat of his.

Finn took a sip of his wine and then placed the glass down as he continued preparing their meal. 'I'm interviewing the key staff at Brackenfield over the next month. I'll offer redundancy packages where it's appropriate, but I plan to do a complete restructure to streamline things to increase efficiency. As a result, some jobs will no longer exist.'

Zoey frowned. 'But some people have been with us for decades. You can't just get rid of them.'

'It's nothing personal, it's a business decision. Increasing profit and mitigating losses have to take priority over everything else.'

'Oh, and I suppose you'll suddenly decide my job no longer exists,' Zoey said, shooting him a glare.

'On the contrary, I'm going to keep you.' He wiped his hands on a tea towel and added, 'June would never speak to me again if I let you go.'

'Could you at least discuss with me first some of the decisions you're making over staff? I know everyone and their skill set and their personal circumstances.'

'Your opinion is likely to be too subjective,' Finn said. 'I don't care what a person's circumstances are— what I care about is whether they are capable of doing their job. I'm running a business, Zoey, not a charity.'

Zoey put her glass of wine down on the counter with a loud thwack. 'Running a business doesn't have to be all about profit. You wouldn't have a business if it weren't for the people you employ. How can you expect to get the best from them if you only see them as cogs in a wheel instead of as human beings? People who have families to feed, difficulties to overcome, mortgages and rent to pay—'

'And I suppose the way you and your father have run Brackenfield Advertising with all that touchy-feely stuff has worked well for you?' His gaze was direct, hard and penetrating.

Zoey couldn't hold his gaze and jumped down from the stool to walk over to the windows and look at the garden lit up with various lights. Anger rumbled through her at his cold-hearted approach to business but, as he said, had her father's way been any better?

Her father had pretended to care about his employees but had exploited them on many occasions, just as he'd exploited her, relying on her to do his work for him, to cover for him, to make excuses for him. She had bent herself out of shape to please him, to keep the company going, yet it had all been for nothing. Just as she had done for Rupert—over-adapting to make things work, when all the time behind her back he was cheating on her.

'I didn't have much to do with running the company,' she said, still with her back to Finn. 'My father refused to make me a director, believing it was a man's job, not a woman's, and especially not a young woman's. He wanted a son, not a daughter, and has spent the last twenty-eight years reminding me of his bitter disappointment.'

She swung round to look at him and added, 'So, maybe if I'd been able to do things my way, we wouldn't have had to sell to you at all.'

Finn let out a long sigh and came over to where she was standing. 'Your father's a fool for not giving you more responsibility. But, even if you had been able to do things your way, it doesn't change the fact that businesses have to produce profit otherwise they go under. And then everyone loses—owners, staff, shareholders, even the community at large.'

Zoey flicked him an irritated glance from beneath partially lowered lashes. Everything he said was true to a point, but how could she stand by and watch long-term staff be dismissed as if they didn't matter? They mattered to her. 'I just think there are ways to conduct a restructure without destroying people's lives, that's all.'

Finn reached for one of her hands and held it between both of his. 'Look at me, Zoey.' His voice was low and had a softer quality in it than she had heard before. She lifted her gaze to his and her pulse rate picked up as his thumb began a gentle stroking over the back of her hand. His touch was electrifying, sending tiny shivers down her spine. 'It's not my goal to destroy people's lives,' he went on. 'My goal is to—'

Zoey pulled roughly out of his hold. 'Make money. Yeah, yeah, yeah. I heard you the first time.' She rubbed at her hand in a pointed manner, shooting him another glare. 'I've put everything into my father's business. I've worked so damn hard, and you come sweeping in and want to change it all. There'll be nothing left to show for all the sacrifices I've made. Brackenfield Advertising will be swallowed up by your company. It will be as if it never existed.'

'I'm not sure what your understanding of a takeover is, but it's not like a merger,' Finn said, frowning. 'And, let me remind you, this was a friendly takeover, not a hostile one. Your father couldn't wait to sign on the line once I named a sum.'

'But you didn't even give me a hint of what was going on.' Zoey banged her fist against her chest for emphasis. 'Why was I kept out of the loop? You had the chance to tell me and yet you didn't.'

He muttered a curse not quite under his breath. 'It seems to me this anger of yours is misdirected. You need to address this with your father, not me. I told him he should involve you, but he wouldn't hear of it.'

Zoey swung away from him, wishing now she hadn't agreed to have dinner with him. 'You don't understand how hard this is for me. I've waited all my life for a chance to prove myself to my father and you've come marching in and taken it all away.'

'Why is it so important for you to prove yourself to him?'

Zoey momentarily closed her eyes in a tight blink, her arms wrapped around the middle of her body. 'Because he's all the family I've got.'

Finn came up behind her and, placing his hands on the tops of her shoulders, gently turned her to face him. His gaze had softened, his expression etched in concern. 'What about your mother?'

Zoey let out a ragged sigh. 'She died when I was four. Horse accident. I was at nursery school when it happened. She never regained consciousness. My father didn't let me see her in hospital or allow me to go to her funeral. He thought it would upset me too much. But it upset me more by not being able to say goodbye to her.'

Finn wrapped his arms around her and brought her

close against his body. He rested his chin on the top of her head, one of his hands gently stroking the back of her head in a comforting manner. 'I'm sorry. That must have been pretty tough on you.'

Zoey leant her cheek against his broad chest, the citrus notes of his aftershave tantalising her nostrils, the steely strength of his arms around her soothing and protective.

'I was lucky that I had nice stepmothers and nannies over the years. Dad remarried several times, I guess in the attempt to have the son he always wanted, not that it ever happened. Only one of his new wives got pregnant but she had a miscarriage and didn't try again, but left him soon after.' She sighed and added, 'I've never been enough for my dad. He wanted a son to pass the business on to and instead got me. And now it's too late.'

'He should be more than happy with you,' Finn said, kissing the top of her head. 'And what's this talk of it being too late?' He eased her away from him to look down at her with a reproving frown. 'You don't need your father to be successful. You can do it on your own. You're talented, Zoey, really talented. You bring a lot of innovation to your projects. They're fresh and original, and I'm sure it won't be long before you get the credit you deserve.'

Zoey basked in the glow of his confidence in her. It was so rare for her to hear praise other than from her close friends and hearing it from Finn, whom she respected and admired professionally, was like breathing in clean air after a lifetime of pollution. 'It's nice of you to say so.'

His brows lifted in a mock-surprised manner. 'Nice? Me?'

Zoey gave a rueful smile. 'You're nice enough to allow me to bore you with all my baggage.'

He lifted her chin with the end of his finger, his eyes dark and unwavering on hers. 'I'm beginning to think it's impossible for you to ever bore me.' His gaze dipped to her mouth and the atmosphere tightened as if all the oxygen particles in the room had disappeared.

Zoey moistened her lips, her eyes going to the sculpted perfection of his mouth. Her lips began to tingle in anticipation, and a soft but insistent beat of desire fluttered like wings deep in her core. 'Oh, I don't think I'm all that exciting...' She touched his lean jaw with her fingers, trailing them down to his lips. 'You, on the other hand...' Her voice dropped down to a whisper.

He captured her hand and held it up to his face, pressing a kiss to the middle of her palm, his eyes still holding hers. 'Is this working or playing?' His tone was gently teasing, his smile doing serious damage to her resolve to resist him.

But how could she resist him? He was a drug she hadn't known she had a penchant for until she kissed him the first time. Now her ardent need of him was a driving force that refused to go away. Every time she was around him, the craving intensified.

Zoey pressed herself a little closer, her lower body coming into intimate contact with his growing erection. 'I don't know why this keeps happening between us. I keep telling myself I won't give in to temptation and then I go ahead and do it.'

'I can tell you why.' He smoothed his hand down

from below her shoulder blades to the small of her back, pressing her harder into his arousal. 'Because we both want each other.'

Zoey let out a shuddery breath, the heat of his body calling out to hers with a fierce, primal energy. 'I don't want a relationship with anyone right now. Maybe not ever.'

He tipped up her chin, locking his gaze back on hers. 'Why?'

She bit down into her lower lip, those horrid images inside her head of her ex with his new lover torturing her all over again. 'My ex cheated on me. It had been happening for months. I came home and found him in our bed with her.' She closed her eyes in a tight blink and then opened them again to add, 'He'd even made love to me that same morning. Told me he loved me and all.'

Finn held her apart from him, his frowning gaze holding hers. 'That is truly despicable. I'm not surprised you're so against getting involved with anyone again.'

Zoey looked at his chin rather than meet his gaze. 'I thought things were fine between us. I mean, we'd been together for years. But, looking back, there were lots of red flags I didn't notice at the time.' Her gaze crept back to his. 'It's only since you and I hooked up that I've realised how boring my sex life with him was. Maybe that's why he strayed. I wasn't exciting enough for him.'

Finn grasped her by the upper arms in a gentle but firm hold. 'Don't go blaming yourself for his shortcomings, Zoey. You're by far the most exciting lover I've ever had. He was the one who chose to cheat rather than discuss any concerns he might have had. You're better off without him.'

'Yes, well, I know that, but I just don't feel ready to date seriously again.'

'The life of having hook-ups isn't always what it's cracked up to be,' Finn said with a rueful grimace. 'It too can get a little boring.'

Zoey arched her eyebrows. 'Don't tell me the hardened playboy is looking for more permanent pastures on which to graze?'

He gave a crooked smile. 'Not a chance.' His hands slipped back down to hold her by the hips. 'But I'm not averse to having the odd extended fling from time to time.'

Zoey began to toy with one of the buttons on his shirt. 'How long do your, erm, extended flings normally last?' She flicked him a glance and added, 'I'm asking for a friend.'

Finn laughed and brought her closer to his body. 'Well, let's see now... I had one that lasted for a month once, but it was a long time ago.'

'Were you in love with her?' The question was out before Zoey could monitor her tongue. Was he capable of loving someone to that degree? Or was love something he avoided out of the fear of being hurt as his parents had hurt him?

'No. I've never experienced that feeling.'

'Would you recognise it if you did?'

'Would you?' His gaze was suddenly too direct, too penetrating, for her to hold.

Zoey looked back at the button she was playing with on his shirt. 'I'm not sure... I really thought I was in love with Rupert, but I can see now that I just cared about him as a person.'

She glanced up at him again. 'My two ex-flatmates have both recently fallen madly in love with their partners. I don't think I felt anything like what they feel for their new fiancés. And I am doubly sure Rupert never, ever looked at me the way my friends' fiancés look at them. As if the world would be an empty place without them in it.'

Finn slid one of his hands up to the nape of her neck, his fingers warm and gentle against her skin. 'Love can be a beautiful thing when it happens.'

She angled her head at him. 'So, you actually believe it can happen?'

His fingers splayed through her hair, sending a shiver down her spine. 'I too have a couple of friends who've been lucky enough to find love with each other.' His lips made a twisted movement. 'But of course, whether it lasts is another question. So many marriages end in divorce.'

'But your parents didn't divorce?'

He made a soft, snorting noise. 'They never tied the knot in the first place. They broke up a couple of times but drifted back together as drinking and drug buddies. Or so I'm told—I haven't seen them since I was thirteen.'

Zoey frowned and reached up to touch his face with her hand. 'I can only imagine how devastated you must have been by them behaving so irresponsibly. Do you know why they became like that? What were their backgrounds like? People who grow up in difficult circumstances often replicate them in their own lives as adults.'

Finn removed his hand from her hair and placed it on the top of her shoulder. His expression became stony, impenetrable. 'I get a little tired of people who excuse their appalling behaviour on their backgrounds. We all have choices in how we behave.'

'I know, but it can be really hard for some people to push past the stuff that happened to them, especially in early childhood,' Zoey said. 'Children's brains can be affected by witnessing violence or experiencing abuse. It can have a lifelong impact.'

Finn stepped away from her as if the conversation was causing him discomfort. He scraped a hand through his hair, his mouth tightly set. 'Look, I know you mean well, but if you're thinking I'll ever have a nice, cosy little reunion with my parents, then you're completely mistaken. I want nothing to do with either of them or the relatives that brought me up.'

Something in Zoey's stomach dropped. 'Why are you so hard on your relatives? Were they…abusive?' She hated even saying the word, wondering if Finn had suffered at the hands of his carers in the most despicable way.

He gave a short, embittered laugh. 'Depends what you mean by abusive. No one ever laid a hand on me, and I was always fed and clothed, but I was left in no doubt of how much of an inconvenience I was to them. I got passed around three or four families over the years. No one wanted to keep me any length of time. They had their own kids, their own tight little family unit, and I didn't belong.'

'Oh, Finn,' Zoey said. 'What about your grandparents? Did either set have—?'

'My father was disowned by his parents for his lifestyle choices. My mother's parents had me for the occasional weekend in the early years but found the task of taking care of a young child too taxing, especially a child born out of wedlock. They were highly religious and were not averse to telling me I was the spawn of the devil. Both of them died within a couple of years of each other and I was farmed out to various great-aunts and great-uncles.' He gave a grim smile and added, 'The only contact I have with any of them is when they ask for money.'

Zoey frowned. 'Do you give it to them?'

He came back to place his hands on her shoulders, his eyes meshing with hers. 'I don't want to talk about my family any more. This is what I'd rather do.' And he brought his mouth down to hers.

CHAPTER EIGHT

FINN WONDERED IF he would ever tire of kissing Zoey's soft and responsive lips. He loved the taste of her, the smell of her skin, the touch of her hands, the way her body pressed against his, as if she wanted to melt into him completely.

But it wasn't just the physical closeness with her that stirred him so deeply. It was the strange sense of camaraderie he felt with her. Both of them were only children who hadn't had things easy and both of them were relentlessly driven to achieve, to prove something to themselves, to leave an indelible mark on the world. He had never felt such affinity with anyone before and it made him wonder if he was getting too close to her. He was allowing her too much access to his locked-down emotional landscape. The barren wasteland of his childhood was normally something even he didn't revisit. But he had allowed Zoey in and it had changed something in their relationship.

Relationship? Was that what this was between them? He didn't do relationships as such. Not the ones that stretched into the future without an end point. He only conducted temporary relationships that didn't go deep enough to engage his emotions. The sort of emotions that made him vulnerable in the way he had been as a child—wanting love, needing it, craving it and yet repeatedly being denied it.

He had taught himself to ignore the human need to be loved. To ignore the need to be connected in such a deep and lasting way to another person. The sort of love that made your bones ache to be with the other person. The sort of love that filled your chest and made it hard to take a breath without feeling its tug. The sort of love that could be snatched away when you needed it the most, leaving you empty, abandoned, vulnerable. And that most awful word of all—lonely.

Finn was not the 'falling in love with your soul mate' type. He had never pictured himself growing old with someone, having a family and doing all the things that long-term couples do. His career was his focus, continuing to build his empire that provided more money than he could spend and gave him more accolades than he could ever have dreamed of receiving.

And yet, with Zoey's mouth beneath his, and her arms around his body, her soft whimpers of pleasure made him wonder if going back to his casual approach to sex was going to be as exciting as it once had been. He was finding it increasingly hard to imagine making love with someone else. Found it hard to imagine how he would desire anyone else with anywhere near the same fervour he had for her. It was as relentless as his drive to succeed, maybe even more so. And that was deeply disturbing.

Zoey lifted her mouth off his to gaze into his eyes. Her cheeks were flushed, her lips swollen from the pressure of his, and he could not think of a moment when she had looked more beautiful. 'I hope the dinner you've been preparing isn't burning to a crisp.'

Finn had completely forgotten about the meal—the only hunger he felt was for her. A rabid hunger then clawed at his very being. He framed her face with his hands and kissed the tip of her nose. 'You have the amazing ability to distract me.'

Her lips curved in a smile. 'Likewise.' But then a tiny frown flickered across her forehead and she added with a slight drop of her gaze, 'I'm not sure what's happening between us...'

Finn knew what *he* wanted to happen—more of what was already happening. The electric energy of being intimate with her, the blood-pumping passion of holding her, the thrill of his senses each time he looked at her. He wanted her like he had wanted no one before. But would the occasional hook-up with her truly satisfy him? For the first time in his life, he wanted to indulge in a longer relationship. Not long-term, but longer than he normally would.

But would Zoey agree to it?

'What do you want to happen between us?' Finn could barely believe he was asking such a loaded question. A dangerous question. He was giving her control over the very thing he *always* controlled—when a relationship started and when it ended.

She ran the tip of her tongue across her lips, her gaze creeping back up to meet his. 'Nothing permanent.'

Nothing permanent. Hearing his own words coming out of her mouth should have delighted him, and would have delighted him if anyone other than her had said it. He was the one who normally set the rules of a relationship, and yet this time Zoey wanted that privilege. And, because he wanted her so badly, he would give it to her without question. 'Okay. So, a fling for as long as we both want it. Does that sound workable?'

Her teeth sank into the fleshy part of her lower lip for a moment. Then her eyes meshed with his with a spark of intractability. 'As long as we both agree to be exclusive. That for me is not negotiable.'

Finn couldn't agree more. He hadn't been too keen on an open relationship—call him old-fashioned, but he wasn't into sharing, especially when it was Zoey, the woman of his sensual dreams and fantasies. The thought of her with anyone else churned his gut, which was surprising to him, because he had never considered himself the jealous type. He had no time for possessive men who thought they owned a woman, but something about Zoey made him want her all to himself.

'It's a deal-breaker for me too. I might be fairly casual with how I conduct my sex life, but I have never played around on a current partner.'

A smile flickered at the edges of her mouth and her arms wound back around his waist. 'I've never had a fling before. I've always been in long-term relationships. Don't you find it ironic that you're the opposite?'

Finn gave a wry grin. 'Believe me, the irony hasn't escaped me.' He brought her closer, hip to hip, pelvis to pelvis, need to need. 'I have an idea. Can you clear your diary for next week?'

'I might be able to, why?'

'I want to be alone with you, somewhere without distractions,' Finn said. 'How does Monte Carlo sound?'

Her eyes lowered from his, her teeth beginning to chew at her lower lip. 'It sounds lovely but...'

He tipped up her chin, so her gaze met his. 'But?'

A flicker of something passed through her gaze. 'It's tempting.'

'That's the whole point.'

She gave a half-smile. 'It sounds wonderful. I haven't been there before, but I've always wanted to go.' But then her smile faded and a frown took up residence on her forehead. 'But what about Tolstoy?'

'I'll get my housekeeper to look after him.' He gave a grimace and added, 'It'll put the peace negotiations back a bit, but hopefully he'll forgive me.'

Zoey made a sad face. 'Poor boy. Cats don't like change and regularly punish their owners when there's a change of routine.'

'Yes, so I'm finding out. You're the only person I've been able to have here since I got him. It will seriously curtail my social life if he doesn't improve his attitude.'

Zoey studied him for a moment. 'If he's turning out to be so much trouble, why haven't you given him to someone else?'

'After all the money I spent on him? No way. He can damn well adjust. I've had to.'

Her lips began to twitch with another smile. 'You love him.'

Finn hadn't really thought about it before, but it suddenly occurred to him that he had developed an attachment to that wretched cat. The thing wasn't even cute and cuddly. It looked more like something out of a horror movie. But he had grown to look forward to seeing Tolstoy at the start and end of each day, even if he wasn't the most congenial housemate. 'Yeah, well, maybe I've developed a mild affection for him.'

Zoey's smile became playful. 'So, the ruthless businessman has a heart after all. Who knew?'

Finn gave her a look. 'Not so big a heart that I would consent to taking him with me to Monte Carlo. I do have my limits. Besides, I want you to myself. My villa is private and secluded, and I often go there when I need to work on a deadline. And, given that Leo Frascatelli has plans for a hotel revamp in Nice, which is only a few minutes' drive away, we can do some on-site research.'

A tiny frown tugged at her forehead. 'But won't having me there be a distraction?'

Finn pressed a kiss to her mouth. 'A shocking one, but I think I can handle it.'

A sparkling light came into her eyes and her arms moved from around his waist to link around his neck. 'You think you can handle me?' Her tone was teasing, her touch electric, and he wished he could clear his diary for a month instead of a week and spend it alone with her. 'You have no idea what you're letting yourself in for, O'Connell.' She pressed her lips against his for a brief moment, making him desperate for more. 'Don't say you weren't warned.'

'Warning heeded,' Finn said and brought his mouth back down on hers.

The following day, Zoey met up with Ivy and Millie for a quick catch-up over a drink after work. She always looked forward to catching up with her friends but, since they had both become so happily engaged, she felt a little on the outer. The irony was, she had once been the marrying type. It was why she had been with Rupert for so long—seven years. Every year that had passed without him presenting her with an engagement ring she had made excuses for him. He was under the pump at work...he wasn't ready for marriage yet...he wanted to pay off some debts first. She had spent years of her life waiting, only to have her loyalty and commitment thrown back in her face.

And now, she was the one who didn't want to settle down.

'Millie told me about your little hook-up in New York with Finn O'Connell,' Ivy said with a smile. 'You do realise I fell in love with Louis after a one-night stand?'

Zoey gave her a droll look. 'I'm not going to fall in love with Finn O'Connell, okay?' She was in lust with him and it was wonderful. She had never felt like this before, so alive and in touch with her body. When he had first suggested the trip, she had been assailed with doubts. Would she be setting herself up for hurt by spending such concentrated time with him? But she reassured herself it was just a fling. She was the one in control and she would stay in control. Five days with him in Monte Carlo would be divine. It was just what she needed right now, a chance to put some of her past disappointments aside and enjoy herself by living in the moment.

Millie leaned forward to pick up one of the nibbles from the plate in front of them. 'How will you stop yourself? I said the same thing about Hunter. When love strikes, it strikes, and you can't do anything to stop it.'

Zoey topped up her wine from the bottle on the table. 'I don't think I've ever been in love, or at least not

like you two are. What I felt for Rupert was… I don't
know… I told him I loved him plenty of times, and he
did me, but…'

'But?' Millie and Ivy spoke together.

Ivy blew out a little breath and twirled the wine
around in her glass. 'I think I might have been in love
with the idea of being in love. Of being important to
someone, you know? Really important to them, not just
someone they lived with who did the bulk of the cooking and cleaning and was available for sex whenever
they wanted it.' She gave the girls a wincing look and
asked, 'Too much information?'

'You've never really talked about your relationship
with Rupert so honestly before,' Ivy said. 'Maybe ac-
knowledging the problems you had with him will help
you to not to repeat the mistakes in a future relationship.'

'That's exactly what I'm doing,' Zoey said. 'I'm
doing what I want for a change. That's why a fling with
Finn O'Connell is perfect for me right now. We want
the same things—a no-strings, no-rings, no-promises-
of-for-ever fling.'

'So, will you bring him to my wedding as your plus-
one?' Ivy asked, looking hopeful.

Zoey gave a short laugh. 'I'm not sure a romantic
wedding would be Finn O'Connell's thing at all. Besides, I don't want to broadcast it too publicly that I'm
having a fling with him.'

Ivy and Millie exchanged speaking looks. Zoey
frowned at them both. 'What?'

'Are you sure a fling is all you want from Finn?' Ivy
asked, with a look of concern. 'Have you really changed
that much to go from having a long-term relationship

history to wanting nothing but flings with people who take your fancy?'

'Of course I've changed,' Zoey said. 'No offence to you two, but I can't see myself settling down with someone any more.' The inevitable hurt, the vulnerability, the crushing disappointment when the person you had committed your life to let you down. Why would she sign up for that? It was better this way, she had way more control.

'I think it's sad that you feel that way,' Ivy said. 'I can't wait to spend the rest of my life with Louis. To think I might have missed out on feeling like this about someone and have him feel the same way about me is too awful to contemplate.'

'But what if Finn wants more?' Millie chimed in.

'Not a chance,' Zoey reassured her and reached for a marinated olive from the plate. 'He's a playboy with no desire to settle down.' She popped the olive in her mouth and chewed and swallowed. 'Look, be happy for me, okay? I'm spending the next five days with him in Monte Carlo. It's kind of a working holiday but there'll be plenty of time for…other stuff.'

Millie and Ivy exchanged *can you believe this?* looks and Zoey rolled her eyes. 'What is it with you two? No one is going to fall in love, okay?'

'We just don't want you to get hurt, Zoey,' Millie said. 'You've been through a lot with Rupert and your dad. The last thing you need is to get your heart broken again.'

'Don't worry, it won't get broken.' Zoey wondered now if it was her pride that had been hurt rather than her heart when it came to her ex.

And, as long as she kept her pride intact during her time with Finn, she would be perfectly safe.

Finn and Zoey flew the next day from London to Nice and then drove the twenty-minute drive to his villa in Monte Carlo in a luxury hire car. Zoey stepped out of the car and gazed at the Belle Époque style three-storey villa, with glossy, black wrought-iron balconies on the two upper levels. She had thought his London home was stunning, but this was on a whole new level.

'Oh, wow, it's lovely…' she said, shading her eyes with her hand from the brilliant sunshine to take in the view over the water in the distance.

Finn placed his hand on the small of her back to guide her forward towards the villa. 'I'm glad you like it.'

'How could anyone not?' She stepped inside the villa and turned a full circle in the marble foyer. A large crystal chandelier hung from the tall ceiling. The floor was beautifully polished parquetry, partially covered with a luxurious Persian rug that picked up the black and white and gold theme of the décor. A large gilt-edged mirror on one wall made the foyer seem even more commodious than it was, and that was saying something, because it was huge. There were works of art on the walls that very much looked like originals and there were fresh flowers in a whimsical arrangement on a black-trimmed marble table in front of the grand, sweeping staircase.

Zoey turned back to face him. 'Oh, Finn, this is truly the most amazing place. How long have you had it?'

'A year or two. It was a little run-down when I bought it, but it's come up well.'

'It certainly has.'

'Why don't you have a look around while I bring in the bags?' Finn said. 'The garden and pool are that way.' He pointed to the right of the grand staircase, where she could see a glimpse of lush green foliage through a window.

Zoey walked through the villa until she came to a set of French doors leading out to the garden and pool area. Finn hadn't been wrong in describing the villa as secluded and private—the pool and garden were completely so. A tall hedge framed two sides of the property, and the twenty-metre pool in the centre overlooked the sparkling azure-blue of the Mediterranean Sea in the distance. The garden beds in front of the tall hedges either side of the pool were a less structured affair with scented gardenias and colourful azaleas. There was an al fresco dining and lounge seating area on one side, and a cleverly concealed changing room and shower and toilet nearby.

Zoey bent down to test the water temperature of the pool just as Finn came out to join her. 'Fancy a swim?' he asked.

She straightened and smiled at him. 'Don't tempt me.'

He came over to her and took her by the hands, his warm, strong fingers curling around hers. 'Look who's talking. Do you know the effort it took for me to keep my hands off you during that flight?'

A frisson coursed through her body at the glinting look in his dark gaze. 'It took an effort on my part too.'

He brought her closer to the hardened ridge of his growing erection, his hands settling on her hips. A shockwave of awareness swept through her body, desire leaping in her core with pulsing, flickering heat. 'Take your clothes off.' His commanding tone sent her pulse rate soaring.

'What, here? What if someone's watching?'

He smiled a devilish smile. 'I'll be the only one watching.'

Zoey shivered in anticipation, for she knew without a single doubt he would more than deliver on the sensual promise glinting in his gaze. 'I've never gone skinny dipping before. In fact, there's quite a few things I haven't done before I met you. You seem to bring out a wild side in me I didn't know I possessed.'

'I happen to like your wild side.' He brought his mouth down to the shell of her ear, gently taking her earlobe between his teeth and giving it a soft bite. A shiver raced down her spine with lightning-fast speed and a wave of longing swept through her. He lifted his head to lock his gaze back on hers and added, 'It turns me on.'

Zoey moved her lower body against the proud ridge of his arousal, her blood thrumming with excitement. 'You turn me on too.' She began to unbutton his shirt, button by button, leaving light little kisses against each section of the muscled chest that she uncovered. 'You taste like salt and sun and something else I've never tasted before.'

He became impatient and tugged his shirt out of his jeans and pulled it over his head, tossing it to one side. 'And do you like it?'

'Love it.' She pressed another kiss to his right pectoral muscle. 'I think I might be addicted to it.' She circled his flat male nipple with the point of her tongue, round and round and round. He made a growling sound deep in his throat and she lifted her head to give him a sultry smile. 'Steady... I'm only just getting started.'

'Yeah, well, so am I.' Finn slid the zipper at the back of her sundress down to just above her bottom. The dress slipped off her shoulders and fell to her feet, leaving her in just balcony bra and lacy knickers. He ran his hands over the curve of her bottom, bringing her back against his hardened flesh, his eyes darkening with unbridled lust.

'I'm not taking the rest off until you take off your jeans and underwear.'

His mouth tilted in a smile and he stepped back to strip them. 'Happy now?'

Zoey drank her fill of his gloriously tanned and toned and aroused body, her insides coiling tightly with lust. 'Getting there...' She stroked her fingers down his turgid length in a lightly teasing manner, and he sucked in a harsh-sounding breath and closed his eyes in a slow blink. She cupped him in her hand and massaged up and down, emboldened by the flickers of pleasure passing across his features.

He made another growling sound and pulled her hand away. He reached around her to unfasten her bra, tossing it in the same direction as the rest of his clothes. He hooked his finger in the side of her knickers, drawing them down until they were around her ankles. She stepped out of them and he ran his hungry gaze over her lingeringly while her body throbbed and ached for his possession. No one had ever made her feel so proud of her body. No one had ever triggered such sensual heat and desire in her flesh. No one had ever made her want them with an ache so powerful. It consumed her totally, it drove out every thought but how to get her needs satisfied. It turned her into a wild and wanton being, driven by primal urges.

Finn cupped her breasts in his hands, moving his thumbs over her already peaking nipples. Her flesh tingled at his touch, tingling sensations coursing through her body in an electric current. She made a soft sound of approval, her breathing increasing as the tingles travelled all the way to her core. He bent his head to caress her breast with his lips and tongue, the exquisite torture making her breathless with excitement. His touch was neither too soft or too hard but perfectly in tune with her body's needs.

It was as if he was reading her flesh, intuitively understanding the subtle differences and needs in each of her erogenous zones. He brought his mouth to her other breast in the same masterful manner and a host of sensations rippled through her. Delicious sensations that made her legs tremble and her heart race.

Finn lifted his mouth from her breast and gazed down at her with smouldering eyes. And, without a word, he scooped her up in his arms and carried her to the sun loungers, laying her down on the largest one, which was the size of a double bed. He came down beside her, one of his hands caressing her abdomen, moving slowly, so torturously slowly, towards the throbbing heat of her mound.

'I love watching how your pupils flare when I touch you like this,' he said in a husky tone. 'You have such expressive eyes. They are such an unusual colour, like winter violets. They're either shooting daggers at me or looking at me like you are now.' He brought his mouth down to the edge of hers and teased her with a barely touching kiss. 'Like you can't wait for me to be inside you.'

'Newsflash,' Zoey said, stroking her hand down the length of his spine, her own body on fire. 'I can't wait. Please, please, please make love to me before I go crazy.'

He tapped a gentle finger on the end of her nose. 'Safety first.' He pushed himself up off the lounger and went to get a condom from his wallet in the back pocket of his jeans. Zoey watched him apply it, her need for him at fever pitch.

He came back and joined her on the lounger, his weight propped on one elbow, his other hand stroking her from the indentation of her waist to the flank of her thigh and back again. 'Now, where was I?'

Zoey pulled his head down so his mouth was just above hers. 'You were here.'

Finn's mouth covered hers at the same time he entered her with a deep, thick thrust that made her shiver from head to foot. The movement of his body in hers was slow at first, then built to a crescendo. Her senses rioted, her feminine flesh gripping him tightly, the exquisite tension in her swollen tissues building and building. She rocked with him, her legs tangled with his, her hands stroking the hard contours of his back and shoulders. And then, as she got closer and closer to the point of no return, she grasped him by the buttocks and arched her spine to receive each driving thrust of his body.

Finn slipped his hand between their bodies, caressing her intimately to push her over the edge of the cliff to paradise. She fell apart with a sobbing, panting cry that rent the air, her body quaking as the pulsating sensations went through her. Her orgasm was powerful, overwhelming, earth-shattering and mind-altering, and it went on and on, faded a little and then resumed with even more force. Finn rode out the second wave of her pleasure with his own release, his deep, urgent thrusts triggering yet another explosive orgasm that left her breathless, panting and wondering how on earth her body was capable of such intense pleasure.

Zoey flung her head back against the sun lounger, her chest still rising and falling, the warmth of the sun on her face and the heat of Finn's body lying over her a blessed weight, anchoring her to the earth. It didn't seem possible to experience such profound pleasure without a price to pay and she suddenly realised what it might be. Her earlier hatred of Finn had faded to a less potent dislike, then somehow it had morphed into a deep respect of him. A growing admiration for the things he had overcome to become the man he was today.

And there was another step she was desperately trying to avoid taking—the step towards love. Not just the friendship or casual love, but the sort of love that sent down deep roots into your very being until you couldn't move or breathe without feeling it. The sort of love that made it impossible to imagine life without that person by your side. The sort of love her friends were experiencing with their partners.

A once in a lifetime love.

The sort of love Zoey had never experienced before… How had she settled for all those years with her ex when she hadn't felt anything like what she was beginning to feel for Finn? The feelings inside her were like the first stumbling steps of a toddler learning to walk. Tentative, uncertain, unstable. But how could she be sure it was actually the real deal—love? What if she was confusing great sex with long-lasting love? It was an easy mistake, and many women made it, becoming swept up in the heady rush of a new relationship when the sex was exciting and fresh and deeply satisfying.

Finn propped himself up on one elbow and used his other hand to cup one side of her face. 'You've gone very quiet.' His gaze held hers in an intimate lock she found hard to hold. 'I hope it's a good quiet, not a bad quiet.'

She lowered her gaze to his mouth and gave a flickering smile. 'It's not often in my life that I become speechless.'

He tipped up her chin to mesh his gaze with hers. 'Same.' His thumb brushed over her lower lip in a slow caress that made her whole mouth tingle. 'You're breathtaking, do you know that?' His voice had a husky edge and his eyes darkened to pitch. 'No one has ever got under my skin quite as much as you.'

'Good to know I'm not the only one who feels like that,' Zoey said, gently caressing his strong jaw. 'But, given this is just a fling, I think we need to be careful we don't start confusing good sex with something else.'

'I'm not confused, but are you?' His tone was playful but there was a faint disturbance at the back of his gaze. A shifting shadow, fleeting, furtive.

Zoey stretched her lips into a confident smile. 'Not so far.'

His eyes moved back and forth between hers as if he was looking for something. 'Better keep it that way, babe. I don't want to hurt you.' There was a roughened edge in his voice. 'That's the last thing I want to do.'

'Ah, but I might be the one who ends up hurting you,' Zoey countered in a teasing tone. 'Have you considered that?'

There was another tiny flicker at the back of his gaze but then his expression became inscrutable. 'I guess I'll have to take my chances.' And he sealed her mouth with his.

CHAPTER NINE

LATER THAT EVENING, Finn brought a bottle of champagne and a cheese and fruit board out to the terrace overlooking the sparkling lights of Monte Carlo and the moonlit sea in the distance. Zoey was leaning against the stone balustrade, her long, dark hair lustrous around her shoulders, her face turned towards the golden orb of the moon. She was wearing a long white shoestring-strap sundress that showcased every delicious curve of her body. He wondered if he would ever get tired of looking at her. His pulse leapt every time he came near her, the memory of their lovemaking stirring his blood anew.

The rattle of the glasses on the tray he was carrying alerted her to his presence and she turned round and smiled, and something in his chest stung like the sudden flick of a rubber band. Maybe it was the moonlight, maybe it was the passionate lovemaking earlier…or maybe it was a warning he needed to rein it in a little.

Her comment earlier about the possibility of her hurting him would have been laughable if anyone else had said it. He never allowed anyone close enough to give them the power to hurt him.

But Zoey was getting close, a little too close for comfort.

She knew him intimately, far more intimately than any other lover. And that intimate physical knowledge had somehow given her the uncanny ability to tempt him into lowering his guard. He had brought her away to spend concentrated time with her because he wanted continuity rather than having one night here and one night there.

Having her to himself, day upon day, night upon night, had deepened his desire for her and also made him appreciate how talented she was and how she hadn't been given a proper chance to shine. He had a plan for her irrespective of the timeframe of their fling—he wanted her on his creative team going forward. He didn't want her to disappear out of his life once their fling was over. Whether she would agree to it was another question, but he would make her an attractive offer, one she would be a fool to refuse.

A part of him was a little disquieted about the lengths to which he was prepared to go in order to keep her. He normally kept his emotions out of business. He hadn't built his empire by being swayed by his feelings but by concentrating on the facts. But the fact was, Zoey was a one in a million person and he didn't want to lose her to someone else. She would be an asset to his business and, since his business was his main priority, he would do anything to keep her. Almost anything.

'Ooh, lovely, a moonlit champagne supper,' Zoey said. 'You really know how to spoil a girl. But then, you've had plenty of practice.'

'Some women are harder to impress than others,' Finn said. 'But worth the effort in the end.'

'And which category am I in?'

'You're in a category of your own.'

Zoey was the first woman he had brought here, and right now he couldn't imagine bringing anyone else. It would seem...odd, tacky...almost clichéd. He knew it was how she saw him. As some well-practised charmer who slept his way through droves of lovers. And there was some uncomfortable truth in her view of him. That was the way he lived his life and he would no doubt go back to that lifestyle once their fling was over.

Finn frowned as he placed the tray on the table and took the champagne out of the ice bucket. The kicker was, what if he didn't want it to be over any time soon? What if Zoey wanted to end it before he did? What if the possibility of her hurting him became a painful, inescapable reality? What if that little elastic band flick in his chest became a thousand flicks? Ten thousand? More?

'Is something wrong?' Zoey asked, catching the tail end of his frown.

Finn gave a crooked smile. 'What could be wrong? I've got the most beautiful woman with me on a perfect night in Monte Carlo.'

Her gaze slipped away from his and her hand left his arm to scoop her hair back behind one shoulder. 'I guess I'm just one of many you've brought here.' She walked back over to the balustrade and stood with her back to him, her slim shoulders going down on a sigh.

Finn put the champagne bottle back in the ice bucket and came over to her. He placed his hands on the tops of her shoulders and turned her to face him. 'You're the first person I've brought here.'

Doubt flickered in her violet gaze. 'I find that hard to believe, given your reputation.'

'It's true, Zoey. I've only just had the renovations done and there hasn't been time to entertain a guest before now.'

'But you'll bring others here once our fling is over.'

Finn removed his hands from her shoulders and frowned. 'Is that a crime?'

'No.' She gave a stiff little smile and added, 'I'll have other lovers too.'

The sting in his chest was not the flick of a rubber band this time but a whip. Finn walked back to open the champagne, a frown pulling at his forehead. He wasn't a card-carrying member of the double standards club, but right now he was having trouble handling the thought of her making love with anyone else. He pulled the cork of the champagne with a loud pop and poured some in each of the glasses, but he had never felt less like drinking it. He brought the glasses over to where she was standing and offered her one.

She took it with another smile and then clinked her glass against his. 'Let's hope my future lovers are as exciting as you.'

Finn put his glass down on the edge of the balustrade without taking a sip. 'For God's sake, Zoey,' he said with a savage frown.

She arched her eyebrows in an imperious manner. 'What? You're being a little touchy, are you not? I'm simply stating a fact. We'll both go back to our normal lives once we end our relationship. In fact, you've done me a favour in breaking my self-imposed man drought. I haven't been with anyone since I broke up with my ex and wondered if I would ever take a lover again. But you've helped me get back in the dating game.'

He scraped a hand through his hair and muttered a curse not quite under his breath. 'Glad to be of service.'

'Why should the mention of my future lovers be an issue for you? You'll probably have dozens after me, hundreds even.'

One thing Finn knew for sure—none of them would be half as exciting as her. 'I'm not sure you'll find the casual dating scene as fulfilling as you think.'

'Does that mean you don't find it so?'

Finn hadn't found it so for months but wasn't going to admit it to anyone. He was barely ready to admit it to himself. Admitting it to himself would mean he would need to change how he lived his life, and he wasn't sure he wanted to explore the possibility of doing that in any great detail. He was used to being alone, apart from brief flings. He was used to being self-sufficient. He was used to having the control to start or end a relationship on his terms. Sharing that control with another person was in the too-hard, too-threatening basket.

Finn took one of her hands and brought it up to his chest. 'I don't want to think about you with anyone else, not while we're having such a good time.' He gave her hand a gentle squeeze. 'You're having a good time, yes?'

Her lips curved in a smile. 'I can't remember when I've enjoyed myself more.'

Finn placed his arms around her and gathered her close, resting his head on the top of her head. 'Nor me.'

* * *

The next few days were some of the most memorable of Zoey's life. They spent considerable time in Nice, looking at the hotel Leo Frascatelli was currently redeveloping. The hotel was situated close to the sweeping arc of the beach and had various restaurants and bars that made the most of the spectacular view. It was in the process of extensive renovations, which were now close to being completed, to coincide with the launch of the advertising campaign.

On another day they toured the ancient fortress town of St Paul de Vence, high up in the hills behind Nice, strolling hand in hand up and down the narrow cobble-stoned alleys, wandering in and out of the galleries and artisan shops. They went to the renowned perfume village of Grasse, where Finn bought her some gorgeous fragrances to take home. They had a leisurely lunch in the resort town of Cannes, famous for its international film festival, and then visited the ancient market place in Antibes, and gazed at the jaw-droppingly expensive yachts moored in the port.

Being in Finn's company every hour of the day, whether they were sightseeing, working or dining or making love, made Zoey realise how dangerously close she was to falling in love with him. He treated her like a princess and yet still managed to make her feel his equal in every way. He was tender and caring, looking at her with such focussed concentration at times, she began to wonder if he was developing a stronger attachment to her than he was prepared to admit.

And, unless she was seriously deluding herself, she had seen that same look on her friends' fiancés' faces.

A look so tender and caring it made her blood sing with joy. Every time she tried to imagine a future without him, a wave of dread swept through her. He was an attentive and considerate and exciting lover and, as much as she had teased him over one day moving on to other lovers, she was beginning to realise it would be near impossible for her to do so without disappointment. Acute, heart-wrenching disappointment. For who could possibly compare to him and his exquisite lovemaking?

But it wasn't just his lovemaking she would miss. She enjoyed listening to his insights into the advertising business. She felt inspired by his work ethic and stamina. And, while he was a hard task master when they were working together on their creative approach to the Frascatelli account, she found herself rising to the challenge, enjoying the repartee and exchange of ideas. He encouraged her to be bold in her vision, bolder than she had ever been, and it freed her to explore and stretch her creativity in a way she had never done before.

But a tiny seed of doubt kept rattling around her brain over her future working for him. Becoming one of his employees was not the same as owning and operating her own business. How could she operate in a business that was no longer hers?

But, then it had never been hers—her father had seen to that.

The takeover would take some weeks to finally settle, in terms of which staff would be let go and which would move across to Finn's company. Could she work with him in the long term once their fling was over? How would it feel to see him every day but not in their

current context? He would go back to his playboy lifestyle and she would have to learn to be indifferent to
him. Indifferent to the many women who came and
went in his life. She would have to pretend it didn't
bother her, pretend he didn't matter to her other than
as an employer.

But he did matter.

He mattered more than she wanted to admit. But it
was beyond foolish to hope she might matter to him too.

On their last night in Monte Carlo, Finn took Zoey to
a restaurant near the Monte Carlo casino and the stunning Hotel de Paris. They were seated at their table with
drinks in front of them, waiting for their meals to arrive. He had been quieter than normal for most of the
day and she hadn't been game enough to ask why. Over
the last few hours, she'd often found him looking into
the distance with a slight frown on his face.

Was he thinking of ending their fling now they'd
had this concentrated time together? His flings were
notoriously short—some only lasted a day or two. What
right did she have to hope he would want her for longer? That he might have come to care for her the same
way she had come to care for him?

Care? What a mild word to use when what she felt
for him was much stronger, much deeper, much more
lasting.

Much more terrifying.

Love was a word she had never thought to use when
it came to Finn O'Connell. But now it was the only
word she could use to describe how she felt about him.
It wasn't a simple, friendship love, although she did

consider him more of a friend now than an enemy. It was an all-consuming love that had sprouted and blossomed over the last few days, maybe even before that. The first time they made love had triggered a change in her attitude towards him, and not just because of the explosively passionate sex. The union of their bodies had triggered a union of their minds, their interests, their talents and even their disappointments about some aspects of their childhoods. Zoey had sensed an emotional camaraderie with him she had not felt with anyone else.

Was it silly of her to hope he felt the same way? That he would want to continue their fling…maybe even call it a relationship rather than a fling and one day allow it to become permanent?

How had she fooled herself that she never wanted to settle down? She wasn't cut out for the single-and-loving-it club. She longed for deep and lasting love, a love that could help overcome the trials and tribulations of life. A love that was a true partnership, a commitment of two equals working together to build a happy and productive life. A family life where children were welcomed, loved, supported and encouraged to grow and be all they could and wanted to be. Zoey had denied those longings until she'd met Finn, but now those deep yearnings were not to be so easily ignored.

Finn reached for her hand across the table, his fingers warm around hers. The candle on the table reflected light back into his dark brown eyes and cast parts of his face in shadow, as though he were a Gothic hero. How could she have thought she wouldn't fall in love with him? How could she have thought she would be immune to his charismatic presence, his admirable qualities, his earth-shattering lovemaking? He was everything she wanted in a life partner but had never thought to find. It wasn't enough to have him as a temporary lover. How could she ever have thought a fling with him would quell the need he evoked in her?

Zoey looked down at their joined hands, his touch so familiar and yet still as electrifying. She glanced up to meet his gaze and found him looking at her with unusual intensity.

'There's something I want to run by you.' His voice was low-pitched and husky.

Zoey disguised a swallow, her heart giving a tiny leap in her chest. Could her nascent hopes be realised after all? Did he want to extend their fling, to make it a little more permanent? 'Yes?'

There was a moment or two of silence. His gaze slowly roved over her face, as if he were memorising her features one by one. His thumb began to stroke the fleshy part of her thumb and a shiver coursed down her spine. His gaze finally steadied on hers. Dark... enigmatically dark. 'How do you feel about becoming my partner?'

His partner? Zoey blinked, as if too bright a light had shone in her eyes. Her heart jumped. Her stomach flip-flopped. Her pulse tripped and began to sprint. 'Y-your partner?' Her voice stumbled over the word, her thoughts flying every which way like a flock of startled birds.

Surely he didn't mean...? Was he proposing to her? No, surely not? He would be more direct if he was proposing marriage, wouldn't he? Should she ask? No, definitely not. Her heart began to thump so loudly she could hear its echo in her ears, feel its punch against her rib-cage. 'I—I don't quite understand...'

'My business partner.' His mouth slanted in a smile. 'I don't just want you to come and work for me, I want you to work with me—alongside me. These last few days have shown how we work brilliantly together and how we balance each other so well. I know we'll make a great creative team.'

A great creative team... He was offering her a stake in his business, not in his personal life. Her heart sank. He was talking business, but she was hoping for happy-ever-after. How could she have thought it would be any-thing else? Zoey pulled her hand out of his before he felt it trembling against his. Her whole body was be-ginning to tremble, not with excitement but an inexpli-cable pang of disappointment. She gave herself a hard mental slap. How could she have thought he was going to propose *marriage* to her? He wasn't the marrying type. She had fooled herself into thinking those tender looks he'd been giving her meant something more. How could she have been such an idiot?

He was offering her a dream—a different dream.

A dream career, working with him in one of the most successful agencies in the world.

A business partnership.

Not the dream partnership she most wanted—a life-long partnership of love and commitment.

'Wow... I'll have to think about it for a day or two...' Zoey gave a fractured laugh and added, 'For a moment there, I thought you were proposing something else.'

There was a thick beat of silence.

'I hope you weren't unduly disappointed?' His gaze was marksman-steady, but the rest of his expression was inscrutable.

Zoey picked up her wine glass to do something with her hands. She kept her features under strict control. No way would she show him how disappointed she was. She had way too much pride for that. He had always been upfront about his level of commitment. She was the one who had gone off-script and begun wishing for the moon and the stars and the rarest of comets too. She was the one who had deluded herself into thinking they had a future together. Finn had never promised a future, only a fling. 'Why would I be disappointed?'

'Why indeed?'

She took a generous sip of wine and kept the glass in her hands, watching one of her fingers smoothing away the condensation marks on the side. 'You seem to have come to this decision rather quickly.' She glanced at him again. 'I mean, there must be other people you've considered letting into the business before now?'

'No one quite like you.'

Zoey looked at the contents of her glass again. 'I'm hugely flattered. More than a little gobsmacked, actually.' She gave another cracked laugh. 'I've been working alongside my father for ten years and he never once offered me a directorship. I've only been sleeping with you for just over a week and you're offering me a dream proposition.'

'This has nothing to do with us sleeping together.' His tone was adamant, his expression flickering with sudden tension.

Zoey raised her eyebrows and forced herself to hold his gaze. 'Doesn't it?'

Finn sat back in his chair and picked up his wine glass. 'This is strictly a business decision. You're extremely talented and haven't yet had that talent properly tapped. You will bring to the company new energy and innovation. I have a good creative team but with you on board it will be brilliant.' He took a sip of wine and put his glass back down, his eyes holding hers and added, 'Besides, I don't want to lose you to someone else.'

He didn't want to lose her. If only he meant those words the way she wanted him to. Zoey ran the tip of her tongue over her dry lips. 'It's certainly a wonderful opportunity. But will my name be on the company letterhead or just yours?'

'Come on, Zoey, you know about branding better than most,' he said with a frown. 'I've spent years building my company's name and reputation. I'm not going to change it now. The deal I'm offering you is generous enough without that.' He named a sum that sent her eyebrows up again. 'How does that sound?'

'It sounds almost impossible to resist.' Just like he was, which was why she needed more time before she signed on the dotted line. 'But I'd still like a day or two to think it over.'

'Fine. But don't take too long. I want to get things on the move as quickly as possible.'

'I understand, but a lot has happened in a short time,' Zoey said. 'The takeover, us getting involved, now this. It's a lot for me to process.'

Finn reached for her hand again. 'Your father was a fool not to allow you more control in his company. If he had given you more creative freedom, then he wouldn't have felt the need to sell to me.'

'It would have been nice if I'd been involved in the process.'

'I'm involving you now.'

Zoey couldn't hold his gaze and stared at her wine instead. 'What if he doesn't stop drinking even though he's no longer running the company?'

Finn placed his hand over hers. 'Look at me.'

She lifted her gaze with a sigh. 'I can't help worrying about him.'

He stroked the back of her hand with his thumb. 'He's not your responsibility. If he doesn't choose to get the help he clearly needs, then it won't be your fault. You have to step back and let him face the consequences of his choices. There's no other way.'

Zoey knew he was right, but the knowing and the doing were as far apart as two sides of a giant chasm. 'He's the only link I have left to my mother. The only person I can ask about her to keep my fading memories of her alive.'

'Tell me about her. What was she like?' His tone was gentle, his gaze equally so.

Zoey gave a wistful smile. 'She was funny and a bit wild at times.'

'Now, why doesn't that surprise me?' His tone was dry.

She smothered a soft laugh and continued, 'She loved to cook, and she made Christmas and birthdays so special.' Her smile faded, her shoulders dropping down on a sigh. 'I missed her so much. I still miss her. She left a hole in my life that nothing and no one can ever fill. I don't think I've ever felt as loved by anyone else.'

'Not even by your father?'

Zoey rolled her eyes. 'No.'

'What about before your mum died? Did you feel loved by him then?'

Zoey thought about it before answering, casting her mind back to the early years before tragedy had so cruelly struck. 'It's funny you should ask that… I've never really thought about this before, but he was a lot warmer to me back then. He wasn't as physically demonstrative as my mum was, but I don't remember feeling like he didn't love me. I'm a bit like him in that I'm not comfortable with showing physical affection.'

'You could have fooled me.'

Zoey could feel her cheeks warming. 'Yes, well, I did tell you, you have a very strange effect on me.'

'Likewise.' His eyes glinted.

She looked down at their joined hands and returned the caress by stroking the strong, corded tendons on the back of his hand. A shiver passed over her at the thought of the pleasure his hands gave her, the pleasure that thrummed in her flesh even now like a plucked cello string.

Why had she thought she could keep her emotions out of a fling with him? Her emotions had been engaged right from the start. 'Losing my mother changed everything between my father and me. It was like the bottom fell out of our world that day. I know it certainly fell out of mine.' She glanced up at him and gave a twisted smile. 'I still see my stepmothers. I haven't told my father, though. He doesn't part with his exes on good terms. But they were each good to me in their own way and I missed having them around—especially the last one, Linda. She's a lot like my mother, actually.'

'Maybe your father was worried about losing you too,' Finn said. 'It can happen after a sudden loss. People become terrified it might happen to someone else they love, so they tone down how they feel to protect themselves.'

Zoey wondered if Finn had done the same after his parents had chosen their drinking and drugs lifestyle over him. 'You could be right, I suppose, but I'm not riding my hopes on it. I'm twenty-eight years old. I don't need to hear my father say he loves me every day.'

'But it would be nice if he showed it in some way.' Finn's hand squeezed hers, his gaze holding hers in an intimate tether that made something warm flow down her spine.

'Yes...'

Finn released her hand and signalled to the waiter for the bill. 'We'd better have an early night. We have a lot of work to do when we get home to London.'

Later that night, Finn reached for Zoey in the dark, drawing her close to his side. He breathed in the scent of her hair, his blood stirring as she nestled into him with a sigh. Their lovemaking earlier had been as passionate as always, but something had changed—or maybe he had changed. It hadn't felt as basic as smoking-hot sex between two consenting adults but a mutual worship of each other's bodies. He began to wonder if he would find anyone else who so perfectly suited him in bed. Their lovemaking got better and better, the pleasure, the intensity, the depth of feeling—all of it made him realise how shallow and how solely body-based his other encounters had been.

Zoey was not just a convenient body to have sex with—not merely yet another consenting adult to have a good time with then say goodbye to and never think of again. He wondered if there would be a time when he wouldn't think of her. She filled his thoughts to the exclusion of everything else.

Finn had never been much of a fan of sleepovers in the past. The morning-after routine got a little tiresome, the attraction of the night before fading to the point where he often couldn't wait to get away. But with Zoey it was completely different. He enjoyed waking up beside her each day, enjoyed the feel of her body against him, enjoyed seeing her sleepy smile and feeling her arms go round him.

But he was surprised she hadn't jumped at his offer of a business relationship last night over dinner. Surprised and disappointed she hadn't been as enthusiastic as he'd hoped. It was a big step for him to take and one he had never taken before. He had run his company singlehandedly from the get-go and had resisted bringing anyone else on board. But he knew Zoey's gifts and talents would be an asset to him and he couldn't allow her to take them elsewhere. He was impatient for her answer so he could get things in motion. There were legal things to see to, paperwork to draw up, contracts to sign—all of it would take time. He had pushed their flight back a couple of hours, determined to get her answer before they went home to London.

Zoey snuggled against him and opened one sleepy eye. 'Is it time to get up yet?'

'Not yet. I delayed our flights a couple of hours.'

She rolled onto her tummy, her slim legs entwined with his. She traced a slow circle around his mouth, making his lips tingle. 'Oh? Why? So we can loll about in bed all morning?'

Finn captured her hand and held it against his chest. 'I want your answer. Today. Before we fly back to London.' He didn't want to waste any more time. He had to know one way or the other.

Her hand fell away from his face and her expression clouded. 'I told you I need to think about it. There's a lot to consider.' She moved away from him and, throwing back the doona, got off the bed, wrapping herself in her satin bathrobe and tying the waist ties.

'Like what?' Finn frowned, rising from the bed as well. He picked up his trousers and stepped into them. 'I'm offering you an amazing opportunity. What's taking you so long to decide?'

Zoey turned away. 'I don't want to talk about it now. Stop pressuring me.'

Finn came up behind her and took her by the shoulders and turned her to face him. 'But I want to talk about it now.'

Her chin came up and a stubborn light shone in her eyes. 'Okay, we'll talk, but you might not want to hear what I have to say.'

'Try me.' He removed his hands from her shoulders, locking his gaze on hers.

She drew in a deep breath and let it out in a steady stream. 'What you're offering me is an extremely generous offer. Hugely generous. But it's not enough. I want more. Much more.'

Finn choked back an incredulous laugh. 'Not enough? Then I'll double it.'

Her gaze continued to hold his with unnerving intensity. 'I'm not talking about the money, Finn.'

He looked at her blankly for a moment. If it wasn't about money, then what was it about? 'Since when is a business deal not about money?'

'I don't just want to be your partner in business.'

A prickly sensation crawled across his scalp. 'Then what do you want?'

Twin pools of colour formed in her cheeks, but her eyes lost none of their unwavering focus. 'I want to be someone important to you.'

'You *are* important to me,' Finn said. 'I've offered you a deal that would be the envy of most people in our field.'

'But why did you offer it to me?'

'I told you before—I don't want to lose you.' He scraped a hand through his hair and added, 'You'll be a valuable asset to me.'

A hard look came into her eyes. 'And what happens once our fling is over? Will I still be an asset to you then?'

'Of course. Our involvement ending doesn't change that. Why should it? This is purely a business decision.'

She gave a hollow laugh, her expression cynical. 'You still don't get it, do you? You talk about your business decisions, but you won't talk about your feelings.'

'Okay, I'll talk about my feelings,' Finn said. 'I feel insulted you aren't jumping at the chance to come on board with me. You complain about spending years pushed to the sidelines by your father, with your talent withering on the vine, and here I am offering you a deal to die for and you're deliberating.'

Zoey walked a little further away, her arms going across her body. 'I don't think I can work with you once our fling is over. It will be too…awkward.'

'Why? We're both mature adults, Zoey. We're not teenagers who can't regulate their emotions.'

She flicked him a glance over her shoulder. 'I think it's best if we end it now before it gets any more complicated.'

Finn stared at her for a speechless moment. End it? Now? The prickly sensation on his scalp moved down the length of his spine and down the backs of his legs. He wanted to move towards her but couldn't get his legs to work. He wanted to insist she change her mind, to beg her to reconsider…but then he realised he would be demeaning himself in pleading with her to stay with him.

His days of begging and pleading with anyone were well and truly over.

'Okay, we'll end it if that's what you want,' Finn said, trying not to think about what that would look like, how it would feel to see her and not be involved with her. 'But the directorship offer is still on the table.'

Zoey turned to face him, her expression difficult to read. 'I can't accept it, Finn. I can't work with you.'

He frowned so hard his forehead hurt. 'You work brilliantly with me. Hasn't the last few days shown you that? We make a great team, Zoey, you know we do. Why would you walk away from that?'

'I'll call Leo Frascatelli and tell him I'm handing the

account over to you,' Zoey said. 'I'll find another job somewhere and—'

'Do you want me to beg? Is that what you want?' Finn said through tight lips. Never had he felt so out of balance. So out of kilter. So desperate, and yet so desperate not to show it. Emotions he didn't know he possessed reared up inside him, clamouring for an outlet. Hurt, grief, despair…loneliness at the thought of losing her. Of not seeing her every day, of not making love to her.

'No, Finn, what I want is for you to feel about me the way I feel about you.'

Finn approached her and, unpeeling her arms from around her body, took her hands in his. He searched her face for a moment, his thoughts in a tangled knot. 'Are you saying you…?' He didn't want to say the word because he couldn't say it back. He had never told anyone he loved them, not since he was a child. And look how his love had been rewarded back then—with abandonment. Brutal abandonment. Loving someone to that degree gave them the power to hurt you, to leave you, to destroy you.

'I used to think I hated you,' Zoey said. 'But, after getting to know you more, I realised I was actually quite similar to you in some ways. That's why I was so confident I could have a fling with you without involving my feelings—but I was wrong, so very wrong.'

'Zoey…' He took an unsteady breath. 'Look, you know I care about you. I enjoy being with you. But I'm not willing to commit to anything more. We agreed on the terms—a fling for as long as we both wanted it.'

'But I don't want it now.' She pulled out of his hold

and stepped back. 'There's no point continuing a relationship that isn't working for me.'

'How is it not working?' Finn asked. 'We've just spent five wonderful days together and you say it's not working?'

'I'm not talking about the sex. It's been perfect in every way, but one day that will come to an end, because that's how your casual flings work. You don't commit in the long-term, you don't want it to be for ever. But casual and uncommitted isn't enough for me any more. I can't be with you knowing you'll end it when someone else catches your attention.'

No one had captured Finn's attention like Zoey. No one. And he wondered if they ever would. But she was asking too much. Long-term commitment wasn't in his skill set. He no longer had the commitment gene. He had erased it from his system. He didn't want to feel so deeply about someone that he would promise to spend the rest of his days with them, always wondering if they would walk away without a backward glance. He strode away a couple of steps, his hand rubbing at the corded tension in the back of his neck.

'What did you think I was proposing last night over dinner?' He gave a bark of cynical laughter. 'Marriage?'

Zoey let out a long sigh. 'You know, I did for a moment think you were considering something a little longer term between us. You've been so wonderful to me over the last few days, so attentive and, yes, loving, even if you don't want to call it by that name. I wondered if you were falling in love with me, rather than just being in lust with me.'

'Marriage was never and will never be on the table.'

'Which is why we have to end this now. I want for ever, Finn. Is it unreasonable to want someone to love me for a lifetime? I want a man to commit solely to me. To love me and treasure me, not just as a sexual partner but as a life partner. I want a partner in life, not just a partner in bed or in business.'

'The latter two are the only ones I can offer. Take it or leave it.'

Zoey hugged her arms around her body. 'You told me a while back when we were talking about my dad it was pointless to expect someone to change if they weren't capable of it. So, I'm going to take your advice—I'm not going to waste any more of my life hoping you'll change because I'll get even more hurt in the end.'

How like her to throw his own words back at him, Finn thought. Words he had lived by for years and which he'd found perfectly reasonable. But now they contained an irony that cut to the quick. Stinging him in a way he never expected to be stung. He was losing her on both counts—she wanted to end their fling and she was rejecting his business proposal.

It was a novel experience for him, being on the other end of a break-up. The one who was left, not the one who was doing the leaving. That hadn't happened since he'd been a kid. But he refused to show her how much it affected him, how much it disappointed and riled him to have the tables turned. 'If you want to end our involvement, then end it. But you're making a big mistake in walking away from the chance to be in business with me. I won't be offering it again if you suddenly change your mind.'

The determined light came back into her eyes. 'I

won't change my mind.' She turned and began to gather her things together.

'What are you doing?'

'I'm packing. I'll make my own way back to London.'

'Don't be ridiculous, Zoey,' Finn said. 'There's no need for such histrionics. I've booked our flight for eleven a.m. You don't need to rush off now.'

She folded an article of clothing and held it against her stomach. 'I think it's best we make a clean break of things, starting now.'

He wanted to stop her. To convince her to rethink her decision, to have just a few more hours with her before they went their separate ways. But the words were stuck in the back of his throat, blocked behind a wall of pride. 'Have it your way, then.' Finn shrugged himself into a shirt and shoved his feet into his shoes and made his way to the door.

'Aren't you going to say goodbye?' Zoey asked.

Finn gave her a cutting look. 'I just did.' And he walked out and closed the door behind him with a resounding click.

Zoey bit down on her lower lip until she thought it would bleed. How could she have thought it would be any different between them? Finn was never going to change, just like her ex had refused to change. And she would be a fool to live in hope Finn would one day develop feelings for her. How many years would she have to wait? One? Two? Seven? Ten?

It was better this way, better for her to make a new start, to put her lost hopes and dreams behind her and forge her own way forward.

Finn was angry at her for not accepting his offer but that came out of his arrogance in believing she couldn't resist any terms he presented her. She could resist. She had to resist, otherwise she would be reverting to old habits. Her old self had toed the line, adapted, lived in hope but been too afraid to embrace her own agency. Too afraid to voice her needs and instead had kept them locked inside.

But Zoey was no longer that person. She had morphed into a person who took charge of her own destiny, who openly stated her needs and was prepared to live with the consequences if they failed to be met. She would no longer stay with a man in the hope of happy-ever-after. And certainly not a man like Finn who didn't even believe in the concept of a once-in-a-lifetime love.

Zoey packed and was out the door and in a taxi within half an hour. It was no surprise Finn didn't return to the villa and try and beg her to change her mind, but she was heartbroken all the same. All her life she had yearned to be loved, to be treasured and valued, and now she had been denied it yet again. By the one man with whom she thought she could be truly happy.

'You were right,' Zoey said to Ivy and Millie a few days later when they caught up for coffee. 'I fell in love with Finn.'

Ivy and Millie leaned forward in their chairs. 'And?' They spoke in unison, hopeful expressions on their faces.

Zoey shook her head and sighed. 'And nothing. I broke things off.'

'Oh, hon, I'm so sorry,' Ivy said. 'What happened?'

'He doesn't feel the same way and I was too stupid to realise it. I thought he was about to propose to me over dinner on our last night in Monte Carlo but he was only offering me a business deal.'

Millie's eyes rounded. 'A business deal? Oh, Zoey, I really feel for you. Under different circumstances that would have been so good. I don't suppose you accepted?'

Zoey screwed up her face. 'I can't possibly work with him now. Can you imagine how hard it would be to see him every day? To hear other staff talking about his latest squeeze in the tea room?' She picked up her latte from the table in front of them. 'I'm looking for a job elsewhere.'

'But what about the account you were working on with him?' Millie asked. 'The Frasca whatsit?'

'Frascatelli,' Zoey said. 'I forfeited it to Finn.'

'I know how upsetting it is to be in your position—we both do, don't we, Millie? But was that wise?' Ivy asked. 'You wanted that project so badly.'

'Maybe not wise, but necessary,' Zoey said with another sigh. 'I never thought I'd fall for anyone the way I've fallen for Finn. He's the only man I could ever imagine spending the rest of my life with but he's dead set against commitment.'

'But he committed to you during your fling, didn't he?' Millie asked. 'I mean, it was exclusive between you, wasn't it?'

'Yes, I insisted on that,' Zoey said. 'And, what's more, I trusted him implicitly.'

'Well, it shows he can commit,' Ivy put in. 'But

maybe he needs more time to realise what he feels for you. You've had a bit of a whirlwind affair. Maybe he hasn't yet come to terms with how he feels. Commitment-shy men can be a bit slow to realise how they feel.'

But how long would she have to wait? Years, as she'd waited for her father to change? She was done with waiting, wishing and hoping for change. 'Finn treated me with the utmost respect and consideration. I know this sounds strange, but I *felt* like he was growing to love me, you know? That's why I thought he was going to pop the question. God, I feel like such an idiot now.' She groaned. 'How can a man make love to you so beautifully and not care about you in some way?'

'I wish I could say it will all work out in the end like it did for Millie and I,' Ivy said. 'But that's probably not all that helpful to you now, while you're hurting so much.'

'Has he contacted you since you came back from Monte Carlo?' Millie asked.

'A text message to inform me of the meetings he's having with the Brackenfield staff,' Zoey said. 'No doubt he's going to fire half of them and not feel even a twinge of conscience about it.'

'The deal Finn offered you,' Millie said. 'Surely he wouldn't have offered it to you unless he didn't think you'd be an asset to the company? It's a huge compliment to you. I just wonder if you're being a bit hasty in rejecting it out of hand.'

'But he only wants me to be an invisible director,' Zoey said. 'My name won't be on the letterhead—he told me so. I've worked for ten years for the Brackenfield name and now it's going to completely disappear, swallowed up by him.'

'You can't talk him into a compromise?' Millie ventured.

Zoey drained her coffee before answering. 'Finn O'Connell doesn't know the meaning of the word.' And her days of compromising were well and truly over.

Zoey called in on her father on her way back from coffee with the girls to find him halfway through a bottle of wine. And it wasn't his first. There was an empty bottle on the bench.

He held up a glass, swaying slightly on his feet. 'Have a drink to celebrate my retirement.'

'Dad, I'm not here to celebrate anything,' Zoey said. 'I'm here to tell you I won't see you again unless the next time it's in a rehab clinic. Your choice—the drink or me.'

He frowned, as if he couldn't process what she was saying. He scratched his head and frowned. 'But you always visit me.'

'I know, and it's going to stop,' Zoey said. 'For years I've visited you, I've had countless lunches or dinners with you, I cover for you, I make excuses for you—and what have I got in return? You continue to drink and embarrass me. Not only that, you sold out on me to Finn O'Connell. I waited for years for you to promote me, to allow me to reach my potential, but you never did. Why am I so unimportant to you?'

He put the glass down, a frown still wrinkling his brow. 'You're not unimportant…'

'But the drink is more important,' Zoey said. 'You

wanted a son. You've made no secret of that and instead you got me. And I tried to be the best daughter I could be but it's not enough. I'm not enough for you.' Just as she hadn't been enough for her ex. And as she wasn't enough for Finn, and how that hurt way more than anything.

'You are enough for me...' Her father looked at her with bloodshot eyes, his voice trembling. 'When I lost your mother...' His hand shook as he rubbed at his unshaven face. 'I kept thinking I might lose you too. I—I found it hard to be close to you after that. I seem to lose everyone I care about. I know I always carry on about wanting a son but that was the way I was brought up. A son to carry on the family name was my dream, but when your mother died, well, that dream was shattered. And when Linda left me a few months ago I began to drink to numb my feelings. I lost interest in everything. Work was just a burden. I couldn't wait to offload the company.'

So, Finn had been right about her father, Zoey thought. He had told her that her dad was most likely protecting himself from further hurt after losing her mother. Was that what Finn was doing too? Protecting himself after the rejection of his parents' love? Strange that he would have such insight into her father but not have it into himself. Or maybe he did have it but just didn't love her. She had been a convenient fling partner but not someone he loved enough to spend the rest of his life with her in marriage.

'Will you promise to get help?' Zoey asked her father, determined not to back down.

He gave a stuttering sigh. 'I've made promises before

and never kept them...' He winced as if in deep pain and added, 'But if it means losing you...'

Tears began to roll down his face and Zoey went to him and hugged him, fighting tears herself.

It would be a long journey but at least her father had taken the first painful step.

CHAPTER TEN

Finn immersed himself in work over the next four weeks to distract himself from Zoey's decision to end their fling. But the endless meetings with the Brackenfield staff were a constant reminder of her. He found it hard to decide on who to keep and who to let go. His emotions kept getting in the way.

Yes, his emotions, those pesky things he never allowed anywhere near a business decision. He offered generous redundancy packages to some, far more generous than they probably deserved. But he kept thinking of Zoey, how she saw the staff as people beyond their desks, people with families and loved ones and worries and stresses to deal with in their personal lives.

But he had his own stress to deal with in his personal life—the stress of missing Zoey.

He missed everything about her—her smile, her laughter, her feistiness when she didn't agree with him on something, her touch, her kisses, the explosive way she responded to his lovemaking. There was a constant ache in his chest, a dragging ache that distracted him during the day and kept him awake at night. He had never reacted to a break-up so badly. But then, he had always been the instigator of his previous break-ups with casual lovers. He never allowed anyone the power to hurt him, to abandon him—he always got in first. Was that why his break-up with Zoey was so hard to handle? He hadn't seen her as a casual lover—she was in a completely different category, but he wasn't exactly sure what it was.

Finn hadn't even thought of taking another lover. His stomach turned at the thought. So much for his playboy lifestyle. He was turning into a monk. A miserably lonely monk. He spent most evenings with only his one-eyed cat for company.

Finn felt a strange sense of camaraderie with his battered and brooding cat. Tolstoy had been hurt in the past and went out of his way to avoid further hurt. That was why, when Finn had gone away to New York and then Monte Carlo, Tolstoy had punished him on his return. Fear was behind that behaviour, fear of being permanently rejected. But, since Finn had been home every evening over the last month, Tolstoy had built up enough trust to lose some of his guardedness. It occurred to him then that Tolstoy loved him and was terrified he might not come back.

Why hadn't he realised that before now?

Maybe it wasn't Finn's dented pride that was causing this infernal pain in his chest. Maybe he was a little more like his cat than he realised. Didn't they say pets and owners became alike? Finn didn't like to think of himself as the sort of man who couldn't move on after a woman had ended a fling. He knew how to let go—he'd been doing it without a problem for years.

But this didn't feel like a cut and dried case of in-jured male pride.

It felt like something else…something he had never felt before…something that was threatening the entire basis on which he lived his footloose and fancy-free life. Something beyond a fleeing attraction…something deeper—a sense that if he never saw Zoey again he would be missing something essential to his existence. Without her, he would not be the person he was meant to be. He would be stunted in some way, reduced, lack-ing. She inspired him, enthralled him, delighted and fulfilled him.

Zoey hadn't said the words 'I love you' out loud but she had told him she had developed feelings for him. Feelings that had grown from negative to positive. Feel-ings he had rebuffed out of fear. Why hadn't he seen that until now? He was as one-eyed as his cat not to have seen it. He'd been afraid to love her in case he lost her and yet he had lost her anyway. He had spent his whole life avoiding love, avoiding emotional attachment in case he was rejected. But he had rejected the most amazing love from the most amazing woman. The only woman he could envisage having permanently in his life. The only woman with whom he wanted a future.

Zoey *was* his future.

Zoey decided there was no more painful thing than watching one of your best friends get married, know-ing you would never experience the same exhilarating joy. It was a month since she'd left Finn in Monte Carlo and, apart from the odd email or text message regard-ing business issues, she had not seen him in person.

Zoey listened as Ivy and Louis exchanged vows under an archway festooned with white and soft pink roses. The love they felt for each other was written all over their glowing faces, both of their voices poignantly catching over the words, 'Till death do us part'. Zoey wasn't a habitual weeper but seeing such depth of emotion in the young couple made tears sting at the back of her eyes. She had so dearly hoped that one day she would stand exactly as Ivy was doing, exchanging vows with the man she loved with her whole heart. But instead, her heart was broken, shattered by the realisation Finn would never love her.

Zoey heard Millie begin to sniffle beside her, no doubt eagerly awaiting her own wedding day the following month. But if there was anything positive to be had out of the pain of the last few weeks it was this— her father was in full-time residential rehab and his estranged wife Linda had been visiting him every day. It was wonderful to see her dad finally taking responsibility for his drinking and, while it would take a while for Zoey to feel close to him, she knew things were heading in the right direction.

Ivy and Louis's reception was a joyous affair and Zoey got swept up in the celebrations, determined not to allow her own misery to spoil her friends' special day.

'Time to throw the bridal bouquet!' the Master of Ceremonies announced. 'Single ladies, please gather in the centre of the room.'

Millie nudged Zoey. 'Go on. That means you.'

Zoey rolled her eyes. 'No way.'

Millie grabbed her by the arm and all but dragged

her to where the other young women were eagerly assembled. 'Come on. Ivy wants you to be in the circle. And make sure you catch it.'

Why? There was only one man Zoey wanted to marry and he was the last man on earth who would ever ask her. But Millie had a particularly determined look in her eye, so Zoey stepped into the circle with a sigh of resignation. The band struck up a rousing melody to get everyone cheering and Zoey had never felt more like a fish out of water. The other women were right into the spirit of the event, cheering and whooping and jumping up and down, arms in the air, hoping for Ivy's bouquet to come their way.

Zoey, on the other hand, was trying to hide behind a larger woman, hoping to avoid the floral missile. The drum roll sounded, the women in the centre of the room became almost hysterically excited and Zoey closed her eyes, figuring she wouldn't catch the bouquet if she couldn't see it. But then something soft and fragrant hit her in the face and she reflexively caught it in her hands. She stared at the bouquet she was holding while the crowd cheered and clapped around her.

But she had never felt so miserable in her life.

Zoey finally managed to escape all the noise and cheering by slipping out of the venue to the garden, where there was a summer house covered in a rambling pink clematis. She sat on the padded seat inside the summer house and looked at the bouquet still in her hands.

'I'm really glad you caught that,' Finn O'Connell said, stepping out of the shadows.

Zoey blinked as if she was seeing things. The way

her heart was carrying on, he might as well have been a ghost. 'Finn? What are you doing here? I didn't know you were invited.'

'I gate-crashed,' he said with an inscrutable smile. 'May I join you?' He indicated the bench seat she was sitting on.

Zoey shoved a little further along the seat, the bouquet still in her hands—or at least what was left of it. She had been shredding it without realising, the petals falling like confetti around her. Her pulse was thumping at the sight of him, her senses reeling at his closeness. 'Why are you here?' She gave him a sideways glance. 'It's not very polite to gate-crash someone's wedding. If it's a business matter, then surely it could have waited?'

He removed the now sad-looking bouquet from her hands and set it to one side. 'It is a business matter—our business.' His dark gaze held hers in a tender lock. 'Zoey, my darling, I have come to realise what a damn fool I've been. I've been fighting my feelings for you for months, even before we got involved. But I was too frightened to admit it even to myself, let alone to you.'

He took her hands in both of his. 'I love you madly, deeply, crazily. My life is empty without you. Just ask Tolstoy. He's witnessed every miserable minute of me moping about my house for the last month. Please forgive me for not telling you sooner. For not realising it sooner.'

Zoey swallowed, her heart beating so hard and fast, she felt light-headed. 'I can't believe I'm hearing this…' Her voice came out as a shocked whisper. Shocked but delighted.

He gave a self-deprecating smile. 'I can't believe I'm saying it. I never thought I would fall in love with anyone. I didn't think I had the ability to until I met you. But you are the most wonderful person and I can't imagine being without you. Please say you'll marry me.'

'You want to get married?' Zoey gasped.

Finn got off the bench and knelt down in front of her, holding her hands in his. His eyes looked suspiciously moist, and her heart swelled until she could barely take a breath. 'My darling Zoey, will you marry me and make me the happiest of men?'

She threw her arms around him with a happy sob. 'Oh, Finn, I will, I will, I will. I love you, love you, love you.'

Finn rose from the floor of the summer house, bringing her to stand upright with him. His arms came round her, his expression as joyful as her own. 'I love you so much. I will never get tired of saying it. I want you to come back and work with me. I want your name as well as mine on the letterhead. We'll hyphenate them— Brackenfield-O'Connell Advertising. It's got quite a ring to it, hasn't it?'

'You mean you don't want me to change my name to yours after we get married?'

His arms tightened around her. 'I don't want to change anything about you, my darling girl.'

'Oh, Finn, I never thought I could be so happy,' Zoey said, gazing up into his eyes. 'Being at Ivy and Louis's wedding has been like torture. Seeing them so happy made me realise how miserable I was without you. And when I accidentally caught the bouquet just then, I wanted to curl up and hide. Millie just about frogmarched me out there to join in. I thought it was a little mean of her at the time, because she knows how unhappy I've been.'

Finn's eyes began to twinkle. 'I heard she's a fabulous jewellery designer. Do you think she'll design our rings for us? She seems the most helpful and obliging sort of person.'

Zoey's eyes widened. 'Oh, my God, she knew you were going to propose! No wonder that bouquet came straight at me. She made sure it did. But she's normally hopeless at keeping a secret.'

He grinned. 'I might have mentioned to her I was dropping by to see you.' He brought his mouth down to hers in a lingering kiss. He finally lifted his mouth off hers to smile down at her. 'How soon can we get married? I don't want to wait for months on end.'

'Nor do I,' Zoey said. 'But I thought you never wanted to get married. And what about kids?'

'I never envisaged making a family with anyone before I met you,' he said. 'But the idea is increasingly appealing. I bet you'll be the most beautiful mother in the world.'

'And you the most amazing father,' Zoey said. 'Speaking of fathers…did you know my dad has been in rehab for the past month? He's doing really well so far.'

'I'm really glad for you and for him,' Finn said. 'And I've even thought of contacting my parents to ask them about their backgrounds. You got me thinking that there may be more to their behaviour than I thought.'

He brought her even closer, his gaze tender. 'You

have taught me so much about love and caring about people. I found it near impossible to trim down the staff from Brackenfield in the takeover.'

Zoey hugged him again. 'I'm glad you found your heart. I knew it was there inside you somewhere.'

He tipped up her face to look deeply into her eyes. 'It was there waiting for you, my darling.'

* * * * *

MILLS & BOON

Coming next month

As the car slowed to go over a speed hump, his fingers briefly fell to her shoulder. An accident of transit, nothing intentional about it. The reason didn't matter though; the spark of electricity was the same regardless. She gasped and quickly turned her face away, looking beyond the window.

It was then that she realized they had driven through the gates of City Airport.

Bea turned back to face Ares, a question in her eyes.

'There's a ball at the airport?'

'No.'

'Then why…?' Comprehension was a blinding light. 'We're flying somewhere.'

'To the ball.'

'But…you didn't say…'

'I thought you were good at reading between the lines?'

She pouted her lips. 'Yes, you're right.' She clicked her fingers in the air. 'I should have miraculously intuited that when you invited me to a ball you meant for us to fly there. Where, exactly?'

'Venice.'

'Venice?' She stared at him, aghast. 'I don't have a passport.'

'I had your assistant arrange it.'

'You—what? When?'

'When I left this morning.'

'My assistant just handed over my passport?'

'You have a problem with that?'

'Well, gee, let me think about that a moment,' she said, tapping a finger to the side of her lip. 'You're a man I'd never clapped eyes on until yesterday and now you have in your possession a document that's of reasonably significant personal importance. You could say I find that a little invasive, yes.'

He dropped his hand from the back of the seat, inadvertently brushing her arm as he moved, lifting a familiar burgundy document from his pocket. 'Now you have it in your possession. It was no conspiracy to kidnap you, Beatrice, simply a means to an end.'

Clutching the passport in her hand, she stared down at it. No longer bothered by the fact he'd managed to convince her assistant to commandeer a document of such personal importance from her top drawer, she was knocked off-kilter by his use of her full name. Nobody called her Beatrice any more. She'd been Bea for as long as she could remember. But her full name on his lips momentarily shoved the air from her lungs.

'Why didn't you just tell me?'

He lifted his shoulders. 'I thought you might say no.'

It was an important clue as to how he operated. This was a man who would do what he needed to achieve whatever he wanted. He'd chosen to invite her to this event, and so he'd done what he deemed necessary to have her there.

'Your business is too important to our company, remember?' She was grateful for the opportunity to remind them both of the reason she'd agreed to this. It had nothing to do with the fact she found him attractive, and everything to do with how much she loved her friends and wanted the company to continue to succeed.

'And that's the only reason you agreed to this,' he said in a deep voice, perfectly calling her bluff. Was she that obvious? Undoubtedly.

Continue reading
CINDERELLA'S NIGHT IN VENICE
Clare Connelly

Available next month
www.millsandboon.co.uk

COMING SOON!

We really hope you enjoyed reading this book.
If you're looking for more romance, be sure to
head to the shops when new books are
available on

Thursday 1st April

To see which titles are coming soon, please visit
millsandboon.co.uk/nextmonth

MILLS & BOON

THE HEART OF ROMANCE

A ROMANCE FOR EVERY READER

MODERN

Prepare to be swept off your feet by sophisticated, sexy and seductive heroes, in some of the world's most glamourous and romantic locations, where power and passion collide.

HISTORICAL

Escape with historical heroes from time gone by. Whether your passion is for wicked Regency Rakes, muscled Vikings or rugged Highlanders, awaken the romance of the past.

MEDICAL

Set your pulse racing with dedicated, delectable doctors in the high-pressure world of medicine, where emotions run high and passion, comfort and love are the best medicine.

True Love

Celebrate true love with tender stories of heartfelt romance, from the rush of falling in love to the joy a new baby can bring, and a focus on the emotional heart of a relationship.

Desire

Indulge in secrets and scandal, intense drama and plenty of sizzling hot action with powerful and passionate heroes who have it all: wealth, status, good looks…everything but the right woman.

HEROES

Experience all the excitement of a gripping thriller, with an intense romance at its heart. Resourceful, true-to-life women and strong, fearless men face danger and desire - a killer combination!

To see which titles are coming soon, please visit

millsandboon.co.uk/nextmonth

MILLS & BOON
Desire

Indulge in secrets and scandal, intense drama and plenty of sizzling hot action with powerful and passionate heroes who have it all: wealth, status, good looks… everything but the right woman.

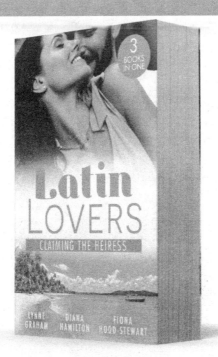

JOIN US ON SOCIAL MEDIA!

Stay up to date with our latest releases, author
news and gossip, special offers and discounts, and
all the behind-the-scenes action
from Mills & Boon...

 millsandboon

 millsandboonuk

 millsandboon

might just be true love...